LIVE TO FIGHT ANOTHER DAY

The battle for Anchorage had been lost in a matter of minutes.

The Japanese rounded up the survivors. An officer barked a command and a roar of laughter came from the Japanese surrounding the Americans. The Japanese pushed and prodded them with their bayonets toward the water and then into it. The Japanese soldiers fired in front of the prisoners and stabbed slow-moving Americans with their bayonets. The message was clear, swim or die.

Swimming only delayed the inevitable. The wounded and nonswimmers had already disappeared under the waves, while others attempted to strike out for the opposite shore and the illusion of safety. When they were maybe a hundred yards out, the Japanese opened fire. It was little more than target practice.

Ruby pulled herself to her feet. She was not going back to Anchorage. She had a cabin a couple of miles away and well into the woods. There, she'd get some decent gear, another weapon, and head farther into the forest.

She left the house and walked into the nearby bushes where she heard strange noises. She stood with the shotgun ready. She lowered it when she looked into the frightened faces of a handful of very young and scared Americassacre.

"Where yo⋯⋯er voice surprisingly c⋯

They hadn'⋯⋯rugged. "Don't know. ⋯⋯arracks."

Ruby slung the shotgun over her shoulder. "Then you'd better come with me."

BAEN BOOKS
by
ROBERT CONROY

Himmler's War

Rising Sun

1920: America's Great War (forthcoming)

To purchase these and all Baen Book titles in
e-book format, please go to www.baen.com.

RISING SUN

ROBERT CONROY

BAEN

Rising Sun

Copyright © 2012 by Robert Conroy

A Baen Book

Baen Publishing Enterprises
P.O. Box 1403
Riverdale, NY 10471
www.baen.com

ISBN: 978-1-4767-3614-3

Cover art by Kurt Miller

First Baen paperback printing, November 2013

Library of Congress Control Number: 2012033440

Distributed by Simon & Schuster
1230 Avenue of the Americas
New York, NY 10020

Pages by Joy Freeman (www.pagesbyjoy.com)
Printed in the United States of America

Seeing a book published never gets old and it is never done alone. I'd like to thank everyone at Baen along with Eleanor Wood and her crew at Spectrum for all their work and for believing that *Rising Sun* has a future. Of course, my wife and daughter were very positive forces.

And finally, to Quinn and Brennan: Not yet but you're getting there.

INTRODUCTION

IN JUNE 1942, WHAT REMAINED OF THE UNITED
States Navy's Pacific Fleet after the disaster at Pearl
Harbor was on its way to destiny at Midway. With
knowledge provided by their top-secret codebreaking
efforts, the American commanders know the intent
and size of the Japanese fleet. With only three carriers and the garrison of Midway against Japan's four,
America's only hope was to pull off an ambush. To
make matters worse, a powerful bombardment and
invasion force was following the Japanese carriers
and would launch the invasion of Midway itself. Yet
another Japanese task force was en route to attack
our bases in Alaska.

The Japanese thought they were in a win-win position. If the American fleet did not show, then they
would seize Midway, a base that would threaten Hawaii.
If the Americans did rise to the challenge, the overwhelming might of the Imperial Japanese Navy would
destroy them.

To get in position, the American forces would have to slip past a picket line of Japanese submarines before they could set up and attack the Japanese carrier force.

In actual history, the U.S. Navy won an overwhelming victory that some have described as miraculous. The Japanese subs were on duty a day late and the proverbial dollar short, and all four Japanese carriers were sunk at a cost of one of ours. In the space of a few minutes, the course of the war in the Pacific was changed forever. Japan's death spiral to ultimate defeat in August 1945 had begun and she would never again be able to seize the initiative.

In this tale of alternate history, some of the Japanese submarines are in place when the American carriers attempt to steam by. Enemy submarines attack, unleashing a storm of torpedoes that sink two American carriers. The surviving ships of the American fleet fall back in disarray to Hawaii. The third American carrier is hunted down and destroyed, all without significant loss to the Japanese. Midway is forced to surrender and the Japanese win another tremendous victory.

Victory fever again grips the Japanese and Admiral Yamamoto is not immune. He'd originally felt that the victory at Pearl Harbor would give him a year before the U.S. could react. Now he feels that he can gain at least two more years of supremacy against the United States, perhaps much longer, by devastating America's West Coast. He hopes that bloody pressure will be enough to ensure a diplomatic peace that will preserve most, if not all, that Japan has conquered.

However, there are those who have doubts. "The fruits of war are tumbling into our mouths almost too quickly," Emperor Hirohito said in real history and before Midway. Events would prove him right.

As I did in my previous novels about the war in the Pacific, I've conveniently ignored the International Date Line. I've also adopted our way of using Japanese names. It's just easier that way.

Also, while the very real problems with American torpedoes are chronicled in my earlier novel, *1942*, they could not be ignored in this story as they were a significant part of the early war in the Pacific.

Regarding the Battle of Midway, a number of fine histories by the likes of Lord and Prange have been written and I've used them extensively. A more recent and very intriguing history of Midway, *Shattered Sword* by Parshall and Tully, was written largely from the Japanese perspective. Along with being well-written and fascinating, it was a great help in sorting out Japanese motives, doctrine, and capabilities.

—Robert Conroy

CHAPTER I

LIEUTENANT TIM DANE, USNR, COULDN'T SLEEP. Going to war for the first time will do that to a man, he thought. Maybe it would happen every time. But then he hoped there wouldn't be a second time. Jesus, what kind of a mess was he in?

Instead of tossing in his bunk, he got up and paced along the flight deck of the aircraft carrier *Enterprise* as she plowed her way through the Pacific swells toward her destiny near Midway Island.

Dane was a very junior member of Admiral Spruance's staff on the carrier, so he was privy to the basic strategy. By this time, of course, so was every one of the two thousand men on the four-year-old, twenty-five-thousand-ton carrier. The *Enterprise* was like a small town in which there were few secrets. Nor was there any need to keep quiet. After all, who could you tell?

The *Enterprise* was accompanied by a second carrier, the *Hornet*. The two carriers were protected by six heavy cruisers, one light cruiser, and nine destroyers. These made up Task Force 16 under the command of Admiral Raymond Spruance. The six heavies were the *Atlanta*, *Minneapolis*, *New Orleans*, *Pensacola*, *Northhampton*, and *Vincennes* and constituted a powerful force by themselves. The light cruiser was the *Atlanta*.

Waiting for the arrival of the two carriers was TF 17, now off Midway with a third carrier, the Yorktown, and her escorts. These ships constituted almost all that was left of the United States Navy in the Pacific after the catastrophe at Pearl Harbor. One more carrier, the *Saratoga*, was reported to be undergoing repairs, probably in San Diego.

Prior to the attack on Pearl Harbor, many naval officers had stubbornly held onto the dogma that the battleship was the navy's primary weapon, and that the carrier's role was that of reconnaissance rather than battle. The attack on Pearl Harbor, in which eight U.S. battleships were either sunk or damaged by enemy airplanes launched from carriers, had done much to change that perception, but it had not totally gone away.

Part of the reason for this sense of nostalgia was because carriers weren't lovely ships. Like all carriers, the *Enterprise* lacked the graceful, rakish silhouette of a cruiser or destroyer, or of the new battleships whose pictures Dane had seen on the wall of the wardroom. The *Enterprise* was frankly a floating block that carried about eighty planes.

Possibly because of a carrier's lack of glamor or tradition, a number of very senior officers still considered the disaster at Pearl Harbor an aberration caused by the incompetence of those in command of the fleet. Guns would sink enemy ships. Always had, always would.

Since Pearl Harbor, the *Enterprise* had undergone modifications to enhance her ability to fight airplanes. A number of 20mm Oerlikon antiaircraft guns had been added to her arsenal.

TF 16 was on its way to Midway Island to rendezvous with the *Yorktown* in a desperate attempt to stop the Japanese from attacking and taking Midway and using it as a base for operations against Hawaii. Dane knew that not only would the three carriers and their escorts be outnumbered and outgunned by the Japanese, but they had to evade a picket line of Japanese submarines that highly classified intelligence said was going to be established in front of their approach. The enemy subs could either ruin the ambush by announcing their presence, or attack the carriers and possibly do great damage. The men of the *Enterprise* and *Hornet* were as ready as they could be, although many, like Dane, were half scared to death.

Tim Dane, however, did not feel he was ready at all. Like everyone else, he'd tried his hand at looking through binoculars for enemy subs and seen nothing. Enough, he thought. He decided to once more try to squeeze his frame into the small navy bunk he'd been allotted, and maybe he'd get at least a little sleep. He hoped the fleet and Spruance would be lucky and the enemy subs would be elsewhere. But every moment brought them closer to Midway and the Japanese fleet.

None of the hundreds of pairs of searching eyes could pierce the night and notice the slight feather of water made by the emergence of a periscope less than a mile away. With cruel luck, the Japanese sub had emerged in the middle of TF 16. She was an older boat, a *Kaidai*-class sub with six torpedo tubes in her bow, loaded and ready to kill, and eleven other torpedoes ready to replace the ones fired. She weighed in at just under three thousand tons, and had a crew of ninety-four officers and men. The oceangoing sub had a cruising range of fourteen thousand knots. This meant she could cruise far away from Japan and stay in position, waiting for her prey.

The Japanese sub and two others had arrived a day earlier than American intelligence anticipated. There had been confusion, perhaps even incompetence, among Japanese commanders regarding when the subs would depart and only these three had left on time. With equally cruel luck, the subs had placed themselves directly in the path of the American carriers that were on their way to a rendezvous at what had been incongruously named Point Luck. This night, however, luck was on the Japanese side.

Lookouts on the *Enterprise* didn't notice the disturbances in the water made by the first of the six torpedoes until they were less than a quarter mile away and approaching at nearly fifty land miles an hour. Screams and alarms were almost useless. Four of the six Type 94 torpedoes fired from the sub hit the carrier. One after another they slammed into her hull and exploded, sending plumes of water and debris high above the flight deck, with much of it landing on the deck. Men were injured and a few swept overboard to their deaths by the sudden assault.

The mighty *Enterprise* shuddered like a large,

wounded animal and immediately began to lose speed. Secondary explosions soon followed as fuel and ammo ignited, further damaging the ship and causing large numbers of casualties. Fires raged while valiant sailors braved the flames to contain them.

Dane had been in his skivvies and sitting on the edge of his bunk when the first torpedo slammed into the carrier, hurling him face-first onto the deck. He lay there for a stunned second and then quickly checked himself out. His lip was split and there was something wrong with the top of his head. It was wet and sticky with blood. He was bruised and shaken, but otherwise he thought he was okay.

Dane's first reaction as he picked himself up was to run and hide, but he quickly calmed himself and tried to gauge what had just happened. And besides, where the hell do you hide on a ship? As a new and minor member of Admiral Spruance's staff, he really didn't have any set place to go in an emergency. But he had to do something, he thought as he threw on some clothes. He would be damned if he would run up to the flight deck in his skivvies.

Cramped passageways were filled with men either hastening to their duty stations or fleeing the greasy black smoke that was beginning to clog everything. The smoke was burning eyes and choking throats. Dane grabbed a life jacket and put it on. He would go to the flight deck, then try to climb up to the flag bridge where Spruance would be, which was as close as he could come to having a duty station. He was also horribly conscious of the fact that the carrier had begun listing to port.

Dane had just made it to the flight deck when a series of explosions knocked him down again. This time, the fuel from the planes parked on the stern of the ship was exploding and detonating ammunition, sending more billowing clouds of smoke and debris over the great, terribly wounded ship. A wave of searing heat blew over him. He screamed and covered his face with his hands. His hair and clothes began to smoke. He rolled across the deck to where an abandoned fire hose was thrashing like a snake and spewing water, and put out the flames by rolling in puddles.

Scores of men lay prone on the deck, either dead or wounded, while others were being brought up from below. A priest was going from one mangled body to another, administering last rites. To Tim, the carnage was a scene from hell. Dane's hands and clothes were covered with something sticky and he saw that it was blood, and that rivulets of the stuff were flowing across the flight deck and over the side.

Sailors with fire hoses tried valiantly to stem the flames, but were in danger of becoming overwhelmed by the size and intensity of the conflagration. Tim saw one man hit by flying debris and fall, leaving a wildly bucking hose understaffed. He grabbed on to help the remaining men who were fighting to keep control of the wild beast.

A sailor glanced at his rank and grinned. "Thanks, sir, it's appreciated."

"Just tell me what to do."

"Hang on!"

Dane anchored the hose while the real firemen played water on the flames. After a few moments, a grimy lieutenant commander replaced him with another sailor. "Nothing personal and thanks anyway, Dane, but you don't know what the hell you're doing."

Dane didn't argue the point. He gratefully handed the hose to a grim-faced seaman and turned to the other officer. His name was Mickey Greene and he'd befriended the bewildered Dane when he'd first come aboard.

"We gonna make it, Commander?"

Greene shook his head, "Beats the hell out of me, Tim. We took at least three torpedoes and water's still coming in. We've got the flooded areas pretty well sealed off, but a lot of things are burning, even though we're throwing tons of water on the fires. The bad news is that all that water coupled with the torpedo holes is causing us to list, and that means we're helpless if Jap planes show up because the list prevents us from launching our planes."

"Christ."

"Yeah, and if you haven't noticed, the *Hornet's* also been badly hit."

Stunned by that piece of news, Dane looked out across the waves and saw that the other carrier was also burning furiously. The cruisers *Atlanta* and *Pensacola* were alongside her and using their hoses to pour water on her, while destroyers frantically searched for the enemy sub. The *New Orleans* and *Minneapolis* were cautiously approaching the *Enterprise*, and water from their hoses began arching over and onto the wounded carrier. Jesus, he thought, most of what remained of the American Navy after the massacre at Pearl Harbor was being destroyed before his eyes. Two carriers with just under two hundred planes were probably going to sink along with God only knew how many pilots and crewmen. And maybe Tim Dane would be among them. Well, not if he could help it, he thought angrily.

Making things even worse, the smoke from the burning ships would be a beacon for the Japanese ships and planes that must surely be homing in on the carnage.

Jochi Shigata was the captain of the Japanese submarine whose torpedoes had hit the *Enterprise*. He knew that he and his sub were doomed and relished the fact as the culmination of his destiny. He would die as a warrior. He and his comrades had severely damaged two American carriers and, with a little luck, at least one of them would sink.

He had radioed his location and his successes and had received an acknowledgment. His life could now be measured in minutes as American destroyers were converging on him like sharks to blood. He laughed. "Sharks to blood" was a wonderful phrase considering all the American blood he'd spilled today. With each hit, his crew had shouted *banzai* until they were now hoarse. He could ask for no better companions to die with. Two American carriers were either dead or badly wounded thanks to his efforts and those of the other two subs who had also attacked. Planes from the Japanese carrier force would soon find the wounded carriers and kill the American ships if they hadn't already sunk by the time they arrived. By that time it would be too late for him.

Depth charges exploded nearby and the sub shook violently. Glass on dials broke and small leaks spouted high pressure darts of water. Crewmen tumbled and fell, sometimes unable to stifle the screams and groans caused by their broken bones. There was no way they could escape their fate.

"Surface," Shigata ordered. "I have no wish to die skulking underwater."

Once he'd had doubts about Emperor Hirohito, a man who seemed more interested in marine biology than the ways of the warrior, but the God-Emperor had proven himself. He had taken Japan on the road to victory. "Now we will die for our emperor!"

His ninety-odd men cheered as he said that. There was no greater honor for a Japanese warrior. The sub surged upward, broaching and exploding onto the surface. She slammed back onto the water, raising a huge wave.

Astonished sailors from American destroyers watched incredulously as the sub's deck gun was quickly crewed and opened fire on the surrounding ships. At the same time, the sub launched her fresh load of torpedoes in the general direction of the American ships.

The destroyers returned fire, killing the gunners and sweeping their bodies into the sea. More shells shredded the conning tower and pierced the sub's hull with multiple hits. Moments later, the sub exploded and broke in two as a shell from a destroyer hit a remaining torpedo. The pieces rolled over and sank. There were no survivors. None of the Japanese wished to survive. Therefore, none of the dying Japanese were able to see that one of the indiscriminately fired torpedoes had struck the badly damaged *Enterprise*, killing any chance of saving her.

Once again, Dane found himself prone and stunned on the gore-covered flight deck. He lurched to his feet. There was something wrong with his left leg. It hurt like hell and it was difficult to stand. He looked for his friend Greene for guidance, but couldn't find him. Many of the men of the damage control parties who'd been trying to douse the flames were also strewn about. Unmanned hoses whipped and snapped, sometimes hitting and injuring sailors who were trying to grab them. Most of the sailors lying on the deck weren't moving, and some of the bodies were smoldering. He assumed one of the bodies was Greene's and others were the sailors he'd been working with just a moment before. He felt sick as he realized the flames were going to win.

Another violent shudder and the ship listed farther to port. We're going over, Dane thought. What do I do now? Men were hollering, "Abandon ship!" But was this an order or were the sailors panicking? Hell, *he* was panicking. Someone yelled that Captain Murray was dead and that it was every man for himself.

An older man with blood streaming down his face grabbed Tim's arm in a strong grip. "Help me," he said.

Dane was shocked. It was Admiral Spruance. He grabbed the admiral's arm to steady him. Spruance's eyes were glazed and he stared intently at Dane. "I know you," he said with a slurred voice. "You're on my staff."

Still another shudder rumbled from an explosion below the deck, and Dane had to hold up the admiral who was quite likely concussed. "Admiral, I think we've got to get out of here."

Spruance mumbled something, but didn't protest as Dane took charge and guided him. The list was so pronounced that people and planes were tumbling off the flight deck like so many toys, falling into the ocean that was, while still quite a drop, much closer than it had been.

"Hang on," Dane said as he half pushed Spruance off the deck and into the sea, hoping that they wouldn't land on anything or that nothing would fall on top of them.

Dane had been holding the admiral's arm, but the impact drove him under water and separated them for a moment. He came up spluttering and choking from spilled oil, but only a few feet away from the now even more thoroughly shaken and confused Spruance. Oil was burning on the water and they had to get away before they were burned alive. Dane's leg hurt and the salt water stung the cuts and burns in his scalp, face, and hands.

Dane grabbed the admiral. He started to look around for a life-raft or even some debris. He flailed his arms frantically until he realized his life jacket would not let him sink, at least not for a while. Other swimmers were doing the same thing as the *Enterprise*, now almost on her side, slowly and mindlessly plowed on, propelled by the energy produced from her dying engines, and escorted by the cruisers who were still pouring water on the fires. He was horribly aware that there were very few men swimming in the water, although a number floated lifelessly. He reminded himself that the carrier had a crew of more than two thousand. Where were they?

An hour later, the two men lay awkwardly and alone on a damaged liferaft that was half filled with water. Dane was afraid that the raft would disintegrate, leaving them with nothing but their life jackets. Getting onto it had proven extremely difficult. Dane's leg wasn't responding and he wondered if it was broken, and the shocked and stunned admiral was little help. Still, they somehow managed.

Far in the distance, the *Enterprise* lay on her side, while the *Hornet* burned furiously and began to settle by the bow. American cruisers and destroyers raced around, plucking sailors from the water. As yet, they hadn't found Dane and his high-ranking companion even though he'd waved his arms in a fruitless attempt to get attention.

A shrieking sound and a plane flew low overhead, bullets spitting from its guns. It was a Japanese Zero and a host of other enemy fighters and bombers followed. The Japanese carriers had found them.

Bombs exploded on and about the helpless and ruined carrier hulks, while still more planes attacked the escorting destroyers and cruisers. It was a massacre. Some enemy pilots amused themselves by strafing sailors in the water. Bullets kicked up spray a few feet from Dane and Spruance, but none hit them.

"Do you have a gun?" Spruance's eyes were clearing, but his voice was still a little slurred.

"No, sir."

Spruance shook his head in an attempt to focus his thoughts. "Of course not. Carrying a heavy sidearm into the ocean is a dumb idea. Forget I asked. Do you have a weapon of any kind?"

"A pocket knife," Dane answered, wondering just what the hell Spruance had in mind.

"Don't lose it. If it becomes necessary, I want you to kill me with it."

"What?"

"You heard me and that's an order. If it looks like we're going to be taken prisoner, you must kill me. If it's a small knife, you'll have to slice my throat. I'll resist instinctively, but you are doubtless stronger and must prevail. I know too many things that would endanger our country's security. Whatever happens, you must kill me. Do you acknowledge that order?"

Dane gulped. This couldn't be happening. Was Spruance even sane or had the blow to his head made him crazy? "I understand and I will obey, but tell me, sir, did you ever read *Ben Hur* or see the movie with Bushman and Navarro?"

"I've done both, Lieutenant, but what the devil does that have to do with our predicament?" Spruance asked, even as understanding dawned. "Of course, there was a scene where Ben Hur and the Roman admiral were adrift in the sea, and the admiral wanted to die because he was shamed by what he wrongfully believed was a defeat. Nice thought, Dane, but I am not suicidal because I'm ashamed of a defeat. No, I want to live to get another crack at them; I simply know too much to be taken prisoner. They would torture me until I told them everything I know and that would be terrible for the United States."

Spruance looked away. He didn't want the young lieutenant to see the anguish in his eyes. He was fifty-six years old and the Midway battle was his first major command, and he'd botched it horribly. His two carriers were destroyed and only God knew how many other ships damaged or sunk and, Jesus, how many young men were dead or wounded? Surely the butcher's bill would eclipse that of the attack on Pearl Harbor. On a purely personal and selfish note, he wondered if he would ever get another command even if he did survive.

He shook his head. He had to think clearly. A new command was the least of his worries. He could not be captured. He did not want to die, but he could not live as a prisoner of the Japanese. He understood full well just how brutal interrogations could ultimately break anyone. He had no illusions regarding his ability to resist torture. Sooner or later and after untold agonies, he would break.

Aside from the sound of the waves slapping against their raft, there was silence. The Japanese planes were gone. A couple of American destroyers and the light cruiser *Atlanta* were burning furiously on the horizon. Worse, all the surviving ships were moving farther away. Dane and Spruance were truly alone in the vast Pacific. There was no drinking water in their damaged raft and their enemy would now be thirst, which Dane was feeling already, thanks to the salt water he'd swallowed. Unless the Japanese fleet arrived and plucked them from the sea they were doomed to die an agonizing death from thirst.

Dane understood what Spruance had said and realized that the admiral was both sane and correct. Word of Japanese atrocities against prisoners was spreading. He didn't want to be taken alive either, but could he kill himself after killing Spruance? He doubted it. Not only did he consider suicide morally wrong, but he simply wanted to live. Could it get any worse, Dane wondered?

Spruance grabbed Tim's arm. "Dane, is that a periscope or am I losing what's left of my mind?"

Dane turned in the direction the admiral was

staring. A submarine's periscope peered at them from a distance of maybe a hundred yards. It looked like a one-eyed sea monster, which, Dane decided, was exactly what it was, but whose? He pulled the pocket knife from his pants pocket and opened it. Spruance looked at it sadly and nodded.

There was a rush of water and the submarine surfaced.

"I can't see too well, Lieutenant. Whose is it, ours or theirs?"

Dane rubbed his eyes to clear his vision. Damned salt water made it difficult to see. He squinted and caught the name. She was the *Nautilus*. He smiled. "Ours."

CHAPTER 2

DANE WAS DRESSED IN HIS UNIFORM, SITTING ON the edge of his hospital bed in the naval hospital in Honolulu, and thinking of how very different he was from most navy officers. After four years of ROTC at Northwestern University, and several more years in the Naval Reserve, he'd never been on board anything larger than a fishing boat in Lake Michigan. Thus, the sheer size of the aircraft carrier *Enterprise* had been both daunting and humbling upon his last-minute arrival. Even though the *Enterprise* had been huge, he knew that many of the carriers and battleships now under construction were much larger. The soon-to-be-completed aircraft carrier *Essex* was a third bigger than the sunken *Enterprise*, and the *Essex* was the first of a class of ships just like her. She had a number of sisters that would be just as large when they were completed.

The doomed *Enterprise* had been capable of going thirty-two knots, which was, he thought ruefully, close to forty miles an hour and was what his old Ford could do on a good day. Dane hadn't seen the car in ten months and wondered if his young nephew hadn't run it into the ground. Tim had been activated in October of 1941 and had been in San Francisco when the Japanese attacked Pearl Harbor.

The other officers on the *Enterprise* had teased him about his lack of seagoing experience and laughed hysterically when he got thoroughly seasick during the early part of the voyage. Some of them did as well, which pleased Tim.

Dane was still mildly puzzled as to why he had been assigned to the *Enterprise* in the first place. He'd had one very brief conversation with Spruance, who'd also wondered, and pointedly asked him just why he thought he'd been assigned to his staff. Dane had prudently decided not to say he had no idea either. Instead, he said he thought it was because he could read and speak Japanese, a skill that was in short supply.

Spruance had smiled slightly and asked if Dane thought there were many Japanese on the carrier who might need interrogating, and whether he thought he'd run into any out in the Pacific.

Before Dane could answer, the admiral had laughed and said the ways of the United States Navy were wondrous indeed and that Dane should simply try to make himself useful. Barring that, he should stay out of everyone's way. That was weeks ago and now he was in a hospital in Honolulu, and the *Enterprise* was at the bottom of the Pacific along with the *Hornet* and a number of other American warships.

There had been time to find out that fewer than

three hundred men had survived the sinking of the two carriers. He was astonished to find that one of them was Lieutenant Commander Mickey Greene, the man who'd said that Tim didn't know how to handle a fire hose. Greene had been burned over much of his body and was wrapped up like a mummy. He told Tim that most of the burns were superficial and that he had no recollection of how he'd survived. He assumed that some of the crew had dragged him into a raft and he dimly recalled being hauled onto a destroyer that had managed to survive the slaughter. Greene said he was lucky and that he would survive. It humbled Dane, who was so much better off.

While horrified by the numbers of dead, Tim felt oddly disconnected. He'd only been on the carrier a short while and, with the possible exception of Mickey Greene, hadn't really known many of men all that well. They were acquaintances, not friends. Even he and Greene hadn't had time to become close.

After seeing Greene and trying to imagine the pain the man was enduring, Tim decided to quit feeling sorry for himself. His head had been shaved, he had six stitches in his scalp, a couple along his mouth, and his leg still hurt. His knee would heal and the dark brown hair on his scalp would grow back and, if it didn't, who cared? Half the men in his family were bald and he thought his hairline was already beginning to recede. He wondered how Mickey Greene would look when his bandages came off. Greene once had thick and curly red hair. Was any of it left? Tim's own burns were rapidly fading and wouldn't likely leave any significant scars.

He realized with a start that a young nurse was standing in front of him, looking at him quizzically.

"Good morning, Lieutenant, I'm glad to see you obeyed the instructions to get properly dressed. My name is Amanda Mallard and I'm a nurse, and unless you want some particularly painful injections in very sensitive parts of your body, you will never, ever refer to me as Ducky Mallard or Nurse Ducky or anything like that. Nurse Amanda, or simply Amanda, will do just fine. Understood?"

Dane smiled, "Totally, Amanda. However, you may call me the Great Dane if you wish and I won't object at all."

Nurse Mallard blinked and then smiled engagingly. "That, Lieutenant, remains to be seen. Also, and in case you haven't noticed, I'm a civilian nurse, which means I'm not all that impressed by anyone's rank, especially a mere lieutenant's," she said as she checked him over, verifying that his heart was working and that he was still breathing. He noticed that both had picked up the pace as she touched him.

"I'm still a civilian at heart myself," Tim said as she worked. He quickly explained that before being recalled to the navy, he'd been employed as an assistant principal at a junior high school where he also coached basketball and track. "Right now I'd very much like to be disciplining kids who talked in class or got caught necking in the park next to the school instead of worrying about Japanese trying to kill me."

Nurse Mallard told him to stand up and he did, wobbling just a bit. "I understand your thoughts," she said. "So how did you wind up in the navy in the first place? I'm from the Annapolis area and noticed that you do not have an academy ring."

She steadied him and handed him his crutches.

Dane was six feet tall and one hundred and eighty pounds and she moved him effortlessly. His leg wasn't broken; his heavily taped knee had been severely sprained and was massively bruised. He grimaced. He hadn't spent that much time on his feet and he felt stiff as a board.

"I had good grades, so I was admitted to Northwestern. They had a naval ROTC program. It looked interesting, and it helped pay the tuition. I wound up serving my active duty in Chicago of all places, but the navy had another series of budget cuts and I was cut loose until Roosevelt decided we needed a bigger navy. I got recalled and sent to Hawaii."

"So you're not a career type?" she asked as she guided him around the ward, ignoring the stares from the men in their beds along with their comments that they, too, would like Nurse Mallard to assist them.

"That may depend on the length of the war, but no. If the war lasts until 1980 like they say, then I'll be a careerist by default and probably still be a junior officer. Like you said, I didn't go to the Naval Academy, which might hold me back forever. Now, how did you become a nurse?"

Nurse Amanda Mallard wasn't beautiful. She was, instead, perky and cute, and when she smiled she exposed two upper front teeth that overlapped slightly. Dane thought it was charming. She had light brown hair that was cut short. He'd seen her walking around before, and some of the other guys in the ward thought she was too skinny and flat-chested, even bookish looking when she put on her glasses. Dane disagreed. He thought she was pretty and seemed very pleasant even though she hadn't spoken to him before now. He'd always thought that the old saying that men don't make passes at girls who wear glasses was nonsense.

"I became a nurse because, even though this is the twentieth century, there aren't all that many occupations where a woman is welcome. Nursing is one, and I do enjoy helping people, so I studied at the University of Maryland. I'm a Terrapin, and I'm okay with a nursing career."

"Going to be a nurse forever?"

"Unless I marry some rich guy, and schoolteachers don't qualify."

He laughed. "If my father's real estate schemes work out, maybe I'll join him and get rich and look you up." His leg stiffened and he winced.

"Don't complain about the pain, Lieutenant," she said as he bit back a groan, "it'll go away if you work at it and, besides, you don't want to be left behind, do you?"

"What are you talking about and why don't you call me by my first name?"

"You'll be Tim when you're out of here; until then, we keep it formal and militarily correct, even though I am a mere civilian."

"All right, but what do you mean about being left behind?"

"You're still on Spruance's staff, aren't you?"

"What's left of it," he said grimly, recalling their two days in the sub and subsequently being picked up by a flying boat and taken to Pearl Harbor.

Spruance was recovering well and already out of the hospital. He was dealing with the terrible fact that, along with the two carriers under his command and most of their crews, almost all of his staff had been killed in the disastrous Battle of Midway, which was commonly being referred to as the Midway Massacre. After destroying Spruance's force, the Japanese had found the remaining third carrier, the *Yorktown*, near Midway and sunk it as well, along with two cruisers and six destroyers. TF 17's commander, Admiral Frank Jack Fletcher, had gone down with his ship.

Thus, all three invaluable and, for the moment at least, irreplaceable carriers had been lost. Japanese casualties had been one damaged carrier, one submarine sunk, and a handful of airplanes shot down.

Midway was the latest in a long litany of defeats in the Pacific that had begun with Pearl Harbor and ran on through Wake Island, Guam, the Philippines, Java Sea, Coral Sea, and now Midway. Some argued that the battle of the Coral Sea was at worst a draw, but Tim thought that it was a loss even though a likely attack on Australia had been blunted. He expected the Japs would be back attacking Australia soon enough since the defeat at Midway. Jimmy Doolittle's bombing attack on Tokyo had momentarily buoyed spirits but had accomplished nothing in the way of a military objective.

Amanda took his arm and steered him down another hallway that led outdoors and he walked gingerly down a street. It felt good to be in the fresh, flower-scented warm air of Hawaii. He could almost forget about the war. Almost, since just about every male was in uniform. He felt his strength returning and could walk fairly steadily now, but he liked the feel of Amanda's hand on his arm. She came a little above his shoulder.

"Lieutenant, assuming you're correct that you are still on Spruance's staff, you are all going back to

California. Same with Nimitz's people. Rumor has it the navy feels that Hawaii is a lost cause since there aren't very many major American ships remaining in the Pacific to protect it."

Tom thought it made a hard and painful kind of sense. He'd seen the admiral once since their rescue when he'd visited Tim. He'd thanked Tim for saving his life—and for not killing him. Spruance had smiled when he said it, but Dane saw the agony in his eyes. All those men, all those ships now resting on the bottom of the ocean, had been his.

Amanda continued. "As I understand it, the rules for evacuation are simple. If you can walk, you'll be evacuated by submarine; otherwise, you'll have to wait for a destroyer or a transport, or even a hospital ship."

"I'll take my chances on the sub," he said grimly.

Tim had hated his first trip in the claustrophobic submarine, but quickly decided a second trip would be better than waiting in Hawaii for the world to end. There had been too many attacks on transports to make them viable alternatives. As for hospital ships, the Japanese record for atrocities included attacks on those unarmed and helpless vessels as well. He handed Amanda his crutches and walked unsteadily but unaided. He was determined to be ready to walk onto a sub.

Amanda was about to comment when air raid sirens went off. This was the first time it had happened since Dane had arrived in Hawaii and he was momentarily perplexed.

"Maybe the Japs are back," she said and grabbed his arm, "There were a lot of false alarms after December seventh, with a lot of Nervous Nellies seeing Japanese bogeymen in their flower gardens, but who knows."

She grabbed his arm more tightly and pushed him. "Let's see how fast you can limp to a shelter."

Shelter was a cement block building that quickly filled with people and Tim moved a lot quicker than he thought he could. Fear was a great motivator, he decided.

In Dane's opinion, the shelter was too fragile to stand up to much of a bombing. Antiaircraft guns began their *crump-crump* firing, and they were followed by the sounds of explosions. Amanda grabbed his hand and held on tightly. Her eyes were wide with fright in the dim light and he thought his mirrored hers. Clearly, this was not a false alarm.

"I thought nurses don't get scared," he said, and put his arm around her. She didn't resist; instead, she shuddered and pressed against him.

"This one does. Right now I wish I had stayed in California. I had a nice job as a nurse in San Diego."

"Why didn't you?"

"Are you trying to distract me?"

"Yes."

Something exploded down the street, sending debris raining on the shelter. "Keep up the good work," she said, and quivered. "I came here because it was an opportunity to earn decent money and see the wonders of Hawaii. I love sailing and it seemed like a heaven-sent opportunity. I never thought going to paradise might actually send me to heaven, or hell for that matter. My contract is for a year, but now it might be forever."

"What will you do if the navy goes?"

"No idea. If there's a way to get back to the mainland, I'll take it. I know of a large enough sailboat that could make it with enough supplies and a little luck, but that would be an act of desperation."

"Are you that good a sailor?" he asked with a smile. She was slender, almost thin, but the way she had steered him toward the shelter indicated she was stronger than she looked.

"We may have to find out. And maybe things are getting desperate. The government has introduced food rationing already and that's not a good sign."

No, it isn't, he thought. Rationing might mean that starvation was right around the corner. As a member of the military he was part of a privileged caste and had all the food he required, at least so far. He felt vaguely guilty for the hearty breakfast he'd had that morning—eggs, bacon, toast, and pineapple juice, of course. What were the civilians eating? He hoped Amanda was eating well enough, too. She didn't look like she could stand to miss too many meals.

The all-clear sounded and they left the shelter. They walked in silence back to the hospital. A petty officer was waiting beside Tim's bed. "Sir, are you Lieutenant Dane? If so, you're wanted right away in Admiral Spruance's meeting room. I've got a car so I'll take you there."

Dane nodded and squeezed Amanda's arm. "I'll call you," he said. She smiled and nodded.

Spruance did not host the meeting. A navy captain in his late thirties glared at Dane for being late, but softened immediately when he noticed his bandages and stitches, and the cane which Tim had swapped for his crutches. The Purple Heart was pinned to his uniform.

"Okay, we're all here, even the walking wounded," he said, nodding at Tim. "Glad you could make it, Dane. For those who don't know me, I'm Captain Bill Merchant and I'm a senior aide to the admiral. My job is to get everyone up to speed on what's happening right now, and what's going to happen real soon. In short, we're evacuating this place. All senior military personnel and their staffs, and that means us, will depart by sub tomorrow night. You will be limited to one small suitcase, so pack light. Take only essential personal stuff as uniforms and such will be reissued in San Diego. Other military personnel and the more seriously wounded will be taken out by transport or hospital ship, and, yes, that does mean that the navy is abandoning Hawaii. Only the army garrison will remain."

A hand was raised. "What about dependents?"

Merchant hesitated then shook his head sadly. "They'll either stay or go by transport if there's enough room. My personal opinion is that there won't be enough room to take everyone."

The man paled. Obviously he had family at what had once been a great duty station, and now was in the front lines of World War II against a particularly savage and barbaric enemy. Dane wondered what happen to people like them and also wondered what would become of Nurse Amanda Mallard. The future did not look pretty for those who would remain.

Captain Merchant went on to clarify what many already knew. There was only one American aircraft carrier remaining in the Pacific. The *Lexington* and the small old *Langley* had been sunk in the Coral Sea, while the *Enterprise, Hornet,* and *Yorktown* had been destroyed at Midway, leaving the *Saratoga* as the only U.S. carrier in the Pacific. The *Ranger, Wasp*, and the partially completed *Essex* were in the Atlantic and no decision had been made to send them to the Pacific where they would be up against nine Japanese carriers. There could be even more enemy ships since no one really knew what they were building back in the Japanese Home Islands.

Merchant added that the U.S. Navy had a number of battleships remaining even after the disaster at Pearl Harbor, including a couple that had been damaged during the raid and subsequently repaired. Merchant said that all of them were old and that less than a handful of other American battleships were in the Atlantic confronting the Nazi U-boat menace. In Admiral Nimitz's opinion, those few old battleships would be destroyed if they attempted to take on the Japanese carriers and their attendant battleships.

"It's rumored that the Japs have at least one monster battlewagon that could blow all our ships to hell," added Merchant, "but we're taking that with a grain of salt."

New battleships and carriers were under construction and in varying degrees of completion, but they would not be ready for battle for some months at the very least.

"To be blunt, gents, we are on our own, which is why the Pacific Fleet, such at it is, will be departing for San Diego. We gave some thought to us being picked up by subs off a beach up north, but decided it would be too difficult and time consuming to ferry people out through the surf. Besides, a lot of our key people are too old for such shenanigans or, like Dane here, too banged up. Ergo, we will be boarding in the harbor and will exit the channel submerged. We will exit behind a tug which we will use as a beacon and a guide."

Merchant looked at his watch. "You have a little more than twenty-four hours before we go, so settle what private matters you have. And Dane, I want to see you."

When the group had scattered, Merchant took Dane into Spruance's empty office. "First off, are you going to be able to get on the sub?"

"I'll have no problem, sir."

"That's good enough for me even though I think you're lying through your teeth. Second, the admiral wants to thank you again for saving his life. You will probably get a promotion and you will definitely get a letter of personal commendation from the admiral, if not a medal. Second, and I don't know what the hell he means by this, but he said you and he had no conversations regarding mortality while in the life raft."

Dane smiled. "Please tell the admiral I have no idea what he's talking about."

Merchant blinked and then grinned. "Damn good answer. See you tomorrow night."

Dane had no bills or any other personal matters that needed settling. He thought about his situation for a moment and made a decision. It took only a few moments sweet-talking another nurse to get Amanda Mallard's phone number and home address. He called her and invited her to dinner. She declined, but said she'd go for a walk with him if he cared to meet her. She reminded him that his leg needed work and he'd better go walking if he wanted to get on that sub.

An hour later, they were strolling in the clean warm sands of Waikiki. Both were barefoot and Tim's pants were rolled up to his knees. Amanda wore a flowered skirt that she tied up and tucked into her waist, providing him with a mid-thigh view of her slender white legs. They strolled along the edge of the water like kids, dodging the waves and getting their feet wet. An occasional larger wave splashed them and they laughed. It was an opportunity to forget the violent world around them and they took it with gusto.

Although she'd declined to go to dinner with him, he brought a couple of steak sandwiches from the officer's club. The meat was tender, rare, and covered with onions and mayonnaise. She'd devoured hers in a couple of minutes after commenting that rationing was already making life difficult. Tim ate half of his and told her to take the rest back to her apartment, which she said she shared with two other civilian nurses.

"Are you feeling guilty?" she asked.

"A little. I'm well fed and mending from my injuries and, tomorrow night, getting out of what used to be this island paradise. I've got to tell you, I'm very unhappy at the thought of you remaining here. I was kind of hoping we'd have time to get to know each other a little better."

She smiled gently. She wasn't wearing her glasses and her eyes were large and bright. "That makes two of us, although the latest scuttlebutt has us going by transport in a couple of weeks. The same rumors have us being escorted by the battleships that either survived the attack or were in California when Pearl Harbor was struck."

She shuddered and leaned against him. "If I live

to be a hundred, I will never forget that morning. When some of the wounded got to me, they weren't humans anymore, Tim, they were just pieces of meat that were somehow still alive. Many of them weren't alive for long, and that may have been a mercy."

Tim mentioned that he too would never forget the dead and dying on the *Enterprise*, or the bodies that floated by the raft he and Spruance had occupied.

In the distance, a handful of sailboats, silhouetted by the moonlight, moved gracefully across the swells. It was a scene from another world, another era. Tim wondered if Japanese warships were just over the horizon or if enemy periscopes were surveying the shore, and if they could see the two of them walking together and what they thought about it. Maybe some Jap captain was laughing and planning their destruction. The enemy planes that had attacked the day before had come from a carrier that had to be out there somewhere.

Amanda looked up at the stars. "If I can't get on a transport, I'll sail to California."

"You're joking."

She bristled and stamped her bare foot, splashing both of them. "I am not joking, and please don't tell me you're one of those men who thinks women are fragile and innocent creatures who can't do anything without a big strong dumb man helping them. You may be big and strong and probably not dumb, and have nice brown eyes, but I can manage well enough alone. I can sail a boat and I have friends who can do it as well, and oh yeah, I know an old guy who owns one. Give me a decent sailboat and enough food and water and I can sail it anyplace."

He took her hand. She did not pull it back. "If it comes to that, Amanda, do it."

The Japanese had committed terrible atrocities when they'd taken Hong Kong and the Philippines. They'd targeted nurses and hospitals for many of their most savage outrages, slaughtering the patients and raping the nurses before murdering them as well.

She managed a smile. "Want me to look you up when I make it to California?"

"I would like that a lot." He pulled her to him and they embraced. He felt her body shake. She was crying. He kissed her and she held him tightly. "We'll meet in California."

Her response was to kiss him back.

The three submarines that were to take the forty men of Spruance's staff were docked in slips located below the fleet headquarters. It was the same building where the now-disgraced and removed Admiral Kimmel had watched both his fleet and his career destroyed.

Along with Tim and Captain Merchant, another ten men would be squeezed into what they had been told were already extremely tight quarters. Tim was well aware what that meant, having spent a couple of days in a sub before the seaplane had picked up him and the admiral. Tim was larger than average, and the average submariner was even smaller than that. For that matter, so too were pilots and many others in the military. There was, he thought ironically, simply no room for larger people in many military professions.

Before boarding, they were gathered in a conference room by their skipper, a very young, short, and lean lieutenant commander named Torelli who gave them a stern lecture.

"I know I am junior in rank to most of you, but let there be no doubt—I am the captain of this sub and I will make all decisions while you are on board. To begin with, you will be assigned bunks and you will spend as much time as possible in them and I don't care how cramped and uncomfortable they might be. This is in order to keep you out of the way of the crew, who have assignments that must be carried out if we are to arrive safely. If we are in danger, you will lie perfectly still in those bunks and not even talk. If you have to piss or crap, do it right there and don't worry about it. We don't believe that the Nips have any sound-detecting devices like sonar, but we're not certain so nobody's taking chances. When necessary, we will run as silent as a mouse. We don't think their radar's all that great either, but a lot of things were proven wrong on Pearl Harbor, weren't they?"

That comment was greated with grunts and growls. The Japanese had been terribly underestimated.

Torelli continued. "The food on board will be shitty at best and the heads are inadequate for the needs of the crew, much less an additional dozen men. Cleanliness might be a virtue in another world, but such virtue will have to wait until we reach California. For those of you who've never been on a sub, it will stink like a sewer when you go on board, so a little more shit odor and body stench won't make a hell of a lot of difference, and it will get worse the longer it takes for us to get to California."

"Will you attack Jap ships if we spot any?" Merchant asked.

"My orders are to deliver you safely and not pick any fights. We will only defend ourselves and then only as a last resort. I have four torpedoes left from my last patrol. Since we're heading to California, the powers here declared I couldn't have any more of their precious supply."

"Have you sunk any ships?" Tim asked.

"Nothing to write home about," Torelli said. "Two small freighters."

Torelli didn't add that most of the torpedoes he'd fired had either malfunctioned or missed, and he didn't think his aim had been off all that often. He'd had a Japanese light cruiser dead to rights and the many torpedoes he'd fired had failed to explode, even though he'd heard two of them clang against the enemy's hull. This was an issue that was very common and a cause of great concern among American submariners. He'd reported it up the line to Admiral Lockwood, who now commanded the sub force and was waiting for the bureaucratic shit to hit the fan.

Like children in grade school, they were paraded single file out to the dock. Tim looked around. It was two in the morning, a time when all good Japanese spies should be asleep, and all but the most essential lights were off in the harbor. Naval intelligence and the FBI said there weren't any spies around, but who could be certain? Tim was one of many who wondered just how the hell the Japs had known so much about Pearl Harbor. The only logical answer was that there had been spies, probably Japanese consular officials, maybe others.

The sky was clear and there was a half moon, so there was some visibility. There was no real reason to suspect any of the population of Hawaii of being spies, but one could never be too careful. What they couldn't see, they couldn't report.

Even though there was a war on, secrets were hard to keep, and several dozen onlookers were present. Both curious military personnel and a handful of civilians were kept behind a tall wire fence by armed sailors. Some of the civilians were dependents and looked distraught. Tim looked to see if Amanda was one of them, and there she was. He waved and she waved back. She didn't smile. He thought she looked a little lost, and he ached at leaving her behind to what might be a terrible fate.

Tim needed only a little help making it down the submarine's deck hatch and into the hull. As promised and as he recalled, the odor of oil, grease, and God only knew what overwhelmed them and a couple of officers gagged.

"Pussies," muttered a sailor and other crewmen laughed.

"I guess we are pussies," said Merchant. "Dane, I've talked to Torelli, and you and I are going to be bunking by each other. I'm taking the top, of course. I'll be the senior officer in the group and rank does have some privileges."

"Understood, sir."

"If we're going to spending a lot of time cheek by jowl, I'm going to pick your mind about anything you know about Japan and the Japanese. If nothing else, it might help pass the time. If you bore me, I'll have Torelli fire you out a torpedo tube. If what you know is useful, you'll be giving some briefings to the staff when we get to California. If we get to California, that is."

The sub began to move and there was a disconcerting feeling when she slid bow down and submerged to periscope depth. The tug led her and the two others out of the harbor and through the narrow channel that led to the ocean. If the enemy was anywhere, they would be waiting for them to emerge from the harbor.

They lay in their bunks with hearts racing. They wouldn't have far to go before they reached relative safety, as the island of Oahu was considered by some to be a mountain that jutted up from the ocean depths; the dropoff to truly deep water would be sudden and soon.

After a surprisingly short amount of time, Torelli gave orders and the sub dived to deeper waters. They had made it out of Pearl Harbor and were on their way to California. They hoped.

A few miles back, Amanda and a handful of others stood by the empty space that once held the three subs and watched and stared. That they could see nothing at all was both frightening and reassuring. For Amanda, it was a terribly lonely feeling and she tried hard not to cry. She felt a sudden and intense kinship with the man she'd so recently met and barely knew. Now, however, she had her own decisions to make, but one thing was tremendously important. She had to get to California.

The train from hell had taken an eternity, or so it seemed to Second Lieutenant Steve Farris, U.S. Army. Hell, the starting point, had actually been Chicago and the train had been overfilled with GIs and their duffle bags and some equipment, minus weapons and helmets. They had been en route to the West Coast to reinforce the troops waiting and watching for a Japanese invasion. Instead of the couple of days a train trip should have taken, the journey from hell had lasted for two long weeks. Two weeks without proper food, not enough water to drink and wash with, and, when they went through the mountains, plenty of scenery, but no heat. The toilets had backed up almost immediately and toilet paper ran out as well.

He'd even seen his first stabbing as two soldiers had gotten into an argument over something. One man wound up with a switchblade in his gut, while the other was placed under arrest and would be charged with attempted murder. Farris been shocked by both the sudden violence and the tremendous amounts of blood that had been spilled.

The men in his brand-new platoon had looked to him for leadership and Farris couldn't provide it. The men, with the exception of Platoon Sergeant Stecher, who treated him with the polite contempt of a veteran for a novice, were all straight out of basic training and scarcely knew how to put on their uniforms. Farris wasn't much better. He was a ninety-day wonder recently graduated from Officer Candidate School and didn't know much more than his men, and he sure as hell didn't know what to do when men settled arguments with knives.

Nor could he get much help from his company commander, Captain Lytle, as that man had spent most of the trip drunk. Lytle had commandeered the only compartment on the train and had filled it with crates he'd brought along. Stecher said that Lytle had owned a bar back in Pennsylvania and had brought most of his inventory.

Robert Conroy

Finally, somehow, they had made it to San Diego and the platoon stood in the train station with several hundred other men in wrinkled and filthy uniforms. Sergeant Stecher stepped up to Farris and made no effort to salute. Farris ignored Stecher's quiet insolence. "What now, Lieutenant?"

"Food, water, and a shower, sergeant. At least that's what I want, and then maybe some sleep." He saw some Red Cross people giving out donuts and told Stecher to send the men over to get something to eat. To his mild surprise, Stecher didn't put up a fuss. Maybe Farris had said the right thing. After all, didn't an army travel on its stomach?

Captain Lytle walked unsteadily up to them. "We are now a recon battalion and part of the Thirty-Second Infantry Division currently stationed here in San Diego. When your men are through stuffing their faces, there are some trucks to take us to temporary quarters, and after some training, out to our patrol areas."

Farris saluted and went to gather his troops. They were part of an understrength and poorly trained National Guard detachment from Pennsylvania that had been fleshed out with a number of raw recruits, brand-new officers like Farris, and a handful of real soldiers like Stecher. They were all part of a civilian army girding for war and were a long way from being soldiers. Well, he thought, so was he. The really disconcerting fact was that he was the senior lieutenant in the company, a de facto second-in-command to Lytle. The other three lieutenants were even less experienced than he and had received their commissions a few weeks after he had.

For the thousandth time he wondered why he hadn't

pulled some strings and gotten into the navy, even if it had to be as an enlisted man. At least sailors had decent places to sleep and even better food, he was told, and they didn't have to march through swamps or climb mountains. He'd envied his uncle and still did, even though Uncle Tim had gotten damn close to being killed in the Midway Massacre. Tim had managed to get a telegram to the family that all was well, which had both relieved and shocked them. Nobody'd had any idea he was out on any ship, much less the doomed *Enterprise*.

Stecher returned and glared at Lytle as the short, pudgy captain departed. "What the hell does he mean by patrol areas? I want to kill Japs, not patrol some fucking beach."

Farris didn't think that patrolling a beach in Southern California was all that bad an idea, especially in the summertime when California girls went out sunbathing. He'd heard delicious rumors that a lot of them swam and sunned in the nude. Yes, he'd like to patrol those beaches.

However, he understood Stecher's concern. The sergeant's brother had been killed at Pearl Harbor and he wanted revenge. Steve had heard the story a dozen times, and it always ended with a rightfully furious Stecher raging that "The fucking Japs murdered him. He was running across a field and one of their planes strafed him. Who the hell would cut down a man who's running away?"

Farris had no answer. He deeply sympathized with the sergeant and said so, but there was nothing he or anyone else could do. The army would send them where it wished.

Originally it appeared that they'd been slated to go elsewhere, and rumors first said it would have been North Africa or some other place that was dry and dusty. This made sense when they were first given some desert gear. But then came the Midway debacle and fears rose that the Japanese would attack the West Coast; thus, they and large numbers of other American soldiers were sent on their way to San Diego.

Base was a tent city outside San Diego. Still exhausted from their trip, Farris and the others were issued additional equipment and uniforms and assigned places in the tents that would be their new home, at least for a short while.

Lytle gathered them around him. He was reasonably sober now. Perhaps it had something to do with the presence of other and more senior officers.

"Tomorrow we'll be issued weapons and we'll start in with physical training and shooting, although it looks like we'll be getting shit for equipment."

"It won't matter much if all we're gonna do is patrol the beaches," Stecher muttered.

Lytle continued. If he'd heard the comment, he didn't let on. "Additionally, there are a lot of Marines in the area, and we're ordered to steer clear of them so there are no incidents."

Stecher wanted to go to war, but even a rookie like Farris knew they were in no condition to fight. They were out of shape, poorly trained, and, he had to admit, poorly led, and that included by himself. If they were sent into war now, they would be slaughtered. Hell, even a bar fight with a bunch of Marines would be a one-sided farce. Perhaps it would be best if all they did for a long while was patrol California's beaches.

CHAPTER 3

THERE WAS LITTLE ROOM FOR A MEETING OF ANY kind in a sub, but Merchant, Dane, and Torelli managed to find space in the glorified closet that served as a dining area. When Torelli found that the other two were going to discuss Dane's experiences as a young man in Japan, he invited himself in. It was, he genially reminded them, his sub. They were running on the surface and fresh air was streaming down the open hatches, trying to make a dent in the accumulated stench.

Dane explained that his father had owned an export-import business mainly dealing with low-priced, often cheaply made, Japanese goods imported into the United States. And, yes, this did include the ridiculous paper parasols that decorated cocktails. His occupation required him to make a number of extended trips to Tokyo and, when Tim was old enough, he scheduled them for the summertime so the boy could go with him. Tim learned Japanese through immersion. His father spoke only Japanese to him during these forays and, to amuse him, taught him how to read it as well.

"Can you write it?" Torelli asked.

"Nope. Never could get those little squiggles in the right order."

"It's amazing they can," said Merchant. "But then, I feel the same way about Arab writing and they probably feel the same way about us. Did you ever speak to any of their military?"

"Yes, sir, and that gets to the point of what I want to say. The first summer I was there, I more or less kept quiet for the first few weeks and just listened to conversations, and some of them were about me since most Japanese didn't see all that many white people, and especially not a teenager. Diplomats and businessmen sometimes, but kids? Never. The average Japanese living outside the big cities and the commercial areas rarely saw anybody who wasn't Japanese like them.

"I wasn't confident enough in my own speaking abilities at first. Then one day I was simply playing the dumb tourist when I heard a bunch of young naval officers talking about me. They never dreamed I could understand them, what with me being an ignorant barbarian and all that, and they were making all kinds of crude comments about the little white boy who doubtless had a tiny white dick. Finally, when I'd had enough, I turned and confronted them. I told them in Japanese that their rudeness was a disgrace to their families and their ancestors. I thought they'd shit they were so shocked."

Merchant laughed. "I'd have paid money to see that."

"They actually apologized and after that we became sort of friends. They were delighted to pick the mind of an American and I enjoyed learning about them, even though some of what I found out scared me. Tell me, have either of you heard of the code of bushido?"

Torelli answered. "Code of the warrior or something like that. Kind of medieval, I've heard."

"Right," said Dane, "but it's something that many of them, particularly the officers, believe in totally and utterly, no matter how insane it may sound to us. Let me give you an example, because I actually discussed this with them. Say you're the pilot of a plane and the plane is badly damaged during an attack on enemy ships. You're not going to make it back to base, so what do you do?"

Torelli laughed. "That's easy. You look for a place to set down or bail out."

"Would you surrender?"

"Of course," Torelli said, puzzled. "I wouldn't like it, but if that's the only alternative to a useless death, why not?"

"But they won't, because they don't consider such a death useless," Dane continued. "Surrender is dishonorable and against their definition of the code of bushido. To them, surrender is a disgrace. They and their families would be humiliated. Any man who surrendered would no longer exist. I've heard that their pilots don't even wear parachutes because it's dishonorable to bail out and try to save one's life. No, what they said they would do is aim that plane toward an enemy ship or installation and crash into it, finding glory in stupid flaming death. We all at least think we might have to die for our country, but the Japanese will actually search it out to satisfy their warped sense of honor."

"That's nuts," said Torelli.

"By our way of thinking, yes, but not by theirs, and even many of their enlisted men believe that, probably in part because it's been beaten into them by their officers, and I do mean literally beaten in. In short, they will not surrender. Oh, they'll reluctantly retreat and regroup and in order to fight again another day, but they won't surrender. They'll die and they will try to take as many of us with them as they can. Picture a wounded Japanese infantryman with a hand grenade hidden on his body. Just when an American medic comes up to help him, he pulls the pin and kills everyone around him; thus dying gloriously."

"And you believed them?" Torelli asked.

"I believe that they believed it sincerely when I spoke with them. Whether they would actually do it, I don't know, but it wouldn't surprise me at all. I did talk with a Shinto priest, and he told me that what the military is professing is a radicalized version of bushido in which death is considered a duty. Taking others along with you would be a bonus."

Merchant took a deep breath. "Dane, to your knowledge, has this craziness happened yet?"

"I don't know. When we get to San Diego, I'd like to look over some reports. By the way, it's only the real Japanese who feel that way. They've drafted others into their army, like Koreans and Okinawans, who definitely believe in surrender and do not feel bound by the code of bushido. But . . . they all look alike, don't they?" he asked wickedly.

"Assuming you're right, I can see a lot of what we used to call atrocities occurring," said Merchant. "Nobody's going to want to take the chance of taking someone prisoner and then having that prisoner try to kill him. They'll just shoot the Jap son of a bitch and I wouldn't blame them."

"There's more, Captain, and this is just as amazing. Their army and navy hate each other. I mean, we have our rivalries, but they really don't go all that much farther than the Army-Navy game and a few drunken brawls afterwards. Can you imagine one service jeopardizing the fate of the country because of really intense jealousies? Can you even think of the American Army invading Mexico without telling either President Roosevelt or the navy?"

"Not really," said Merchant. "In fact, it's utterly inconceivable, almost as illogical as suicide."

"But that's exactly what the Japanese Army did in Manchuria and China, and the Japanese Navy boys I talked with are totally, thoroughly pissed. I'll bet you a dollar the attack on Pearl Harbor was at least in part a payback for the army's unannounced move into China."

Merchant stood up abruptly and bumped his head on a pipe. "Damn it," he snarled and rubbed his skull. "Dane, when we do get to safety, I want you to write up a report, a paper, on what you learned."

"Yes, sir."

"Just curious," Torelli asked, "but did the combination of war and Depression damage your father's business with the Land of the Rising Sun?"

Dane chuckled. He was very proud of his old man. "Not really. He saw the war coming and sold out a few years ago to a group of Japanese businessmen who probably, hopefully, lost their shirts. He thinks the combination of the war and the Depression is going to cause a real-estate explosion in the United States when the war ends, so he's buying up vacant properties in areas around major cities. If he's right and the war doesn't last beyond 1950 or so, he'll probably be rich. I'll be his heir, of course."

There was a sudden commotion on deck and the conversation was over. Torelli shouted orders as men tumbled down from the conning tower in a well choreographed dance that only looked like chaos. Ships had been spotted on the horizon, and the submarine quickly and quietly slipped under the sea. Ships meant the enemy. There were no American warships in this area of the Pacific. With luck, their low silhouette had not been spotted.

Back in their bunks, they waited, helpless to do anything about the peril they were in. Dane wondered if the air had just gotten staler and hotter, or was it just his imagination. He'd never been claustrophobic, but being prone and helpless in a too-small cot in a sub maybe hundreds of feet under the ocean was a truly frightening experience.

An explosion shook them, rattling everything in the sub. They were being depth charged. Dane wanted to run and ask Torelli what was happening, but that was painfully obvious. The Japanese had somehow spotted them and were attacking.

Another explosion, this one much closer—it almost threw him out of his bunk. He held on tight and the lights went off. For an utterly horrible instant, they were plunged into total darkness. Dane thought they would plunge to the bottom of the Pacific and be there forever, dying slowly, gasping like fish on the floor until the air finally ran out.

After an eternity, the lights flickered and came back on. Someone in the group was screaming and sailors pounced on him, stuffing a rag in his mouth. Dane was shocked to realize that cold water was dripping on him. Were they sinking? His heart began to pound as if it wanted to explode from his chest.

He smelled urine and wondered who'd pissed himself. He checked, and thankfully, it wasn't him.

Another set of explosions shook them, but these were farther away. Even better, the leak had stopped. After what seemed an eternity, Torelli approached them.

"I think we got away. One of their floatplanes saw us and we were damned lucky. Maybe they thought they got us or maybe they just don't give a damn. From now on we'll travel submerged during the day and on the surface only at night. In the meantime, we'll stay submerged for a couple of hours to make sure the Japs have cleared the area. It may take us a little longer to get to San Diego, but I'd rather be safe than sunk."

Only Torelli's eyes betrayed the fact that he was as frightened as they were. He took an obvious deep breath and the fear disappeared. "We identified two *Kongo*-class battleships and two aircraft carriers. We were too far away to get a specific make on them, although one carrier might have been the *Akagi*, but their course said they were headed toward Hawaii. We got off a radio signal, fat lot of good that will do. Hawaii's got nothing to fight with, at least nothing that flies or floats, and the army in Hawaii will just be a sitting duck. I hate to think what those carrier planes and the battlewagons' fourteen-inch guns could do to a defenseless city like Honolulu."

Dane sagged back on his too-small bunk and thought about the Japanese flotilla headed toward Hawaii. What would happen to the people in paradise, he wondered? What would happen to Amanda Mallard?

Amanda and her roommates cowered amid other tenants and passersby in the basement of their two-story frame apartment building while waves of Japanese planes flew over Honolulu and Pearl Harbor.

"There can't be much left to bomb," said Grace Renkowski. At thirty-five, she was the oldest of the three roommates. The Japanese planes had been overhead almost constantly since morning. Hawaii was almost defenseless, little more than a punching bag. When the attacks began, they'd watched as a handful of American planes rose to meet the Japanese horde. They'd been saddened and sickened as the brave American pilots had their planes blown from the sky by Japanese Zeros that seemed to dance among them. There were few parachutes and those that did blossom were attacked by the Japanese and shredded, the pilots falling to their deaths.

"Why don't we have any good planes!" lamented Sandy Watson, the other roommate. She was twenty-three and, like the others, a civilian contract nurse.

Or good leaders, Amanda thought. Somebody should go to jail for this litany of disasters. Why weren't we prepared when the first attack on Pearl Harbor occurred? She'd been in bed on December 7th after a normal Saturday evening dancing with young officers. She'd awakened to the explosions and the improbable fact that Pearl Harbor was being attacked and the fleet slaughtered before her eyes. Why did so many good young men have to be killed and wounded before somebody woke up to the fact that the Japs wanted to kill us? And now it was even worse and not very likely to change.

The explosions changed in volume. One of the older men in the basement with them nodded solemnly. "Those aren't bombs, girlies, those are shells. The damned Japs are close enough to shoot at us with their ships."

Normally, Amanda would have resented being called a girlie, but this was too serious for trivialities. If Japanese warships were close enough to shoot at land-based targets, would the Japanese soon be landing troops? God help them if this was the invasion they all feared and anticipated.

After half an hour, there was silence. The all clear sounded, and they left their shelter and went outside. The area around her apartment was largely untouched, although a few small fires burned and were being attacked by neighbors with brooms and buckets. The old man explained that the fires were probably caused by American shells being shot into the air and coming down on something flammable. The harbor was again in flames as the giant fuel tanks that provided oil, the lifeblood of the fleet, sent enormous clouds of black smoke billowing thousands of feet into the sky. The only good news was that there didn't appear to be a Japanese landing force approaching the shore.

Shouting and screams distracted them. Scores of people were headed toward a grocery store. The plate glass windows were broken and a small elderly Japanese man was futilely waving a broom at the mob pouring in while others left with armloads of bread, beer, canned goods, and anything else that struck their fancy.

The owner grabbed a looter's arm and was knocked down. The looter and a couple of his companions kicked and stomped the poor man until he lay bloody and still. A woman, probably the grocer's wife, emerged screaming. Her face was bloodied and bruised. She fell down beside the injured man and continued to scream. A police siren wailed and the crowd vanished as quickly as it had appeared.

Amanda and the others ran to the fallen man and began to check him over. "He's breathing," she said. The woman's howls diminished into sobbing. Grace tried to comfort her while Sandy and Amanda helped the man, who was having trouble breathing.

"Maybe broken ribs," Sandy said, and Amanda concurred. "And perhaps a heart attack, too."

An ambulance arrived and they helped put him inside along with the woman who was indeed his wife. Some neighbors tried to board up the store even though it had been pretty well stripped of anything valuable. The cops took their statement although they could add nothing to the obvious. Nor did anyone recognize any of the looters.

"I wonder if the stupid bastards in Washington can see this," Grace said as she looked at the desolation that had once been a family's livelihood. That it had been caused by Americans and not the enemy made it even more difficult to swallow. "I voted for Roosevelt and look what he's gone and caused."

"I don't think the politicians in Washington can see much of anything," Amanda said. She too had voted for FDR over the Republican Wendell Wilkie, as had most of America. "But I do think this shows just how helpless our situation is. Are we all agreed that we have to do something?" They were. "Good, now let's go see Mack."

The Japanese Marines were formally called "Special Naval Landing Forces," and were proud of their training, their skills, and their ferocity in combat. They were well led, and always fought efficiently and bravely. And they never surrendered. Like their elite counterparts in the U.S. Marine Corps, they were the ones who would land on hostile beaches and fight their way to victory. A number of them had even been trained as paratroopers and they rightfully thought of themselves as a truly elite force.

There were those who thought this was a suicide mission, but Captain Seizo Arao dismissed such complaints. He had a hundred men on the tramp steamer. Her counterfeit markings said she was Spanish, a neutral, which meant that she was safe from undue notice as she approached the Pacific coast of Panama.

A clumsily applied paint job proclaimed her as the *Santa Anna Maria.* She was tawdry and harmless looking, which offended Arao's sense of military professionalism, even though he recognized the necessity for such a slovenly disguise. Soon the time for skulking would be over and his men would commence attacking, bringing the war to one of America's economic and military treasures, the Panama Canal.

In the ship's hull, the hundred men of the Special Landing Force detachment waited eagerly and stoically, shrugging off their discomfort as a temporary and trivial inconvenience. They were honored to have had been chosen to attack the Panama Canal, which they all knew was a vital means of moving American ships from the Atlantic into the Pacific where they would confront the Japanese Navy.

Not only would the hundred men fight as soldiers, but they would also be mules, carrying large amounts of explosives. The normally stern and stoic Captain Arao had joined in the laughter when he heard his men joking that one accident with the dynamite and they'd all be back in Tokyo in time for dinner. It was good to have men like that.

They anchored a few miles north of the Pacific terminus of the canal and waited for darkness. They were not alone. A number of other ships were waiting for their turn to cross to the Atlantic. The Americans who ran the canal had stepped up their security, especially before ships could enter the canal; but they could not closely watch so many ships still at sea. Perhaps they'd ultimately get curious and check the hold of the *Santa Anna Maria*, but the men should be gone before the Americans even began to wonder about the Spanish-flagged tramp. With only a little luck, she would journey safely back to a Japanese base.

The Americans had a small army base at Fort Clayton, close to the Miraflores Lock, but it was on the other side of the canal. National Guard soldiers were supposed to be garrisoned there, but Japanese intelligence could not tell how many men were in the fort, or their state of preparedness. It probably wouldn't matter. National Guard troops were known to be poorly trained and would be not present much of a problem. No matter, Arao thought, they would be through with the Miraflores Locks before the bumbling Americans could react.

Shortly after midnight, the Japanese Marines departed the freighter by lifeboat and landed on a sandy beach south of the canal. The *Santa Anna Maria* would wait for two weeks in case there were survivors from the attack on America's military strength. Arao's wish was for complete success and many survivors, but he would gladly settle for success and a glorious death.

The Panama Canal was only fifty miles long, a short distance for Arao's men; especially since they were only going a few miles inland to the first series of locks at Miraflores. However, they soon found themselves exhausted and confused as they traveled through the steamy heat and the dense jungle foliage, which they had to do to stay hidden. The Americans doubtless had soldiers near the canal and, no matter how poor they were, Arao's men didn't want to meet them, at least not yet. Prudently, Arao decided to wait and let his men rest. They were tough and hardened as only a Japanese soldier can be, but a well-rested soldier was a much better fighter than a fatigued one, and the next several days promised to be exhausting enough.

Thus, it was after midnight of the third night when they finally made their move. Their entry was laughably easy. Barbed wire surrounding the locks was cut and half of Arao's men poured through. These had the job of neutralizing American security while the rest carried double loads of explosives and detonators.

They had no idea how well the locks were protected, so they simply swarmed out, looking for the enemy. Their instructions were to use their rifles only as a last resort. Bayonets and officers' swords would be best.

Arao led his men around a corner of a building that looked like a maintenance shack. Two men in overalls looked up in disbelief at the apparitions racing toward them. Arao's sword whipped the air. The first man was beheaded in an instant, and a Japanese Marine rammed a bayonet into the chest of the second. Arao laughed and wondered if it would it all be this simple?

It wouldn't be. Screams and gunshots split the air. Damn, he thought, somebody was awake. He laughed and howled with pleasure. Let the fight begin. Sirens wailed and lights came on. Rifle fire increased in volume and a machine gun opened up, chattering insanely and shooting wildly. It looked like some American soldiers were on duty and willing to fight.

Arao exhorted his men to move more quickly and place their charges, while his lieutenants established an effective perimeter to keep the Americans from interfering with them. His plan was uncomplicated—he would blow the gates closest to the ocean and move inland in the direction of Gatun Lake, destroying as he went. Both Miraflores Lake and Gatun Lake were artificial, created by the construction of the canal itself. The lakes not only served as a highway for ships, but as reservoirs for the canal area. They were well above sea level, and a few well placed charges would drain the entire complex. He laughed as the first charge went off, blowing a set of gates to smithereens and sending a torrent of water gushing down to the ocean. Wouldn't it be marvelous, he thought, if any ships attempting to use the canal had to slither through the mud of what used to be Gatun and Miraflores Lakes?

Hours later, Arao realized his error. He should have begun his destruction of the locks farther up at Pedro Miguel where the water from the Calebra Cut waited to flow to the Pacific and not so close to the ocean itself. Still, success was within reach. The Americans had been slow to realize the threat, but when they did, they'd attacked with a vengeance. He'd lost nearly half his men, many of them to low flying and obsolete American biplanes who'd caught them out in the open and cut them down with machine guns. His men had shot down one plane that had flown too low. They'd ambushed Americans who were slow to recognize the artfully placed traps he'd set for them. Americans were brave, he concluded, just not very smart. Now he was at the last of the locks he needed to destroy.

Rifle and machine-gun fire ripped through the air and mortars exploded around him. All the charges were placed. He gave the signal and drew his sword, then dashed up the wall of the cut to where the rushing water wouldn't reach him. He would die with his sword in his hand and not beneath a wave of scummy water rushing from the lake like a Pacific tsunami. The explosion ripped the final gates and water from a few miles above him began to flow freely to the sea. Arao laughed harshly. It had taken the Americans many years to dig the Canal. How long would it take them to fix it?

Bullets ripped into his body and he fell to the ground, gasping in pain and shock. His sword flew out of his hand and, before he could reach it, an American soldier picked it up and shot him again.

"Leave him be," yelled an American officer. "We want a prisoner, not another dead Jap."

Arao didn't understand the words, but their intent was plain. The Americans wanted to take him prisoner. He would not let that happen. He had succeeded, but his men were all dead and soon he would be as well. He was lying on his stomach and he managed to take a grenade from his belt. He pulled the pin but kept the trigger down. He groaned piteously to gain sympathy. It was easy, and it was the truth. He was in agony from his wounds and death would be welcome.

The officer who wanted him alive and a medic rolled him over. The last thing Arao saw in this world was the look of horror on the Americans' faces when they realized he was holding a live grenade.

The women had earlier guessed that Mack was somewhere between fifty and eighty. He was small, wizened, and withered. His skin was baked brown by the sun, and covered by a multitude of tattoos. He never said where he came from and no one knew if Mack was his first or last name or none of the above. He lived in a shack on the beach near the small town of Nanakuli, a few miles west of Honolulu. Mack was one of the few residents of the area not of Hawaiian ancestry. Nobody minded. He was friendly, spent his money locally, and sometimes brought business to the area's poor restaurants and bars.

He greeted the three women with a smile and threw his cigarette into the ocean. The nurses had been customers, good customers who'd enjoyed both his tours and his company. Mack owned a forty-foot twin-hulled sailboat of a type called a catamaran, and he made a living of sorts taking tourists and locals sailing in the clear waters around Oahu. He especially liked taking scantily clad young and not-so-young ladies out on his boat. As he told his few friends, he was old, not dead, and, besides, every now and then one of the vacationing old maid school teachers from New Jersey or some other dull place felt liberated enough by being in paradise to get herself laid by a genuine tattooed Hawaiian who owned a sailboat.

These three nurses had been fairly frequent visitors and, while not raving beauties, were pleasant enough in the two-piece bathing suits many young women liked to wear, or with their regular clothing wet and plastered against their young bodies. He hadn't screwed either of them yet, but that was correctable. In his opinion, Amanda was too thin and Sandy too plump, but either would do in a pinch. Grace, however, was a little older and shapelier, and seemed more worldly. In Mack's opinion she was prime for the plucking.

The women were skilled enough sailors that he didn't have to hire others to crew his cat when they were on board, which saved him money, and they got free rides. He smiled and thought he'd really like to give Grace a free ride.

It was not a bad life, but war clouds had gathered and he was afraid his pleasant and near-idyllic life was coming to an end. Fuck.

"Ladies, how can I help you?"

"How far can you sail this thing?" Amanda asked with a smile.

Mack shrugged. It was a most intriguing question. "How far do you want to go?"

"California," Grace said.

If Mack was surprised, he didn't show it. "Kinda been thinking along those lines myself. I think paradise is about to get damn near ugly, hellish, if you will."

"Will you take us?" Amanda asked.

Mack paused before answering. He hadn't anticipated

the question. "Do you know what you'd be getting into? I'd rather have three men than three women. Men are stronger."

Amanda smiled tightly. "But no men are lining up to go with you, are they? And besides, we asked first. And since we're smaller than the average male, we won't take up as much room or eat as much, now will we? And don't forget, we do know how to sail the cat."

"Like I said, do you have any idea what you'd be getting into? It's maybe two thousand miles or more to California and even if we got lucky, it'd likely take us a month or two. For us to make it, we'd need a lot of food and water so we don't die. There'd be no privacy whatsoever. There's a cabin on the cat and a one-holer inside leading to the ocean, but that's for tourists. If we sailed, the cabin and everyplace else would be full of supplies. Any of you genteel ladies want to pee or poop, you'd have to hang your butts off the boat and solve your problem that way."

"Or we could jump into the ocean to relieve ourselves and scare all the little fishies away," Amanda said sweetly. "Don't worry, we can do it. Besides, we've done it before."

"And if we guess wrong about the currents or the wind doesn't cooperate," Mack continued, "we could die a long and painful death in the middle of the ocean where nobody will find us."

"On the other hand," Amanda rebutted grimly, "we could die of starvation here on Oahu, or be raped and murdered when the Japs come ashore, which they will surely do, sooner or later. We've talked it over and we'd rather take our chances on your sailboat. We'd much rather do something to save ourselves than wait for the worst to happen. We'd also rather do it sooner rather than later, while we're still strong enough to do it."

Mack appeared to think for a moment, then nodded. "I want money, a thousand dollars apiece, and that'd be above and beyond anything we spend getting set up for this cruise."

"Why?" asked a surprised Sandy.

Mack smiled. "Because, sweetmeat, this catamaran is my living here. Assuming we make it to California, I'm going to have to pick up the pieces of my life and actually start earning a living. California ain't Hawaii. There they actually expect you to work instead of letting the sun bake your ass. Shit, I might even have to get a job in a factory," he said in mock horror.

Amanda thought quickly. She had fifteen hundred dollars in the bank. Whether they sailed or not, pulling it out before there was a run on the banks now seemed like a prudent idea. Sandy was a saver, too, but she had no idea how much Grace had. Whatever it was, they would make do.

"A deal," she said.

"Fine. Now we ain't leaving tomorrow or anything like that. I say we take a month to get ready, and that includes you nice ladies getting the money, finding supplies that won't perish or need cooking, and spending every weekend and any other time you can with me learning more about how to sail this beautiful boat that I named after my ex-wife."

Amanda was surprised. She hadn't known Mack had an ex-wife or that the catamaran had a name. "What's the cat's name?"

"The *Bitch*."

CHAPTER 4

ONLY TWO OF THE THREE SUBS THAT DEPARTED Pearl Harbor made it to San Diego. The third was never heard from again. Whether an accident or a Japanese attack caused the sub's death they would likely never know. Maybe someday the wreck would be discovered on the bottom of the ocean and the grieving families given some solace. Dane could only be thankful that it hadn't been him on that sub. The old phrase, there but for the grace of God go I, now carried great meaning for him.

The loss of more key personnel put an additional strain on Spruance's rebuilding staff, especially with his new job. Spruance was now chief of staff to Nimitz. It also resulted in Dane being promoted to lieutenant commander sooner than expected and his being given a more senior position in Captain Merchant's intelligence gathering group that was now reassigned directly to Nimitz.

On arrival at San Diego, Dane swore that he'd taken two trips on a sub and that there wouldn't be a third.

After being rescued from the sinking of the *Enterprise*, he'd spent much of the trip in his bunk enduring the pain from his knee. Along with the claustrophobia of the second trip, there'd been another scare when, approaching San Diego, overeager American fighter pilots decided that any sub was a Jap and strafed them. There were now several holes in Torelli's sub and he was thoroughly pissed off.

The staff officers were given fresh uniforms and assigned quarters in overcrowded facilities, and told to be in Admiral Nimitz's conference room by eight the next morning. Admiral Ernest J. King was on the base and he was going to get an overview of what was happening in the Pacific Theater, and Spruance, who had arrived safely a day earlier in the other surviving sub, wanted all of them to hear it.

The conference room was more of an auditorium and at least fifty people were present. Dane, as a newly ordained lieutenant commander, was one of the lowest-ranking officers present. As he took a seat alongside Merchant, Dane had the nagging feeling he still smelled of diesel and shit. He'd showered several times, but he still felt unclean. Torelli, also present for the briefing and unawed by the presence of all the brass, teased him mercilessly.

Admiral William Halsey—nobody who wanted to live ever called him "Bull" to his face—ran the meeting. He'd been hospitalized with a skin infection, shingles, when the Battle of Midway took place, and he still looked awful. Painful-looking blotches and scabs covered his arms and extended under his clothing, and Dane wondered how he could refrain from scratching himself to shreds.

Halsey looked for a moment at Admirals Spruance and King, who was just in from Washington. King had been appointed Chief of Naval Operations in the spring, replacing his good friend, Admiral Harold Stark, who was one of those blamed for the disaster at Pearl Harbor. King was reputed to be a lecher, a heavy drinker, and a hater of all things English. However, and despite all the rumors regarding his personal issues, he was considered a tough and highly qualified leader and, despite reservations, now supported the Europe-first strategy as the best way to win the war and ultimately get back at the Japanese.

Still, he wanted as much pressure as possible brought to bear on the Japanese as long as there were no major actions against Germany either occurring or planned for the near future. It was rumored that he was going to get his way but not for the reasons he'd anticipated. King's normally sour expression looked even more depressed. Stark had been blamed for Pearl Harbor, but it was King who was currently in charge. He bore the responsibility for Midway and the current dismal situation in the Pacific where the Japanese fleet could strike anywhere, anytime.

Halsey began. "First let me say that those of you who piss and moan that we have no major warships in the Pacific, and that means Hawaii, California, and the rest of the West Coast, are largely correct. The cupboard is pretty Goddamned bare, especially when it comes to carriers."

There were muted gasps and the sounds of chairs and feet shuffling. Halsey wasn't going to be handing out dollops of happy bullshit this fine morning.

"The Japs have bombed and shelled what was left

of our installations in Hawaii," he continued, "and the islands are now of little military use. The Japanese can take them anytime they wish. However, they might just decide they aren't worth the cost since we reinforced them after the attack on Pearl."

Halsey grimaced and continued. "We are not totally toothless. We still have one fleet carrier in the Pacific, the *Saratoga*, and for the time being she's anchored here in San Diego. The Japs, unfortunately, have maybe a dozen carriers with several more under construction. Since the Japs aren't telling us much, that's only a guess; but it does mean the *Sara* isn't going out alone. We do have two fleet carriers in the Atlantic along with a couple of smaller ones, but they aren't moving out here either. FDR says they are needed in that ocean to fight Nazi U-boats and, besides, the odds against us would only be slightly reduced. Any confrontation between our carriers and the Japanese fleet at this time would be suicide. We do have a number of fleet carriers under construction and they will start coming on line next year, which won't do us a whole lot of good today."

Halsey paused to let harsh reality sink in. "We are outnumbered in battleships as well, although not as badly. Admiral Pye has six battleships available, seven if the *Pennsylvania*'s repairs are completed soon. However, they are older ships, and the Japs have ten that we know of with at least two under construction, and those are reported to be real monsters. The *West Virginia* and *Nevada* are still being repaired and cannot be counted on for the near future.

"However, we will soon have some new battlewagons of our own. The *North Carolina* will arrive shortly, and Admiral King says the *Washington* will be shifted here from the Atlantic Fleet. No matter how many battleships we have, they aren't going anywhere without carrier planes to fly cover for them."

There were murmurs of agreement with that statement. Only a few months earlier such an assertion would have been heresy. But England had lost the battleship *Prince of Wales* and the battlecruiser *Repulse* to Japanese planes the previous October when they'd steamed into the Pacific Ocean without air cover. Whereas the battleship had been queen of the seas at the beginning of the war, that title was quickly passing to the aircraft carrier.

"In effect," Halsey continued. "We can do nothing major. We will be postponing any offensive actions, including planned moves into the Solomon Islands. That means the Japs will be free to build an airfield on Guadalcanal that can threaten Australia, which is too bad for the Aussies. It also means that the army will be pulling back on building defenses in Alaska since the navy can't protect them, and any planes up there will be flown back here because we cannot supply or support them."

Dane looked around. Shock was evident on many people's faces. Not only were American forces in Australia now threatened, but so too were the people of Alaska. The Japanese had landed army detachments on the Aleutian Islands of Attu and Kiska and could possibly attack the mainland.

Halsey took a swallow of water and continued glaring. "So what will the Japs do? First, they will either invade and conquer Hawaii or leave her to starve. My money is on the latter. We also feel that they will likely strike at Alaska. It's just too damned vulnerable. Finally, they will not invade California."

Dane looked around and saw his own puzzlement reflected on other faces. How the hell could Halsey be so certain?

"All the same, the Japs will not leave us alone," he continued. "We believe there will be bombing raids from their carriers and shelling from their battleships, and this will cause panic in California and elsewhere. Our army is moving a number of divisions to key spots along the West Coast to defend the cities and keep the politicians at bay."

That brought laughter. California's governor, Culbert Olson, had been strident in his pleas for military help. He'd called for the internment of Japanese civilians and wanted an endless wall of soldiers along the coast. The governors of Oregon and Washington weren't much better. All politicos were being inundated by calls from people in coastal towns for a ship of their own or a regiment for their personal use to protect them from the rampaging Japs, who hadn't arrived yet.

King interrupted. "Unfortunately, people like Governor Olson have a point. The Japs control the seas, so they can land with overwhelming force at any point they choose. If I ran their navy, that's exactly what I'd do, and I'd stay to loot and pillage until we put enough pressure on them to leave. Fortunately for us, we do have a number of cruisers and destroyers remaining and they, along with Pye's old battleship force, will run combat patrols along the coast. Our subs, of course, will be out scouting and patrolling."

Merchant nudged Dane and whispered, "He's saying the Japs will pull out from a raid if pressured. How does that square with your theory about Japanese fanaticism?"

"Withdrawing is not the same as surrendering," Dane answered, and realized King was glaring at him.

"Do you have anything to add, Commander?" the CNO asked.

Dane swallowed. It was like being a kid in school who'd been caught talking in class. "Sir, I was wondering what the current status of the Panama Canal is and when we're going to get reinforcements through it?"

Halsey took back the floor. "Good question, Commander. As you're all aware, a Japanese commando force landed and destroyed the locks on the Pacific side. This caused much of Lake Gatun, which is needed to float ships, to flow down to the ocean. As the lake receded, it left a number of ships in transit literally stuck in the mud or damaged by the sudden flood of water downstream. Work's already begun on repairs, but God only knows how long it'll take. At least we've stopped the flow of water from Gatun by pushing dirt into the cut and making a rude dam. The rough estimate is at least several months and maybe up to a year before the canal will be back in operation."

This brought more gasps. Any naval reinforcements would now have to go either around Africa and across the now-hostile Pacific, or around South America and up to California. In either case, the time for the trip had more than doubled and been made significantly more dangerous.

"The attack was made by a company-strength contingent of Japanese Marines," Halsey added. "They succeeded, but all were killed after inflicting heavy casualties on our troops. Their commanding officer took

out two of our men with a grenade while he was dying."
Dane looked at Merchant and the captain nodded. They
would request a copy of the report from Panama.

"Furthermore, they came in a tramp freighter which
the Coast Guard only belatedly identified. The freighter
tried to run away, but was shot up by a Coast Guard
cutter and one of our old gunboats that was in the canal
area. The enemy ship then rammed the cutter. The
gunboat continued to pound the freighter and, when
they thought she was dead, sent over a boarding party.
At that instant, the ship exploded, killing everyone
on the cutter and most of the people on the gunboat.
Needless to say, everyone on the freighter was killed.
We don't know if the explosion was accidental or not."

"Let me give you some reassurance, gentlemen,"
Admiral King said. "The situation Admiral Halsey has
described is totally accurate, but you are not going to
be hung out to dry. We know you need carriers and
more carriers. I've spoken with Secretary Knox and he
assures me that warship production will be shifted from
cruisers and destroyers to carriers. Thus, we will be able
to accelerate the completion of the *Essex* by at least several months, even if her shakedown cruise is truncated
and she sails with a couple of hundred civilian workers
still finishing her. She will be done early and she will
be sent to the Pacific. So too will other carriers, such
as the smaller *Independence*, when she is completed."

After a few more questions, the meeting broke up.
Merchant grabbed Dane's arm. "How's that report on
Jap fanaticism coming?"

"Haven't started, sir."

"Start."

✻   ✻   ✻

Steve Farris had reluctantly come to the conclusion that Captain Lytle might be more of a danger to the American army than the Japs were. His platoon had been issued helmets and rifles and now at least looked like soldiers. The helmets were the new bowl type and not the World War I pie tins. The new models were said to provide more protection for the occupant's skull. Farris was in no hurry to check out the hypothesis.

The rifles, however, were the venerable but still lethal 1903 model Springfields, and not the new Garands that were just beginning to be produced. The Springfield was a .30 caliber bolt-action weapon that took a five-shot clip. It might be old, but in the right hands, the Springfield was a deadly weapon. The next day, Lytle took them to the rifle range where the company largely succeeded in hitting the ground, much to the amusement of their Marine instructors. Farris, who considered himself a good to excellent shot, had lost any edge he might have had and was as bad as anybody.

To Steve's astonishment, Lytle had appeared satisfied and announced that the next day they would head ten miles north and build a post near the small village of Bridger. Bridger was located a mile inland and had a population of two hundred, some of whom farmed and others fished.

Along with being satisfied with the company's miserable shooting, Lytle was preoccupied with building what Farris considered a resort for himself and his men after they arrived at their destination. Patrolling and recon work were not on his agenda. Instead, a comfortable tent village was constructed with the largest and most luxurious tent going to the captain.

Farris and Lytle soon had a number of arguments regarding this and other matters, but to no avail. Steve once again worked up the nerve to protest and did so in Lytle's tent when the two of them were alone.

"Sir, when are we going to start doing our job of scouting?"

Lytle laughed mirthlessly. "For what? Do you really think there are Japs coming? Hell, there are thousands of miles of coastline. The odds of the Japs landing here are astronomically small."

Farris had to admit his lush of a commanding officer had a point. But they had their orders and there was such a thing as doing their duty. "I think we should be doing at least a little recon work instead of painting the rocks white."

"I think it makes the base look good," Lytle replied, not catching the sarcasm. Several paths were outlined by brightly painted rocks. Lytle's breath reeked of booze. Away from San Diego and the sobering presence of more senior officers, he'd again been drinking heavily.

"Regardless, I think it's a waste and I also believe we should have built elsewhere."

"Nonsense, we have a great view of the ocean."

"And that's the point, Captain. We can see for miles, which means we would stick out like a sore thumb to lookouts on any enemy ship. We should have built behind the hill where we can't be seen and have lookouts watching the ocean. I agree with you that it's a long shot that any Jap will show up, but any enemy ship that might happen by would know right away that this is a military post and shell it from a distance, and we'd be unable to do a damn thing about it."

He declined to say anything about white rocks serving as aiming points. Lytle sat down in a camp chair and leaned back, clearly off balance. For a moment it looked as if he would fall over and Steve relished the thought.

"Farris, just because you had a year of college, it doesn't mean you're smarter than I am. I am the captain and in command of this company, and you are a lieutenant and you are rapidly becoming a pain in the ass. If I could, I would send you back and get someone more reasonable, but I can't."

Farris was undeterred. "And instead of painting the damn rocks, we should be training. Our men are out of shape and, like you saw on the range, can't shoot worth squat. Sir, I would like to start patrolling and training instead of just sitting here and admiring the scenery."

"Lieutenant, instead of wasting our time patrolling, I would like to either relieve you of your command or have your worthless ass court-martialed. Like I said, though, I can't do much about you. Instead, I am going to do you a big favor. You can take your platoon and your grumpy fucking Sergeant Stecher the hell out of here and build your own little castle a couple of miles up the coast where you can hide behind hills to your little heart's content. I'll replace your platoon with Sawyer's."

Farris had mixed emotions. Sawyer was the youngest and least experienced officer in the company and was totally intimidated by Lytle. They would do a marvelous job of painting rocks and anything else the company commander wanted, except prepare for war.

There was, however, a good side to Lytle's orders.

Away from Lytle, Farris would indeed be able to get his men as close to fighting trim as circumstances would permit.

Outside, Stecher asked how it went. "Well, we get a little independence," Farris said and explained that they'd be moving.

"Half a loaf is better than nothing," Stecher said. He was impressed that his lieutenant had a pair of balls and had stood up to their sot of a CO. He also had a sense of duty.

Farris smiled. "Lytle may be right, and the only Japs we'll ever see will be running a laundry or something, but if the worst should happen, we'll be as ready as we possibly can be."

Stecher laughed. "Chinese run laundries, not the Japs. No Pearl Harbor on our watch then?"

"Not if I can help it. If anybody dies on my watch, it won't be because I didn't do the best I could."

"Uh, Lieutenant, I know you don't approve of our captain's drinking, but I hope you agree there's a time and place for everything."

"Of course."

"Then you might like to know that a case of beer has appeared as if by magic in my tent, perhaps sent by the beer fairy, and I'd enjoy sharing one or three with you."

Farris grinned. "I'd be honored. Tomorrow we move this hot dog stand to a new location."

"Any of you ladies own a gun?" Mack asked.

Amanda, Sandy, and Grace shook their heads in surprise at the question. Sandy said she hated guns.

"Well, thank God I own a few," Mack said. "I'll be

bringing a twelve-gauge shotgun, a thirty-two-caliber revolver, and an 1873 model Winchester carbine that I was told was used by the Sioux against Custer. That's probably a lie, but it shoots straight. Oh yeah, there'll be a box of ammo for each."

"But why," Sandy asked. She was tired. They all were. They'd managed time off from the hospital and had spent the last several days learning how to improve their handling of the catamaran. Sandy had started as the plump one, but was now slimming down. Mack thought she looked good, but not as good as Grace, who had just unbuttoned the top three buttons of her blouse, which gave him a good view of her ample cleavage. Regardless, all three were becoming skilled sailors.

When the nurses weren't there, Mack had worked hard to improve the sailboat. The decking connecting the twin hulls had been reinforced and compartments made to store food, water, and other supplies, including a spare set of sails and an extra mast. The cabin just behind the single mast in the middle of the boat had been enlarged so they could fit inside in case of bad weather, although sleeping would be difficult for more than two people at a time.

"We need guns because of sharks," he answered, "and I don't necessarily mean the ones that swim in the sea. I'm thinking of the two-legged ones who might try to take the *Bitch* from us before we can leave, or jump us at sea. Tell me, does anyone in your real world know what we're up to?"

"Not to my knowledge," Amanda said. "You told us to keep it under our hats and that's what we've done. If anybody's followed us here or figured things out, I don't know. What about here? Any of the locals suspect anything?"

Mack nodded. He'd already decided that Amanda, the quiet-looking one, was the smartest of the three and the leader. He wondered if she knew it yet.

"I don't think any of my neighbors have noticed anything," Mack said. "Fixing up the cat isn't unusual, and I've been storing stuff at night so nobody should suspect that we're preparing for the end of the world. As to the guns, I'll be teaching you how to handle them just in case."

"I hate guns," Sandy said again with a shudder.

"You don't have to like them," Mack said, "just respect them and learn how to use them. It might just save your life."

Amanda looked at him stonily. "Are you also suggesting that we save a bullet each for ourselves?"

Well, Mack thought, you figured it out. You are indeed the smart one. "If we're about to be captured by a Jap warship, or if we're dying of thirst or starvation, the choice'll be yours, now won't it."

"When are we leaving?" Grace asked.

"Next Saturday'd be good. No sense waiting here any longer than we have to. Wait too long and the Japs'll be crawling all over the beaches."

The Japanese Zero was simply the finest plane in the world and it was flown by the finest pilots in the world. This was not only the opinion of twenty-four-year-old Ensign Masao Ikeda, but of everyone else who had half a brain, and that included the deluded Americans who'd been dying in large numbers because they'd underestimated Japan.

The official designation of the Zero was the A6M. The letter A indicated it was a carrier plane, the number 6 said it was the sixth model, and the M said it had been made by the Mitsubishi corporation. The Zero was a one-man fighter that could fly more than three hundred miles an hour, soar to more than thirty thousand feet in the sky, and maneuver on the proverbial dime. Ikeda's plane had two 20mm Type 99 cannon and often carried a pair of 132-pound bombs slung under her wings.

The Zero simply outclassed anything the Americans had sent against them so far, but there were rumors that the Yanks had newer and better planes coming into play. Let them, Ikeda thought. None would be better than the Zero. Let the arrogant Americans learn to die. They'd tried so hard to humiliate Japan and her revered emperor, they deserved nothing less.

Ikeda was proud beyond words to be a fighter pilot in the service of the emperor. Training had been more than grueling. Ninety percent of the pilot candidates had flunked out. The ones who made it through were the best of the best, the elite of the elite.

He'd heard some officers complain that too many good pilots were being dismissed because they weren't quite excellent enough. Ikeda scoffed at that idea. The successful pilot candidates, like him, would be more than enough to slaughter the larger number of poorly trained Americans who thought that Japanese were ignorant, buck-toothed, and too nearsighted to fly a plane effectively. The Americans and British also thought that Japan could only produce junk, and both were paying terrible prices for their hubris.

Rigorous training had continued after his commissioning as a officer three years earlier so that now he and his plane were almost as one. The same was true of his comrades. No one could stand against them. They were modern samurai. They could not be beaten. They would bring honor and glory to Japan and the emperor.

Masao was not afraid to die, although he would not recklessly seek it out. Should it come to him in the course of battle then he would be at peace with his honor. He would have fulfilled his obligations to the code of bushido. Before leaving Japan, he'd left fingernail clippings and a lock of hair with his parents. Should he be killed and his body not returned, they and his little sister could honor him and themselves by enshrining his scant remains at the Yasukuni Shrine in Tokyo. He planned to live a long and prosperous life. However, death in war was a real possibility. He would not, of course, allow himself to be taken prisoner. The shame would be unendurable and his family would disown him. Should that remote possibility arise, he would endeavor to take as many Americans with him as he possibly could.

If the Zero did have a fault, it was a minor one in Ikeda's opinion. There was no armor. It had been sacrificed for speed and agility. If hit, the plane was prone to burst into flames. Therefore, his fellow pilots all joked, don't get hit. Avoiding enemy guns was not all that difficult as both the American planes and pilots were slow and awkward.

Nor did the pilots have parachutes. They'd been issued and their commanders had ordered the young Japanese eagles to wear them, but no true warrior would even think of it. If the plane was too badly damaged to make it back to base or be rescued, they would simply seek a target of opportunity and crash into it. Again, skeptics said that was a waste of highly trained pilots, but those who said that didn't understand the code of bushido.

Ikeda longed for the chance to shoot an American out of the sky. He'd strafed a couple of planes on the ground at Pearl Harbor's Hickam Field, along with trucks and fleeing personnel, but those did not count as true kills in his mind. His thinking was that he might as well have shot up as many parked cars.

This day he and a dozen others flying from the air-craft carrier *Kaga* were searching for ships that a scout plane reported had departed Honolulu at night. These were transports and freighters escorted by a cruiser and a pair of destroyers. Killing the three warships was a goal, but attacking the other ships was something that would usually be beneath him. However, he'd been informed that they were full of soldiers trying to flee Hawaii, which made them marginally worthwhile targets. He'd also been given specific orders and, while he could get away with not wearing a parachute, he could not refuse an assignment, however lowly. He and his fellow pilots would sink the lowly transports.

His radio crackled. Directions and orders were given. There were no American planes flying cover for the transports, which further frustrated Ikeda. At least a few Americans had attempted to stop them when they'd attacked Honolulu a couple of weeks earlier, but other Japanese pilots had destroyed them before Ikeda's chance had come. Back on the *Kaga*, they'd boasted about how easy it had been, laughing that there weren't enough Americans to go around, unintentionally humiliating the young ensign.

But now they were over the convoy. The American ships were in no formation to speak of. They were simply running away, now scattering in all directions as they spotted their attackers. Nor did the escorts have much in the way of antiaircraft guns. Only a few streams of tracers searched for them. Ikeda aimed at a transport and dropped his bombs. He cursed when splashes that hit near the ship's hull told him he'd missed. One bomb might have been close enough to cause internal damage from the pressure of the explosion, but he doubted it. He would have to work on his bombing technique. It wasn't easy for one moving object to hit another moving object unless they were very close to each other, which he now intended to do.

He swung his nimble plane around and lined up his cannon at a destroyer. He flew lower. He opened fire and walked the 20mm shells up to it and they ripped along the hull. He laughed and returned to attack the transport.

Ikeda exulted. This one is mine. He swung about and launched another deadly attack. The transport began burning and he could see scores of men jumping overboard. It was a sight being repeated throughout the fleeing enemy ships as the Americans were again being slaughtered.

He made another pass and now the American ship was disgorging hundreds of people, some of whom looked like civilians. If they were, so be it. They should not have been traveling with soldiers. Besides, they were Americans and it was the Americans who'd started the war by depriving Japan of her rightful place in the world by trying to contain her with insulting restrictions.

Ikeda decided that his target transport was a burning ruin and sought out another. He fired and heard only a click. He cursed again. He was out of ammunition. The Zero carried only enough 20mm shells for seven seconds' sustained firing and he had used up too much on the helpless transport. He turned and flew back to the carrier. Next time he would show more patience.

A thought intruded. Why the hell don't the Americans surrender? They were cowards who did not live by bushido and had surrendered elsewhere, so why not surrender Hawaii? He had another thought and it made him laugh. Perhaps, instead of painting an American warplane insignia on his Zero, he'd have the silhouette of a ship painted instead.

The mighty new battleship *Yamato* was Admiral Yamamoto's flagship and she, along with a couple of other older and smaller battleships and three carriers, was anchored in the waters off what had been the American base at Midway Island. The mighty *Yamato* was a floating citadel, a fortress that could cruise at nearly thirty knots. She was eight hundred feet long and displaced more than seventy thousand tons, which made her twice the size of most navies' battleships. Anchored alongside her, destroyers and cruisers were absolutely dwarfed. While her top speed was over thirty land miles an hour, she could cruise more than seven thousand miles at a more conservative twenty miles an hour.

Her main weapons were nine massive 18.1-inch cannon and a dozen six-inch guns, and it was thought that she represented a technological leap forward that had not been seen since the British had launched their revolutionary battleship, the *Dreadnaught*, in 1906. In particular, 18.1-inch guns were thought to be so large as to be impossible to make and fire efficiently. The *Yamato*, it was hoped, would prove them all wrong. Once again the Americans would pay for underestimating Japanese technological skills.

It was firmly believed that the *Yamato* and her still-building sister-ship, the *Musashi*, could simply stand off at a distance and pound every American and British warship to pieces. Just as important, her very name, *Yamato*, was synonymous with Japan.

At least that had been the theory, but that was then and this was now, and wars, even victorious ones, never go as planned.

Admiral Yamamoto flew his flag in the great ship because it was such a symbol of power and authority, but he now believed that he'd set up his headquarters in a giant dinosaur. The recent carrier battles, fortunately all won by the superb planes and pilots of Japan, had changed the face of warfare and shaken the proponents of traditional big gun battles. American and British battleships had been destroyed by small airplanes, little more than flying gnats, and the great decisive battle Japan wanted to fight and win was unlikely to include the great ships as major players.

The admiral's left hand throbbed, as it sometimes did. He had lost two fingers during the epic battle of Tsushima against the Russians in May of 1905. That battle had propelled Japan into the first rank of world powers, even though some of the Europeans and Americans had a difficult time dealing with yellow-skinned men as equals.

In this latest war, the victories at Pearl Harbor,

Midway, and a host of other places reinforced the fact that the Imperial Japanese Navy was second to none. It was strange, he thought, how the missing fingers seemed to still be attached. Were they trying to tell him something?

Yamamoto turned to greet Prime Minister Hideki Tojo with all due pomp as he crossed the deck of the *Yamato*. He could see the minister's look of awe as he took in the immensity of the world's most powerful ship. Tojo had seen the ship before, but it never failed to impress, which was why Yamamoto was holding the meeting on board her and not on nearby Midway Island. The admiral smiled to himself as he recalled that Tojo was a general and knew little of the sea. The prime minister was devoted to the emperor and a strong supporter of the war against the United States.

After the obligatory review of the crew, there was a tour of the ship which included an examination of the great guns and the interior of a huge turret. This was followed by a formal dinner, after which the two men retreated to Yamamoto's elegant wood-paneled office. The prime minister would sleep on the island and fly back the next morning in the same Kawanishi flying boat that had brought him to Midway. That the fifty-eight-year-old would deign to make such a trip showed the seriousness of concerns back in Tokyo.

"You have done wonders," Tojo said with genuine admiration. "You have defeated the Americans at every turn and with minimal loss to Japan. Everything you've done has displayed an almost magical touch. The emperor is more than pleased."

Yamamoto's nod was almost a bow. "I have been fortunate, prime minister, that the Americans so totally underestimate our abilities. That happy situation cannot last forever. Sooner or later they will develop the leaders and the resources to fight us more evenly. We are aware that they have a monstrous fleet building and that we cannot match their productivity. And kindly recall that we have not escaped totally unscathed. One of our carriers, the *Soryu*, was badly damaged and will be out of action for at least a year. The *Shoho*, of course, was sunk at the Coral Sea. Even what you correctly refer to as minimal losses cannot be sustained for very much longer. We cannot construct ships and planes at anything resembling the rate at which the Americans can. I am afraid that they will soon overwhelm us."

"Hence, you will smash them with this marvelous instrument," the prime minister said, beaming.

"Indeed. As with our pilots, we must substitute excellence for quantity. Yet I am concerned that the results of our battles for Midway and in the Coral Sea, as well as our attack on Pearl Harbor, show that the age of the battleship has passed and that we must have carriers, not more *Yamatos*," he said sadly.

Tojo sucked in his breath. "The battleship in general and the *Yamato* in particular are symbols of the Japanese Navy and our nation's pride. Are you telling me they are obsolete after all the fervor, money, and resources we've showered on them?"

"Yes," Yamamoto said, and grimaced. "I will not lie to you, prime minister. War has a nasty tradition of making its own rules as the action develops, and war leaders have a habit of planning to fight a new war with an old war's weapons and tactics. There were no carriers in 1918, in part because planes were so crude, but there are now, and, in every confrontation carriers and planes have prevailed over battleships. Oh, there will be a role for the *Yamato* and her sisters, but it will be as support for the carriers."

"So be it," Tojo said glumly. "What do you need?"

"Almost everything, prime minister. Carriers, planes, pilots, food, and oil. We should consider converting some of our existing battleships and cruisers to carriers. In particular, the *Shinano*, which was intended to be a third *Yamato*-class battleship, should be converted to an aircraft carrier of immense proportions. Perhaps that will give us a tactical advantage in battle with the Americans.

"However," he added sadly, "it will only be a temporary and tactical advantage. The Americans still have large numbers of cruisers and destroyers and, as I said, are making them at a far faster speed than we can. I believe they will produce them four times faster than is possible for us. Since they too are likely to believe that the carrier is the capital ship of this war, they will be making those in great numbers as well. Also, they are likely to be converting merchantmen to small carriers in even larger numbers."

"What about the *Musashi*?" Tojo inquired softly.

"The *Yamato*'s sister is practically completed and about to begin her trials. We can do nothing about changing her. The *Shinano*, however, is a different story. Also, we must put an end to the draconian way of weeding out less-than-perfect pilot candidates. The Americans are beginning to turn out thousands of only slightly inferior pilots who will simply overwhelm our eagles."

Tojo nodded agreement. He'd hoped for news of

continuing victories, but now his favorite admiral was dashing those hopes. The prime minister wondered if the war against the United States was going to bog down the Japanese Navy as the war against China was sapping the strength of her army? Of course he would never admit that the Japanese Army was in trouble in China.

Nor would he criticize Yamamoto's candor. The admiral was a hero in Japan even though his earlier prewar comments about not wishing to fight the U.S. had not been appreciated by many whose philosophies were more militaristic, and that included the prime minister himself.

Yamamoto had been dubious about Japan's ultimate success, and fanatic militants had been so upset by his statements that he'd been sent to sea in part to prevent his being assassinated.

Nor could Tojo forget that Yamamoto knew more about the United States than most Japanese. He'd lived and traveled in America, served in Washington, and had even attended Harvard. It was said that his English was excellent and he'd developed a taste for Scotch whisky and playing poker.

Yamamoto continued. "Regarding battleships, the Americans are building at least a dozen larger and newer battleships that, while not equal to the *Yamato*, could easily overwhelm her and her sister should they get close enough. The same holds with carriers, although their superiority will be both numerical and qualitative. Simply put, the Americans make excellent battleships and carriers. Soon, also, they will produce vast numbers of planes that will at least be the equal to the Zero. Please recall that, in my travels, I was permitted to see the giant factories in Detroit and Pittsburgh that are now producing planes and tanks in great numbers, along with the shipyards whose output will consume us sooner or later. We must win decisively before all this happens."

Tojo shook his head. This dire report was not what he'd expected. "What else do you need?"

"A forward base of operations, but I do not see that as likely. Hawaii and Midway are too far away from California to be useful, so food, oil, and reinforcements must come by a stream of ships from Japan. We have taken the islands of Attu and Kiska in the Aleutians, but they are not useable as a base."

"That stream of ships will be vulnerable to attack."

"Good," the admiral said with suruprising emphasis. "Then perhaps the Americans will come out and fight and we can destroy them. Ironically, our successes seem to have made the Americans want to conserve what they have left, which is one carrier and a handful of old battleships much smaller and totally inferior to the *Yamato*."

The admiral sipped his tea and paused for effect. "We have perhaps a year, two at the most, before already growing American strength will, like I said, overwhelm and crush us."

"The emperor," Tojo said and nodded his head reverentially, "is also concerned about that. He said that 'The fruits of war are tumbling into our mouths almost too quickly.' He too wishes an end to the war with the United States as soon as possible."

Yamamoto nodded agreement. "While you pursue a diplomatic end to this war, I will continue to harass, sting, and destroy Americans everywhere I can. We will raid their cities and wreak havoc. This will occur as soon as I can get the campaign organized and supplied. We did not expect such an overwhelming victory so soon and were not prepared to exploit it."

Tojo smiled grimly. "Such are the unintended consequences of unexpected victory."

"Hopefully, the Americans will be so demoralized by our assaults that they will seek a negotiated end to the war and a return of the many thousands of prisoners we now hold. Those prisoners are a great concern to them. I was dismayed to hear that so many died in what the Americans are calling atrocities and death marches. As bargaining chips they should be kept in good shape."

Tojo sighed. "You are right, of course, and I will give the necessary orders. However, many of the men guarding the prison camps are inferior soldiers and it will be difficult to control them insofar as they consider surrendered soldiers to be less than human."

"But we must try, prime minister."

"Indeed. Will your forces invade Hawaii or Australia?"

"No. My intent is to let the Hawaiian Islands starve, and perhaps their lamentations will provoke the Americans to try and relieve them. We will do much the same with Australia and New Zealand. They would be a distraction. We must focus on the real enemy, the United States. A number of transports recently tried to escape Hawaii in a desperate venture and were slaughtered."

Tojo brightened. "Then they will not try it again. What else do you require?"

Yamamoto smiled, "Diplomatic help from our erstwhile allies, the Germans. Our victories have doubtless caused the Americans to send hundreds of thousands of soldiers and thousands of planes to their west coast to forestall an invasion that will never come. That relieves significant pressure on Germany, does it not?"

Tojo nodded. "It does."

"Then I would like German saboteurs to destroy American installations like our brave men did to the Panama Canal. I would prefer to use Japanese soldiers, but they cannot hide in the American population, while a white-skinned German could, especially since local Japanese in California are being imprisoned by their army. Give me well-trained Germans who speak excellent English and let them raise havoc with their shore installations."

CHAPTER 5

DANE WAS SICKENED BY THE RESULTS OF THE carnage. A dozen ships in all had departed Hawaiian waters and all but two had been sunk by Japanese planes flying from an unexpected carrier.

Approximately ten thousand people, most of them civilians and the rest wounded military personnel, had been killed along with the crews of the escorting warships. Only a few hundred survivors, many of them badly wounded, had been picked up by fishing boats and other ships whose captains were brave enough to help. So far, news of the slaughter had been kept from the civilian population, which was still reeling from the litany of disasters since the initial attack on Pearl Harbor. That couldn't last and soon the American public would find out about this latest round of bloodletting.

He couldn't help but wonder if one of the dead was Amanda Mallard. She'd said that she would try to get out of Hawaii, hadn't she? Worse, he might never know her fate. There were no accurate lists of those who'd been on the ships, so she and so many others might be listed as missing forever. Nobody should ever be "missing," he thought angrily. Family and friends and lovers should know what happened to the ones they cared for. Even as he thought that, he knew there were thousands of such missing from previous wars, so many that nations had tombs dedicated to them. There was a tomb in Washington for an American unknown from the First World War, and there would certainly be one from this conflagration as well. He wondered if they'd put up a separate tomb or just add another body. What a hell of a happy thought, he concluded.

"Captain, when the devil are we going to start winning?" he asked Merchant as he passed by Dane's desk.

"Possibly when we stop underestimating the damned Japs and realize that they are extremely smart and dedicated people. A number of senior officers still think that Nazi Germany both made their planes and are flying them because little yellow-skinned Japs can't possibly be that good. The same people don't think it's possible that the Japs have giant battleships, either. Or even better torpedoes than we do. Christ, the stubbornness of some people in command is enough to make you want to punch someone, but you didn't hear that from me, did you?"

Dane grinned. "Not a word."

"Good. I submitted your paper regarding their suicidal tendencies, and the reaction around the fleet and the Marine Corps has been less than overwhelming. Some of those I talked to don't believe humans would do that. One of our admirals actually said it wasn't Christian. He got a little annoyed when I reminded him that very few Japanese were Christians. Well, fuck him. The Marines said they weren't planning on taking prisoners anyway, which is good thinking."

"So once again we're doomed to learn the hard way."

"Looks like it, Dane. You going to watch the *Saratoga* leave?"

The Pacific Fleet's one remaining carrier, along with three of Admiral Pye's old battleships and a handful of cruisers, would be departing San Diego that night. It had been determined that she was just too vulnerable in the narrow confines of the bay and, since there was a civilian population of more than a hundred thousand in the area, there was little possibility of keeping her presence a secret. Once upon a time, this particular incarnation of Task Force 16 would have been a powerful force. Now, her ships were going to run for their lives and hide from the overwhelmingly strong enemy. The battleships were there not because they were strong, but because they might delay or distract a Japanese assault, and possibly pay with their lives, permitting the carrier to get away. Dane wondered if their crews understood that.

How the hell did the United States Navy ever get itself into this position? Dane wondered. Where the *Sara* and her sisters would go, neither Dane nor Merchant knew. Perhaps Halsey, sick but still commanding America's one remaining carrier force in the Pacific, didn't know either. Maybe he'd make it up as he went along. With a touch of whimsy, Nimitz had told the staffers and newspaper reporters that the *Sara* was headed for Shangri-la, the mythical takeoff point for Doolittle's raiders for their attack on Tokyo.

Later that day, as Dane and a number of others

looked on the empty anchorage, he realized that
Amanda must have felt much the same sense of loss
when the three submarines left Pearl Harbor. At least
he hoped she had, he thought, and wondered if he was
being greedy. Sometimes the depth of his feelings for
a woman he'd known for such a short time surprised
him, but she had moved him and he thought he'd at
least gotten a little bit to her too.

He laughed harshly. Maybe someday the gods of
chance would smile on them and they'd be reunited
only to find out that they didn't care for each other
at all. He realized that he desperately wanted to know
one way or another.

Damn it to hell, he felt like a lost kid.

Tonight they would leave. To Amanda and the
other two women it was both exhilarating and frightening. It was a long way from Hawaii to California,
and so much could go wrong on a journey that was
dangerous to begin with and could easily prove fatal.
Granted, they had all learned a lot about sailing and
each other in the last few weeks, but did they know
enough to make it across the Pacific? There was only
one way to find out.

Every spare inch of the catamaran was packed with
food and water. Each person was allowed one small
suitcase, which meant that a lot of personal treasures
would be left behind. Amanda was fortunate in that
all her really important possessions were still at her
parents' house back in Maryland.

Mack had decided to leave this night because
of still more rumors of Japanese ships in the area,
coupled with the fact that their preparations were

beginning to attract attention. He said he was afraid that a panicky mob might storm the boat and either steal it or destroy it while trying to get away. They had guns, but shooting other islanders was not part of the plan, at least not yet. Mack said he'd chased away a couple of scrawny local would-be tough guys who seemed far too interested in the *Bitch*. Their names were Ace and Mickey and they seemed interested in the three women as well as the cat.

Amanda was back at the car, which was parked a good hundred yards from the boat. She'd gone there for one last check to see if she'd left anything important behind. She hadn't. On a whim, she decided to leave the keys on the front seat. She sure as hell wasn't going to be driving it any longer. Let some islander enjoy it and the half tank of precious gas, along with tires that still had some tread life on them.

Screams and shouts pierced the air, paralyzing her for an instant. She got control of herself and moved slowly and stealthily toward where the catamaran was anchored in shallow water. It was just off the beach and in water that was barely knee deep. As she got closer, she saw two men whom she quickly identified as Ace and Mickey. They were struggling with Sandy and Grace, while Mack was down on his hands and knees and apparently unable to get up.

Ace and Mickey were obviously hellbent on hurting her friends and stealing the *Bitch*. It was what Mack had feared. People were so afraid of what might happen that they would take desperate measures to get off the island. Amanda and the others were ready to leave; however, it looked as if they might have waited too long.

The attackers had their backs to the water and the

sailboat, which presented Amanda with an opportunity, however slim. The two men had knives, but apparently no guns. Mack looked badly hurt, but there was nothing she could do for him right now. The men were wrestling with Sandy and Grace and pulling at their clothes. They would be raped before the men departed, and possibly killed. They knew it and were fighting back desperately, clawing and screaming, despite the unlikelihood of anyone hearing them.

Keep up the noise, Amanda prayed as she slipped into the shallow, warm water. She crawled silently to the cat and hauled herself on deck. She slid on her belly to the cabin where Mack had stored the weapons. Of the three, she liked the Winchester the best and quietly took it from the container. She checked and found it loaded.

She couldn't see Mack, but Ace and Mickey were still ripping the clothes off Sandy and Grace, who were screaming and wrestling while their attackers yelled and laughed. She couldn't shoot at them because they were all twisted up together. Amanda took a deep breath and fired one shot in the air. The noise stunned everyone.

"Drop them!" she yelled, wondering if that was quite the thing to say.

"Bullshit," yelled Ace, the one holding Sandy. She was already naked from the waist down and one of his hands was between her legs. Grace was totally nude and being held by Mickey. He threw her aside and pulled out a knife.

Amanda fired and hit him in the leg. He fell screaming as blood began to gush from his wound. Ace twisted Sandy to use her as a human shield.

"Drop the gun or I'll kill her."

Amanda wavered. Once again, she didn't have a clear shot. The man she'd shot had stopped moving and was glaring at her. His blood-covered hands clutched his wound and it didn't look like she'd hit an artery.

"Don't believe me?" Ace snarled. "Watch."

Before Sandy's attacker could move his knife into position, he flinched and a look of disbelief crossed his face. He staggered and reached behind him only to find Mack was pulling his own knife out of the man's back. Mack quickly sliced it across Ace's throat. Ace fell forward as blood pumped out. His arms and legs flopped for a moment and then he stopped moving.

Mack walked across to Mickey, the man Amanda had shot. He was whimpering and trying to crawl away. Mack reversed the knife and hit him hard on the back of the head. Mickey quivered and lay still. His leg wound continued to bleed.

Mack looked around coldly. "Good job, Amanda. Always knew you were the strong one. Now, the two of you get dressed and get all your shit onto the *Bitch*. We're leaving right this minute, and anything we don't have we don't need. I don't know if that shot and all the other noise is gonna scare anybody up or not, but I really don't feel like explaining any of this to the police or the army."

Grace had put on her torn blouse and panties and pointed to the unconscious attacker. "You're not going to kill him?"

"You want me to?"

"He wanted to rape me, so yeah, I do."

Mack nodded. "What about you?" he asked Sandy, who had managed to put on her shorts.

"I don't want you to kill anybody on my behalf."

Grace sagged. "I don't either, I guess. Why don't we just get the hell out of here?"

"I've got the gun and I don't want any more killing, either," said Amanda.

Mack laughed. "You got all the votes, then." He walked over and checked the wounded man's pulse. "Not that it matters, Amanda, but you didn't kill him."

In the distance they heard sirens. Someone had heard the shooting and the screams and called the cops. "Now it's really time to go," Mack said, "unless you want to spend the next several days or longer explaining what we're up to, and maybe having all our stuff confiscated because we might be hoarding."

"But we've done nothing wrong," Amanda said.

Mack laughed harshly. "Maybe you haven't, but let's just say that maybe I'm not a virgin and my past might not stand up to a serious investigation. They do a little digging and find out what I used to do and we'll all be in jail while they sort things out."

Shit, thought Amanda. Why hadn't they realized that Mack really was a crook? Too late now. "Then let's get going," she said.

Headlights were visible on the road leading to the shore. They climbed aboard, hauled up the anchor, pushed off, and set the sail. The catamaran moved slowly at first and they tried to help out by paddling. She soon picked up speed as her large square sail filled with the wind. The surf was wondrously calm and they made deep water quickly. Amanda looked back and saw several people walking around where they'd just left. She wondered if the police could even see the cat as they sailed away.

"Don't worry about the cops," Mack said. "They'll probably think those two jerks hurt each other fighting, and the living one won't disagree. He'll claim it was self-defense and maybe even get away with it. Can you even imagine him telling the cops they were trying to steal the cat and were going to rape you ladies as an explanation for getting shot and stabbed? Not a chance."

Amanda had to agree with Mack's logic. But what had he done in the past that made him afraid to talk to cops?

Mack laughed. "Ladies, we are on our way. California, here we come!"

Farris thought his little command was shaping up fairly well, especially with Stecher around to yell at his platoon of rank amateurs. While one squad patrolled the beach and the dirt road leading to it, the others worked on being soldiers and that included plenty of marching and running. The men were losing a lot of fat and getting into shape. Stecher had set up a firing range and they'd used a few clips of ammo each until they could at least get close to hitting the target. Nor did Captain Lytle seem to mind when Farris asked for more ammunition. Just as long as Farris's military exercises kept him away, the captain was happy.

The men had bitched, but they really couldn't complain too much since Farris made a point of leading them on all their endeavors. Steve found he could march and run and keep up with the best of them, which pleased him no end. At the end of a long march, Farris generally called for a race to the finish with about a quarter mile to go. To his amazement, the men jumped at the chance to beat their lieutenant who, to their mock dismay and his total astonishment, generally won. He even beat Stecher, who loudly proclaimed that every good NCO always let his officers win. This was met with even more good-natured laughter.

After a while, it was clear that no one missed being with Captain Lytle even if it meant being farther away from the pleasures of San Diego.

Farris had found a nice spot for their new camp two miles north of Lytle's base, which was itself north of La Jolla, and positioned the platoon behind a low hill. Lookouts could see in all directions, and their tents were concealed from the sea and from the land. Borrowing a small boat, Farris had confirmed that the camp wasn't visible until you were almost onto it.

And no rocks were painted white.

The dirt road led inland to a village that was little more than a settlement. The locals called it Bridger, maybe after the frontiersman, Jim Bridger, or maybe not. Nobody was certain. Farris was of the opinion that it didn't matter because it would be swallowed up as San Diego inevitably grew and sprawled. Bridger had a loose population of just over a hundred and was centered on a combination store and gas station owned by an old-timer named Sullivan. The store carried food that supplemented their rations and, even better, a decent selection of beer, which Sullivan made sure never ran out. Thousands of soldiers and Marines were stationed nearby, but their presence hadn't yet made it felt this far from San Diego. It was like living in another world.

They had a shortwave radio and there was a phone line in Bridger that one of Farris's men had managed to extend to their camp. The phone company would probably pitch a fit if they found out, but who cared? Hey, there's a war on. The area was scenic, with sandy beaches and rocky hills, and even Stecher had begun to come around to the idea that not going anyplace wasn't all that bad, although he still wanted to kill every Jap who'd ever been born. His grief was becoming manageable and he definitely looked on Steve with a growing measure of respect.

Their first patrols along the shore had produced shock. There were many footprints and they wondered if they were from Japs sneaking ashore during the night. One night they'd waited in ambush and found only the local people fishing for pleasure, or drinking and watching the surf, or drinking and making love and watching the surf. To their dismay, the majority of people having sex in the sand were older, and they made a conscious effort to not look. Some of them reminded Farris too much of his parents.

"I gotta get my uncle up here," Farris said to Stecher. He'd gotten mail from home saying that Uncle Tim Dane had been promoted and was now at San Diego. Farris bet he'd enjoy some time on the beach, and maybe he knew some women he could bring along. All the women in Bridger were old, at least in their thirties, and some of the seals and otters cavorting in the waves were beginning to look really good. It was rumored that Sullivan had a family, but no one had seen them. If true, Farris wondered why.

Tim Dane considered himself far from stupid, so when he was told to be on the alert for saboteurs, he wondered if anybody knew for certain or if it was someone's wildass guess. If they did know for certain, then how did they know? He was in Intelligence, which meant everyone was paranoid, and why not? Overconfidence had led to Pearl Harbor, hadn't it? However, nobody in the office knew anything specific; therefore, it must be more fear of the Japanese bogeyman, which was on the increase since Midway and the slaughter of the refugee ships.

Of course there was another reason for paranoia. German saboteurs had landed on America's Atlantic coast and, even though they'd been either rounded up or killed, everyone had to wonder if all of them were accounted for, or if there were others hiding and waiting for the opportunity to attack America at home. Thus, there was real concern that the Japanese would try the same thing.

Dane was relatively alone in thinking that such attacks would not come from what remained of the local Japanese community in California. On the other hand, Governor Olson and Lieutenant General James L. DeWitt, commander of the Fourth Army and the Western Defense Command, were adamant that all Japanese were potential subversives. They would be rounded up and held until further notice. When it was brought to their attention that most of those being rounded up and interned were American citizens, including many native born, DeWitt's response was quite simple, "a Jap is a Jap."

Sadly, he had a point. The Tokyo government had decreed that all who'd immigrated to the U.S. were still considered Japanese citizens whether they'd become U.S. citizens or not. Tokyo further said that this also applied to their children, who were native-born

American citizens. This had caused a great deal of confusion and even more distrust because of the disasters at Pearl Harbor, the Philippines, and Midway. Intelligence was an inexact science, and neither Dane nor anyone else could say with certainty what the native Japanese population in California was thinking or what they would do. Being able to speak and read the language was some advantage for Dane, but he could say nothing with confidence. He could not read people's minds or peer into their souls.

Nor did it help that Yamamoto himself had been quoted as saying that it might be necessary to invade the West Coast and even Washington, D.C., to bring the United States to the peace table. Dane thought the Japanese admiral had been engaging in hyperbole, since such was clearly far more than the Japanese could accomplish, but many people thought otherwise.

The Japanese internees were sent to a camp at Manzanar in the Owens Valley, east toward the mountains. A number of local Japanese had been rounded up and were being held in a warehouse near the San Diego waterfront and were waiting for transportation. Dane was ordered to see them and interview them, a task that he found totally odious.

Only a score of Japanese waited for him, older people, a few small children, and a handful of youngsters in their early teens. They were sitting on the cement floor of the warehouse and looking confused. A couple of the young teenagers appeared angry.

"I was born here," one of them said. He was no older than fourteen. "And so was my mother. So why the hell are we being sent away?" It didn't go unnoticed that the boy spoke perfect, unaccented English.

Major Cullen was from the 32nd Division and in charge of the ragtag group. He turned and snarled at the boy. "Because you're Japs, that's why, and the only good Jap is a dead Jap."

When the kid looked like he was going to say something more, Dane told him not to lest he get his skull cracked. He said it in Japanese, which surprised the boy and stunned Cullen.

"You speak Jap?" asked Cullen.

"Looks like it, doesn't it?"

"No matter, they all speak English."

Dane shook his head. "I find it very hard to think that any of these people are saboteurs. Did you find any weapons, any radios?"

Cullen shrugged, "A couple of hunting rifles, but no shortwave radios. You're probably right, Dane, none of this group is any threat whatsoever. However, until we sort them out they stay locked up, and I don't care what the bleeding hearts say. You know what they're doing to our people in the Philippines and Hawaii, don't you?"

Dane knew all too well. American prisoners of war were being brutalized, while many American civilians in the Philippines had been jammed into a concentration-camp-like place called Santo Tomas in Manila, where they were being poorly fed and probably abused. Americans in Hawaii were slowly starving while the Japanese Navy blockaded the islands and prohibited food from going in. He couldn't help but think of Amanda and whether she'd made it out or was dying in Hawaii. She had been fairly thin in the first place. How would she survive? He had a nightmare vision of someday returning to Hawaii and finding a skull with a twisted front tooth and realizing it was her.

Or had she survived at all? Or, damn it to hell, was her body rotting at the bottom of the Pacific as a result of the attack on the doomed convoy? For a second the cluster of Japanese civilians didn't look all that harmless. He shook his head and put things back in perspective.

Cullen softened. "Look, I'm not a total goddamn monster. I know these old ladies and little kids are no more a threat to the country than are one of Orson Welles's little green men from Mars," he said, alluding to Welles's *War of the Worlds* broadcast that had terrorized so many people a few years earlier. "But I do have my orders and I'm going to obey them."

"I understand," Dane said, and he did. Japanese were not the only ones being interned. Some Germans and Italians had also been rounded up, although selectively and in much smaller numbers. FDR had signed Executive Order 9066 authorizing just such actions, and Dane could do nothing to prevent the roundup unless he wanted to risk court-martial.

And what did he really want to do? Prior to Pearl Harbor, numbers of Japanese-Americans had been proud of the advances Japan had made in less than a hundred years, emerging from a medieval period to become a technological and military power of the first rank, and that included their military advances in China. Japanese-language newspapers had praised their homeland with bold headlines and pro-Imperial articles. So too had millions of German-Americans and Italian-Americans when Hitler and Mussolini led their respective homelands to victory after victory. Did that make them all suspect as traitors? War with the United States had quieted them and made many choose between their new country and their old homeland. The overwhelming majority had chosen the United States. But had it changed their hearts? And what about the minority who felt more strongly for their origins than for their new homes?

And what would happen to this pitiful handful of people staring at him if they were released back into the population? Many Japanese ran small farms or owned little shops. A number of their businesses had been burned and looted by angry white Californians in an orgy of violence that had gotten worse after the disaster at Midway. Censored reports said that more than a hundred Japanese men had been lynched, and an unknown number of women raped by angry whites in California. For the most part, the police had done an admirable job of enforcing the law, but they couldn't be everywhere; thus, there was some logic to the thought that interning the Japanese was for their own protection.

Some of General DeWitt's staff had read Dane's report on Japanese fanaticism and, to his dismay, it was being used as another excuse to round up the unreasonable Japs as opposed to more reasonable Germans and Italians.

"What are you thinking, Commander?" asked Cullen.

"That I should go back to base, write a little report about how I spent my day, and then go get a drink."

"My thoughts exactly," said Cullen.

Perhaps a drink would help him to not wonder what might be happening to Amanda. Maybe he would phone his nephew and take him up on the invitation to see how the other half lived just a few miles up the coast.

❋   ❋   ❋

Their first day sailing out of Oahu, they'd sighted a number of small craft like theirs, but nobody made any attempt at contact. Were these others trying to flee, or were they fishermen busy at work, or perhaps they were smugglers? Neither Amanda nor the others cared—they just kept their distance, and the other vessels did as well. Leave me alone, and I'll leave you alone, was the clear message.

A few hours later, just before nightfall and what they hoped would be the safety of darkness, they saw a Japanese cruiser on the horizon. They quickly dropped their sail in hopes that they wouldn't be spotted. They were, and the cruiser headed their way, even firing a shell that landed a few hundred yards away when they wouldn't follow the order to heave to. Mack handed them each a gun and the message was clear—use it on yourself. Don't become toys for the Japanese Navy to play with, torment, and then throw overboard to the sharks. They took the guns and looked at each other, was this the way their lives were going to end?

To their astonishment and relief, the enemy ship suddenly turned and raced away. "I guess they found something more important than us," Mack said as he collected the weapons. The cruiser fired a second shell, apparently just for spite, and it raised a giant splash a ways away from them. There was no third shell and Amanda imagined the Japanese officers on the bridge of the ship laughing at the silly sailboat whose occupants they'd just terrified.

Late in the second day, they were practically alone in the vast sea. The other small boats had scattered and were out of sight, although a few were doubtless attempting the same trip to California. The food riots and the menace of the Japanese Navy were too much, as it had been for them.

The weather remained warm and good, with largely clear skies. The seas were calm and the catamaran clipped along, eating up miles and easily climbing over the gentle swells. If it wasn't so deadly serious and their journey just beginning, it would be pleasant.

"Don't get used to this happy little vacation," Mack warned. "The ocean can turn into a monster in a heartbeat."

Amanda agreed. It was noted that this was the first time that the catamaran with the girls sailing it had ever been out of sight of land. It was a profound and disconcerting feeling and one that was not at all pleasant.

Seasickness was not that much of a problem, although Grace had spent a little time sending her meals into the briny deep before managing to shake it off. They were just too busy sailing the catamaran to indulge in the luxury of being sick. Even though the weather was calm, at least two of them were alert at all times.

When there was time, Amanda couldn't help but wonder whether she'd actually killed Mickey, the man she'd shot. If so, what did she truly think about it? He and the other one had been trying to rape her friends and steal the boat, leaving them stranded in Hawaii. Desperate times called for desperate measures, didn't they? And what she had done was self-defense, wasn't it?

Despite the fact that Mickey was a sleazy and violent criminal, she found herself hoping she hadn't killed him, although she concluded that she'd likely never know unless Mack confessed that he'd lied and that the man was dead when he'd checked on him.

That she was coping so well with the possibility that she'd killed was another surprise. The fact that Ace and Mickey were out to rob and possibly kill them made it a justifiable killing, which must be what went through the minds of men in combat when they had time to think about it. Her father had been a corpsman in the Argonne in the first war and never talked about it, politely but firmly refusing to be drawn into any discussions. Now she had a small idea why.

But what about Mack? He'd stabbed the other man without hesitation and then didn't want to get involved with the cops. If and when the time was right, she'd ask him. There must be a very dark side to his past. She had a thought and almost laughed. Maybe the catamaran wasn't his and an investigation would prove it. Maybe he'd stolen if from the rightful owners and murdered them. If so, Mack was a thief as well as a killer. Despite belated misgivings, she had to accept the fact that she was on a small sailboat with a man who killed, even though it was in self-defense and on behalf of herself and her friends. Of course, she realized, she had done much the same thing. She hadn't been aiming for Mickey's leg. No, she'd shot at his chest and simply missed. So much for her being the next Annie Oakley, she laughed softly.

Mack gathered them for yet another class in navigation. "Remember, ladies, we've got to go north as well as east in order to hit California. Hawaii's just south of the Tropic of Cancer and San Diego is about eight hundred miles north of that, with San Francisco another several hundred miles beyond. It we make a mistake and go too far north, we'll hit stretches of coast that are as wild and rugged and dangerous as you can believe, and filled with really large bears who like to eat little girls like you. White meat is their favorite, I've heard.

"Too far south, and we'll land in Mexico, where the land is equally crappy, and I'm not too sure whose side they're on right now. Therefore, we've got to hit somewhere between San Diego and San Francisco or we could be in shit as deep as if we'd stayed in Hawaii."

A couple of days later, their luck with the weather continued and it rained. They happily refilled their water containers and anything else they could, and let the cool but comfortable fresh water wash the salt out of their clothes and off their skin. Amanda was mildly shocked when Mack stripped naked and soaped himself before letting the rain rinse him.

Grace laughed. "What the hell." She undressed as well and, a moment later, so did Amanda and Sandy. Mack was surprised and grinned happily, but said nothing. After that, neither nudity nor lack of privacy while performing body functions was ever an issue, and lack of clothes not only felt liberating but sometimes enabled them to work better. Mack, however, did at least usually put on an athletic supporter.

"Got to protect my most prized possession," he laughed.

That night, Grace and Mack commenced having noisy and exuberant sex in the cabin while the other two sat outside and grinned.

When Grace emerged after the first time, her comments were succinct. "What's the point of taking a Pacific cruise if you're not going to get laid by the captain?"

Mack made no effort to get Amanda and Sandy into his bunk. He was content with Grace, and the others were fine with that. "He's so withered," Sandy giggled. "Even his wrinkles have wrinkles."

And he's a killer and likely a thief, Amanda thought.

They had a radio and they listened but did not transmit. The war was still raging, although Hawaii hadn't been invaded. They caught broadcasts from the islands beginning to beg for food, and they knew they'd made the right decision. Now all they had to do was find California.

Wilhelm Braun looked admiringly at the U.S. passport that gave his name as William Brown. Braun had been the assistant military attache at the German embassy in Mexico City until Mexico declared war on Germany. Braun was a distant cousin of the cowlike blonde woman who, if rumors were correct, was Hitler's mistress. Some were shocked at the thought that the beloved Fuehrer was anything but celibate in his total dedication to the Reich, but Braun didn't care. If Hitler wanted to screw Wilhelm's dumb and plump cousin, then let him. Apparently, she had been the Fuehrer's mistress for six or seven years and, while the relationship was unknown to the average German, it was common knowledge to those in the Nazi hierarchy as well as the diplomatic corps, and, of course, the Braun family.

Braun had another passport that proclaimed his Swedish identity and gave his name as Olaf Swenson, and a third that said he was from Denmark and named Oosterbeck. Since Sweden was neutral and likely to remain so, it and the others were aces in the hole. Denmark had been conquered by the Germans and the world was sympathetic to her plight.

He shook his head. If he was going to pass muster

north of the border, he'd damned well better get used to being either Swenson, Oosterbeck, or Brown. In either case he'd be a fifty-year-old mining engineer from Wisconsin who'd been working for the Mexican government. Claiming to be from Wisconsin was safe since he'd lived there for several years with an elderly aunt and uncle who'd died a few years earlier.

But first he had to get across the border with a truck full of very special and dangerous material.

He'd been in San Francisco doing nothing more sinister than taking a vacation and doing some shopping when the Japanese attacked Pearl Harbor and war unexpectedly broke out. He'd quickly checked out of his hotel and driven to the border, where he crossed easily, and only a day before Germany declared war on the United States. The Americans were suddenly watching out for those entering their country, but blithely unconcerned about who left. Americans, he concluded, were stupid and had no concept of security.

Once back in the embassy, he'd tried to figure out ways to help Germany in her increasingly desperate struggle against England and Russia, and now the United States. Braun was neither a fool nor suicidal. He knew he now had little chance of getting back to Germany, and, if he stayed in Mexico, might even be interned for the duration of the war, or at best, forced to wait many months until exchange arrangements could be made. That he considered intolerable.

Even if he did somehow make it back to the Reich, he didn't much feel like getting killed in the steppes of Russia as the initially dramatic and far-reaching German advances into the Soviet Union had become more like a bloody brawl between two equally matched titans. His age and the leg wound he'd endured in the last war and which caused him to limp in bad weather were no guarantee he wouldn't be sent to an SS line division.

Although no one would say it out loud, there were those who thought that Germany had been badly bloodied and needed to focus on destroying Russia before the United States got over its lethargy and stupidity and began to fight for real. Braun had traveled extensively throughout America and seen firsthand her potential warmaking capabilities. He wondered if the leaders in Berlin had any concept of that, or had they recalled the fact that the United States had a population much larger than Germany's, which was already dwarfed by that of the Soviet Union and the British Empire?

Yes, the Americans were decadent, corrupt, incompetent, and ruled by Jews, but they could cause great damage to the Nazi cause. He despised the Americans, but he did not underestimate them. Curiously, he understood that the Japanese admiral, Yamamoto, had also lived in the U.S.

German advances toward Moscow, Leningrad, and now Stalingrad had slowed. Russian winter had proven to be a shock and Braun was delighted to be in the warmth of Mexico instead of frozen Russia even though it was now summer outside of Moscow. Another terrible and murderous winter would come soon enough to Germany's Eastern Front.

When it first became apparent that Mexico was going to declare war on Germany, Braun and a couple of others simply disappeared from the embassy and, using their several aliases, set up a bogus import-export business north of Mexico City in the industrial city of Monterrey.

While official Mexico declared war on Germany, the average Mexican cared little about a European conflict and many totally despised the United States for being the greedy gringos who'd stolen her northern provinces.

In the First World War, the Kaiser had tried to take advantage of those hatreds by inducing the Mexicans to invade the United States. A shame nothing had come of it, Braun thought, although it had been a primary cause of America's declaration of war on Imperial Germany and had led to the shameful Treaty of Versailles. Even though the Mexicans were squat and ugly, nearly subhuman as the Jews, their hatred of the United States could be channeled to Germany's advantage.

Braun held the SS rank of *Obersturmbannfuehrer*, which was equivalent to a colonel in the American army. When word came that a landing on the American east coast was planned by German saboteurs, he thought it was insane and was quickly proven right. The would-be saboteurs had all been captured or killed. He was sadly confident that the ones captured would be hanged. Thus, when the request came down for Germany to take the war to America's west coast in support of Japan, he was delighted to volunteer. He knew he could do far better than the buffoons who'd been landed by sub on the east coast. Anything that aided Japan would help keep America's growing military forces from aiding Britain or Russia in their war with the Third Reich.

He recognized the irony that he would be helping apelike little yellow subhumans defeat the Jewish-dominated United States. Well, he thought, one can't always choose one's enemies any more than one can choose their own relatives, like his fat cousin Eva. Sooner or later, the Jewish-controlled United States would fall into the gutter of history, and he would be a part of that glorious effort, whether he did it directly for Germany or indirectly in behalf of Japan. He would do anything to destroy America and the Jews. While he wanted no part of Russian weather, he did envy others in the SS who were wreaking bloody havoc among the Jews as they advanced.

A handful of other staffers were fluent enough in English to function in the U.S., but he rejected them for the time being, instead keeping them in Monterrey and Mexico City, literally watching the store and prepared to relay reports. Braun was concerned that their accents would cause suspicion at the border, while his very slight accent could be explained away as Midwestern, or Swedish, or Danish. He would go alone, at least initially. He liked that idea. The Americans at the border would not suspect a middle-aged and slightly overweight man who walked with a little limp and drove a truck filled with junk. If he later decided he needed more help, he would send for it. *If* he decided he needed help, he would send for Gunther Krause. Although not an SS man like him, Krause had combat experience and possessed good English speaking skills and had been a loyal Nazi party member for some time.

He bought a decrepit junk-hauling truck, and, instead of junk, loaded it with weapons, ammunition, and dynamite bought with money provided by the German embassy before it was closed. In a couple of weeks at the most, he would cross the border even though he had no clear idea what he would do then. He did not think there would be a shortage of targets, however.

CHAPTER 6

THE MASSIVE PBY FLYING BOAT TOOK OFF FROM San Diego bay with a crew of eight and Lieutenant Commander Tim Dane along as an observer. Built by Consolidated, the flying boat initially looked as if it would never leave the surface, but her powerful Pratt and Whitney engines soon lifted her off the bay's protected and gentle waters.

Dane was along for what he hoped was a long but pleasant ride. The idea had been Merchant's. Dane was along not just to see the ocean below, but also the large numbers of ships traveling the Pacific coast, and try to get some idea of the difficulty involved in tracking any vessel that might be carrying enemy soldiers or contraband for enemy subversives already in place. Merchant and Spruance also wanted him out of the office for a while. The report he'd written about Japanese-Americans not being threats to American security and the abuses they were suffering at the hands of cops and the army had ruffled some high-ranking feathers. General DeWitt had gotten a copy and he was furious, as was Governor Olson. Olson was a politician who was in deep trouble with the electorate, but John L. DeWitt was a three-star general in charge of the Fourth Army and the western states. Even though he was in the army, he had to be respected until he calmed down.

The PBY could fly at over ten thousand feet and her top speed was a hair under two hundred miles an hour. Her pilot was an ensign named Ronnie Tuller who appeared to be a teenager, although he insisted he was twenty-two.

"There's a whole boatload of ships out there," Tuller said, laughing at his own bad joke, "and we have to check them over visually. If we fly at a conservative speed, say one hundred and twenty-five miles an hour, we can stay out here for a very long time. We'd likely run out of food and toilet paper before we ran out of gas."

Dane was seated in the co-pilot's seat. "Could you fly this thing to Hawaii?"

"Stripped down, stuffed with fuel, and with a lot of luck, yes. Realistically, we'd probably get close, and then have to land in the ocean because we'd probably hit a headwind or have to detour around a storm. Why?"

"Just thinking of all the people trying to get off the islands," he said. Thoughts of Amanda kept intruding. Where the hell was she?

"Understood," Tuller said. "I have heard that the Japs have a seaplane that is even larger than this baby and can fly twice as far. Too bad we don't have some of those. Maybe we could run a shuttle to Hawaii and back." Too bad indeed, Dane thought.

Tuller banked the massive plane. A freighter was in view, heading north, and he skillfully turned toward it.

"Just so you know, Commander, the idea of using our seaplanes was kicked around, but it just wasn't feasible. Filled with refugees, it would be too heavy to make it back. Getting there we'd doubtless have to land short and refuel, and that'd be a mess what with Jap ships and planes all around. That and the fact that there were so many people on Hawaii who'd want to leave, and so few planes, kinda nixed the idea."

Dane nodded and reluctantly accepted the logic. The people on the Hawaiian Islands were trapped. But was Amanda?

Observers on the PBY checked out the freighter. It was flying an American flag and several of her crewmen waved at the plane. No one in the PBY was taking chances, however, and guns were trained on her. Memories of an innocuous-looking ship unloading Japanese troops at the Panama Canal were still too fresh.

Tuller waved back. "We'll attempt to contact them by radio and try to determine that they are what they say they are and that no one's being forced to do anything bad because there's a gun to their heads. Odds are, everything's okay, but you never know. Even if we do make radio contact, we can't always believe what they're telling us if we're to do our job. They may not be saboteurs but they could be smugglers."

Dane smiled tightly. "I suppose if they start shooting at us, we'll know everything isn't on the up and up."

"Absolutely, Commander. If they do, we get to shoot back. It hasn't happened yet, but we're ready."

The Catalina carried three .30-caliber machine

guns and two fifties. She could also carry two tons of bombs, but had none on this flight. If the bombs weren't dropped, landing with them still on their racks was dicey at best and could result in an explosion. The other alternative was to dump them into the ocean, which was a waste of good bombs.

They left the freighter behind and flew on to the next one, gave it a look-see and moved on. Dane was coming to the conclusion that this excursion was a waste of time. A steady stream of ships was flowing both north and south and generally staying fairly close to the coastline. Despite her long-range capabilities, the PBY wouldn't fly too far out into the ocean this trip. Other long-range planes were doing that and trying to prevent the sort of sneak attack that had devastated the fleet at Pearl Harbor. Long-range radar installations were being constructed on the hills around major cities and would also provide warnings. Still, everyone knew that nothing would or could be foolproof. The coastline was just too long and the ocean too vast.

Many military personnel wished the Japanese would make an attack. While the American fleet was virtually nonexistent, just about every airfield, airstrip, or even flat piece of land around the major West Coast cities was lined with American fighters and bombers, all piloted by young men eager to take on the bastard sons of Nippon. Dane had seen figures saying that almost fifteen hundred U.S. planes were ready to be launched at the enemy, with more on the way. Types of fighters included a few of the older P39 and P40s, which were outclassed by the Japanese Zero. Planes lined up in growing numbers included the army's

P47, the navy's F4F fighter, which was a carrier plane without carriers, and the army's twin-tailed P38.

Tuller coaxed the plane to a higher altitude. "I know there are Jap subs out there. I think I might have spotted one a couple of days ago, but the damn thing dived before I could turn and attack it. Hell, maybe it was a whale. I just don't understand why they don't hit our shipping. Jeez, the ships down there are so vulnerable. They aren't even sailing in convoys, which is stupid if you ask me." He laughed. "Nobody does, of course."

Dane looked at the distant ships with his binoculars. "The Japs have a different mentality," he answered. "The Germans think it's a great idea to attack our civilian ships, especially oil tankers, and they're right. On the other hand, the Japs see attacking anything other than a warship as an insult to their manhood. 'Warriors attack warriors' is their philosophy according to their interpretation of bushido. I think some Jap skippers would actually disobey orders to attack a freighter or a tanker and save their torpedoes for warships instead."

Tuller rolled his eyes. "That ain't too smart. Those ships are our lifeblood."

That's right, Dane thought. And maybe they'll regret that someday. He also realized that he'd been calling the Japanese by the derogatory term *Japs*. So much for absorbing the culture of Japan when he was a kid.

The great wall of water came on them like a giant black train in the middle of the night. One moment, Amanda was lightly holding the wheel and simply steering in the direction of California by keeping the boat aligned with the correct stars, and the next, the swiftly moving wave had blotted out the stars and the night. Before she could do anything more than scream, the wave crashed over the catamaran, inundating it and her under several feet of roaring water.

She lost her grip on the wheel and thought she was going to be swept overboard as the wave knocked her about. She swallowed what felt like gallons of salty, nauseating water. The lifeline Mack insisted everyone use, especially at night, caught and held her while her fingers tried to grab and claw at anything that would keep her on the cat. She was wearing a Mae West life jacket that might keep her afloat if she was swept overboard, but that was not what she wanted. If that happened, she'd be alone in the ocean and condemned to die a terrible death. She thought about that and desperately hung on to the deck and prayed that the line would hold.

The cat lurched upward and she thought it would flip over on its back like a turtle and kill her as it climbed the wave. A part of her mind recalled Mack saying that killer waves, rogues, sometimes appeared out of nowhere, squashing everything in their path. She also remembered him saying that a catamaran could go bow-down into the water and sink like a rock. She prayed for the boat to make it through the torrent.

After an eternity, the cat reached the wave's peak, teetered, and lurched forward, skimming down the other side. It was a deadly and terrifying roller coaster ride.

It was over as quickly as it began. The rogue disappeared and continued on its journey. Amanda lay on the deck, gagging and vomiting the sea water she'd swallowed. She grabbed the lifeline and clawed her way back to the wheel, steadied it, and looped a rope around a spoke to keep it steady on course.

"Somebody!" she yelled. "Talk to me!"

She heard moans. Sandy had been on deck with her, and she was a few feet away, trying to get up. She was on her hands and knees, retching and shaking, but otherwise seemed unhurt. Okay, Amanda thought, now where were Mack and Grace? In the cabin, she recalled.

At first the cabin seemed okay, but then she saw that a wall had caved in. From inside came the ominous sound of silence. Reluctantly, she unclipped her lifeline and moved into the cabin. Grace lay on the floor. She was moaning softly and beginning to move. Her pulse was strong, so Amanda moved on to Mack. To her horror, she saw that his skull was distorted and he was drooling blood.

"Sandy, get in here."

"I'm sick."

"You're a nurse and these people are hurt. Get your butt in here."

Sandy came in a few seconds later. "Sorry," she said sheepishly. "My mind wasn't working."

Grace was coming around. Her eyes were clear and she seemed more stunned than injured. Neither she nor Mack had been wearing their lifelines, nor anything else, Amanda noted. They checked Mack over and looked at each other in dismay. Grace crawled to them and confirmed their diagnosis—Mack had a depressed skull fracture along with several broken ribs, maybe a punctured lung, and God only knew what other internal injuries. Maybe he'd be able to tell them if he regained consciousness.

"I don't think he's going to recover," Amanda said sadly. "He might stand a chance if we were first-class surgeons instead of nurses and if this was a great hospital instead of a dinky sailboat."

"You're right," said Sandy while Grace sobbed. "All we can do is make him comfortable and hope for the best."

There was one bunk and it was damaged. They repaired it as best they could and carefully laid Mack on it. He groaned but didn't wake up. They tied him to it, tried to give him some water, and then went out on deck. A beautiful multihued Pacific dawn was rising but they didn't see it. They were only dimly aware that the seas were as calm as an inland pond, with nothing to remind them of the horror of the night and the killer wave.

Amanda was aware that the others were looking at her for directions. Grace was the oldest, but leadership was never her strong suit.

She took a deep breath. "Okay, first of all we take inventory. What's left in the way of food and water, is the sail damaged, and, oh yeah, is the radio working?"

It didn't take long to confirm that the news was mostly bad. The radio was smashed, and some of the food had been swept overboard along with a couple of containers of precious water. They'd all thought their provisions had been secured, but obviously not well enough. Their sail had been slightly damaged, but it could be repaired and, besides, they had a spare. Fortunately, the mast was solid.

"We should all pray for rain," Grace said.

"And for Mack," Sandy added.

Amanda shook her head sadly. "He might die without

us knowing much about him except that he was our friend."

Grace smiled shyly. "His name is Maxwell Garver and he was an embezzler from Kansas City."

"You're joking," Amanda said.

"Nope. He worked for a bank that doubled as a brokerage house and he was stealing from them for about five years. He took the money and put it into cash and securities because he thought opening an account, even in another bank, would attract attention. When the Crash came, both the bank and the brokerage disappeared before they caught on to the fact that they were short some money."

"How much?" Sandy asked.

Grace shrugged. "Who knows? Mack said he wasn't interested in going back and claiming it because he was perfectly fine with his current life. Right now, it is sitting in a safe-deposit box in San Francisco. He did, however, write up a will a few days ago leaving it all to the three of us to be divided equally. The Three Stooges was the way he put it. If he doesn't live, it's ours, whatever it is."

Amanda laughed sardonically. "Are you telling me we could be filthy rich and dying of thirst in the middle of the world's largest ocean?"

"He gave me the key to the box, but I couldn't do anything with it unless I had something to prove it belonged to me, like the will. When we get there, I guess we'll find out."

"But first we have to get there," Sandy said.

Mack died that night, never regaining consciousness. They waited until morning, said some prayers, and gently pushed him into the sea. They'd wrapped him in a sheet so they didn't have to look at his face as his body bobbed up and down. Nor did they have anything to use as an anchor. Fortune was kind, and the catamaran soon outdistanced Mack's body. Unspoken was the fear that they'd have to watch while he was devoured by sharks, but that didn't happen either. In a few minutes, he was gone, out of sight but not out of their minds. He'd been the one who really understood the boat and the ocean.

"We're all alone, now," Sandy said.

"Think we'll make it?" Grace muttered.

"I don't think we have a choice," Amanda whispered. She wondered what Tim was doing now and what he would do if he was in such a predicament.

Admiral Yamamoto was angry and frustrated. Once again the foolishness of the code of bushido was hampering operations. His submarine captains had reported numerous sightings of American merchant ships, but few had done anything about it. A score of long-range submarines lay in wait off the major American cities like Los Angeles, San Francisco, San Diego, and, farther north, off Portland, Tacoma, and the British base at Vancouver. They, however, were waiting for the American Navy to emerge, not contemptible merchant ships. Sinking the American merchant ships could help cripple the American economy, but that point was lost on the devotees of bushido. He recalled a phrase from his time spent in the United States—with friends like these, who needs enemies?

Their excuses had been piously clever. They reminded him that they only carried a limited number of torpedoes; therefore, the precious weapons should not be

wasted against lowly merchant shipping. Once the torpedoes were gone, it meant that the submarines would
have to return to Japan for resupply while American
and British warships cruised unimpeded. The fact that
major American warships did not cruise at all in the
Pacific did not deter the devotees of bushido. The
goal of the submarine was to kill other warships, and
merchant shipping was beneath them.

Regarding the supply of torpedoes, the sub captains had a point, so the first step toward solving
their torpedo problem was to seize the large island
of Hawaii and utilize Hilo Bay as a base. The other
islands, including Oahu and the city of Honolulu, they
would continue to ignore. The reinforced American
Army garrison was no threat. It was stranded on Oahu.

The distance from Tokyo to San Diego was just under
fifty-six hundred miles and using Hilo would cut the trip
more than in half. With the American garrison on Oahu
helpless and under long-range siege, the attack on Hilo
would be a walkover and would largely eliminate the
excuse that there weren't enough torpedoes.

An attack on the Alaskan city of Anchorage was
planned. It would give the Japanese Army, now suddenly cooperating with the navy, a North American
base and one only twenty-four hundred miles from
San Diego. Army Colonel Yasuyo Yamasaki commanded
the garrison on Attu. His would be the invasion force.
His unit would be reinforced, removed from Attu for
the invasion, and the northern flank of the Japanese
Empire would be protected. He had spoken with
Admirals Nagumo, Toyoda, Kurita and Koga and all
were in agreement that submarines and other surface
warships must attack merchant shipping. Even though

Yamamoto was admiral of the Combined Fleet, and senior, the others would also use their considerable influence to get the more junior and more aggressive commanders to comply.

Another solution to the supply issue was the usage of Japanese civilian tankers and freighters to provide the subs with fuel, food, ammunition, and, of course, Type 94 torpedoes while submarines were on station off America's West Coast. These were just getting into place and would be situated far enough in the central Pacific where it was hoped they wouldn't be noticed by American patrols. Japan had begun the war with sixty-five submarines, although twenty-one of them were obsolete, with another thirty-seven under construction. They would never be able to keep up with America's production capabilities.

Therefore, Yamamoto's goal was to keep at least five subs on station at each of the major American ports where they could inflict maximum damage, while the others were resupplied or were repaired. There were scores of other cities on the coast, but he would need an infinite number of subs to cover them all.

Of course, the Americans were confronted with the same dilemma. They could not place warships all along the length of the American-Canadian coastline. Nor could they protect all their ports even with the many hundreds of airplanes intelligence reports said they were assembling. Nor could their radar cover everything as well. The coast was just too vast.

Even better for Japan, the Americans were condemned to fight from stationary positions while his ships, the subs in particular, could move stealthily and at will to any place and attack in strength before the Americans could respond. At least that was the theory, he thought. He had allowed the Americans far too much time to gather strength after their defeat at Midway. Yamamoto had to admit that he hadn't expected such an overwhelming victory either and, therefore, had little in the way of concrete plans when it so suddenly occurred.

At least Japanese torpedoes worked, he thought. It didn't matter how many submarines the Americans had if they couldn't sink anything with their flawed weapons. There had been so many reports by Japanese captains of American torpedoes going under Japanese ships, or bouncing off their hulls, that he didn't doubt there was a major issue that must be driving the Americans insane.

When Dane arrived at his nephew's camp, Steve Farris immediately and facetiously asked whether he should salute, shake hands, or kiss his uncle on both cheeks. After telling him to go screw himself, Tim laughed and hugged his nephew. It felt good to laugh. It took his mind off Amanda and the litany of defeats the country was enduring.

"Where the hell's my car?" Dane asked with mock anger.

"Sitting on blocks back home and quietly rusting away. I took the tires off and put them in the basement."

"Good thinking." Tires were as valuable as gold. While there was a sufficient amount of gas available if everyone paid attention to the rules of rationing, rubber for civilian uses had virtually disappeared.

Dane had brought enough steaks and beer to feed

the platoon, and distributed them, keeping two of the best pieces of sirloin and half a case of beer for the two of them. He assured his nephew that he'd paid for it, and that nobody was going to jail. Steve assured him that he didn't much care. A third of the platoon was on duty and enough was saved for them. Even though it was Sunday, they would be on duty with their eyes open. It would not be like what happened at Pearl Harbor, that never-to-be-forgotten Sunday in December.

After agreeing, however, that the Japanese were not likely to invade California this particular day, they changed into swimsuits and traipsed down to the water's edge. The sea was fairly calm and the temperature warm. A pair of seals stared curiously at them from perches on rocks, decided that the two men with pale white skin were insignificant, and went to sleep.

"Rough duty," Dane said, and Farris only grinned. "If it wasn't for my CO, Lytle, it'd be pretty good."

"I met him on the way in. I decided a courtesy call was in order. He was clearly drunk and didn't much care what I did. I was going to leave him a steak just to show what a good guy I am, but screw him."

"And leaving him some beer would be like taking coals to Newcastle," Steve laughed. "I'll probably hear about my not telling him you were coming. I'll just lie and say you surprised me as well, but now you know what I'm dealing with. I keep him informed about everything I see, including ships that I identify thanks to a copy of *Jane's* that I had to buy out of my own money. He's as much as told me to quit bothering him."

"How does he get away with it?" Dane asked.

"Easy. Major Harmer is the battalion CO and he's totally dominated by Lytle. Rumor has it he's as big a lush as Lytle. A lot of us wish the Japs would swoop in some dark and stormy night and carry them away. Of course, with our luck they'd be returned."

Dane smiled. "Give me some time and maybe I can arrange for somebody in the army's chain of command to make a surprise visit."

"That'd be nice. I admit there's likely only one chance in a million that the Japs will show up here, but I think it pays to be at least a little vigilant. Now, what are you up to with the navy?"

Dane told his nephew about his ordeals on the *Enterprise* and his rescue of Spruance. He didn't spare the details, including Spruance's wish to be killed rather than captured. He knew his nephew would keep his mouth shut. Farris's eyes widened as he took in the gruesome firsthand story of the U.S. Navy's second major defeat in the still-young war.

"That landed me in intelligence, which would better be named lack of intelligence, but not because people are stupid, far from it. Some of the brightest people I've ever known are trying to figure out what the Japs will do next. Some people say that military intelligence is an oxymoron and, to some extent, they're right. However, we're like kids trying to put together a jigsaw puzzle but are never given all the pieces. Generally we've only got a few. From them we have to extrapolate what the whole picture is, and a lot of times it later turns out to be a picture of a cow instead of a tree. We do the best we can with what we have."

"Like Kimmel and Short in Pearl Harbor?" Farris asked.

"Yes. They did what they thought best with the information on hand. They guessed wrong and paid for it with their reputations and thousands of American lives."

"So they're scapegoats?"

"That's an opinion question, and here's mine. Yes, they are scapegoats but only to a point. They willfully and foolishly didn't cooperate with each other, and neither realized they were the equivalent of a frontier outpost surrounded by potentially hostile Apaches or Comanches. Instead, they continued to run the base like it was a country club in Virginia. They didn't send out enough scout planes and did nothing to coordinate their defenses. If they'd been prepared and we'd fought like bandits, and still lost, they'd be heroes, tragic heroes, but still heroes. Maybe they didn't know how to prepare for a war? Hell, I didn't. Still don't."

Dane took another beer. "Look, here's the problem with intelligence and the Japs. Even if they send radio messages, which they didn't before Pearl Harbor, the important messages will be in code, which we can't read, although I presume we're trying to. Most communications aren't encoded because they are routine, mundane, and unimportant, but are still in Japanese, which only a precious few, like me, can understand."

"Is that why you're on Spruance's staff?"

"No, it's because of my good looks. Yes, it's because I can understand Japanese. There are literally tens of thousands of Americans who understand German, probably a lot more, but maybe only a few score who can do the same with Japanese and who can be trusted because their ancestry's not Japanese. Nobody's quite ready yet to enlist the help of local Japanese, although necessity might force that to change. So, even if we do intercept a radio message and manage to translate it, we find that most of them are innocuous, like requests for rations, complaints about the weather, and other stuff. Even if we find something referencing a future action, it's going to refer to something like Plan Jupiter and Objective Fred. Then we have to figure out what Jupiter and Fred are."

"Sounds like great fun," Steve laughed.

"It's a royal pain in the ass, which is why I finagled a day off to come out here. There's no way I can succeed and provide the higher-ups with a clear picture. I convinced them I needed a break. At least I got promoted and my group now reports more to Nimitz than Spruance."

Dane changed the subject and told about his trips on a submarine and the girl he'd met in Honolulu.

"Wow," said Farris. "You really think it's possible she's trying to sail from Honolulu to here?"

"Yep."

"Jesus, I'd like to meet her."

"And I'd like to see her again."

They cooked their steaks over a fire made of driftwood, ate, drank beer, and swam in the warm water, always staying in the shallows. Neither was a strong swimmer and they were concerned about tides and, of course, sharks. They talked about families and home, topics that seemed like they were from another galaxy. They only touched on their futures, since they would be in the military for the foreseeable future. Soldiers and sailors everywhere joked that they'd be discharged in just time to collect Social Security.

"I wonder when the war really will end," Farris said.

"You think we should negotiate with the Japs?"

"Someday, we'll have to," Steve said. "I don't think we should cave in to them, especially not after Pearl Harbor and all the other crap they've done to us, but yeah, sooner or later there'll have to be some talks unless this is really going to be a second Hundred Years War."

"They've kicked our asses up and down the street," Dane said. "What should we give up in order to stop the killing and get our people back?"

His nephew jabbed the opener into the can of Budweiser and took a swallow. "I don't know. Do we need the Philippines? Hell, we were going to turn them loose anyhow. Does it really matter who gets them next?"

"But we promised them independence, not brutality and slavery."

"But, Tim, how many Americans will have to die to get those islands returned, just so we can give them away? Certainly we want to keep Hawaii and get Midway, Wake, and Guam back, and they sure as hell are going to have to pay for Pearl Harbor and all the atrocities, but I guess I can't totally rule out negotiating with the little yellow bastards. Just count your fingers when you shake their hands and cover your ass when you bow."

Steve belched before continuing. It was his fourth beer and he was starting to feel it. There hadn't been all that much opportunity for serious drinking lately. "First of all, we've got to start winning some battles so we can bring them to the table. When the hell is that going to start?"

Dane opened his own beer. "How the hell would I know? I'm a lieutenant commander, the equivalent of a major to you army types, and there's a million of us wandering around thinking we know what's going on, and none of us do."

It was midafternoon when they heard Sergeant Stecher's voice calling for them from up on the hill. They stood as Stecher ran down to them, upset and out of breath.

"Commander, you just got a call from a Captain Merchant."

Dane shook his head. He didn't want the war to intrude. Besides, what would happen if he ignored it for a few more minutes?

"And you didn't salute me, Sergeant," he said with a smile.

Stecher blinked in surprise and then laughed. "I wasn't aware I had to salute an officer in a baggy bathing suit."

"True enough. So what's so important?"

"Damn Japs just invaded Alaska."

Ruby Oliver's small, shabby restaurant in the gray and undistinguished city of Anchorage specialized in large servings of mediocre food fried in bacon grease, or whatever she could get that was close to it. Anchorage itself was on the flat, low ground at the end of Cook Inlet. It was as far inland as decent-sized ships could go. On a clear day, the mountains to the east glowered down on the small city.

Seating a mere twenty people, the restaurant was in a small one-story frame building with a good view of the channel that led from the Cook Inlet to Anchorage itself.

Of course it was named Ruby's and it provided enough income for her to be comfortable. What people were calling the Great Depression had pretty well left Alaska alone since nobody'd had that much money in the first place. Can't lose what you never had, went the joke.

Ruby was forty, divorced, had badly dyed red hair, and was at least twenty pounds overweight, the result of a tendency to eat the leftover food, a practice she referred to as profit sharing. Even though the Depression had largely missed Alaska, she'd been hungry enough in past years to know that you didn't let food go to waste.

The restaurant rarely served beef as it was too expensive to import, but fish and venison were regular staples brought in by local fishermen and hunters. Fruits were almost unknown and a few vegetables were homegrown during the very short growing season. That or she'd occasionally buy foodstuffs, if they weren't too expensive, from ships plying their trade from the south. Oranges, she'd discovered, were as rare as hen's teeth and out of her price range.

She had a clientele that wasn't too particular about what they ate, especially if it was cooked in that bacon grease. They liked Ruby, who was gregarious and friendly. A few of the boys had tried to get her drunk enough to get into her pants, but she'd outlasted all of them, sometimes to her regret. Her ex-husband, now living somewhere in Oregon, had been a complete jerk who'd slapped her around when drunk, but, when sober and aroused, was a helluva lover. Sometimes she missed that part of her life, but not enough to go back to him.

Ruby was beginning to have money worries. When

war with Japan had first commenced, there was hope that the military would find Anchorage, one of Alaska's major ports and a bustling town of two thousand, indispensable. Elmendorf Army Air Force Base had been built and Fort Richardson reinforced, and she'd dreamed of all the new customers frequenting her restaurant. But then came Midway and the Air Force had shuttled its planes out, and Fort Richardson's garrison was reduced to only a couple of hundred men.

This morning, she had a slight hangover thanks to several drinks taken alone in the back of the restaurant, and was serving coffee to her one customer when she thought she heard thunder. She looked out the window and saw a nice bright summer morning and no reason for thunder, but hell, this was Alaska, wasn't it? In five minutes they could be hit with a blizzard, even though it was summer. Some people said Alaska's weather was God's idea of a joke.

She was about to comment to her customer, when the lawyer's office across the street disintegrated and shock waves blew through her window and hurled her across a table and into the wall. Her customer landed on top of her and she realized to her horror that he had borne the brunt of the explosion and was a bloody, dead mess. Large wood splinters and shards of glass protruded from his back and head like an obscene porcupine.

She screamed and clawed to get out from under him, finally succeeding as more explosions rocked the area and their concussions knocked her around. The front door wouldn't open so she ran out the back. Anchorage was in flames. Many of the buildings were wood frame like hers, and they were burning furiously.

"Look down the channel!" someone yelled, and she did. She could see the gray shapes of large ships approaching. Smaller boats were alongside them, and these were heading directly for Anchorage and Ruby Oliver. She'd seen enough pictures and newsreels to know that the smaller boats were landing craft and that the larger ones were doubtless Japanese transports and warships. A dozen or so Japanese planes flew overhead and inland, seeking targets. It was common knowledge that the Japs had already landed farther out on the Aleutians on Kiska and Attu, and now they were headed directly for her.

Ruby ran back into the restaurant, now also afire, grabbed her shotgun and a box of shells and began to run down the road toward Fort Richardson. As she did, a column of trucks roared by her, forcing her off the road. They were coming from the fort and were filled with grim-faced soldiers carrying their Springfield rifles and wearing the tin-pot helmets that were leftovers from the last war. She was surprised they'd responded so quickly, but realized that spotters farther up the channel must have radioed the information to the fort. She wondered why the hell the military hadn't warned the city. At least some civilians could have fled before the shelling began and maybe saved some lives. Several bodies were visible, and other civilians were running away from the burning town.

As some of the trucks approached the town, Ruby found an undamaged two-story house with the door open. She entered and went upstairs so she could see. She soon wished she hadn't. As the column entered Anchorage and approached the waterfront, shells from the Japanese ships exploded in and around the

American soldiers who were trying to deploy. She watched in horror as some soldiers simply disintegrated from the explosions while others were sent hurling into the sky.

The Japanese landing craft disgorged scores of men. They raced down the street toward the stunned and confused remaining American soldiers. The fight was at short range and she cheered when some Japanese fell, but many more Americans lay still, and the remnants of the column were soon standing with their hands up. The battle for Anchorage had been lost in a matter of minutes.

The Japanese rounded up the survivors. Ruby estimated there were thirty all told, and a number of them were wounded. One, an officer, tried talking to a Japanese counterpart. The Japanese officer shouted something, and the American was rifle-butted to the ground and stabbed with bayonets by several soldiers while the Japanese officer looked on. The soldiers stopped stabbing him and he lay still in an enormous pool of blood. She thought she could hear the other prisoners moaning.

More landing craft unloaded several hundred Japanese; most of whom headed down the road to what was likely a now abandoned Fort Richardson. A number, however, surrounded the prisoners, shouting and pointing bayonets at them. Ruby had heard that the Japs treated their prisoners brutally and fearfully wondered just what they'd do. She knew most of them, if only by sight. Some had even eaten at her place.

An officer barked a command and a roar of laughter came from the Japanese surrounding the Americans. The Japanese pushed and prodded them with their bayonets toward the water and then into it. It might be late summer, but the water was very cold and Ruby could hear the screams coming from the prisoners as they were pushed into water that came up to their chests.

The Japanese soldiers fired in front of the prisoners and stabbed slow-moving Americans with their bayonets. The message was clear, swim or die.

Swimming only delayed the inevitable. Tears streamed down her face as a couple of GIs tried to return to shore and were shot. The wounded and nonswimmers had already disappeared under the waves, while others attempted to strike out for the opposite shore and the illusion of safety. When they were maybe a hundred yards out, the Japanese opened fire. It was little more than target practice. Splashes surrounded the dozen or so heads remaining, and soon there were none.

Ruby pulled herself to her feet. She was not going back to Anchorage. Doubtless there were civilians still there who would also become prisoners of the Japanese. She might not be killed because she was a civilian, but she'd also heard what they did to women.

Along with her sleeping quarters behind the kitchen of the restaurant, she had a cabin a couple of miles away and well into the woods. There, she'd get some decent gear, another weapon, and head farther into the forest. But where to go? South to Seward or Valdez was an easy choice, but were the Japs landing there as well? Maybe heading inland toward Fairbanks and the Canadian border was the best idea.

She left the house and walked into the nearby bushes where she heard strange noises. She stood with the shotgun ready. She lowered it when she looked into the frightened faces of a handful of very young and scared American soldiers who'd escaped the massacre.

"Where you boys headed?" she asked, her voice surprisingly calm.

They looked at each other. They hadn't thought that far. They'd run like they were on fire when the shells cut their unit to pieces. One, a PFC, shrugged. "Don't know. Sure as hell can't go back to the barracks. The Japs'll be sacked out in our bunks pretty damn soon."

Ruby slung the shotgun over her shoulder. "Then you'd better come with me."

CHAPTER 7

WITH A FEW BEERS AND A FINE STEAK COOKED medium rare causing an overfull belly, Dane drove cautiously back to his quarters, fearful that he'd doze off and get into an accident. A couple of cups of coffee had helped, but he still felt fuzzy when he finally made it back to the base. He'd planned to shower and change, but a message told him to get his ass to Spruance's offices right now.

When Dane arrived, it was clear that a number of others on the admiral's staff had also been off base and were still arriving. Like Dane, some even in civvies. Thus, it was early evening before Spruance let Merchant begin. He stood in front of a large map of Alaska and the western states and started with the obvious. The Japanese had landed troops at Anchorage and did not appear to be planning to leave. It was an invasion, not a raid.

"They were first spotted by military personnel on the Kenai Peninsula along with a number of civilians

who promptly contacted everyone they could by ham
radio or by telephone. Just for the record, most tele-
phones in the area are still working, so we're getting
a lot of good intelligence."

Merchant continued. "The spotters said there were
half a dozen Jap battleships, which is clearly an exaggeration. Cooler heads and some ex-navy types said
there were two cruisers and four destroyers followed
by a dozen or so transports. There were planes, so we
have to assume at least one carrier, although probably
a small one. We estimate they landed approximately
five thousand soldiers and we think most of them came
from their existing garrisons on Attu and Kiska, which
we believe were heavily reinforced just recently. It
is also likely Attu and Kiska have been abandoned."

"So what are their plans?" asked a clearly annoyed
and impatient Spruance. Merchant had used the words
"think" and "likely" too often. The admiral wanted
something more precise. The damned Japs had just
invaded the mainland of North America and were
again showing how impotent the United States Army
and Navy were.

Merchant was unfazed. "Sir, they don't have enough
men to conquer Alaska, much less threaten the United
States, although people in Alaska and the West Coast
are starting to panic over the possibility. Even if they
do heavily reinforce their men on the ground, they
might be able to take some nearby towns, but Alaska
is so vast it'd still be an enormous undertaking and a
logistical nightmare to maintain. Hell, it's almost six
hundred miles from Anchorage to Juneau and much
of it is truly miserable going. In my opinion, Admiral,
they took Anchorage because they could, and because

they could rub our noses in it, and maybe because they think it'll goad us into doing something stupid."

"Which is not going to happen," snapped Spruance. "But you will tell me what we can do."

"Which isn't much," Merchant said and earned a glare from the normally even-tempered Nimitz, who had just entered. Dane stifled a smile. Merchant wasn't afraid of the brass, which was good. Too many intelligence officers fed their superiors what they thought their superiors wanted to hear, rather than the unvarnished and sometimes painful truth. On the other hand, Nimitz, for all his apparently easygoing personality, was reputed to be a solid tactician and a proponent of attacking. Doing nothing had to be killing him, Dane thought.

Merchant continued. "The problem is distance. I assume we have some submarines heading for Cook Inlet to try to make life miserable for the Japs, and I also assume that any surface ships have been told to stay clear."

"True," said Nimitz. "We had two old destroyers patrolling Cook Inlet and they were lucky enough to neither see nor be seen. If they had spotted the Japs, they might have gotten off a slightly earlier warning, but it wouldn't have mattered, and they likely would have been sunk for their efforts."

"Right now," Merchant continued, "Alaska cannot be reached by either road or rail. As you're aware, we're building a so-called highway to Alaska, but it won't be ready for some months and will likely close down during the winter if it's not through to Fairbanks. All supplies for the engineers working on the road coming down from the north have to come in by ship and I presume that lifeline has just been cut. I've been told by General Bruckner, who commands Alaska, that the army wants to pull those men out since they are so exposed and they aren't combat troops in the first place. Many of them are Negroes and there is serious doubt as to how well they will fight. I assume we'll try to speed up its construction from the south, but there's only so much you can do. As to rail, there ain't none. Also, the handful of planes we had at Fairbanks got shot up pretty badly by Jap carrier planes."

Spruance shook his head. "Damn place is larger than Texas and might as well be on the moon."

"Sir, the army's admitted that they have a true Hobson's choice regarding the troops they now have in Alaska. Even if the road-building troops up there are poorly trained, they are still soldiers and should be able to help in the defense of Fairbanks and Ladd Field. However, we must have that road through Canada, so the army doesn't want them to stop road-building. Also, the Alaska National Guard has fewer than three thousand men and they are scattered all over the territory."

"So that leaves air," Spruance said, uncomfortably acknowledging that the Japanese controlled the seas. He had a good idea what was going to be said next.

Merchant smiled grimly. "That's right, sir, and we have little to work with right now. We have plenty of planes, but they don't have the range to make it to Anchorage or Fairbanks and back. Hell, some of them couldn't even get there in the first place, much less return. Even if we based our planes on Canadian soil, at Vancouver for instance, it's more than thirteen hundred miles from Vancouver to Anchorage, and those are crow-fly miles that would require a lot of flying over the ocean and maybe running into Jap carrier planes on the way. If we take the overland route, we'd add several hundred more miles each way. The air force has B17, B24, and B25 bombers that could make it from Vancouver to Anchorage, but couldn't make it back. They'd need a place to land and refuel. There's a small base near Fairbanks called Ladd Field, but it's not adequate and needs a lot of improvement. Besides, the Japs just bombed it."

"Suggestions?" said Nimitz.

Merchant jabbed his pointer at the map. "Juneau. It's six hundred miles from Anchorage to Juneau, and eight hundred from Vancouver to Anchorage. It'd be tight, but the planes should make it. Unfortunately, it's going to take time to prepare a proper base. I don't know if Vancouver has an airport that can handle planes as large as our bombers."

Nimitz shook his head. "Of course, the navy has no planes that can make it, either."

"No, sir," Merchant said, "Maybe in a year or two, but not today."

Dane raised his hand and earned a quick glare from Nimitz. "What, Commander? You've got an idea?"

"Yes, sir, or at least it'd be a stopgap until we get things rolling at Vancouver. A PBY can fly two thousand miles and carry a ton of bombs and doesn't need an airfield. I suggest we stage them out of the waters of Puget Sound, fly up to Anchorage via the overland route, and bomb the place. We might not accomplish all that much with just a few tons of bombs, but they'll know we're alive and kicking."

"It's a great idea," Merchant said. "In a way it'd be like Doolittle hitting Tokyo. Not much damage, but we sure as hell got their attention. We don't even have to wait for an airfield to be developed. The Catalinas can land in the water off Juneau, or anywhere else for that matter, refuel, take off, and be on their way."

Everyone seemed pleased that they could soon be striking back. "Hopefully, our people in Alaska can pinpoint some good targets for us." Nimitz said. Then his mood turned dark. "The PBYs are large, slow targets. We might get in one or two raids before the Japs figure that out and either land their own planes at Anchorage or station a carrier nearby and slaughter our boys."

"But it's a lot better than doing nothing," Spruance added softly. "We have to strike back. We're all sick and tired of being kicked."

"May I ask one more question?" Dane inquired, and Spruance nodded. "Sir, who is commanding the Japs in Alaska?"

Spruance laughed, recalling Dane's background. "Think you might know him?"

"Yes, sir, I did meet some army officers."

"His name is Yasuyo Yamasaki and he's a colonel," Spruance answered.

"Admiral, I never met him, but some of the people I knew in Japan said he had a reputation. Sir, he's a fanatic. He's cold, hard, and cruel, and one of those who will fight to the last man."

Amanda was so weak she could barely stand up, much less work the sails or stand at the wheel. With food and water at dangerously low levels, they'd cut down to what they hoped was subsistence levels. Now she wondered if they'd gone too far. There was only a little left, and they were wondering if they should finish everything in one almost literal gulp that would build up their strength, however temporarily. Of course, when it was gone, it was gone and they would go back to dying slowly. No, it was decided, they would stretch it out. Every day they still lived was a triumph.

There had been no more rogue waves or storms. Instead, just the opposite. Too much of their time was spent floating in the calm seas and praying for a wind to take them to safety.

Nor had it rained. They'd seen cloudbursts in the distance dumping tantalizing loads of water into an ocean that didn't need it. Once, a storm had been close enough for them to see the raindrops lashing the waves. They'd tried to steer the cat toward it, but the cloudburst ended as quickly as it had begun, leaving them with the feeling that they and their puny efforts were being mocked by the gods.

"I'm a Christian," Sandy had said weakly. "I don't believe in plural gods. At least not until recently. Get us to safety and I'll believe anything."

They'd managed to catch a few fish. They'd devoured them raw and gotten diarrhea that had left them weaker and sicker than before they'd eaten. Their joints hurt, their teeth were beginning to feel loose, and their gums were painful, sure signs of developing scurvy. Soon they would be unable to work the catamaran. Soon they would die.

Far, far worse was the horrible feeling that they were lost. They'd done their best to keep on course, but their navigational skills weren't up to Mack's and they had zero confidence that they knew precisely where they were going. That they were headed east and north was the best they could conclude. Assuming they could keep sailing, sooner or later they would hit the Americas. They could only hope and pray that they were still alive when it happened.

"I think I was falling in love with him," Grace announced a couple of days after Mack's death.

"We'll have a memorial service for him when we reach California," Amanda said, rubbing her aching jaw and wishing she had an orange or a lime. And *that's assuming we reach California*, she thought.

When they left Hawaii they knew that the amount of time necessary to make the trip was impossible to estimate. Still, they had the feeling that they should have bumped into something as immense as North America by now. They were well north of the equator and should be on track, but they couldn't be certain. They knew by the stars that they were headed in the right general direction, but that didn't tell them how near or far landfall might be. In a few days, their reduced rations would run out, and a few days after that they'd be dead with no one to know what had happened to them.

They'd begun keeping journals in case the catamaran was found drifting at some time in the future with their desiccated, mummified corpses on board. Or maybe they wouldn't be on board. Maybe their bodies would tumble into the ocean and be devoured by the fish. They wondered how long the last to die would want to spend staring at the bodies of her friends before she heaved them overboard. How long would the last one survive before going mad or killing herself? And what about cannibalism? Would the last one have the strength to devour the flesh of the others? They all said no, but nobody could truly rule it out.

Amanda wondered how long her parents and sisters in Annapolis would grieve for her, especially since they didn't know that she was out in the ocean in the first place. Someday, when Hawaii was again free of the Japanese, her family might hire someone to look for her. She'd left messages in her apartment and "mailed" some letters to her family that might not be delivered for years, but that was it. All three of them wondered if they had done something truly foolish and tragic by setting out from Hawaii in the first place. At least starvation in Hawaii might mean a marked grave, Grace remarked bitterly.

Sandy was the one who first noticed the difference. The swells were higher, but that was nothing new. The size of the waves differed all the time. If it meant a storm was coming, however, it might mean that their end might be sooner than they thought. They all doubted that they had the strength left in their frail bodies to fight a storm. In that area alone had they been fortunate. With the exception of the rogue wave, the seas had not been at all treacherous.

"Quiet," Sandy said. They did as they were told. "Do you hear it?"

"I don't hear anything but the wind and the waves," Amanda said. "I hurt too much to hear anything else."

"Listen for the waves," Sandy insisted. "They're different."

Amanda listened intently. They were surrounded in the rolling sea by a fog so thick they'd tried to lick its moisture off their arms. Sandy was right, the sound was different. She thought she heard breakers. "Oh, God," she yelled, "we're near shore!"

"Or rocks," Grace said, quickly dampening their sudden enthusiasm. They lowered the main sail and attempted to coast toward the sounds, which were becoming louder. If they were headed toward rocks, they didn't want to crash into them. They might be close to shore, or the rocks might be part of a reef scores of miles away from land. Either way, they had to get through them unscathed. They grabbed poles to use to push the cat away from the still unseen rocks.

Sandy went to the bow of the cat and tried to peer through the fog. "I still can't see a thing, but we're definitely near land. I can almost smell it." She giggled almost hysterically. "God, I hope it's California and not the Galapagos, or Easter Island."

An unseen force suddenly lifted the cat and threw it forward, causing them to fall backward, again held tight by their lifelines. They felt the hull grate on sand and another wave pushed it onto land. "Get out," Amanda yelled. "Get out and pull the boat farther onto the shore."

With the remnants of their strength, they managed to drag it a few feet farther onto the sand where they collapsed, gasping and choking from their exertions. The catamaran wouldn't run away, at least not for a while. Maybe they'd find a little water, or some food. Maybe they'd find out just where the hell they were. Of course, it would help if they could see through the fog.

They stood, but it was difficult to walk. The steady ground was so different from the plunging of the cat that they fell down like a trio of drunks. They lay there, helpless and exhausted until a breeze stroked them and blew away the fog. The gods had not mocked them. They had somehow landed between a number of large rocks, any one of which could have smashed the catamaran into pieces and sent them into the ocean to drown. A few feet away, two men with rifles stared at them incredulously.

"What the hell are you people doing out in that damn thing?" the older of the two said. They were wearing armbands. "You idiots are gonna catch hell for violating curfew."

Curfew? Amanda began to laugh, which angered the man. "Don't piss me off, young lady. Where'd you come from? Which yacht club let you go out in violation of the law, and how long ago did it happen?" His eyes widened and his tone changed as he took in their ragged and gaunt condition. "Good lord, what is going on here? You people look like refugees."

Sandy managed to stand up and smile through chapped, torn lips. "We came from Oahu."

The man blinked, and then smiled. "You tellin' me you little girls sailed that piece of crap catamaran all the way from Hawaii?"

"That's right," Amanda said, and accepted his helping arm. The men sat them back down on the beach and let them drink from their canteens. The water was warm, brackish, and delicious. With each swallow they felt life returning.

Amanda smiled. "Now, where the heck are we, and please don't tell me we've been blown back to Honolulu."

"Not a chance," laughed the second man as he

guided them toward a truck that was parked on the hard ground above the beach. "You're just about ten miles south of San Francisco."

Wilhelm Braun drove his rickety old truck slowly and carefully down the dirt road toward the dilapidated shack occupied by U.S. Customs outside the small, dull town of Campo, California.

The wretched wooden building did little more than keep two American customs agents out of the sun. Before reaching the post, Braun left his truck behind a hill that overlooked the border and was out of sight of the Americans. He'd crawled over the hill and reconnoitered the area just before dawn, confirming that only two men were in it. He wanted to get there before any others showed up to relieve or reinforce them. Two he thought he could handle, but any more would be just too much. Another concern was that the army was building a base somewhere nearby and he didn't want to run into any military personnel.

The main crossing point from Mexico to California was to the west at Tijuana, and he hoped that this spot was far enough away to have little traffic or witnesses. He'd passed an empty Mexican customs post a half mile back. It looked like no one had been in it for quite some time. There were no cars in view behind him and the road coming from California was likewise devoid of traffic. Perfect.

Braun drove on and stopped the truck a few feet from the wooden bar that separated the two countries. He stepped out, feeling only a little foolish wearing the cheap but colorful Mexican serape over his shoulders. It was baggy and hid the pistol in his belt.

The two customs agents approached with their hands on their holstered revolvers, but relaxed visibly when they saw that Braun was neither Mexican nor Japanese, just a slightly overweight middle-aged white man in a ridiculous outfit. They relaxed even more when he showed them identification that showed he was an American citizen named William Brown.

"Watcha doin', mister?" the older of the two asked as he looked over the truck.

Braun grinned in what he hoped was an ingratiating manner. He wanted to get through without incident if he could possibly do it.

"What I've got here, gentlemen, is a load of cheap Mexican souvenirs that I intend to sell to the troops in San Diego. This is my first trip by truck. In the past, I've sent them by ship, but that's not a good idea anymore thanks to the fucking Japs. So I'm driving this stinking relic filled with my inventory."

The guards laughed, but the leader of the two had a question. "We heard a truck an hour or so ago and then it stopped. Was that you, and, if so, why did you stop?"

Braun rolled his eyes in mock dismay. "Because I had dinner in a little place south of here and I've been sick ever since then. I stopped for a while to let things pass, literally, and thought it was a good idea to make sure I had control over myself and my bowels before continuing on."

The second guard nodded solemnly. "Damn greaser food'll kill you. I've been in your position a few times." He laughed again. "And that position is squatting and crapping your brains out. Goddamned Montezuma's Revenge is gonna kill us all some day."

The leader shook his head. "We can't spend all day out here. Who knows, maybe somebody else'll come along and we'll have a traffic jam. Mind if we see what's in your truck?"

"Of course not," Braun said hopefully.

The two guards walked to the back of the truck. A tarp hid what was inside. The contents could stand a cursory inspection, but something told Braun that the two bored guards might pay a little more attention if only to kill the time. He briefly wondered if he shouldn't have chosen the busier Tijuana route, but it was far too late for second thoughts.

"I hope you don't mind if I stand back a ways," he said, "my stomach's still grumbling and I'm not fit company."

"Not a problem," they said in unison and began to undo the tarp. The leader stuck his head in and began to poke around. "What the hell is this?"

Braun already had the pistol gripped tightly in both his hands and fired before they could turn. At fifteen feet, two bullets struck each of them in the back and they crumpled to the ground. He checked and they were still breathing, although probably dying. He wouldn't take any chances. He rolled them on their stomachs and shot them once each in the back of the skull.

Braun looked around and saw nothing. Still nobody coming down the road in either direction. Killing the two men was a shame, but also his duty. Nor had the shots aroused any interest from the few distant houses scattered in the area. Live and let live seemed to be the rule in this area.

He dragged them by the feet into a shallow ravine maybe a hundred yards away from their post. He dumped them in and covered their bodies with brush after taking their badges and their weapons. He thought about burying them, but decided he didn't have the time. Or a shovel, he thought, and laughed harshly.

He wiped away scuff marks and footprints and traces of blood and brains as best he could. With a little luck, it would be hours before the two bodies were discovered. It was the first time he'd killed an enemy since the Great War, unless he counted a couple of Mexicans, but Mexicans don't count at all.

A slowly moving dot and plume of dust in the distance marked another vehicle heading toward the United States. When they saw the abandoned post, Braun hoped they'd continue on, thanking their good luck that said they didn't have to declare what they were bringing in. At least that's what he would do. Finally, he cut the telephone line leading to the shack.

Humming softly, he lifted the wooden bar, left it open, and drove into California.

"Why me?" Dane asked. "I thought I was going to be an observer on the PBY raid on Anchorage?"

"You are," said Merchant. "It's going to be your punishment for suggesting it. But it'll be a couple of days before we've got the planes all in a row and ready to fly."

The navy was gathering a dozen of the Catalinas and sending them to Vancouver where bombs would be added. In the meantime, Merchant had a job for him. There had been an incident at a border crossing and there were concerns about Japanese saboteurs crossing into California. For a variety of reasons, Dane had his doubts about that, but kept silent. Whatever thoughts and doubts he had, he would bring them back from the border and discuss them with Merchant.

Two hours later he had been flown to the border in a Piper Cub piloted by a kid who said he was fourteen and wanted to kill Japs when he was old enough to enlist in the navy. Dane also found that the kid's parents were divorcing and that his father drank a lot and beat up on his mother. Dane wished him well. They landed on a road near the border, where a stocky middle-aged man in a rumpled suit met them.

"You Commander Dane? If so, I'd like to see some ID. I'm Special Agent Roy Harris, FBI," he said and flashed his own credentials. Dane did as well and also showed Harris his hastily typed orders. Harris grunted and seemed satisfied that Dane was for real.

"Commander, do you understand what's happened here?"

"Very little. I was told there'd been an incident and, since I'm with intelligence and otherwise free for a couple of days, I was tagged to come down here. I also read and speak Japanese, if that's important."

Harris looked impressed. "It might come to that, but not today. What we have here, however, is a double murder. Sometime early this morning, either somebody or a group of somebodies murdered two border guards. Shot them in the back and then in the back of the head just to make sure. The bodies are on ice in town and, unless you have a strong stomach and a devout wish to see them, you can take my word about the shootings. The bodies are in terrible shape after being swollen by the sun and chewed on by a host of animals."

Dane grimaced. "I'll pass, thank you. I saw enough torn up bodies when the *Enterprise* went down."

Harris was clearly impressed, then recognized the Purple Heart Dane had thought to wear. "You'll have to tell me about that some time. I had a cousin on the *Hornet*. He's missing and his family can't deal with the fact that he's probably dead."

Harris shook his head. "In the meantime, here's what we do know. The two men were likely first shot in the back and then in the head to finish them off, and their bodies dragged into the brush. We don't know how many people were involved in the shooting, and we have no idea how many vehicles they drove, or how many went by the border afterwards and just drove by since nobody was in the post.

"Finally, some good citizens got curious about the buzzards congregating off a ways and seeming to have a good time, and checked it out. They tried to call on the post's phone, but the line had been cut. They went into town and called the sheriff, who called me since it was federal property and federal agents have jurisdiction. I got here an hour ago. The sheriff says it was Japs trying to sneak in. We found some tire tracks where somebody had tried to erase them and we think they came from a truck. What do you think?"

They walked to the border and looked around. The tracks in question were barely visible. He'd take the agent's word that they came from a truck. Dane stared in disbelief at the shack. "Do people actually work in there?"

"Yeah, and for damn little pay, which makes it worse. They were good guys. Each was married and had kids."

Dane looked around and tried to think. Japs? It just didn't seem right to him.

"Agent Harris, I think the sheriff's wrong about it being Japs and I think you know it. It just isn't logical. If the guards were shot in the back, that means they had turned away from their attacker or attackers and they wouldn't do that if they were dealing with Japs, even ones born in the U.S. National paranoia's just too deep for border cops to let that happen. I also think there was only one person, and likely a man, since the guards didn't seem concerned enough to split up and keep an eye on somebody else. I also think it was a white guy and someone who probably appeared to be an American. Anything other than a white man, even a Mexican, would have set off alarm bells."

Harris grinned, "Damned good. I'm almost impressed. Now, do you think it was a smuggler?"

Dane gave it some further thought before replying in the negative. "I had an uncle who was a cop in Texas and he liked to tell a lot of stories. Once he told me that smugglers tend to be locals who know all the back trails and how to avoid problems with border crossings like this. He told me that driving right up the road to a customs post is something you do only if you absolutely have to. Given the openness of the border, real smugglers wouldn't have been caught. I think the killer isn't from here and very likely not smuggling in anything more than himself."

"And the contents of the truck," Harris added. "And they all had to be worth killing for. I've got a local doctor pulling out the bullets and he's said they might have come from a Luger. However, he's more certain that they came from the same weapon. We'll know for certain when run a ballistics check."

Harris walked to his car and popped the trunk. A

cooler was inside. He opened it and handed Dane an ice-cold bottle of Coke, taking another for himself.

"Not bad thinking for a navy guy," Harris said. "I'm glad they sent you. I was afraid they'd ship me the least qualified person they have just to say they were trying to help out."

Dane took a swallow and belched lightly. Coke always did that to him. He thought he might still be the least qualified person in the office for this kind of work, but kept quiet.

"How come nobody heard gunshots?" Dane asked.

Harris shrugged. "They probably did and thought it was either hunters or something else, like a backfire. Either way, people don't get involved in somebody else's business down here. I've asked around and a couple of the local yokels think they maybe heard a truck driving off about the right time we think this happened. Nobody saw it, of course. It wouldn't surprise me if a lot of people around here did some periodic smuggling, so they'd all believe in live and let live."

Dane took another long swallow and controlled the belch. "Now where do we go?"

Harris shrugged. "I guess you go back to your normal duty while I try to figure out what this guy is planning. My guess is sabotage. And unless he does something truly stupid that makes him stick out like a sore thumb, we're going to have a devil of a time finding him before he strikes."

"Firebells in the night" was a term Farris remembered from a history class he took in college before he left to join the army. He thought it was Thomas Jefferson who said it but couldn't remember when

or why. Maybe it had something to do with a possible slave rebellion in the American south before
the Civil War?

Since there wasn't a quiz coming up, he really didn't
care. His real concern was the burning oil tanker that
was clearly visible a couple of miles offshore and closer
to Captain Lytle's headquarters than to Farris's position.
The explosions had awakened everyone and the entire
platoon was armed and ready. This was the first time
any of the many ships passing in front of their post had
ever been attacked and the first time carrying a rifle was
serious business. People were being killed out there on
the ocean and it was a sobering experience.

A second explosion sent another cloud of flames
billowing into the night. Oil was burning on the water
and Farris thought he could hear screams as people
burned to death. He prayed it was his imagination.

"That ship's gonna take a long time to die," Stecher
said. "Maybe it'll give the crew time to get away."

"God, I hope so," Farris said.

They had binoculars and were looking for lifeboats
as well as the submarine that had torpedoed the tanker.
Trying to find the sub was futile; the roaring, billowing
flames had destroyed their night vision. They'd only
see a sub if they picked up its silhouette, although
just maybe they'd be able to spot lifeboats in the light
caused by the fires. Farris commented that the spilled
oil was going to leave a mess on the shore and kill a
lot of wildlife. Stecher replied that war was hell and
that he was more concerned about the crew than the
seals. Farris agreed.

A distant pair of lifeboats came into view. The
bulk of the dying ship had hidden them from sight,

but now they were backlit by the flames. They were rowing toward shore and Farris thought they would come close to his position, but more to the south and closer to Lytle's spot. He told his men to be ready with blankets and water and to stack their weapons. The Japs weren't going to invade this night. He radioed his company commander for more blankets and water and for medical help as well, and the call was acknowledged. Farris wondered if that meant Lytle would actually send more help or was just noting the request. On a positive note, people from the little town of Bridger were arriving with all kinds of first-aid equipment. Sullivan, the store owner, was organizing the efforts. Apparently shipwrecks had occurred before. Farris wondered if the locals also scavenged for valuables that washed up on the shore.

"Jesus," yelled Stecher. Tracers from shore-based machine guns south of them snaked out toward the burning ship, which was well out of their range. What the hell were Lytle's men shooting at?

"Did you see a sub?" Farris asked Stecher with a feeling of dread.

"No, sir, just those lifeboats and the bullets are coming damn close to them. Aw shit, sir, you don't suppose that our beloved captain ordered his men to shoot at the survivors in the boats, do you?"

Farris didn't know what to think. Finally, the firing stopped. The two lifeboats had veered north and were now definitely heading right toward him. As they crashed through the surf, soldiers ran out and grabbed them, pulling them onto the beach. Other soldiers and civilians helped crewmen out and onto the sand. Many were unhurt, but others had broken bones and suffered horrible-looking burns. A few were covered with oil and were shivering uncontrollably. One crewman didn't have an arm from the elbow down, and a buddy was trying to keep him from bleeding to death with a tourniquet. From the way the wounded man's head was lolling, it was a losing battle.

Farris's men laid the injured on the ground and tried to administer first aid. Vehicles were arriving, including still more civilians from Bridger. One man, clearly the tanker's captain, strode up to Farris. He was livid with anger.

"You weren't the asshole who opened fire on us, were you?"

"No, Captain, I wasn't. The firing came from farther south. Was there a sub near your boats when it happened? I mean, could you actually see the one that hit you?"

"Hell, no," he said and wiped some greasy blood from his face. "We never saw a thing, never knew there was a Jap out there until we got hit. One torpedo and we become a torch and the little Jap bastard is well away from here. Whoever shot at us from shore must be either blind or drunk or totally stupid. Or all three, dammit. Whoever he was is just damned lucky he only hit the boats and not us in them."

He held out a large dirty hand. Farris took it and felt his fingers being crushed. "My name's Ed Neal and I've been skippering that ship for ten years now. I guess I should be thankful I still have my life. And I am grateful for the help all you people here are providing. However, I guess I'm now unemployed. If you ever find out who the prick was who shot at us, let me know. I'd like to have a little talk with him."

Farris assured him he'd look into it. The angry skipper strode away to check on his men.

Steve shook his and wondered if he should have told the tanker's captain of his suspicions. He walked over to an arriving jeep. Lytle was in the passenger seat and got out unsteadily. He reeked of alcohol.

"Did we hit the sub? Goddammit, we had him in our sights and I wanted to sink the fucker."

Farris seethed. The man was totally drunk and had just tried to kill a bunch of American merchant seamen. "Sir, the tanker captain and crew said the sub was long gone before you opened fire, and that you were shooting at his lifeboats."

"Bullshit, Farris. I'm not blind. I saw the conning tower of a sub. Some of the men, like your buddy Sawyer, tried to argue with me, but I gave them a direct order to shoot. I know there was a sub and I know we hit it."

"Sir, the captain of the tanker might disagree with you. He says gunfire from the shore wounded two of his men and shot up one of the boats." Farris kept a straight face as he lied to his captain. Nobody'd been hit by Lytle's machine guns. "He's really angry and looking for somebody to kill and maybe send to jail when he's done with him. He's a big, mean-looking son of a bitch, so you might not want to talk to him right now."

That finally got through to Lytle, who paled at the idea of the threat. He staggered back to the jeep and ordered the grim-faced private to drive him back to his headquarters. As they pulled away, Farris saw the private looking at him and shaking his head as if to say "get me the hell out of here."

The tanker captain had calmed down seeing that none of his men had been killed or hurt by Lytle's actions. Farris decided not to stir things up by saying he knew who'd done the shooting. Neal said he could almost understand how somebody could panic and shoot at shadows. He really wanted vengeance against the Japs and not necessarily against some trigger-happy son of a bitch, but he would knock the man's head right out his ass if he was to find him anytime within the next ten years. Farris decided to keep that happy thought in a mental pocket for future reference.

"This may be the first attack on an American ship so close to shore," Neal said, "but it damn well won't be the last."

Farris concurred. He wondered why it had taken this long.

CHAPTER 8

AMANDA AND THE OTHERS WERE TAKEN BY AMBU-
lance to a small private hospital a few miles south of
San Francisco on the Oakland side of the bay. They
were checked over, cleaned up, and given food and
water, quickly followed by a very short haircut. They
drank several glasses of orange juice like it was an
elixir from heaven. They thought they could feel the
effects of their scurvy receding with each swallow.

It was better than marvelous to have a full belly and
be in a bed, lying on clean sheets, and not have to
be afraid of rogue waves, thirst, or starvation. They'd
been surprised by the number of cuts and bruises all
over their bodies, but these were beginning to heal
and salves had been applied to their worst sunburns.
With their physical recoveries beginning, their minds
began to clear from the shock of their ordeal. They'd
answered a few questions asked by local police, but
otherwise were left alone.

The hospital they'd been sent to overlooked San

Francisco Bay and the view from their window was breathtaking. Even so, it was difficult to realize that they'd actually made it across the ocean, and that they were back in the bosom of civilization.

They had their own small ward, including toilet and shower, and reveled in the privacy. Sandy was the first to notice that there was an armed sailor on guard at the door and wondered why. Surely they weren't prisoners, were they? Amanda decided to try him. He looked harmless enough, just a skinny teenager, even though he did have a .45 strapped to his waist.

"Mind if I go down the hall and visit some of the other nurses?" Amanda asked sweetly even though her chapped lips hurt when she smiled. She thought she must look like a half-bald, half-starved monster to him.

The young sailor was clearly uncomfortable. "Sorry, ma'am, but I have my orders to make sure you stay here for the time being."

"And if I pushed my way past you?" He wasn't that big and she thought the three of them could do it easily enough, and she wondered if he even knew how to use the pistol.

The sailor gulped. "I would really appreciate if you didn't. Look, I have no idea what's going on and I would really thank you if you didn't get me into trouble. Captain Harding will be back in a bit."

"Are we prisoners?" Sandy inquired bluntly.

"No, ma'am. I'm here mainly to keep people out and leave you alone. And nobody told me why, so please don't ask."

They looked at each other and sat back on beds that didn't seem quite so comfortable anymore. They checked their meager personal possessions, each in their own hospital pillowcase. Along with salt-crusted watches that didn't work anymore and rings that wouldn't fit their swollen fingers, they had Mack's money belt containing over five thousand dollars. The cash included what remained of the three thousand they'd given Mack along with other money Mack had brought along.

"For an embezzler, he didn't have all that much dough," Grace said, "but we do have his will."

Other than the inadequate hospital gowns and bathrobes they had on over them, they had no clothing. What they'd been wearing on the catamaran had been properly identified as rags and disposed of. They had an urge to go shopping.

There was a knock on their door and a Marine captain entered after a suitable pause. "Ladies, I am Captain Harding and I'm sorry I'm late, and I hope I can answer all your questions. I'm also happy you didn't bully that poor young man at the door. He's much better with a typewriter than a weapon."

"Are we prisoners, and if so, why?" Amanda said.

Harding smiled slightly at the blunt question and sat down in a wooden chair. "You are not prisoners. We—the government, that is—just want to be sure of what is said by you when you leave here. We're primarily concerned about your amazing story getting too much publicity at this time."

"Why?" Grace asked.

"Because," Harding said sadly, "we don't want others in Hawaii getting the idea they can do it as well. To the best of our knowledge, maybe twenty small boats like yours have tried to sail from Hawaii to here, and you here are the only ones who've made it. The rest have just plain disappeared, swallowed up by the ocean. I don't know if you have any idea just how fortunate you were."

They looked at each other. "There were times when we thought we'd disappear as well," Amanda said softly. A tear ran down her cheek and she wiped it away. "We'd almost lost hope and were on our last legs when we landed here."

"And you had advantages that no longer exist to anyone else who might want to try now," Harding continued. "When you started you had a goodly supply of food and water, which others won't have, and you were in pretty good physical shape which is no longer the case in Hawaii where people are already going hungry and getting weaker by the day. In short, few people in the islands would be strong enough to take on the Pacific like you did. This may surprise you, but we still have radio communication with the islands, and we don't want those poor people getting any ideas about leaving if they find out you made it."

The three women looked at each other in silent agreement. They'd had such a small margin of error and nearly died. Others would surely perish.

"So what do we do?" Sandy asked. "We've all got families and we want them to know we're all right."

"Just send them telegrams saying that you are safe in California and that you got out via a neutral freighter. Tell them you'll elaborate later. And later will come when we either liberate the islands or the war is over. When that happens, you can write a book or proclaim your truly wonderful story from the mountaintops for all anybody cares. In the meantime, we just don't want anybody else to die trying."

"That's good," said Amanda. "We're all nurses, you know, and we'd like to go back to being that. Along with needing to earn a living, we'd like to be helpful. Now, how do we get back to work, and we'd prefer San Diego."

Harding grinned. "Ever think of enlisting? We'd make you officers right off."

"No," Amanda said, and the others nodded. "We enlist and we could get sent anywhere in the world. No, thank you, but I'll stay in California." She didn't add that she wanted to find Tim Dane, although Harding's expression told her he understood her motives.

Harding stood. For the first time, Amanda noticed that his left hand was permanently set in a claw and that he had a Purple Heart on his chest.

"Where?" she asked, looking at the medal.

"The Philippines. I was in the Fourth Marine Regiment and got lucky. I was wounded very early on and evacuated before the place was cut off by the Japs. All I lost was the use of my left hand. I'm right-handed so it's not that much of a loss."

Grace took his arm and examined the hand. There were burn scars on his wrist and forearm. "Can you use it at all?"

"A little, and they say it'll get better." Harding gently pushed her hand away. "Based on the info you gave us, we've been contacting your schools and places you worked before going to Honolulu to establish your credentials so you can go to work in your field. When that is done, you'll be free to travel to San Diego or wherever else your hearts desire. Do you agree to keep this whole thing quiet, at least for the time being?"

As usual, Amanda spoke for them. "Of course. We wouldn't want anybody to die as a result of our actions. However, I do have to wonder if staying in Hawaii is the better choice for starving people."

"So do I, and so do a lot of people," he said. "We can all only hope and pray that we make the right decisions."

"Are we still restricted to here?" Stacy asked.

"Nope. Now that we've talked and come to an agreement, you're free to go and do whatever you want. Housing's really short around here, so you might want to stay here for a while, gather your strength, and let the government pay for your room and board until things get squared away regarding your work status."

They agreed that it was a splendid idea. Harding said his wife lived a couple of miles away and would get them some clothing so they could get started on some real shopping without having to wear hospital gowns.

"Just curious, but what would you have done if we'd said we wouldn't cooperate?" asked Grace.

Harding smiled grimly. "Then we would have moved you to a place in the desert with real guards and it would have taken decades to find your nursing credentials."

Grace nodded. "Keeping mum sounds like a splendid idea to me."

Harding turned and smiled at Amanda. "And I do hope you find your boyfriend in San Diego."

Amanda blushed. "Are my motives that transparent?"

He laughed. "Yes."

Amanda flushed. "He's a navy officer and his name's Tim Dane and he was supposed to leave Hawaii on a sub. Have you heard of him?"

Harding shook his head. "No, but it's a big navy. I'll check around. Any of you other ladies have anybody you want me to check up on?"

Ruby Oliver and her little band of soldiers had been augmented by one more GI who carried a tattered duffle bag instead of a rifle. He explained that he was the base photographer and that the major had told him to take pictures of his troops fighting off the Japanese.

"And I did what he said, Miss Oliver, and it made me sick," said Private Perkins.

Ruby took him aside so they could talk privately. "First of all, call me Miss Oliver again and I'll be forced to kill you and it will be painful. Understand?"

Perkins was a scrawny kid who was well outmanned by Ruby. "Okay," he said with a shy grin. "Ruby."

"Now, what kind of cameras do you have in that bag?"

"Ah, one eight-millimeter movie camera and a couple of regular cameras. The eight-millimeter's one of those that's sixteen millimeter and takes pictures on two halves."

Ruby had no idea what he was talking about, but decided it didn't matter. "And you took pictures of everything?"

Perkins face fell and his lips began to tremble. He had seen much too much for a young kid. "Yeah. I started shooting when we pulled out of the base and kept it up when Jap shells started clobbering us. I started to help some of the wounded, but the major told me to keep filming so people would know what had happened, so I did. Then he got killed along with the wounded I was trying to help. When I realized I was alone, I ran into the town and watched as the Japs massacred the prisoners by shoving them into the ocean."

"You got that on film?" Ruby asked incredulously.

"All of it, Ruby. Every second of it," he said and started to cry. "They were my friends."

"How old are you, Perkins?"

"Seventeen. I lied to get in. I'll never tell a lie again. I'd really just like to go home."

She held him to her bosom and hugged him until he calmed down. None of the others could see the exchange, so no one would mock him for being a sissy and breaking down in front of a woman. If they had, she would have chewed them out until they'd cried as well. None of them had handled this disaster very well, and a couple looked like they too were on the verge of emotional collapse.

"You have any film left?"

"Lots, and of both types."

She took him back to the others and introduced him. They were from different units and didn't know him very well. The men were uninterested until she told them he was going to take their pictures and send them home to loved ones. At that point they brightened up. Maybe life wasn't so futile after all.

First, though, they had to find a place that was far enough from the Japs and where they could communicate with the rest of the world either by phone or radio. Maybe she could arrange for a small plane to land somewhere and pick them up along with Perkins's films. Remembering the massacre of the prisoners made her angry once more, but having proof of it would be vindication. Let the world see what miserable, barbaric sons of bitches the Japs were.

She looked at her nervous and frightened flock, and wondered—what have I done to deserve this? "I know you're all soldiers and the highest ranking one of you is supposed to lead, but let me make a proposition. I'm from here and I know the area. I'm confident I can get us all to safety, including Perkins and his magic cameras. If you don't want me to work with you, that's okay too, and I'll just strike off on my own and leave your worthless asses here to either starve, be eaten by grizzlies, or be captured and you know what'll happen to you then."

One of the soldiers, a PFC, stood and smiled. "My name is Crain and we've already talked it over and I guess I'm senior and would normally be in command. However, back at the fort I was a cook and not really much of a soldier. None of us are so stupid that we'd reject your idea, and we're all willing to follow your lead."

"Good."

"One thing, though. When we get back to the real world and the real army, please tell them you were just advising us, won't you?"

Dane's first view of the attack force that would strike the Japs at Anchorage came from one of the inadequate windows of the C47 that was carrying him and others to Puget Sound. Below, the twelve PBYs looked like either strange toys or a flock of large but truly ugly birds sitting on the water. More and more he doubted the wisdom of launching an attack on the Japanese invaders with such unwarlike planes. He was beginning to deeply regret opening his mouth and putting both himself and others in peril.

He asked for and got permission to fly again with Ensign Tuller who openly called it a suicide mission and berated him for coming up with the idea. "Look, Commander, it's one thing for us to attack a sub or a relatively unarmed freighter, but we're no good at hitting ground targets and we'll be nothing more than low, slow targets for Jap gunners."

"Which is why the plan calls for us to fly low and slow and come in over from land, rather than water. Hopefully, they won't expect us to come from that direction."

"With respect, Commander, 'hopefully,' my ass. Low I'll give you and slow is the only way we can fly, and coming in over land might just give us the element of surprise, but that won't last long. Maybe ten seconds if we're lucky. Besides, I'll give you a dollar for every real target we hit."

Dane could not argue with Tuller's assessments. What was now referred to as "Dane's idea" had taken hold and would be implemented regardless. As Spruance had explained to him as he was departing, "It's vitally important for us to hit back at the Japs, or at least be perceived as hitting back. The American public is demanding that we do something, anything, to strike back at our enemies. Even though Alaska isn't a state, it's damn close to us and we just can't let them get away with invading us and not do anything."

When Dane had been on the verge of saying something, the admiral had put his hand on Dane's shoulder. "Doolittle's raid was a mission with little chance of success and it managed to rile the Japanese government into doing something foolish. With just a little bit of luck, the Japs would have suffered the disaster at Midway and not us."

"Even if we do nothing other than dig holes in the ground with bombs and lose a lot of planes?" Dane asked.

"No. It won't be like flying over Japan and then having to bail out over China like Doolittle's boys did," Spruance said. "You'll have a much greater chance of survival."

Dane shuddered. While many of Doolittle's pilots had escaped, some had been shot down and captured. Rumors had it that they either would be executed or had already been killed.

Spruance continued. "The Catalinas will come in, hit, and fly back out just as fast as they can. There is no indication that the Japs have any planes on the ground or much in the way of antiaircraft guns, and we're certain there are no carriers out there."

Dane wondered how the admiral could be so certain, but again kept his mouth shut. He was getting good at that. He did wonder if the navy had some superior source of intelligence regarding the Japanese he wasn't being told about.

The next day, they flew the PBYs from Puget Sound to Juneau, which was still an incredible eight hundred miles from Anchorage. "Jesus," said an incredulous Tuller. "Don't they make anything close to anything else up here?"

They and the rest of the PBY's crew were in a bar in Juneau having a meal. To a man they resisted the urge to call it their last supper. Since they would be flying over land, the actual flying distance would be much longer than crow-fly miles, more than a thousand miles altogether. Days were getting shorter, so they would have to leave before dawn to arrive over the target before nightfall. Their cruising speed was a lowly one hundred and twenty-five miles per hour, which meant at least an eight-hour trip each way.

Tuller accepted the inevitable. "Commander, don't forget to bring a change of socks and underwear, and some nice warm pajamas would also be a good idea."

"Tuller, go screw yourself," Dane said and then ordered another round of beers for "his" crew.

The next morning they took off before dawn as planned and formed to four groups of three each. They did not keep radio silence; instead, only mimicked casual conversations between bush pilots to maintain order and help keep in visual contact.

Alaskans on the ground had set up radio beacons, and the Ugly Duckling Flight, as they now called themselves, duly turned west after several hours and headed to Anchorage. As they got closer, a female voice identified only as Ruby Red chatted inanely about food and fuel shortages, and the flight followed her signal. At a certain point they dropped down to less than five hundred feet.

"There we are," yelled Tuller. "Finally."

The small town of Anchorage was coming up fast. Rows of tents were visible in a field alongside the road leading to Fort Richardson. Tuller laughed. "God, we can't miss a field full of tents, can we?"

The Japanese were not asleep. Spotters on high ground had seen the planes, but only at the last minute. As PBYs dropped their loads, machine-gun and rifle fire blazed up at them.

"We're hit," yelled one of the machine gunners who was busy returning fire. To Dane's horror, holes had appeared in the plane's hull.

"One down," yelled Tuller. One of the PBYs had been mortally wounded and had just crashed in flames. Another was burning but still staying aloft.

"We're done," Tuller yelled and turned his plane due south.

More Japanese machine guns opened up and more planes were struck. Dane saw that one of the Catalinas was attempting to land in the water off Anchorage. Not a good idea, Dane thought. What the Japanese would do to the survivors wasn't pleasant to contemplate. They should have tried for land farther south, but maybe they didn't have a choice. Tuller was screaming into his radio, but Dane couldn't hear it. One of the bow gunners nudged him and Dane looked back to where the bombs had dropped. Yes, they had managed to hit the field. A total of forty-eight five-hundred-pound bombs had been dropped on the tent city, but, he wondered, had anybody been in the tents?

He also wondered how many Americans had perished in this exercise, and the thought that it had been his idea made him slightly ill. How the hell do people like Spruance or Nimitz get away with sending people to their deaths and not cracking up over it? If that was one of the privileges of rank, he thought, the brass could keep it.

The little town of Grover, California, was about halfway between Los Angeles and San Francisco. It consisted of a couple hundred frame houses, some stores, and a few churches. It also had thirty-five-year-old and unemployed Fred Hanson, who was waking up on the beach after a long evening of drinking with some friends at the hotel where he once worked. Sleeping on the beach had been a little chilly but much better than going home and confronting his wife.

Maria was half Mexican and had a temper that was half volcano. When Fred had a little too much to drink, she was not rational, in Fred's highly biased opinion. Thus, he'd made the decision to sack out on the sand. If he had been a truthful man, Fred would have admitted that he wouldn't have been able to walk to his house in the first place. Being unemployed, he had a lot of time on his hands. Even he had to admit that he was jobless by choice. Sometimes he thought about going to nearby San Diego or even Los Angeles and getting a job in one of the burgeoning war industries, but that never quite appealed to his minimal sense of ambition. So far, too, he'd been declared too old to be drafted, but he knew that could change at any time. What the hell, he thought, he'd face that problem when it came along, which was pretty much the way he ran his life.

The Town of Grover was its official full and pretentious name. It had advertised itself as an affordable tourist location before the war, but there were damn few tourists nowadays.

Fred rubbed his eyes and splashed water on his face. He was careful not to swallow. The salt water would have upset his stomach even more than it was, and the last thing he wanted right now was a case of the heaves. Damn, Maria was going to be pissed. He couldn't put it off, though. It was Sunday morning and maybe the good, devout Catholic woman would be at church when he sneaked home.

Speaking of piss, he stood, smiled, and relieved himself hugely into the ocean, sending a multibeer stream arching well into the sea, hoping as always that he hadn't killed any of the little fish that swam around in the shallows. He blinked and noticed a pair of warships a mile or so offshore. They looked different. He wasn't an expert, but they looked, well, foreign. He'd seen a number of American ships cruising by, but there was something not right about these two. What the hell, he thought as he carefully zipped up his fly. Maybe the navy got some new style ships and why not? The old ones hadn't done them all that much good so far. Every time they went out, it seemed that they got themselves sunk.

Lights flickered on the ships, and, seconds later, something shrieked through the sky and impacted in the town, sending debris and dirt high into the air. The explosions were shocking and ear-shattering and threw him to the ground. When he looked up, he saw that several buildings in Grover had been damaged and were on fire. Jesus, he thought, those were Jap ships and the Japs were shelling Grover. Why? What had the people of Grover done to deserve it?

More shrieking shells flew over him and landed in Grover. People spilled out of their homes and ran around, confused, terrified, and aimless. Fred lurched to his feet and watched as a number of them headed to the nearby Baptist church for what they might have thought was sanctuary. But that was a mistake as another shell hit it squarely, causing what could only have been incredible carnage inside. Outside, torn bodies littered the ground. Fred could hold it no longer. He threw up all over himself.

Fred regained control and took off for his home as fast as his legs would propel him. Others were heading out of town in cars, on bicycles, or, like him, just running like hell.

More shells struck around him. One of his neighbors grabbed Fred's arm. His eyes were wide with terror. "What the hell's going on, Fred?"

Fred pushed him away angrily. "How the hell would I know?" He had to find his family.

Finally he saw Maria and the two boys running toward him. At least she wouldn't be mad at him right now unless she was blaming him for the disaster. She was wide-eyed with fear and the boys were crying uncontrollably. Maria threw herself into his arms and, sobbing, asked him what was happening and told him that she was terrified. Welcome to the club, Fred thought.

He grabbed her arm and she took the kids. They didn't own a car so they would have to walk to get out of Grover. People from everywhere had the same idea and soon the two-lane dirt road that led inland toward the mountains was choked with people. Behind them, the bombardment continued then, as suddenly as it began, stopped. When he was certain it was safe to look back, Fred saw that the two Japanese warships had turned and were heading toward the horizon. Scores of buildings were on fire and the flames were beginning to spread. Unless somebody took charge, the town of Grover would be ashes in a very short while. However, it didn't look like anybody was interested in fighting fires, only running.

"Where's our fucking navy?" Fred raged. Maria tried to shush him, but she suddenly began screaming and swearing when she realized that their two-bedroom home was burning furiously. Everything they owned except the clothes on their backs was being consumed by flames. For once Fred was grateful that they rented instead of owned like Maria wanted.

Almost half an hour later, a dozen American fighters flew overhead and out to sea. "Where the fuck have you been?" Fred yelled impotently. "Where the fuck is Roosevelt and all the assholes who are supposed to protect us?" Before this, they had been poor, poor but proud. Now they were destitute. What would happen to them?

Long lines of people from Grover and other towns in the area headed inland toward what they hoped was safety. It was a regular exodus, Fred thought, or maybe it was like the newsreels of French civilians fleeing the Nazis. Where they would go and who would feed them, they didn't know. Maria had stopped crying and hung onto his arm with grim determination. He commented about the French refugees, and she clutched his arm and asked him if they'd sunk to that level. Fred said he had no fucking idea but it sure looked like it. Maria didn't chastise him for swearing in front of the boys, and she hadn't said anything about the puke on his clothes. She was too busy crying again. Fred quietly decided that getting a job in a factory wasn't such a bad idea after all.

CHAPTER 9

THREE AMERICAN PLANES HAD GONE DOWN IN the attack on the Japanese facilities at Anchorage. The first had crashed near the city in a blaze of flames and the explosion of a bomb that hadn't been released, which told Ruby and the others that finding survivors was highly unlikely.

The second one landed in the water a mile down Cook Inlet and was quickly surrounded by Japanese soldiers in small boats. As they watched from a prudent distance, the surviving crewmembers were becoming prisoners whose fate was grim. They were punched and shoved as they were thrown into the Japanese boats, heedless of any possible injuries they might have had. The enemy was furious at the attack that had left a number of Japanese soldiers dead and wounded, along with a score of small fires where the bombs had landed in their tent city. Helping the downed airmen was impossible. Their fate was in the hands of merciless Japanese.

183

The third PBY had gone down a couple of miles south of Anchorage and in dense woods. The plane was burning when they got there, but the wind was blowing a smoke plume low and away from the town. Ruby hoped the Japs couldn't see it, at least not for a while.

When Ruby and the others arrived at the scene after some hard hiking, the Japanese hadn't yet shown up. The plane, however, was a charred and smoldering skeleton, and the stench of burning flesh was heavy in the air. The surrounding trees had been scorched, but it had rained heavily recently, and a forest fire had not developed.

Two living crewmen had been pulled out by other quickly arriving civilians and were stretched out on the ground. Each appeared to have multiple fractures and cuts. Caring for them would be well beyond their capabilities, which didn't go much past first aid. People were very self-sufficient in Alaska, but they couldn't perform major surgery. Broken arms and legs would be splinted and cuts stitched, but anything more serious would be beyond them.

Ruby decided they would pack the two men onto makeshift litters and take them to the small fishing village of Valdez, a hundred miles south on Prince William Sound. From there, maybe they could find a boat that could take them south to Juneau, or perhaps even a plane could land on the small strip that served Valdez. Taking the road from Anchorage inland to the larger city of Fairbanks was doubtless a bad idea. The Japanese had likely already cut it.

She had a thought. If the Japs had the road, would they move inland to Fairbanks? It was less than three hundred miles between the two cities. After this raid, she didn't think they'd sit still and wait to be clobbered again. The Japs didn't look like they were ready to move out just yet, but that could change at any time.

The two wounded men were secured onto the litters and a small group of local men and women said they'd transport the men to Valdez. It would be a rough trip and the men would have to be carried. They were unconscious and she hoped they'd stay that way. She wondered if they'd survive.

After the bearers left, Ruby's group returned to a lookout point from which they could see into Anchorage. A large number of Japanese soldiers was milling around an undamaged school building. She surmised that the American prisoners were being held inside and being interrogated. Having seen what the Japanese did to other prisoners, she pitied them. She wasn't a particularly religious person, but this time she prayed for them. If nothing else, she wanted them to have a quick and merciful death, even though she didn't think it would happen.

The Japanese would want revenge for the surprise bombing attack. What looked like a couple of hundred heavily guarded American civilians were also gathered to see Japanese justice. Closer inspection showed that the men in the crowd had been beaten and many of the women's clothing had been ripped and torn leaving them in a state of semi-nudity. It was an obvious indication that they'd been sexually assaulted. Once again, Ruby was thankful that she'd decided to flee rather than run the risk of being a prisoner of the Japanese.

After about an hour, the door opened and a half

dozen Americans were dragged outside and forced to kneel while an officer seemed to be screaming at them.

"He really looks pissed," Perkins said.

"Shut up and keep taking pictures."

Perkins was using a telescopic lens and Ruby was watching through a fine set of German binoculars her uncle had brought back as a souvenir of World War I. Ruby had the terrible feeling that she was going to regret that the picture they provided was so clear and so vivid.

The Japanese officer finished his harangue. She thought he might be the commander of all the Japanese forces from the way others deferred to him, but she had no way of being certain. She groaned when he unsheathed the long curved sword that officers carried. He waved it around in the air and his men cheered him, the sound carrying up to them.

The officer waved it a couple more times and then sent it slashing down on the neck of a kneeling American. The prisoner's head was sent flying and blood gushed from the man's trunk. His body continued to kneel for a second and then toppled slowly forward while the soldiers laughed and the civilians moaned.

"Fuckers," Perkins said.

Ruby forced herself to be calm even though she wanted to both kill and vomit. "Pictures, keep taking the damned pictures."

The Japanese officer walked slowly down the short line of kneeling men and repeated the process five more times, each to the loud cheers of the gathered soldiers and the further groans of the civilians. When they were done, the heads and bodies were tossed into the inlet.

"Ruby, you think they know we're up here?"

"They've got to know somebody's likely watching them from the trees and they don't care. That was a lesson. Now the Japs'll use the civilians as hostages and probably have them working for them, repairing roads and maybe building an airstrip."

"So what do we do now?"

Damn good question, she thought. "First, we get to the radio and tell them all about these latest bullshit murders. Then we head inland to Fairbanks. Three hundred miles is a long ways to walk, but maybe we can commandeer a car. I've got a feeling that Fairbanks is where all the action is going to be. Hopefully, we can find an airplane there and get your pictures south to somebody who'll publish them and let the world know what first-class pricks the Japanese are."

"Ruby?"

"Yes?"

"Is commandeering the same as stealing?"

On his return to San Diego, Dane was informed that the brass wanted his opinion of the PBY raid. He'd been deposited at Vancouver by Tuller and stuffed into the back seat of a Douglas Dauntless scout plane. They took off immediately and, after refueling at San Francisco, arrived at the base. Dane was so exhausted and drained that he'd managed to fall asleep in the Dauntless.

"Once again, I don't get a chance to clean up," Dane lamented jokingly.

Merchant laughed and slapped him on the shoulder. "I believe the admirals think you dress like a slob all the time. By the way, once again Nimitz is going to be there as well. We've issued a press release telling the world how the navy has struck back at the Japs who dared to invade Alaska. All the boys on those planes are heroes. Now all we have to do is figure out what they accomplished."

Before Tim could make the scathing comment that was on the tip of his tongue, he was ushered into a conference room where Nimitz and Spruance were holding a meeting with others who wore stars on their shoulders. "Congratulations on making it back safely," said Nimitz. "Spruance says you have a habit of doing that."

"A damn good habit, if you ask me," added Spruance. "Now, what can you tell us about the raid? And don't pull punches."

Dane turned to Nimitz. He was the senior man in the room. "Sir, if you wanted a public relations coup, you got one. We came in low and they didn't notice us until we were just about on top of them. We dropped our bombs and started to fly away. At that point, things began to fall apart. We were so low that we began to take a lot of small-arms fire, and the Catalina is far from bulletproof. Three of our planes went down for certain, and we have to assume that the crews are all dead or captured."

"But what damage did we do to them?" asked Spruance.

"Sir, we bombed a field full of tents. I saw a lot of Japs running, and bombs exploding, but I doubt very much if we did any substantial damage. We didn't have all that many bombs and they were small ones anyway. That, and I've been told that bombing a field doesn't cause all that much damage."

Merchant interrupted. "Spotters on the ground say that at least twenty Japs were killed. They determined that by counting graves dug the next day, and they don't know how many were wounded. They also say that at least six crewmen were captured, and beheaded by this Colonel Yamasaki, or some other Jap officer."

Nimitz's face turned red. Normally mild mannered, the admiral was outraged. "That bastard's going to burn in hell."

Dane continued. "We sent in twelve planes and three were shot down. Every other plane was damaged in some manner, and there were wounded on several others. The PBY I was flying was fortunate. We only had two men lightly wounded, although I did count at least thirty bullet holes in the fuselage."

Spruance shook his head. "So we just about traded casualties with the Japs, but we lost three valuable planes destroyed and nine others damaged. If we put the raid in that context, we lost."

"However," said Nimitz, "morale has jumped with the announcement. Just like Doolittle's bombing of Tokyo, the price was high, but we showed the Japs that we could and would strike back. Dane, what's your opinion of using the PBYs for a repeat raid, and be blunt."

Dane was not in the mood for candy-coating a report for admirals under any circumstances. "It'd be a disaster. The Japs will be ready next time and they will have some kind of an early warning system in place. Our planes would be cut to pieces. The PBY is simply not a fighter or bomber. A regular bomber could hit them from higher up, fly faster and hit them with more bombs, and make them squeal. In my opinion, it'd be murder to send PBYs again. Like it or not, we should wait until the field at Vancouver is ready."

"Even then we'd need an interim field for them to refuel," said Nimitz. "We're developing runways at Juneau and Fairbanks. When those are ready, the army'll hit the Japs hard from the air. In the meantime, you're right. No more PBY raids."

With that, Dane and Merchant were dismissed. Dane went to his desk and sat down wearily. His body still ached from all the hours in the PBY and then in the cramped Dauntless. At least he could move around a little in the Catalina. Even the kid lieutenant who'd flown him in the Dauntless teased him about being too big for a fighter cockpit. Maybe he should go to the gym and work out, maybe get some kinks out of his body. Maybe he should have a couple of drinks and take a nap. That sounded like a much better idea. On leaving the meeting, Merchant had as much as told him that the war would get along fine without him until the next morning.

A young sailor Dane recognized as being from the mail room walked up with a puzzled look on his face and a letter in his hand. "Sir, this has been kicking around a bit, but we think it's for you since there aren't that many Danes around. Whoever wrote it didn't know your correct address here and had your rank wrong."

Puzzled, Dane thanked the kid and took the envelope. Whoever it was indeed had the right name but had his rank wrong. It was amazing that the navy figured out that it might be for him. He opened it and gasped in shock and pleasure. It was from Amanda.

Dear Tim,

Obviously we arrived safely in California and I'd love to fill you in on the details, but I can't at this time. I'll explain later, I hope. "We" consists of two other nurses named Sandy and Grace along with yours truly. Let it suffice that we are all weary, hungry, sunburned, and know a lot more about the ocean and ourselves than we ever thought possible. Or ever even cared to know. Otherwise, we are fine and nothing that a few good meals and a little rest won't cure. For a variety of reasons, my hair is cut shorter than the average marine's and I'm even thinner than I was before. I didn't put a return address on the envelope because we are going to be moving soon and I don't know exactly where we'll wind up. I just hope this letter finds you and that you too are well. A very nice marine captain and his wife helped track you down. I hope.

We are planning on picking up the pieces of our nursing careers and have collectively decided that San Diego would be a good place to be, what with all those good-looking sailors hanging around in seedy bars. I hope that meets with your approval. Because of paperwork, it could be a couple of weeks before we get there. We have some money, so we've been able to get some new clothing and I've even bought some new glasses. Mine were lost in the journey.

I just realized I'm being presumptuous in assuming that you even want to see me at all. I thought we started something very interesting and special back in Honolulu a thousand years ago, and I hope you would like to continue it as well. If not, I'll understand.

In the meantime, like it or not and ready or not, I'm coming down, and I'm bringing the other two musketeers with me. Know any other good-looking sailors?

Love and aloha,
Amanda

Tim put down the letter. His hands shook and he felt emotions he hadn't felt since he was a kid. He felt his eyes start to moisten. Amanda was safe.

Merchant stepped by and looked down. "What's the problem, Tim?"

He took a deep breath and regained control. He remembered a rule that said "thou shalt not cry in front of a senior officer." "No problem, sir, far from it. Remember the young lady I told you about? The one I met in Honolulu? Well, she somehow made it to San Francisco."

Merchant laughed and slapped him on the back. "Fantastic. You've been moping like a lost dog since you got here what with your worrying about her."

"Was it that obvious?"

"Worse. Now, fill me in."

Tim did, at least as much as he knew. "She's going to be coming here and it's such a big location, I don't know how we'll find each other when she does."

"You're an intelligence officer, right? Well, just use your damn intelligence, and figure it out. Or, hell, if she could make it across the Pacific, I'm reasonably certain she could find you in San Diego."

❋   ❋   ❋

Wilhelm Braun was frustrated and angry. He had made a mistake. In fact, he had made several of them and he was not used to that. It did not behoove a field-grade officer in the SS to make so many errors. At least, he thought ruefully, there was no one senior to him around to notice.

First, he had underestimated the complexity of the situation confronting him. The American buildup around San Diego was truly massive and security was surprisingly tight the closer to the more tempting targets. It rapidly became evident that he was not going to be able to blow up ammunition depots, fuel storage facilities, or ships. Nor would he be allowed to get close to senior military and civilian personnel in the area without committing suicide, and that still was not on his agenda. He was willing to die for the Reich, but not in a futile gesture.

He laughed harshly. Let their little Jap allies do that.

Doing it all alone was also no longer practicable, if it ever had been. He would need help. He sent a signal to Gunther Krause, the embassy aide he'd thought could come north and meet him should the need arise. Krause was a senior sergeant who'd been masquerading as a low-level clerk in the embassy, and would be an invaluable help. He would also provide muscle and was more than willing to kill for the Reich. Braun was as well, but two men with guns were much better than one.

When Krause arrived at the bus station in San Diego after crossing without incident from Tijuana, he was dressed in a combination of clothes that made him look like a refugee. At least his hair was long enough to not look military. Even to Braun it was clear that Krause would need help in becoming inconspicuous.

"My dear Sergeant, I am delighted to see you," Braun said as they drove away, "but there are a number of changes that we will have to make."

"I understand, sir."

Braun wondered if he did. Braun knew that Krause wasn't well educated formally, but he was surprisingly intelligent and, somehow, had become fluent in English along with Spanish. Apparently the man had a feel for languages.

"First, Sergeant, we will get you some American clothes. You stand out in what you are wearing. All of your clothing, including underwear and socks, will be of American make."

Krause nodded. It made good sense.

"Second, you and I will speak only English, and that includes when the two of us believe we are alone. Anyone speaking a foreign tongue will attract attention, and that is something we don't need. I'm sure we'll both make slips and people will surely notice your accent, but we must fight against them. The accent can be explained because your identification says that you are Swedish, which practically nobody speaks, while German is a fairly common language.

"Further, you and I will not speak loudly as that, obviously, will attract unwanted attention. Nor will we whisper as that will make people lean forward to try and eavesdrop. Human nature, I'm afraid."

Krause laughed. "People are nosy and gossipy, sir. May I ask how you will explain me?"

"Good question. Quite simply, you are my assistant in my engineering business. May I assume you know nothing about engineering?"

"I know how to blow up a bridge, but not build one. Does that count?"

"Actually, it does. However, if anyone asks, and I doubt that they will, you are my wife's nephew and I had to take you despite your shortcomings. You are my clerk and assistant and you are definitely not an engineer. I'm not either, but I believe I can fool people for long enough to get out of trouble."

"Understood, Colonel. Is that it? I would like to go shopping and get out of these rags."

"Not quite. I want you to never refer to me as sir or colonel again and I will never call you sergeant. We are civilians in the United States, and we must act and speak like they do, however uncomfortable that might make us at first. Therefore, you will refer to me as Bill, and not sir or colonel, and I will call you Gunther. I used the name of Brown when I crossed the border, which turned out to be unnecessary, but now I'm using Swenson as my last name. Americans are far less formal than we are, and civilians almost uniformly, and despite differences in their hierarchy, refer to each other by their first names. It would be especially so for two people working together. Such social intimacies would be normal."

"I understand, sir."

"What?"

Krause laughed. "I understand, Bill."

Some things had gone well. The two-story rental property he'd arranged through the shell company provided a shop and a place to store the truck, while the second floor above the shop included a comfortable apartment that would house both men. It amused Braun that his landlord was an annoying Jew lawyer named Zuckerman. When the time came, perhaps he would kill Zuckerman the Jew just for pleasure.

The freshly painted sign on the front of the building proclaimed it as the home of Swenson Engineering, which matched the Swedish passport he would use for identification if anybody asked. So far, nobody had, which also amused him. Once again, he concluded that Americans were gullible fools. Gunther Krause had become Gunther Swenson.

In Germany, Gestapo informants would be watching his every move and reporting everything he did. But not here. Apparently the Americans thought that nobody would use false identification or that Germany would be even slightly interested in America's war against Japan.

The staff he'd left behind in Mexico had also given him some marvelously created fictitious contracts between the United States government and Swenson Engineering, including phony purchase orders, which enabled him to get rationed food and gasoline. Since his papers said he was a defense contractor for the government, he was eligible for more gasoline then he'd ever use.

The truck he'd driven across the border was a ruin, and he'd decided to drive it only in an emergency. Instead, he bought a 1937 Ford station wagon from a lady whose husband was in the service. It had wood paneling on the side and was commonly referred to as a "woody." He made a removable sign identifying it as belonging to Swenson Engineering, along with several other business signs which he kept out of sight. This evening, however, there were no signs on the Ford.

✳ ✳ ✳

It was getting dark by the time he and Krause had driven the station wagon out toward the small town of Lakeside, north and east of San Diego. A rail line ran through it and it was time for the two of them to earn their pay. He'd planned to do it alone, but it would be so much easier with Krause's help. Braun thought a couple of sticks of dynamite and an impact detonator would do the job and Krause concurred.

Braun parked the Ford among some trees a few hundred yards away from the railroad track and walked slowly toward it with Krause a few paces behind. He found a place where the rail bed was built up and crawled onto it, after first looking around to see if anyone was in view. The dynamite went under the rails and the detonator, built to act like a land mine, went on top. When the train's wheels ran over it, a spark should be created which would cause the dynamite to explode. The track would be shattered and the train would be sent hurtling down the embankment.

It was easy, almost too easy. The tracks were normally deserted. He'd checked it out before and seen no signs of activity, not even kids or bums or patrols checking for sabotage. Well, he said with a laugh, all that might change after tonight.

They looked around. There were people who spent a lot of time doing nothing more than train watching. However, he did not think he'd run into them as the late afternoon sky darkened. If the trains in California ran on anything resembling a schedule, the freight train they were waiting for should be along within an hour.

Even though it was dangerous, Braun felt compelled to stay and see the results of their handiwork. They drove to a spot where they could look down on the tracks and still remain out of sight. The place where he'd placed the dynamite was a good mile away and he hoped an innocuous Ford station wagon would go unnoticed.

He pulled out a cheese sandwich and ate slowly. He offered half to Krause, who said he wasn't hungry. After what seemed an eternity, they heard a train whistle in the distance. Braun tried to will it to come closer, sooner, but when it finally appeared, it was a very long one and moving slowly. Braun was delighted.

Two steam engines sending clouds of white smoke into the sky were locked in an almost sexual embrace and pulling a line of freight cars and flatcars that stretched to the horizon. It was the type of train that blocked roads and drove drivers to distraction. Braun thought that blocked roads would be the least of people's worries in a little while.

Braun smiled as he saw that the flatcars carried a number of M3 Stuart light tanks. They were the best the Americans had at this time, but were pieces of shit in comparison with German armor. He was confident the German Panzer III and the new Panzer IV would destroy them with ease. What disconcerted him was the fact that the tanks would be replaced by the Americans who turned them out like Ford used to make cars.

He wondered what the dirty little Japs had in the way of tanks and decided he really didn't care. He just wanted this train to crash.

The whistle sounded again, loud and strident. Here I come, it seemed to proclaim. Not for long, Braun laughed, and Krause sighed.

He held his breath as the first locomotive passed over where he'd placed the charge. It drove on and, for a second, Braun thought he'd failed and set the detonator improperly. Then a white flash suddenly appeared underneath the second engine and was followed by an explosion. The train shuddered like a drunk trying to keep his balance. But it couldn't. The rails had been destroyed. The train lurched and stumbled, and slowly turned to its left and began to career off the tracks and down the embankment. The sound of metal crashing and tearing ripped through the sky. Car after car played the game of follow the leader and ran down onto the field to their destruction.

The sound of metal and wood colliding and ripping became deafening. Some train cars fell on their sides while others stayed upright and a few actually turned turtle. The despised Stuart tanks ripped free of their shackles and fell onto the field. In a couple of cases, the turrets came loose and rolled around. Braun was mildly disappointed that their crews hadn't been traveling with them.

Smoke clouds began to obscure the site. The boilers on the locomotives exploded, sending shock waves across the wreckage and white clouds of steam roaring upward.

Braun and Krause exulted as scores of freight cars kept falling to their destruction, screeching as more metal ripped apart, taking large sections of the track with them. When it seemed it couldn't get any better, something in one of the cars exploded and started a chain reaction. Moments later, a score of freight cars was burning and others threatened to catch fire.

Curiously, they could hear no sounds of screams

although a couple of figures could be seen running around in apparent shock and panic. Doubtless what was left of the crew, Braun thought. Too bad it wasn't a passenger train. Perhaps the next one would be.

As he pulled the station wagon onto the road and drove away, he could see emergency vehicles heading toward the crash site. He turned to Krause and laughed. It was a good start.

Harry Hopkins was a confidante of Franklin Delano Roosevelt and had advised him on many important and delicate issues. He'd traveled on his president's behalf to Moscow and London and was noted for his bluntness when dealing with foreign leaders. He was so valued by FDR that he now lived in the White House. However, the chain-smoking Harry Hopkins was dying of a stomach cancer, and he looked far older than his fifty-two years.

Hopkins looked at Admiral Nimitz and Lieutenant General John Lesesne DeWitt. Even though he was gaunt, disheveled, and dressed in an ill-fitting suit, Hopkins was clearly in charge. He was also a little annoyed that he'd been sent west to negotiate what amounted to a truce between the army and the navy and the nation's overall war goals. At least, he thought wryly, he didn't have to deal with the arrogant General Douglas MacArthur, who was busy trying desperately to hold onto Australia.

Hopkins coughed and began. "Gentlemen, enough is enough. We are now certain that the Japanese will not invade California or anyplace else on the West Coast. Therefore, we have to make some changes consistent with plans for coming events. In short, we now have more than a million American soldiers sitting on their thumbs, waiting in trenches and pillboxes along the Pacific coast for an enemy who isn't going to come."

"Is your intelligence that good?" DeWitt asked with a trace of sulkiness.

As a three-star, DeWitt was junior to Nimitz and strongly suspected that he wasn't getting all the information the higher-ranking admiral was. He was also getting a lot of flack for interning Japanese civilians even though he was convinced that the actions were necessary and his efforts were supported by FDR. DeWitt was painfully conscious that most of his experience in the army was as a quartermaster and not as a combat officer. He now commanded the sprawling Fourth Army area, which also included Alaska, and was being heavily criticized for the ease with which the Japanese had taken Anchorage.

The internment of Japanese civilians and American citizens was another major problem. The short-tempered DeWitt had been infuriated by the lack of preparedness and common sense shown by civilian authorities. This included failure to black out cities and several absurd false alarms when people thought the Japanese fleet was approaching. The sixty-two-year-old DeWitt felt all of those years.

"Our intelligence is excellent," answered Hopkins as Nimitz looked down at his hands. The admiral was among a chosen few who knew the United States had broken at least some of the Japanese codes. DeWitt was not.

Hopkins continued. "I assume everyone has heard the rumors that we are going to invade North Africa. Well, the rumors are true and, in order to do that, we are going to need an army. Specifically, General DeWitt, we are going to need many of those several hundreds of thousands of troops who were sent here after the Midway battle to protect against what we now know is a nonexistent invasion, and to forestall the hysteria among the civilian population that was assuming epic proportions. Gentlemen, there never was any threat of an invasion. The Japs can and will continue to raid, but they will not invade. Therefore, we need significant components of the Fourth Army sent back east pronto so they can be prepared to land in North Africa in November."

DeWitt was angry. He'd been an officer in the army for more than forty years and didn't like the bullshit that was being shoveled in his direction.

"And just how the hell am I supposed to forestall raids without an army? And how also am I supposed to recover Alaska, or do we let the Japs keep on beheading people?"

Hopkins glared at him. He wasn't used to people arguing with him. "General, it has been noted over and over again that your Fourth Army cannot ever be large enough to defend literally thousands of miles of coastline. We have to depend on air and naval patrols along with coastal radar to identify the Jap fleet's location and plan accordingly. Yes, I understand that the enemy can cruise up and down the coast causing the army to run up and down as well. Nor can we stop the Japs from shelling small towns like they've been doing with impunity since we don't yet have enough ships to stop them. It can't be helped. The president is under extreme pressure from the Russians to open up a second front against the Nazis and support Stalin."

DeWitt was not impressed. "The Russians are a long ways away, while the Japs are here on our soil. Even worse, the shelling of small towns has resulted in hundreds of thousands of refugees heading inland. We can't handle all that. We need more help here and to hell with the Russians."

Hopkins seethed. He felt his stomach aching, but he chose to continue, ignoring DeWitt's outburst. "It is also imperative that we prevent Rommel from defeating the British in North Africa. If that happens, fascist Spain is likely to decide that allying with Nazi Germany is the better good bet and scrap its neutrality. Don't forget that Hitler supported Franco in Spain's civil war and has been pushing for that debt to be repaid. We believe Spain is wavering and, if the British are defeated by Rommel, they will either attack Gibraltar directly or permit German troops to cross Spain and take it. If Gibraltar falls, the Mediterranean almost automatically becomes a German lake, which could cost us a fortune in blood to retrieve. Therefore, the forces arrayed against Japan must be reduced."

"What do you suggest I do about the Japs?" DeWitt snarled.

"You can do whatever the hell you want, General," Hopkins snapped back. "I'm not going to strip your cupboard bare. You'll still have more than a half million soldiers and Marines along with more than a thousand planes. I expect you'll move your troops in detachments large enough to defend the major cities from an attack that isn't going to come in the first place. The Japs simply do not have an army tagging along with their fleet and they don't have the ability to bring one across the Pacific and supply it. And as to the shelling of our cities, until and if we get radar all up and down the coast, they will have to be endured."

"What do I tell Governor Olson?" DeWitt asked. Culbert Olson was the Democratic governor of California and a long time supporter of Franklin Roosevelt. It was a clear implication that Olson would complain to the president, who might then change his mind.

Hopkins smiled. "Tell Olson he's fucked up so badly he's going to lose to the Republican candidate, Earl Warren, in November. Olson once described hell as being governor of California. He'll be glad to be able to blame someone else for his screwups."

Nimitz leaned forward to Hopkins. "In all fairness to the general and me, we still don't have a radar wall in place and the Japs will be able to strike heavily at certain points without our knowing it until the last minute. You're right, though. We could have millions more men and there would still be gaps in the coverage. When will the North African invasion take place?"

"Mid-November is the target," Hopkins said and fished in his jacket pocket for a cigarette. People with stomach cancer weren't supposed to smoke, but he didn't care.

"Which is why we have to move as many troops as we can back to the East Coast as soon as possible. And when we do win in Africa, don't expect the troops to return. North Africa will be only the first step in the reconquest of Europe."

"Do you have any good news for us poor souls in the Pacific?" Nimitz asked.

"Yes. The Panama Canal will be back in business very shortly and we'll be sending some new submarines out to you."

"What about carriers?" Nimitz asked, even though he was certain he knew the answer.

"None until we have enough on line to make a difference, and that includes the merchant ships we are converting to smaller carriers," Hopkins responded. "The same holds with your getting new battleships, although additional cruisers and destroyers can be expected. Until then, the *Saratoga* will have to cruise alone. By the way, where the devil is the carrier?"

Nimitz smiled. "Truthfully, I don't know."

CHAPTER 10

DANE STEPPED OUT OF HIS STAFF CAR AND WALKED across the field to the ruins of what had once been a very long freight train. Now it was little more then piles of charred wood and metal. Blackened train wheels stuck out of the debris, incongruous and looking totally and pathetically out of place. So too did a number of tanks, their guns pointing uselessly in all directions.

FBI agent Roy Harris waved him over to a section of track. Dane had to walk past a locomotive that lay on its side like some mortally wounded animal, an iron whale that had washed up on an unfriendly shore. He could see where the boiler had exploded, ripping the guts out of it.

"This is where it happened," Harris said. "Right here is where the son of a bitch placed the charge that blew the track and sent the train down the hill. Along with destroying all that material and equipment, he also killed four people and injured two others. The engineer and fireman in that locomotive you walked by were killed, scalded to death when the boiler exploded. I hope to hell they died quickly because their bodies were pretty damn awful to look at. The other engineer and fireman got out although they were injured."

Dane looked up and down the tracks which had been ripped up for quite a ways. "And you're certain this is the place?"

"Never doubt the FBI, Dane, we know everything. Seriously, kindly note that while other rails are damaged, none are twisted quite as sharply as this one, and that none of the rails ahead of the train are in any way disturbed. Ergo, this is the spot. We also found dynamite traces and pieces of what he used as a detonator."

Dane looked down the tracks at the chaos. A number of small fires continued to smolder and there was the smell of ash in the air. Four dead wasn't a large number in the middle of a war, but they were civilians who were supposed to be alive, even protected by the military. It was like the execution of the customs agents.

"Well," said Dane, "we were waiting for him or them to do something and now he has. You're going to tell me this is only the beginning, aren't you?"

"Yep. And it also means we're going to have to expend manpower to try to prevent it from happening again. The army is going to start patrolling the train lines as well as looking under bridges and along roads. Sad part is, we have no idea who or what we're looking for. Some people saw vehicles leaving the area, but nothing of note, just the usual litany of Fords and Chevrolets, with the odd Hudson or Packard thrown in. Assuming the obvious, that he or they drove here, and I think it's likely more than one man, they're using a nondescript vehicle."

"Like a Ford or a Chevy."

"Exactly, and that narrows the field down to a few hundred thousand cars."

"Would they need a truck to carry the explosives?"

Harris smiled. "Good question, and the answer is no. It's shockingly easy to derail a train, and only a little bit of dynamite would be needed to blow up a track and set the whole calamity in motion. It could all be carried in a suitcase with plenty of room left over to stuff in some underwear and socks."

"So what now?"

"Since they've started up, we can assume two things. One, they'll do it again, which means stepped-up security and patrols, and that means your navy as well as the army. We don't know if these guys have access to any military bases or not, or whether they'll strike closer to San Diego or farther away. In short, we don't know much at all."

Dane shrugged. "What else is new? Knowing little is standard with the navy."

"Same goes where I work. However, Dane, we must also assume that someone's in charge and has to report his successes back to the Reich so they can inform the Japanese, if he is indeed trying to help out the little sons of Nippon. In order to report, he must be using the mail, telephone, or telegraph, or shortwave radio. Mail's too slow and telegrams can be monitored. International mail can be opened, too, but don't tell anybody that. We can have operators listen in on international phone calls, although we haven't been paying all that much attention to calls from the U.S. to other countries."

"Obviously, that's going to change."

"Absolutely. Therefore, we think he will start to use shortwave. If he stays on the air long enough, we can locate him, but odds are he won't. He could set up a transmitter, broadcast for a minute or two at a prearranged time, and shut down quickly without us being able to find him."

"What if he uses messengers, couriers, to go back and forth across the border and send their reports from Mexico?"

Harris paused thoughtfully. "Another good question, but I don't think so. My gut says that would take too long, and also leave him or his messenger open to getting caught."

"You paint a depressing picture, Agent Harris."

"Indeed I do, Commander Dane. So far, we've told the public that this was a tragic accident that we are routinely investigating because of interstate commerce implications and all that bull-crap. If he strikes again, like at a civilian installation, and if the public realizes it's sabotage, we could have a genuine panic on our hands."

Dane thought of Amanda and her friends coming down to San Diego from San Francisco. A well-placed bomb could destroy a passenger train and all its occupants as easily as a freight train. Where the hell was she, and why didn't she make it down to him? And what was so important about her journey to California that she couldn't tell him?

Lieutenant Commander Lou Torelli's new sub was a *Salmon*-class boat built in 1939. Named the U.S.S. *Shark* after a sub of the same name that had been lost earlier in the year, she carried a crew of ninety, and was larger and faster than his previous sub. She carried twenty-four torpedoes, which could be fired from eight tubes, with four each located at the bow and stern. The *Shark* had a three-inch gun on her deck and four machine guns to fight off enemy aircraft. Torelli, however, had no intention of being on the surface long enough so that enemy planes could either find or attack him. He'd learned that lesson transporting people from Hawaii to San Diego. He'd been lucky once. He would not count on luck again.

Like most smaller warships, the *Shark* had no radar, which many still considered unreliable anyhow. Until radar was perfected, most sailors preferred a wide-open eyeball to unproven technology. Torelli was reasonably confident that no Japanese ships or planes carried radar either, although there were rumors that the Japs did have knowledge of it and were building sets. It was yet another blow to Anglo-American egos. The Japanese were too primitive to understand radar, it had been thought. Another stupid miscalculation, he thought ruefully.

Even though fairly new, the *Salmon*-class subs were already being outclassed by newer categories of subs that were being built by the dozen. Soon, it was joked, subs would have to be outfitted with old tires on their hulls because there would be so many of them they'd be bumping into each other while underwater.

He had the dismal feeling that this patrol was his punishment for complaining about the quality of U.S. torpedoes. The powers in the navy's Bureau of Ordnance in Washington had accused him and other sub captains of incompetence or cowardice and insisted there was nothing wrong with their damn torpedoes. It was a debate that now raged far above his pay grade.

Perhaps in order to get him out of the sight of BuOrd, his patrol area included the waters off the Cook Inlet and the Gulf of Alaska to its south. Rear Admiral Charles Lockwood had recently arrived from Australia to head up the submarine force in place of the ailing Admiral Thomas England. Torelli and other submariners felt that Lockwood was a stern fire-breather, but a man who would be sympathetic to the needs of submariners and would fight hard for them.

The *Shark* was at periscope depth and creeping along to keep any wake from the periscope to a minimum. The day was gray and bleak with pockets of fog obscuring their view. Torelli wished he did have radar. In the lousy weather, the Japs could be a few hundred yards away and nobody'd know. Of course, the Japs wouldn't either, but he was not going to risk running on the surface just so he might be able to see a little better.

Torelli had turned the periscope over to his XO, Lieutenant Crowley, who was peering intently through it. "What do you make, Ron?" Torelli asked genially.

"Visitors for Anchorage, Skipper. I make two Jap heavy cruisers and six destroyers all escorting at least half a dozen transports."

They'd spotted the enemy force a half hour earlier as gray shapes moving through the intermittent fog. The Japanese ships were well out of range and Torelli was torn between the need to try an attack and his duty to inform the brass of his discovery. He decided to do both. Catching up to the convoy was out of the question. They had too much of a head start.

He would wait until they were out of sight, surface, and send off a message. After that there might be the opportunity to seek out and hit the Japs where it hurt. Right now, the Japanese commander was skillfully keeping his convoy against the shore with the warships protecting their port flank.

Torelli did not entirely agree with Crowley. "Not only am I better looking than you, my eyes are sharper, young Lieutenant. I make two heavy cruisers and one light along with five destroyers. No, change that. I see another light cruiser. If my math is correct, that makes nine of the fuckers heading straight for Anchorage."

Crowley whistled softly. According to his latest copy of *Jane's*, a Japanese heavy cruiser generally carried eight-inch guns. "Lord, Skipper, one of them would look great on our trophy rack, although we'd need a helluva big trophy rack."

Torelli didn't respond. He had some decisions to make. If he decided that the transports were the more valuable targets; he'd have to shoot his way past the cruisers and destroyers to get at the transports. He wondered what important materiel the transports carried to make them worthy of such a strong convoy. Planes, artillery, more troops, supplies, and all of the above came to mind, and there was no way he could close the distance in time. He swore. So much materiel would soon be landed to reinforce the invasion of Alaska before he could do anything about it.

As soon as he could he surfaced and sent a detailed message. He stayed on the surface to recharge his batteries. Torelli had the nagging feeling he was going to need them fully charged soon. Bad torpedoes or not, he wanted to strike back at the Japs.

A couple of hours later, he got the response. The *Shark* was to stay and observe, but not attack, at least for the time being. The message didn't quite say it, but Torelli felt that something nasty was being planned for the Japanese. He fervently hoped he could help out.

Japanese ships on patrol off the American coast could not see through the persistent fog, and they could not get too close to the hostile shoreline when the gray shapes of American ships slipped out of Puget Sound and headed north a week earlier. Hugging the shore, they'd made it to Yakutat Bay, south of Anchorage, where Alaska became a finger of land running alongside the border with Canada. The bay was dominated by Mount Hood and Mount Hubbard, and, if the weather was right, they could see the mountains and glaciers farther up where Yakutat Bay changed its name to what the sailors of the American force thought was the wonderfully appropriately named Disenchantment Bay.

There was a town called Yakutat, but none of the crew showed any inclination for shore leave in such a dismal-looking place, even if liberty would be permitted.

Admiral Jesse Oldendorf had recently arrived from a command in the Atlantic. It was rumored that he would take over from Admiral Pye, who was under severe criticism for his handling of his part of the fleet after Pearl Harbor. The criticism might not be deserved, but scapegoats were needed, and Pye had pulled his ships back from reinforcing Wake Island. Wake had subsequently fallen after heroic fighting and Pye had been blamed for not making a strong enough effort to help. Cooler heads said Pye's efforts would have been doomed, but Pye would still be sacrificed.

Oldendorf's command consisted of two of Pye's old battleships, the *Mississippi* and the *Colorado*, along with four destroyers. The admiral flew his flag in the *Colorado*, in part because her eight sixteen-inch guns mounted in four turrets were larger than the *Mississippi*'s twelve fourteen-inch guns. Bigger is always better, the admiral had said with a smile.

Their presence in Yakutat Bay was in the hope that the Japanese would do exactly what the *Shark* had reported, make a reinforcement run to Anchorage, and they had been waiting anxiously for several days. The two battleships, however old, were much more powerful than three Japanese cruisers and a handful of destroyers. Better, both the *Colorado* and *Mississippi* had recently been equipped with radar. The Japanese were supposed to be superior at night fighting, but how well could they fight in a fog? Truth be told, Oldendorf wanted very much to see the enemy face to face, but it would be just as nice, he thought, to be able to sneak up on the sons of bitches before they had a chance to react. "Never give a sucker an even break" was his motto, adopted after hearing the line in a movie.

In single file, with the two radar-equipped battleships leading, Oldendorf's ships slipped out of Yakutat Bay and said farewell to the thoroughly disenchanting Disenchantment Bay. They headed north, again hugging the coastline.

Naval intelligence insisted that there were no other major Japanese warships in the area. All carrier and battleship units were well to the south, they said, and concentrated in two roughly equivalent forces, one off San Francisco and one off San Diego.

On the flag bridge behind Oldendorf, Tim Dane shivered, and not just from the cold. He hadn't had time to draw cold-weather gear before being sent up north, and the jacket he wore was too thin.

"Tell me again how I got here," Dane asked.

Lieutenant Commander Mickey Greene smiled benignly. His face was a mass of red and healing scars and, like Tim's, his head had been shaved, but he was upbeat. Perhaps the thought of striking back at the Japanese helped.

"Because Oldendorf asked for you after I told him you could speak Japanese. Nobody else in the squadron can perform that trick."

"Thanks a lot."

"He was also impressed that you'd saved Spruance and had led that raid on Anchorage, which means you know a little about the area."

"Damn little and I didn't lead any raid. I just flew along as a spectator and was as useless as when I was on the Enterprise. We flew over the Jap base at a hundred miles an hour and at a height of only a few feet. It was just a blur of trees and people shooting at us."

Greene chuckled. "Well, that still puts you miles ahead of anybody else."

As with his impression of the *Enterprise*, Dane was overwhelmed by the size of the *Colorado* and her monstrous sixteen-inch guns. At just under forty thousand tons, the battleship was much larger than any carrier in the U.S. Navy, including the *Enterprise*. More than two thousand men were on her and they all seemed to have a job and know what they were doing, which, once again, was more than Dane could say.

Dane had to admit that battleships, however obsolescent they might be, looked more like warships than
carriers. Greene concurred.

"Oldendorf's a big-gun man," Greene said, "but he
ain't no fool. The days of the battleship are numbered
and he knows it. It's just that we have a chance to
strike back at the Japs and we don't have any carriers
to play with anyhow. I guess the *Sara*'s too valuable
to risk right now, wherever the hell she is."

Greene reminded Dane that the U.S. Navy hadn't
won a surface battle since the Spanish-American War,
and that the only time they'd tried it in this war, it
had met with defeat in the Java Sea. Dane wondered
if this coming fight would be the last naval battle that
didn't involve carriers.

Greene continued. "Don't forget that these are
old ships, at least two decades old. Yeah, they've
been updated, but they are still at least a generation
behind the newer battleships in technology and, most
important, in fuel efficiency. These two battleships are
real pigs when it comes to guzzling fuel and they have
to provide fuel for short-legged ships like destroyers.
New battlewagons like the *Washington* are not only
far more fuel-efficient, but a helluva lot faster and
better armed. It's too bad, but this is likely the last
ride for these old warriors. Oldendorff wants to make
it a ride to remember."

Dane had briefly met Oldendorf, who asked him
to confirm that he indeed spoke Japanese and then
told him to stick close to Greene. Dane's job would
be to listen to Japanese radio transmissions and try
to figure out if they had any idea what was going to
hit them. The admiral was in his mid-fifties and this

was his first combat command. He had a craggy face that made him look tougher than he was, but Greene had told Dane that this was probably Oldendorf's last hurrah as well as his first.

"But two battleships against four heavy cruisers and one light? Isn't that overkill?" Dane said.

Greene smiled and rubbed the scars on his cheeks. He'd said he was glad to go to sea so he wouldn't scare little kids until he got better. Dane wondered if he would be so calm about life and his future if he'd been burned like that.

"The admiral said it would be wonderful if a couple of arthritic old battleships could give the Japs a bloody nose. Besides, my friend, the odds aren't so well stacked in our favor. Heavy cruisers still pack a helluva kick."

Dane thought about the bloated and mangled bodies he'd seen floating around the dying *Enterprise*. "I'd like to give them more than a bloody nose."

Oldendorf planned the attack for four AM, a time when it was believed that people were drowsiest and least on their guard. The American force moved in single file, again with the two radar-equipped battleships slowly leading the way up Cook Inlet.

American observers near Anchorage had reported that the transports were unloading cargo while the warships were arrayed in a loose defensive perimeter. Ominously, their cargo was confirmed as disassembled airplanes, and were the Type 43 fighter code-named "Oscar" by the Americans. The Oscar had a range of a thousand miles and could carry a pair of two-hundred-fifty-pound bombs. The Oscars would be able to blunt future bomber attacks and hinder naval assaults like the one coming down the inlet.

Dane was able to listen to radio chatter between the various Japanese ships and quickly confirmed that nothing unusual was happening. Chatter was in the clear and not encoded, which was normal for talk between ships. It took time to encode a message and more time to decode one; since most message traffic concerned mundane matters such as supplies and mail, very few messages were coded.

Dane turned to Greene. "Tell the admiral that it's the middle of the night and the radio operators are simply killing time. They think it's funny that Admiral Hosogaya asked Colonel Yamasaki if there were any decent restaurants in Anchorage. Apparently, he inquired before actually seeing the place. One can only imagine his disappointment."

Greene nodded and reported to Oldendorf, who laughed harshly.

Spotters on the hills overlooking the town reported that the transports were clustered near the limited docking space and struggling to unload their cargoes. The space was so cramped that only one transport could unload at a time and then with great difficulty. Large ships were infrequent visitors to Anchorage.

The destroyers were farthest out and the cruisers about a mile offshore. Two destroyers were patrolling while the rest of the flotilla was at anchor.

"Do we have any other ships in the area?" Dane asked.

"A sub's been spotting for us as well, but she should be well to our north and west and lying low so she doesn't get mistaken for a bad guy." Greene reached into his pocket and pulled out a small package. "Here, have some ear plugs. You're going to need them when the big guns fire, unless you want to wind up deaf for the rest of your life. And, by the way, hang on to something sturdy. The blast could also knock you silly."

Dane paused. The tone of Japanese radio communications had changed. Now there was the sound of worry. One of the patrolling destroyers had reported strange ships approaching through the light fog.

"Are we in range?" Dane asked.

"Of the destroyers that spotted us, yes," Greene answered. "So put in the damned ear plugs."

Dane complied and, seconds later, the forward guns of both battleships opened fire, violently shaking the ship and, despite warnings, almost causing Dane to fall. Even with the ear plugs, the sound was deafening.

A moment later, someone yelled that the shells were short. Corrections were made and another salvo was fired, and one of the destroyers simply disappeared. One moment she was a blip on the radar, the next, nothing. The second destroyer was racing at high speed toward the rest of the squadron.

The cruisers were the battleships' primary targets, while the American destroyers streaked in to rake the Japanese destroyers with gunfire and torpedoes. Each battleship carried three floatplanes and these had been launched to aid in targeting.

The heavy cruisers had been identified as the *Nachi* and *Maya*, and the light cruisers as the *Tama* and *Abukuma*. Dane wondered how they knew that for certain. Greene told him that observers all along Cook Inlet had confirmed it. He added that some were retired navy and even had their own copies of *Jane's*.

Distant flashes showed that the Japs were firing back. Their shells, however, landed well short, although they did create mighty plumes of water. Without radar and in the dim light, the Japanese weren't all that certain where the Americans were. The Americans fired a big gun salvo at the cruisers, and spotters reported they too were short. Oldendorf raged while adjustments were made. Dane thought he could see the faint shapes of the Japanese ships against the shoreline, and wondered if that was confusing the fire-control radar. The Japanese were beginning to move.

Another salvo and Dane watched incredulously as the glowing red shells, each the size of a small car, sped through the sky. False dawn was rising and with his binoculars he could indeed see the enemy ships just as the second salvo impacted.

A plane reported. "Hit! We got a hit on the *Nachi*."

Japanese cruisers were big, but they couldn't stand fourteen- and sixteen-inch shells ripping through them. The *Nachi*'s superstructure collapsed on her forward turrets as near misses sent columns of water higher than the ship.

Another plane reported. "*Nachi*'s on fire and the *Maya*'s trying to get underway."

The *Colorado* turned violently to port. "What the hell?" asked Dane.

Greene laughed harshly. "Torpedo. Remember them? This one missed."

A second torpedo didn't, and the battleship shook as a plume of spray shot to the sky. A few moments later, damage control reported water, but that it could be contained. The Japs had teeth, but the battleships were not going to succumb to their bites.

Another report came in. "*Nachi's* burning and slowing down. *Maya's* hit, too."

A bright light flared in the distance. After a minute it was reported that the light cruiser *Tama* had blown up and that the *Abukuma* had taken a hit that had blown one of her stern turrets completely off the ship. The spotter quickly added that the *Maya* had capsized.

On the *Colorado*, men were cheering, Dane among them. The rational part of his mind said he shouldn't exult because men were dying. The emotional side, however, said they were Japs who'd invaded and massacred, and deserved what they were getting.

In a matter of moments, all four enemy cruisers had been destroyed. Oldendorf ordered the battleships to focus on the remaining Japanese destroyers. One of them was already burning, but so too was an American destroyer. The big guns of the *Colorado* and *Mississippi* turned on the surviving enemy ships with a vengeance. One Japanese destroyer managed to make it through the gauntlet of fire and out toward the ocean end of Cook Inlet.

The sun was up and the small city of Anchorage was in plain sight. The transports were huddled like sheep waiting to be slaughtered and Oldendorf accommodated them. The battleships cautiously moved through shallowing water to near point-blank range where their secondary batteries of five-inch guns ripped through the transports' thin hulls. In short order, they too were exploding, burning, and sinking. Naval fire was then lifted to targets of opportunity, including trucks, buildings, and anything that looked like it might be useful to the Japanese. The recently offloaded supplies received special attention and were blown to pieces, including a half dozen Oscars that would never get off the ground.

Finally, the slaughter was over. A very satisfied Oldendorf had his victory, and the U.S. Navy had finally defeated a Japanese surface force. It didn't take back the sting and shame of Pearl Harbor, Midway, the Philippines, and the Java Sea, but everyone in the task force was pleased, and the American public would rejoice once the news got out. Four Japanese cruisers and four destroyers had been sunk, along with half a dozen transports. One enemy destroyer might have escaped, but so what, was the consensus. One American destroyer was badly damaged and would be scuttled. It would be too time-consuming and dangerous to try and tow her all the way back to Puget Sound. Fifteen were dead aboard her, along with forty wounded. Apart from bumps and bruises, there were no other casualties on the other ships. The admiral announced that it was time to leave.

Motion was seen in the ruins of Anchorage. At first scores, and then hundreds of people could be seen running toward the shore, frantically waving their arms.

"What the hell is going on?" Oldendorf asked.

Dane had binoculars on the throng. "Those are civilians, sir. They want us to pick them up."

Oldendorf shook his head grimly, "Can't do it. We've stayed long enough."

Dane was appalled at the answer. "Sir, those are the Americans the Japs have been torturing and using as slaves. Admiral, if you don't save them, the Japs will likely kill them in retaliation for this disaster. Their commander, Colonel Yamasaki, is a real fanatic and he will want revenge for what we've done. He will have them all beheaded or shot, or maybe used for living bayonet practice."

Oldendorf looked stunned. He nodded grimly and made his decision. "That will not happen on my watch. Get the destroyers in close and everyone launch boats. We'll pick up every goddamned one of them."

An hour later, a score of lifeboats had each made several trips to the shore, returning with as many civilians as they could find. Without exception, they were dressed in rags and showed signs of starvation. Multiple bruises were evidence of repeated beatings, and some looked maddened by their ordeal, especially the women. Many of them were nearly nude despite the worsening weather. Hundreds of helping hands lifted or carried them onto the warships and hardened sailors were moved to tears by what they saw. Finally, there was nobody else, only dead Japanese, although they could sense the angry survivors among the enemy invasion force glaring at them through the woods.

"Now it's time," Oldendorf said grimly. The sight and condition of the civilians had shaken him. "Let's get the hell out of this place. But first, let's lob a few shells into the woods and maybe we'll get lucky and hit something Japanese."

A few miles north and west of the fighting, the *Shark* remained submerged. As the morning brightened, Torelli could see smoke coming from the Anchorage area. He could also see a ship heading for him and racing at great speed.

He grinned. "Damn if it isn't a Jap destroyer," he announced after carefully checking his *Jane's*. "And he's running like a bat out of hell, which means we probably won the fight, and damned if we aren't going to sink the fucker."

"Want me to put that in the log, sir," Crowley asked innocently. "I feel that using exact quotes are best for historical purposes."

"Screw you, Mr. Crowley," Torelli said amiably. "We will fire when she's broadside to us. I don't want any misses running toward any of our ships that might be coming out of the fight."

He also added that, when the four torpedoes were fired from the *Shark*'s bow tubes, the boat should turn as quickly as possible so the stern torpedoes could be fired. Torelli had no confidence in his torpedoes and wanted to minimize the chance of a thoroughly pissed off Japanese destroyer commander running up the torpedoes' wakes and depth-charging them. The Jap might be fleeing, but who knew how he might react if he thought he could sink an American sub.

They fired at a thousand yards. Four torpedoes streaked toward the destroyer and this time fate smiled on the men of the Shark. Two of them exploded against her hull, shattering her and breaking the destroyer in half. Both parts floated for a while and then slipped beneath the sea.

"No lifeboats," Crowley said as he took his turn at the periscope, "and nobody swimming in the water. I guess that means no prisoners."

Torelli recalled his conversations with Dane. "From what I hear, young Lieutenant, the sons of bitches would rather die than be taken prisoner."

Crowley grinned. "Sounds good to me, Skipper."

CHAPTER 11

JAP FLEET SUNK

REVENGE FOR MIDWAY—
NINE JAP SHIPS DESTROYED

FINALLY! WE WIN A BIG ONE!

The headlines on the San Francisco and Oakland newspapers said it all. The United States Navy had won a major victory over the Japanese and the nation was exultant. The string of agonizing defeats had ended and there would be more victories.

Amanda, Sandy, and Grace were not immune to the festive air as they walked down Funston Avenue near the Presidio in San Francisco on their way to the law offices of Goldman and Swartz. The articles following the headlines made for sparse reading, as it was obvious that the government wasn't releasing much in the way of information. Nothing was said about which Japanese ships had been sunk, except to say that four were cruisers and five were destroyers. It was painfully evident that no Japanese carriers or battleships had been involved, which meant that the main Japanese battle fleet remained unscathed. Nor was anything said about what American ships were involved or where they'd been based, except to say that two battleships had done much of the work. The article also said that Japanese army shore installations had been pounded and destroyed, and that a large number of terribly mistreated American civilian refugees had been saved from Japanese clutches.

It was like a cloud lifting. The litany of defeats had come to a screeching halt. Now the United States would continue to strike back; at least, that was the prevailing hope and thought. There was, however, the nagging sense that the Japanese would seek revenge for the slaughter.

Even reading between the lines, it did not look like something Tim Dane would be involved in, and for that Amanda was thankful. Captain Harding had dropped by that morning with copies of their nursing credentials, which meant they could get a job, and gasoline ration coupons that would enable them to drive to San Diego in the '38 Buick they'd purchased.

The law firm of Goldman and Swartz consisted of one person, Richard Goldman, Swartz having died several years earlier. The offices were on the second floor of a nondescript building that had a men's clothing store on the first floor. Goldman was a small, frail man in his sixties and the women had asked for an appointment with him because Mack had suggested him.

"I'm sorry to hear of Mack's passing," Goldman said. "I've known him for a very long time, and yes, he did do some very questionable things when he was young and aggressive, but nothing that would have put him on the wrong side of the law. I think what you heard was his conscience speaking. He felt responsible when he made money while others lost theirs. Perhaps it was best that he wound up on a beach in Hawaii. Maybe I'll go there myself someday." He sighed. "Of course, I'd look like the devil in a bathing suit, so perhaps it's best I don't."

Goldman took the envelope containing Mack's will. "Alleged will" is how the lawyer phrased it.

"We have to prove its authenticity and, unfortunately, the only ones who witnessed it are the supposed heirs, you people, which is an obvious conflict of interest. You shouldn't be witnessing something that will reward you; however, I don't know what else you could have done. Also, we'll have to prove that Mack is actually dead, and, since you are the witnesses as well as the heirs, the police might want to talk to you about the possibility that you killed him for his money. Again, however, since any alleged crime took place on the high seas, and likely out of anyone's jurisdiction, that would be an uphill fight for the cops unless one of you wanted to confess, of course. If one of you would kindly implicate the others, I'll get whoever confesses first a light sentence."

"I didn't kill him, I loved him," lamented Grace.

"And I'm joking," said Goldman. "Unfortunately, it was a bad joke."

"I'm confused," said Amanda. "Are you implying there's enough money involved for someone to want to murder him?"

Goldman shrugged. "Who knows? He apparently

cashed out all, or at least most, of his investments and put whatever he got into the safe-deposit boxes for which you have the keys. What's in them we won't know until and if they are opened."

"Do you think it's worth the effort?" Amanda pressed.

"I'd say probably. By the way, the legal effort will include someone, me, locating any of his living relatives who might file a claim that the will is invalid as well as dealing with the State of California, who might also say that the will is invalid and the contents of the boxes belong to the oppressed citizens of the state. What they'll probably do is negotiate a percentage if it looks like you might prevail in court. By the way, we haven't discussed my fee."

Amanda sighed. "And how much will that be when you consider that we don't have all that much money?" She decided not to mention the cash "refund" they'd recovered from Mack.

"Normally, I charge twenty-five percent of the proceeds. But, since you're Mack's friends, I'll only charge a third."

"What!" said Amanda.

Goldman laughed. "Glad to see you're paying attention and understand basic math. Twenty-five percent is my fee."

They agreed, signed a contract and some other forms, and left. It was time to go to San Diego and start earning a living. Goldman had a relative named Zuckerman in San Diego and they would communicate through him. Zuckerman was an attorney as well as an investor in real estate.

"I hope we're doing the right thing," Sandra mused as they waited for the ferry that would take them across the bay to Oakland and their car, "but I don't know what the wrong thing could be."

Amanda was about to answer when air-raid sirens went off. They looked about and scanned the skies along with thousands of other people who were staring skyward, puzzled and confused.

"There," Grace shrieked and pointed. Hundreds of tiny dots were approaching from the south and heading over the Bay.

The Japanese were striking back.

Masao Ikeda piloted his Zero with the consummate skill of an experienced Japanese pilot, the best in the world. He and close to two hundred others flying both Zeros and the Nakajima B5N2 two-man carrier-based bombers had approached from the south of San Francisco because senior officers said that American radar likely did not extend that far. So they had circled behind where they thought radar would be, and apparently they were right. Radar was only dimly understood by the average pilot, and Japanese planes and most ships did not have it yet.

The waves of Japanese planes had flown at very low levels, well below what the experts also said were the limits of the radar devices that could identify a flying plane that could not be seen by the human eye. They had flown only a hundred feet above the ground and had been more concerned about trees and power lines than American warplanes. By coming from the south, it looked as if they'd also managed to avoid being spotted by any patrolling planes and ships.

The flight was both stressful and intoxicating. The terrain south of San Francisco surprised Ikeda. Unlike

Japan, where cities were jammed with teeming multitudes, there was so much empty space and room for growth. He idly thought that he would like to visit the place some time. Perhaps after the successful conclusion of the war, where he would be treated as a conqueror and take his pick of white-skinned American women.

Today, though, he and his comrades would take revenge on the Americans for their disgraceful ambush of the Japanese convoy in what was a massacre unworthy of warriors. The planes from four carriers were taking part in this raid that saw them sweep unmolested over the rugged terrain south of San Francisco. Their knowledge of the area was minimal and they'd been reduced to reading road maps and magazine maps from sources like automobile clubs and *National Geographic*. Even so, it was impossible to miss the coastline and San Francisco Bay. Once over the bay, they turned north and east and headed toward the naval base at Mare Island. The bombers, referred to by the Americans as "Kates," would drop their loads while the hundred and fifty Zeros dueled with American defenders. The Japanese did not think they could destroy the massive base with the fifty bombers and their relatively small loads. The purpose of the attack was to show the arrogant Americans that Imperial Japan could and would strike their home cities at will.

Ikeda had another hope. He was still a virgin when it came to enemy kills, and he was sick and tired of the teasing from his comrades. He would not even think of discussing the fact that he was a virgin when it came to women as well.

"Many enemy fighters!" came shrilly over his radio. "All directions."

Ikeda looked around. Yes, American planes were swarming like angry bees from a hive. He exulted. There was no way he would not emerge with a kill; perhaps several enemy planes would fall to his guns. Another order sent the Kates back toward San Francisco, their secondary target. There were far too many American planes between them and Mare Island for the Kates to force entry. Now they were to bomb the city itself and then return to their carriers.

A shape flew across his nose. It was gone too quickly to fire at and Ikeda again cursed his luck. There! An American P47 was in his sights. He fired a burst and his tracers showed that the shells had fallen short. He fired again and the American plane lurched as pieces fell off. It began to smoke and headed toward the ground.

A kill, a kill! He howled with pleasure. He got his Zero on the tail of another P40 and blew it apart. A third plane, another P47, fell to his 20mm guns. He had to be careful, now. He didn't want to run out of ammunition while surrounded by enemy wasps. He looked down and saw a number of parachutes. He thought about strafing the cowardly American pilots, but that would be a waste of ammunition.

"Break off. Return home."

He snarled at the order, but it had to be done. A flash to his left and he saw a Zero explode. He fired a last burst at a P47, saw the shells hit but not kill the plane. Rumors said that the American plane was sturdy and the rumors, he thought ruefully, were correct. A flaming Zero fell from above him. He looked around and saw many, many American planes. The far fewer Japanese planes were all headed out to sea.

The Americans would chase the Japanese planes far to where the carriers waited along with the planes left behind to ambush any pursuit force. Ikeda tried to count the Japanese planes now flying west with him. He presumed that almost all the Kates had left the area and flown to safety, which meant there should be close to a hundred and fifty Zeros left. But where were they? Ikeda roughly counted much less than a hundred. Could the Americans have shot down so many? Nonsense, he thought. They must be scattered or following farther behind. Japan had won another great victory by bombing an American city and shooting down scores of enemy planes.

Even better, he, Masao Ikeda, was a virgin no more. Three confirmed kills and a possible fourth would tell all his comrades that he was a Japanese warrior.

Amanda cowered in the doorway of an office building while sirens continued to wail. There were many large plate-glass windows and she could visualize explosions sending knifelike splinters into the many hundreds of people running around screaming in panic. She saw a little girl knocked down and trampled. Amanda ran out and got the screaming child. Luckily she was only scared and bruised. A moment later, her sobbing mother took her and ran off. There were no bomb shelters. Of course not, she thought. San Francisco would never be a target despite all the hysteria regarding the possibility of a Japanese invasion. Damn politicians were wrong again, she thought angrily.

Explosions rocked the area. Bombs seemed to be dropping indiscriminately, which caused even more panic. Which way to run when you didn't know what was the target? There was no safety. She saw a handful of Japanese planes fly overhead, heading west. They were low enough to see the empty bomb racks. There was a pause but no all-clear signal. After a few minutes, a large number of Japanese fighters headed west and they were followed by an even larger horde of American planes.

"Shoot the bastards down," Grace yelled, and others joined in. How dare they bomb a helpless American city! How dare they attack civilians?

With bombs no longer falling, the panic slowed and ceased. Previously terrified people took a deep breath and regained control. Amanda realized that there appeared to have been very little real damage. She could smell smoke in the distance, but there were no massive conflagrations, and the San Francisco fire department seemed to have the situation under control.

Amanda dusted herself off. She was thankful that she'd not worn any stockings as her leg was bruised and she'd likely have torn them. Even cotton stockings were rare and nylons almost impossible to find. She shook her head at the inanity of worrying about stockings during an air raid. The sirens decided it was time to sound the all clear.

"Well, should we find a hospital and volunteer?" asked Sandy.

They did, and found that their services weren't needed, that everything was under control. Only a small number had been killed or injured, and most of the injuries had occurred as a result of panic, not the bombing directly. A few dozen people had broken bones and bruises from being shoved and trampled, although few of the injuries seemed serious. A nurse in the emergency room was of the opinion that the bombing raid had been a bust.

"Police radio said a lot of Jap planes had been shot down. What a shame, huh?" the ER nurse said with a grin.

"What do we do now?" Grace wondered.

Amanda smiled. "We do what we planned. We cross the bay to our car and start driving south. On to San Diego!" she laughed, and thought, on to Tim Dane. Ready or not, here we come.

Masao Ikeda landed on the *Akagi* with empty guns and only fumes in his tanks. The engine actually sputtered as he pulled up on the flight deck. He dismounted from the cockpit to the cheers of his fellow pilots. As he walked by they congratulated him on his kills and that he was no longer a cherry. He laughed and took a moment to swallow a few mouthfuls of rice and half a gallon of water while mechanics refueled the plane and replaced ammunition. There was no time to waste. The American planes that had pursued him and his companions were overhead and fighting with the planes left behind to protect the precious carriers.

A moment later and Masao was airborne again and dodging among the American planes. He was astonished at the number and variety of Yank fighters. Models included the pitiful P40 and the very rugged P47, along with a couple of types he didn't recognize. One, with twin tails, looked very interesting and also very lethal.

The Americans were not interested in dueling with Zeros. Their goal was the carriers, just as it had been the Japanese Navy's goal back at Midway. They sent enough planes to skirmish with the Japanese cover force and keep them at bay, while torpedo planes and dive bombers attacked the four carriers that made up the Northern Force. The *Akagi, Ryuju, Shinyu*, and *Soryu* were arrayed in a square and their antiaircraft guns were killing Americans as they approached.

Even though Masao hoped and prayed for the best, it was inevitable that some American planes would get through. He watched in horror as a dive bomber dropped its load on the flight deck of his own *Akagi*, blowing a hole in it and clearly destroying the elevator. Fires erupted but were quickly brought under control. However, no planes would be landing on the *Akagi* for quite some time.

Another American plane strafed the *Ryuju*, starting fires in the bow area as poorly stored fuel ignited. Someone would be severely punished for neglect, he thought. Unless, of course, that the poor person had been immolated, and that would be poetic justice.

In the meantime, Masao had shot down two more planes, including one of the twin-tailed ones. He wondered just how much longer the Americans could linger over the Japanese fleet before they ran out of gas. The carriers were already more than a hundred and fifty miles offshore, and heading westward at top speed.

His question was answered when he suddenly realized that there were no more American planes in the air, instead they were dots fading in the distance.

He'd had a marvelous day and so, he thought, had Japan. They'd avenged the ambush of Admiral Hosogaya's force in Cook Inlet and bombed the city of San Francisco. But at what price, he found himself

wondering as the exhilaration of battle faded and cold
reality set in. Had they really won a victory? Two
carriers were burning and would be out of the war
for months, if not longer. They had not succeeded
in bombing the base at Mare Island, and he was
certain that the few bombs the Kates had dropped
on San Francisco had been too few and too small to
be significant.

He was ordered to land on the *Soryu*. She and
the *Shinyu* were undamaged. Masao wondered just
where they would find room on two carriers to park
the planes from four carriers when he realized to his
dismay that there would be plenty of room. Victory?
Where were the Japanese eagles? Where were his
comrades? What kind of price had Japan just paid?

An angry and frustrated Admiral Yamamoto held
court in his quarters on the massive *Yamato*. Was
ultimate victory slipping away? Again he clutched his
mangled hand. It was reminding him of his mortality.

The two men with him were his senior admirals,
Takeo Kurita and Chuichi Nagumo. Kurita's northern
force now consisted of only two carriers and escorts,
while Nagumo's southern force included five carriers.
It was an imbalance that he would have to correct.
He would send the carrier *Zuikaku* north in partial
replacement for the two that had been damaged in
the attack on San Francisco.

"I have radioed my apologies to the emperor for
the disaster in Cook Inlet," Yamamoto said. "Both he
and Prime Minister Tojo were polite and consoling,
but nothing can change the fact that Cook Inlet was
the first defeat the Japanese Navy has suffered in

modern times. Our only consolation is that the defeat is a minor one. No carriers or battleships were lost."

"Our intelligence failed us," Nagumo said. "No one expected two American battleships to suddenly appear so far north."

"And without air cover," Kurita added grimly.

It upset them that the Imperial Japanese Navy possessed overwhelming air superiority but hadn't used it. Nor had the Americans used any of their air power, including their lone carrier, the *Saratoga*. They had sent their battleship force naked and vulnerable in an attack that was both bold and unexpected. For the Americans to not use their planes had been an act of desperation, for the Japanese to not use them was an act of stupidity. At least one carrier, even a small one, should have been sent to cover the relief force.

Yamamoto nodded. "We must accept the fact that the Americans are getting more aggressive. They have great numbers of planes protecting their major areas; therefore, we will not attack large cities again. Our planes and pilots are superior, but the Americans are good enough and can overwhelm our pilots by sheer weight of numbers. We will not directly challenge their air fleets again. There are more than enough smaller targets to satisfy our needs and make the Americans squeal. Nor will we use our carriers when we attack them. Instead, we will again use cruisers and destroyers, along with our submarines, to bombard them and bring pain to California and the northern coast."

"Then what of the carriers?" Kurita asked. "I hope you're not suggesting they stand idle."

Yamamoto laughed bitterly. "While some of our carriers are looking for the *Saratoga*, the others will be in reserve and will hopefully be able to ambush overeager Americans."

The other two admirals nodded their approval. Carriers and battleships were too valuable to waste in smaller skirmishes. Japanese battle doctrine called for the Japanese fleet to engage major enemy forces in a climactic battle that would end the war. There had been some hope that Pearl Harbor would have accomplished that, but the absence of American carriers there had dashed that hope. Later at Midway, when the American carriers had been sunk, hopes had risen that the Americans would see reason and negotiate an honorable end to the war, one that would see Japan keeping her conquests. Those hopes had ended in disappointment. The Americans were not ready to negotiate and were not going to come out and fight a great battle; therefore, the Japanese fleet must change its strategies.

Yamamoto continued. "I did not tell the emperor of our losses in the San Francisco attack. After all, we suffered no ships sunk even though the *Akagi* and *Ryuju* will be out of action for at least six months, probably longer. And we shot down nearly two hundred American planes, if our pilots can be believed."

They all laughed. Even at this late date in the war and with almost all pilots being experienced, they were still prone to unintended exaggerations. For too many, any plane they fired on had to have been destroyed.

Yamamoto continued. "We lost seventy of our own planes and, of course, their pilots. That is roughly the equivalent of a fleet carrier's entire flight crew. Replacement planes and pilots will be sent as soon as possible, of course, but it is doubtful that the pilots will be of the caliber of the men we lost. It does not help that our inventory of replacement planes is so small. We simply cannot produce enough planes to replace out losses."

"Have we had any success in locating the *Saratoga*?" Kurita asked. Like so many of his contemporaries, Takeo Kurita was a battleship admiral, but he recognized the need to eliminate the one remaining American carrier. Yamamoto felt that Kurita was not totally a supporter of the war. Well, he had his own doubts as well.

Yamamoto laughed. "No, and perhaps she too is back in Shangri-La."

The others laughed as well and then grew somber. "What about our forces in Alaska?" inquired Nagumo. "Admiral Hosogaya and the survivors of the defeat have joined with Colonel Yamasaki's army forces and are moving toward the Alaskan city of Fairbanks."

Yamamoto shook his head sadly. "For the time being they are on their own. The Americans are doubtless building airfields at several locations and will soon be able to bomb Yamasaki's forces at will, as well as being able to inflict too much damage on any forces attempting to relieve or evacuate them. In short, our forces in Alaska are doomed. I have spoken with Prime Minister Tojo and he understands the situation. He is confident that Colonel Yamasaki and his men will fight on to the end as true Japanese warriors and will honor the code of bushido."

Yamamoto scowled. "In the meantime, we must double and redouble our efforts to find that one remaining carrier. She and her escorts must be sunk if we are to continue with our position of strength.

We must put pressure on all our intelligence resources to find her."

More likely, he thought, she was no longer in the Pacific. He had to find out one way or the other. If the *Saratoga* had moved to the relative safety of the Atlantic, so be it. But if she was somewhere within striking range, she had to be destroyed, if only as a symbolic gesture.

CHAPTER 12

LIEUTENANT STEVE FARRIS WAS HOT, TIRED, AND
dirty. As a result of the train crash, the army's duties
had expanded to patrolling roads and railroad tracks,
along with keeping track of who was using the beaches
of the area. Some of his men wondered why, since
it was announced that the crash was merely a tragic
accident, but Farris knew better and some of his men
suspected the truth. His uncle had quietly and confi-
dentially told him that it had indeed been sabotage,
and that there had been several other minor incidents
as well. Nobody'd been hurt and damage had been
minimal in the other incidents, and it was not definite
that it had been the same person or persons as those
who'd derailed the freight train.

Both the navy and the army decided that the rail
lines would be patrolled, and a several-mile stretch
of tracks was now the responsibility of Lytle's recon
company, with Farris's platoon having its own section
to patrol.

Farris initially thought he'd exercise his prerogatives as an officer and ride in a jeep while others actually walked the tracks in the hot sun, but two things changed his mind. First, the tracks did not run parallel to most roads, which meant that he would at times be a long ways from his men and, second, it didn't seem right that he would be in relative comfort while his men hiked. Sometimes he thought it was hell to have both a conscience and a sense of responsibility. But if he didn't, then he'd be just like his prick of a company commander.

Stecher was back at camp with one squad, while the third patrolled the beaches. Another reason for taking a hands-on approach was the fact that this squad's leader, Sergeant Adamski, was a tall raw-boned kid from Chicago who'd recently gotten his third stripe. Farris wanted to see how the young buck sergeant operated with a number of men, many of whom were older than he was. So far, so good, he thought. Nobody seemed to be taking advantage of the young sergeant.

Farris let Adamski take the lead while he brought up the rear. It was a pleasant though warm day and the scenery was pretty. As tail end, he could dawdle and enjoy the view as well as observe his men. The sun was shining brightly, so the mountains in the distance could be seen clearly. One of these days he thought he'd like to go hiking or camping up one of them. The only times he'd slept in a tent were while bivouacking during basic and OCS, and that hadn't been fun at all. He'd only fished a couple of times in his life and thought he might like to try that as well. Then he thought that cleaning and cooking fish might be a little more than he wished to take on.

Farris also thought it would be nice to camp out with a real live girl and maybe both get naked in a sleeping bag. Maybe she would even clean and cook the fish he would catch. Damn, it had been a long time since he'd even talked to an attractive and single young woman. He thought it funny that the enlisted men were certain that young officers like him got all the women they could handle.

Sure. The army was sexless and monastic, and he was in command of forty horny young guys, including himself. He'd heard that there were whores in town and really cheap hookers down across the border in Tijuana, but there was no way he was going to take a chance on getting the clap and fucking up his life. He laughed at his pun and wondered if he'd be young enough to start a family when the war finally ended. If the pressure got too bad, he could always resort to Rosie Palm or Mother Five-fingers if he had to, but it hadn't gotten that bad yet. Jesus, what if he ever got caught playing with himself? A couple kids had gotten caught and became objects of scorn and ridicule.

"Lieutenant! Come quick!"

Adamski was standing over the tracks and the rest of his men had scattered. Farris ran up and looked down on the tracks.

"Oh, shit," Farris said. "Is that what I think it is?"

A small device sat over the rail and it was connected to a box underneath. If it wasn't a bomb, it would do until a real one came along. He checked his watch. According to the schedule he'd gotten, a large freight train was due to pass by in less than an hour.

He sent the sergeant and a couple of men up the tracks to try and wave down the train if they had to.

He radioed the captain and was told he was unavailable, which meant he was too drunk to answer the call.

"Damn it," he muttered as he fumbled for a piece of paper he'd been given by his Uncle Tim. A phone number had been written on it, and Farris had one of his brighter troops climb a telephone pole and tap into a line. He called and an FBI agent named Harris responded and said he'd get the train stopped and would be there as quickly as possible.

Harris said that Steve should not touch the device. "Don't you worry," Farris said.

The soldier up the telephone pole called out and pointed. A dark-colored Ford station wagon was pulling into a dirt road a mile or so away, and it looked like one of those with wooden paneling.

An hour later, Harris drove up in a civilian car and showed his credentials. A few moments later, a navy sedan arrived and Dane emerged.

"Glad you called me right away instead of trying to get through channels," Harris said.

Farris smiled. "Channels were sort of interrupted."

Harris nodded. "I understand. Your CO's an asshole. Your uncle said you were smart and he was right. You did the correct thing."

"We'll take care of Lytle later," Dane said, acknowledging that it was touchy for a navy officer to complain about an army equivalent.

A couple of army trucks arrived and half a dozen men climbed down. Harris explained that they were ordnance experts who were skilled in demolitions. Hopefully, they could disarm the bomb, if it was a bomb.

"On the off chance they can't and something bad

happens," Harris said, "let's say we get a few hundred yards away where we can't be hurt if it goes off. Of course, the bomb disposal guys would be fucked, but that's life."

When the three of them were at a safe distance, Harris asked if anybody had seen anything and was told about the dark-colored Ford wagon. Harris nodded. "One of the witnesses at the first explosion said he thought he saw a black Ford station wagon along with a small group of other vehicles, but that doesn't prove a damn thing. One sighting means nothing, two could be a coincidence, but three or more is a pattern. I just hope we end this before there are many more sightings."

"All clear," yelled one of the ordnance men, who put an object down and stepped away. He'd been told to leave any evidence as close as possible to where it had originally been.

Another car with two more FBI agents arrived and began interviewing Farris's soldiers. Farris, Dane, and Harris walked over to the dismembered bomb.

"Nothing much at all," Harris said on examining the device. "A couple of sticks of TNT and an impact detonator. It's just like the last time. We'll check for prints, but I'll bet you a dollar, gentlemen, that we won't find a thing. Even if we did it's a snowball's chance in hell that we'd be able to connect them with anyone."

"Can we trace the dynamite?" Dane asked. "At least this time the sticks are intact."

Harris shook his head. "No unique markings on the sticks, and there's got to be a couple of hundred construction companies, mining enterprises and such around here who are supplied by a score of businesses legitimately selling explosives. They could have been bought anywhere, or even stolen."

"At least he didn't cause any damage," Farris said hopefully.

Dane laughed. "Didn't he? This is a single line track, which means trains come and go both ways all according to an elaborate dance so nobody runs into someone else. Now that schedule is all fucked up and it'll be some time before it gets straightened out. Yeah, you're right in that nobody got killed or injured, but the saboteur is still messing with the war effort. And who knows what might happen the next time. We got lucky that your man spotted it. If the saboteur had put it down at night, who knows what might have happened."

"Worse," Harris added, "there's no way we can keep this quiet. Just too many people know about it now. We can and will try to keep it out of the newspapers, but rumors will be all over Southern California and people are going to think twice before they go on a train or drive over a bridge."

"What do we do now?" Farris asked.

Dane smiled and slapped his nephew on the shoulder. "Well, you get to keep walking up and down train tracks while Agent Harris and I get a bite to eat."

Wilhelm Braun was even more frustrated than usual. Another attempt to derail a train had gone awry. Even with the help of the skilled and physically powerful Gunther Krause he was accomplishing nothing. He'd tried to blow up a couple of vehicle bridges and underestimated the amount of dynamite it would take. He had a goodly supply of explosives, but it would

not last forever. Braun was not confident he would
be able to buy any more locally. Logic told him that
merchants had been warned to be on the lookout
for anyone buying dynamite, especially someone with
an accent, and to report it to the police or FBI. He
would live with what he had.

So far, the best that had happened after destroying that first freight train was that he'd caused some
traffic tie-ups and delayed a few other trains.

It was not what he or Berlin had in mind. To
complicate matters, he had just received a coded
message that he was to concentrate on finding out
the location of the American naval squadron that
included the carrier *Saratoga*. He snorted and took a
swallow of his beer. The Americans made miserable
beer. The only thing this bottle of something brewed
in California had going for it was the fact that it was
cold. Mexican beer was even worse. A friend in the
Mexico City embassy had described it as cold horse
piss and, even though he had never tried horse piss,
he thought the description was likely apt. To make
matters even worse, the alcohol content was low.

"What now?" asked Krause.

"Where would you look for an aircraft carrier?"

"Why, in the ocean, sir," he said cheekily, forgetting
the fact that they were to use first names.

"Krause, when we get back to Germany I will have
you broken to the rank of private."

The sergeant took his own beer from the old refrig-
erator, popped the bottle top, and took a swallow. He
shook his head and grimaced. "At least it's cold," he
said, and Braun chuckled.

"Seriously," Krause continued, "do you think we

will ever get back to the Reich? There's a huge ocean between us and Europe and a number of belligerent nations who'd like nothing better than to kill us. And what the devil are we doing playing at helping the fucking slanty-eyed Japs? They should be waiting on tables for us at best, or even going to camps like we are sending the fucking Jews."

Braun couldn't argue with him. He'd tried so many times to rationalize the point that helping the Japs helped Germany, but he had done so little to help the Japs it was sad.

"What are you suggesting?" Braun asked.

"I suggest we lie low for a while, unless some target of opportunity pops up and is irresistibly tempting. The Americans are doubtless checking mail and monitoring phone calls, so that leaves our radio, which, if we use it too often, will enable the enemy to triangulate and find us."

"We could, of course, move the radio," Braun said thoughtfully.

"Excellent to a point, but every time we'd dismantle it we'd be running the risk of damaging it, or, worse, being stopped by the police for any reason. A simple speeding ticket or a small accident and we would be found out. How would we explain the existence of a shortwave radio in our truck?"

Krause was right, of course. He was smart and more than a thug, which was why Braun had wanted him as the second man on his two-man team. Despite the disparity in their ranks, their long relationship went beyond simple respect.

"Krause, have you heard anything about the *Saratoga* in your wanderings through San Diego's bars?"

Krause laughed. "I wouldn't dream of bringing up the topic, but every now and then somebody wonders where she is and when she'll be coming back, but nobody seems to know."

In his own wanderings and listenings, Braun had picked up pretty much the same thing. One rumor that kept repeating itself was that the top brass had told the admiral in charge of the *Saratoga* and her escorts to get lost and not tell anyone in the Pacific Fleet where they were or what their plans were. That, of course, killed any idea of ferreting out the carrier's location.

Nor could he and Krause get any help locally. They were swimming alone in a hostile sea. They had to maintain the facade of Swenson Engineering, which meant they periodically had to drive the truck or station wagon to fictitious work sites, lest the neighbors get suspicious and call the police.

Braun took a long swallow of the cold horse piss and weak beer. "What we will do is quite simple. We will continue to send reports saying how hard we are working and what difficulties we are encountering. In the meantime, we will continue to look for targets to destroy, along with anything new that comes up. I am not quite ready to write this off as a useless venture, no matter how frustrating it might be."

Ruby Oliver thought that Colonel James Gavin was the handsomest man she'd ever seen. The rugged-looking thirty-five-year-old commander of the 505th Parachute Infantry Regiment had arrived at Fairbanks a couple of days earlier along with the leading elements of his regiment and immediately made his presence known.

The first units of the 505th had parachuted in, which was dramatic and joyous to the Americans in Fairbanks. They'd waved and cheered as the paratroops floated down from the sky. Ruby and her group had arrived the day before by truck. She would not admit that they'd stolen it from an abandoned farm.

On first meeting her, Gavin had laughed and stripped her of her own little detachment of soldiers, but not until commending all of them for jobs well done. They had been interrogated by both Gavin and other officers. They told all they knew about the Japanese force that even now might be heading toward them. Ruby was able to confirm that the Japanese had no armor, little artillery, and few vehicles. They were not going to come up the road at thirty miles an hour like she had. Ten miles a day was more like it and she assured Gavin that the weather would begin to get truly shitty before long.

Now she was part of a volunteer group led by a big professional hunter and trapper named Bear Foley. Bear was well named. Although he was only a little over six feet tall, he weighed more than two hundred and forty pounds and he was indeed hairy. Foley now had close to four hundred men and fifty women in his volunteer brigade that Gavin chose to use as scouts. They'd already picked up on the fact that the Japanese were beginning to probe up the road to Fairbanks, which was why Gavin was there with his new command.

The lead elements of the 505th quickly improved the small and primitive airstrip to where C47s could land with their cargo of either twenty-plus troops or three tons of supplies. Both men and supplies were kept below maximum load weight because of the need to conserve fuel. Ruby and her cohorts noted with amusement that many of the military planes were painted over civilian DC-3s, and some still had passenger seating.

What was maddening was the time it took to develop a base so far away from the forty-eight states. The first planes unloaded fuel, much of which they promptly consumed for the trip back. After that, planes alternated between men, fuel, and supplies. Now, after a couple of hectic days and nights, more than two thousand men of the 505th were on the ground along with several hundred support personnel and a working supply of fuel and food. Talking to the troops, Ruby found that the regiment was someday going to be part of the newly forming 82nd Airborne Division and be entirely made up of paratroops.

Gavin was openly concerned about their lack of ammunition and artillery. The Alaskan Volunteer Scouts and other sources estimated the Japanese force at close to six thousand men now that it had been "reinforced" by the few survivors of the naval force the battleships had sunk.

Ruby sat on her sleeping bag in the tent she shared with Foley. He was a couple of years older than she and they'd hit it off immediately. He was a skilled hunter, something she admired since she thought she was pretty good herself. She was dressed in bra and panties and was intent on sewing a tear in her blouse.

"Looking good, Ruby," Bear said with a grin as he stepped in.

She returned the smile. She'd lost twenty pounds and firmed up dramatically since the first Japanese attack. One thing good about war—it kept the weight down. Her dyed red hair was returning to its normal reddish-brown with disconcerting hints of gray that Bear didn't seem to mind.

War also heightened the senses. She hadn't slept with a man in more than a year, but now the urge was imperative.

"Join me," she said. He laughed again and stripped down to his shorts after first closing the tent flap. He reached for her and she held up her hand.

"First tell me what Jim said."

Bear laughed. "Jim? Damn it to hell, Ruby, he makes me call him Colonel. Anyhow, he said that the Japs will be heading for us because they have no place else to go. He says they're starving since their support ships were sunk and they see Fairbanks as a way of staying alive. He says they'll attack us with unbelievable ferocity because getting our supplies is their only hope of not starving to death. He says they would rather die in a suicide attack, not starve, which they feel would be cowardly. Gavin said he was stationed in the Philippines and helped them prepare for war with the Japs, so he's studied them extensively. So, yeah, he sees a suicide attack by the Nips if things get real bad for them."

Wonderful, she thought. She slipped out of her bra and panties and he got out of his shorts. She smiled when she saw he was more than ready. We could all be dead very, very shortly. Live and love while we can.

Beer runs qualified as emergencies, or so Stecher happily thought. Using rank for the privilege, he commandeered a jeep and drove the few miles to the hamlet of Bridger. Neither he nor Lieutenant Farris thought much of anything was likely to happen at nine o'clock this sunny Tuesday morning. As to their beloved company commander, it was highly improbable that Lytle was even awake, much less likely to stop by on an unannounced inspection. And who gave a shit if he did, he thought happily.

There had been a euchre tournament last night, and the men off duty had managed to wipe out their supply of suds; thus, the beer run to Sullivan's small store in Bridger. Usually the lieutenant did it, but he was off someplace.

Stecher thought that life was not bad at all. He'd begun to get control over his fury regarding the loss of his brother. He recognized the helplessness of his situation. Until and if something changed dramatically, he would continue to spend World War II in southern California. And after talking to some navy pilots, he'd grudgingly come to accept the fact that soldiers on the ground were fair targets for pilots in planes. The enemy you spared today could come back and kill you tomorrow. What had happened to his brother was war, not murder.

He'd talked with a number of others who'd lost loved ones in the all too numerous defeats suffered by the United States. They'd commiserated, had a beer or six, and told how they controlled their anguish and sealed off their hate. If they didn't it would consume them. Stecher would never get over the loss of his brother and would never want to, but he was beginning to understand what older people had said about life moving on after the death of someone dear. Someday, though, he would like his chance to personally kill at least one fucking Jap.

He pulled up in front of the single-story white frame store owned by Sullivan. He'd recently found out that Sullivan's first name was Patrick. What else, he thought.

Stecher entered the store. No one was behind the counter, which was unusual. There was no way he could have sneaked up on Sullivan. There wasn't that much else around in Bridger and anyone in the store had a clear view down the road, so somebody should have been there to greet him. Maybe Sullivan was in the can? He waited a few moments but heard nothing. He tapped on the wall by the door to announce himself, but still no one came. Should he help himself? Sullivan's was an old-fashioned store where you told the clerk what you wanted and he got it for you. None of that supermarket stuff where you wandered around with a cart and filled it. Sullivan said there was too much opportunity to steal in such a situation.

So where was everybody? What the hell's going on, Stecher thought. He heard the sound of something scurrying in the storage room in the back of the building. An animal? His rifle was in jeep only a few feet away. Should he get it? Hell, would he need it?

He heard a groan. He stepped around the counter and pushed open the door to the back room. There were no windows and it was illuminated only by the shaft of light from the open door. He heard more sounds.

Stecher fumbled by the doorway until he found a light switch and flipped it on. Two women were on the floor. They were bound hand and foot and there were rags stuffed in their mouths. They were Japanese.

One was older and her face was bruised. There was blood on her torn blouse. The younger one stared at him in primal fear. She did not appear be hurt and she looked very young, maybe fourteen.

Japs or not, they were suffering. He took the gags out of their mouths and gave them some water. He was not quite ready to untie them before he found out why they had been bound in the first place, although he didn't think they were spies or saboteurs.

Stecher heard a metallic click behind him. "Stand and turn slowly."

He did as told and found himself looking down the barrels of a shotgun held by Patrick Sullivan, the store owner.

The older woman jabbered something in what Stecher presumed was Japanese and Sullivan lowered his weapon. "Miko just told me you had nothing to do with this and were freeing them."

Sullivan pulled a knife and deftly slashed the ropes holding them. Both women hugged each other and then Sullivan. The older woman, Miko, managed a smile for Stecher, while the younger one looked away. She seemed more embarrassed than hurt.

"It was two very young men who looked like Mexicans," Miko said in unaccented English. "They came in and overpowered us before we could do anything. Thank you for helping," she added to Stecher, who nodded.

She turned to Sullivan. "And just so you know, they did nothing other than take the few dollars in the register."

Miko gathered up the younger woman. "Sergeant, this is my daughter, Nancy. Until the war started, she was a sophomore in college in San Francisco. We decided she was safer here."

So much for being only fourteen, Stecher thought.

Maybe Asian women matured differently. She also didn't look totally Japanese. With a jolt, he realized that Sullivan was her father.

"So what are you going to do now?" Sullivan asked. "You going to turn them in and send them to a concentration camp?"

"I don't know what the hell do to, Mr. Sullivan. Hey, they are your family, aren't they? If so, they won't be sent to a camp. Isn't that the rule?"

Sullivan shrugged. "Nancy is my daughter and Miko is my wife. One problem, though, we never managed to get married formally. This is California, you know, and some of the traditional rules don't always apply here. Both of these ladies were born here in California, which makes them citizens, and Nancy is only half-Japanese, so I guess only half of her will go to a camp."

Stecher was at a loss. Technically, maybe the mother should be interned since she was hiding, which was against the law, and Sullivan was doing the hiding, which was also illegal. Damn. He hated the Japanese, but the rational part of him said that neither this woman nor her skinny daughter posed a threat to the United States. And would turning them in to the authorities do anything to help America win the war?

"So what are you going to do, Sergeant?" asked Sullivan. Stecher noted that the shotgun was still in the crook of his arm.

"Mr. Sullivan, I'm going to do what I set out to do in the first place and that's get me a couple of cases of beer. What you do with your life is your own problem."

✳ ✳ ▌✳

Emotions were running high. Everyone in Nimitz's offices was sickened, angered, and disgusted by the photos and films that had finally made it down to them from the brave men in Alaska who'd taken them. Men cursed and pounded their fists and a few men cried in frustration as they saw American soldiers and airmen being shot, drowned, and beheaded.

Dane had a hard time not being nauseated when the surviving crewmen of the PBY were chopped with the sword swung by the Jap officer. He'd known a couple of those guys. Granted, he had just met them before the takeoff and only shook their hands and wished them well, but he was part of the reason they were being murdered before his eyes. It had been his lamebrained idea to launch an attack by relatively defenseless flying boats in the first place that had led to their being shot down and captured. But for him, they'd still be flying long, dull, safe patrols over the endless Pacific.

Spruance, still functioning as Nimitz's chief of staff, might have been reading Dane's mind. "What happened to those men is nobody's fault but the Japanese and, to a lesser extent, mine. I see Commander Dane looking miserable because he thinks he's responsible, but he isn't. I totally and enthusiastically supported the idea of the PBY raid, and I thought we would take even more casualties than we did. What I didn't expect was that the Japs would kill those men in contravention of the Geneva Convention."

The admiral took a sip of coffee. "Admittedly, the Japs never signed it and neither did we, but that does not permit them, or us, to behave like barbarians. When the war is over, or if they are captured, the men responsible will be brought to trial."

"Can we behead them?" snarled Merchant.

"A lovely thought," Spruance responded with a grim smile. "However, I don't think that'll be allowed under our rules. Hanging or a firing squad are our traditions. First, of course, we have to capture those people. We have been reasonably assured that none of the actual killings were done by their commander, this Colonel Yamasaki. That doesn't absolve him. He's responsible for the conduct of his men, just like General Homma is responsible for the Bataan Death March in the Philippines, and Hirohito's responsible for the sneak attack on Pearl Harbor. When the time comes, those men will pay."

"I don't think they would have done it without Yamasaki's approval, sir," said Dane. "He might not have given direct orders, but I'm certain his men knew that he approved, at least tacitly."

Merchant was still angry. "May I register my disapproval with the decision to withhold the photos from publication?"

"Duly noted," Spruance said. "However, nothing's going to change. The public is inflamed enough right now. The pictures will be saved for the proper time, and that may be a long ways off in the future. Word is, the president is concerned that families will recognize their loved ones being murdered and, even though they are aware that they were killed in action, it would serve no purpose to show them in the act of being slaughtered."

Dane silently agreed. How would his father and mother feel if they went to the movies and the newsreels showed their only son being sliced to bloody pieces by a crazy Jap with a sword? The military had been quite strict so far—no pictures of American dead had been released, except for a couple taken at Pearl Harbor. Of course, everyone knew that the ships at Pearl, especially the *Arizona*, were tombs containing many dead.

Merchant shook his head. "It just doesn't seem fair, Admiral. Those guys risked their lives taking those pictures and we're going to sit on them?"

"Life isn't fair, Captain, and you know that."

Dane interrupted. "Sir, how many know about these pictures?"

"Only a few have actually seen them and after we're done, they get locked up, so let's pass them back." There was a shuffling of papers as the men complied. "Let the rumors flow, and don't deny their existence, but they won't be released without permission from Washington."

Disgruntled and still dissatisfied, Dane and Merchant went back to their desks. Dane had gotten some uncoded Japanese radio broadcasts from the night before that had been recorded. He would listen to them and try to make an intelligent observation about the state of mind of the people in and around Tokyo. In his opinion, it was an exercise in futility, although it was intriguing the way the Japanese propagandists were still portraying the American attack on the Japanese squadron at Anchorage as a victory for their side. Also, they hadn't admitted a thing regarding the two carriers that had been damaged after the attack on San Francisco, although a number of American pilots had confirmed that the ships been hit and were burning.

Well, Dane thought grimly, I don't suppose we'd admit to losing any ships either, unless we had to.

He wondered if there were photos of the Japanese carriers burning and if they would be released or locked up for a future date. He made a mental note to ask Merchant.

A young seaman first class came up to his desk. He didn't salute or come to attention. There were far too many officers around for that kind of military formality. As Spruance had said with a smile, "Making an enlisted man salute every time he spoke to an officer in this place would mean the poor man would have no time for his work."

"Commander, I don't know how they got on post," the sailor said, "but there are some civilian-type people outside the building asking for you."

Dane was puzzled. Just about everyone he knew was within a few feet of him. "Any idea who?"

"No, sir, I was just asked to come and get you."

Dane got up, told Merchant where he was going, and followed the sailor to the lobby of the building that had once belonged to a civilian contractor.

When he entered the lobby, two women approached him. One was a short-haired blonde in her mid-thirties with the kind of full figure that Captain Merchant always said he loved. The second was a short young brunette with equally short hair. He wondered if this was a new style. Both of them had terrible sunburns.

"Lieutenant Tim Dane?" asked the blonde.

"It's lieutenant commander, but that's not important, and yes, I am Tim Dane."

"Well, I am Grace and this is Sandy, and we just wanted to check you out and make sure you were worth the trip. What do you think, Sandy?"

Sandy shrugged and walked around him, examining

him quizzically. "He looks reasonably human, but I don't know if he's really the right person. Tell me, Lieutenant Commander But-that's-not-important, are you a good guy?"

Dane had to laugh, even though he was puzzled. "I hope so."

"You got yourself a girlfriend here?" asked Grace, who was clearly enjoying herself.

"Maybe. I got a letter from her a few days ago, but nothing since. I'm not even sure she's my girlfriend although I'd sure as hell like her to be, and why am I telling you all of this since I don't even know you?"

Then it hit him. Sandy and Grace were the women Amanda had mentioned in her letter. "Oh, Jesus, where's Amanda?"

Grace smiled warmly and Sandy giggled. "Right outside that door," Grace said.

Tim nearly knocked over two startled ensigns as he raced outside. She was standing a few feet away, just by the curb. She was wearing a short-sleeved white blouse and a flowered skirt that came to her knees. Her hair was as short as that of her friends and she was thinner than he remembered, but she was even lovelier. She smiled and he saw the two crooked teeth. Her skin was red and blotched, just like the other two women. They paused for a second and embraced. They didn't kiss, just held each other tightly and swayed gently.

Grace and Sandy followed him outside. "I really think they do remember each other," said Grace. Sandy, who was crying softly, silently agreed.

CHAPTER 13

TIM AND AMANDA SAT AS CLOSE TO EACH OTHER
as they could on a park bench across the street from
where they'd reunited. Their hips and thighs were
pressed against each other and their hands were
grasped tightly. Neither knew quite what to say and
neither wanted to spoil the moment.

Finally, Tim took a deep breath and spoke. "I was
so worried. I had no idea if you were still in Hawaii,
or out in that sailboat you spoke about, or even on one
of those ships that had been sunk by Japanese planes."

She squeezed his hand even tighter and told him of
their voyage across the Pacific in Mack's catamaran. She
told him of Mack's death from the rogue wave, her own
fears that they'd made the wrong decision and that they
would die lonely and painful deaths. She then added
that she wasn't supposed to tell anyone lest people in
Hawaii find out and try the same thing. Tim said his
lips were sealed.

"It was almost a miracle when we washed up near

San Francisco. Another day or two at the most and we'd all have been too weak to sail the cat. I had scurvy, a touch of dysentery, and had managed to lose twenty pounds that I didn't know I had in the first place. We would have come down here sooner, but we had to gather our strength, learn how to eat again, get some clothes, and, of course, identification and ration cards."

She held out her bare arms. For the first time, he noticed that they were red and raw, and that dry skin was flaking off them. Her thin legs were in the same condition.

"It took a couple of days and a gallon of salves to get the sunburn down to where we could even stand the feel of cloth against our skins."

A few people walking by glanced at them and a couple of enlisted men grinned. None of them saluted. Amanda touched Tim's cheek. "We've been out of touch for so long and I was worried that you hadn't made it yourself."

"One of the subs didn't. We were attacked but got away."

"At least you were safe here in San Diego after that."

Dane laughed. "Did you hear about the bomber raid on the Japs at Anchorage and the battleships hitting them a while later?"

"Of course. While we were convalescing, we spent a lot of time reading old newspapers and magazines and, oh God, you weren't involved in them, were you?"

Tim told her he was and she shook her head. "I don't believe it. Here I was so happy thinking you were safe and sound in San Diego, assuming you'd made it, of course. Please promise me you won't do anything foolish like that again."

"Sometimes it's not my call. By the way, you made the right move in leaving Hawaii. The Japs have landed on the big island and set up a base by Hilo where they're out of reach of the army garrison on Oahu. Much worse is the fact that the population of the islands are on near-starvation rations. They're subsisting on fish and whatever they can grow, which isn't much. Someday we'll send in a relief fleet, but not for a while. If you have any friends there, and I'm sure you do, they are having a pretty rough time and it's not going to get better."

She wiped away a tear. "There aren't any right decisions, are there? If we hadn't sailed, Mack might still be alive although we'd probably be just as hungry as we were the last week or so on the boat, and we'd be terrified that the Japs would invade and take even that away."

They were silent for a moment. Tim took a deep breath. "Amanda, where do we go from here?"

She smiled, "Just what I was thinking, too. Where would you wish to go, and don't suggest an apartment? First of all, I don't know you that well and, second, the three of us are bunking in a Quonset hut with a dozen other nurses. Seriously, my Great Dane, I would like for us to move slowly, get to know each other a whole lot better, and see where the world takes us."

Tim took a deep breath. He was thrilled and happy beyond words that she was safe and by his side, but were they ready to make a commitment based on a couple of hours together? Wartime romances had a tendency to be intense and quickly consummated and often just as suddenly dissolved. No. However much he liked her and desired her, they would take it slowly.

"Sounds great to me. Just so you know how luxuriously I have it, I live in a two-man room in a miserable barracks that's been designated as Bachelor Officers' Quarters. The walls are so thin maybe a hundred men can hear each other snore."

Amanda nodded and smiled warmly. "That's probably just as well. When the time for privacy arrives, I'm sure we'll work it out. Now, who is that navy captain talking to Grace and is he trying to pick her up?"

Tim laughed. "That's my boss, Bill Merchant. He's an Annapolis guy and pretty decent."

"Is he married? I wouldn't want Gracie to meet up with the wrong sort, even though I kind of think she can take care of herself."

"Bill was married, but he got a Dear John letter a few weeks ago. His wife left him for a guy who works as a supervisor in the post office. He got her pregnant, so she's divorcing Bill and going to marry the guy. He took it pretty hard for a bit, but looking at the way he's staring at your friend, he may be recovering."

Amanda stood and straightened her skirt. "Do you have any money?"

"Uh, a little. What do you have in mind?"

"I'm meeting you here at six and you're taking me out to dinner."

"Great. What would you like?"

"A great big thick and juicy steak cooked rare, thank you. I will eat it very slowly and have a glass of nice red California wine to go with it. Maybe two glasses if you promise not to take advantage of poor helpless little old me."

"Anybody who sailed across the Pacific is far from helpless. But will I get to kiss you?"

"Plan on it, Commander, but just not on a park bench in front of half the fleet."

Tim laughed. "Do I get to call you Mandy now, or should I stick with Amanda?"

"Amanda, always Amanda. Call me Mandy and you'll suffer the excruciating pain I told you about in Honolulu a thousand years ago."

Tim gestured to where Sandy and Grace were still talking to Merchant. "What about your good buddies?"

Amanda smiled sweetly and again patted his cheek. "Tim, I didn't come all this way to find you so I can share you."

Farris couldn't sleep, so he decided to walk his platoon's small perimeter. His little kingdom had been enlarged by the addition of a pair of 81mm mortars and another squad of soldiers to man them. They'd first been assigned to Lytle's headquarters platoon, but he decided he didn't want them around. Farris thought they probably looked too military for Lytle's taste, or maybe they interfered with the decor provided by his seemingly endless rows of painted rocks.

Regardless, Farris had the mortars set up so they could fire out over the ocean, logically concluding that any attack would come from the sea and not from the land behind. He'd gotten a few dummy rounds and watched as the men operating the mortar attacked the Pacific. The mortars had a range of a little more than two miles. No one was manning them now, in the middle of the night. Only sentries and guards were awake and he was pleased to see that they were reasonably alert.

He'd gotten a phone call from his uncle with the

good news that his girlfriend had made it from Hawaii to San Diego after all. He was amused at the thought of bachelor Tim Dane having a girlfriend and that he'd found her in the middle of a war. How the hell had he managed that? Damn, maybe it was true that sailors had all the luck. Once again he wondered if he was in the wrong service. He sure was having a fine time staring at the seals and sea otters, who, he was sure, were laughing at him.

He had a thought and it made him smile. Clever Steve Farris would invite Tim and his girl for a picnic or cookout and maybe this Amanda had a young woman friend of her own she could bring along. It would help if Amanda's friend was cute, but, lord, it wasn't all that necessary. All he wanted was a chance to talk with a real live girl and maybe wind up going a little farther than just talking. Maybe a lot farther. Excellent thought, he decided. Perhaps the world wasn't such a bleak and lonely place after all.

Steve was still mildly concerned about how well Stecher had taken the existence of Sullivan's wife and daughter. The sergeant was a little annoyed when he realized that Farris had known about them for quite a while, and had even chatted with them. Stecher finally admitted that the two women weren't a threat to national security and would forget he ever saw them.

A sudden flash of light off the coast was quickly followed by the bark of what could only be a ship's cannon. An explosion erupted down the coast near Lytle's headquarters. The gun from the ocean fired again a few seconds later and commenced firing more rapidly, with shells pulverizing the tents and the damned white-washed rocks that beckoned like a beacon.

Steve's platoon was stumbling in the dark as the alarm was sounded. Again he thanked his decision to place his men behind the low hill. Lytle's position was getting creamed while his was invisible.

Stecher plopped down beside him as they looked over the hill. "Can you see anything, sir?"

Both men had binoculars. The ship fired again and for the briefest of instants, they saw it was a submarine.

"Damn it, Lieutenant, he's killing our guys."

Farris forced himself to stay calm. This was like the sinking of the tanker. Maybe it was the same damned sub. It had to be. This spot was just too innocuous to attract random attention, however foolish Lytle had been.

"What's the range to the sub?" Farris snapped.

Stecher swore and said that he wasn't certain and couldn't tell all that well in the dark. He asked the men who were standing by the mortars and was told maybe two miles. Farris nodded. They reminded Farris that two miles was about it for an 81mm mortar.

"Shoot at the damn thing," he ordered. "We won't likely hit it, but maybe we'll scare him off or at least distract the bastard."

Seconds later, mortar rounds went arching toward the dimly seen outline of the Japanese sub. Shells splashed well away from her, and short. The mortar men made corrections and the next salvo landed much closer, but the sub was still not in range.

"That's about as close as we can get, Lieutenant," said the corporal in charge.

A searchlight arced out from the shore and now they could see the enemy boat. The deck gun fired again and another explosion chewed up the American base.

"We need more range," Farris shouted. He took a sandbag and shoved it under one side of the base plate. This would lower the angle and maybe increase the range.

The mortar fired again and the shell landed over the sub. They were within range. The second mortar was similarly fixed and Farris gave the order to fire at will.

The corporal grimaced. "Just so you know, sir, we've only got twenty shells apiece. They'll all be gone in a couple of minutes."

"No point saving them, is there?" Farris said harshly. The corporal agreed.

The sub located its tormenters and the deck gun fired toward them, the shell exploding just inside the beach line. Farris realized it would take a miracle to hit the sub.

But miracles do happen and one of the last rounds they fired slammed into the conning tower. The explosion threw one of the deck gunners into the ocean and Farris's gunners cheered their unlikely achievement. The sub's skipper had had enough. She turned and headed out to sea but, curiously, wasn't attempting to dive. Was the water too shallow or—Sweet Jesus, he thought—had they actually done some damage to the bastard?

A moment later, a dark shape flew low over Farris's position. Machine-gun bullets and rockets streaked over the water to where they could still see the dark shape of the fleeing Japanese sub. They cheered as a second and a third plane raced in for the kill. The sub was doomed. She had to be too hurt to dive. The planes were shredding her hull with rockets. A bomb landed in the water near her. Then, suddenly, she rolled over on her side and bobbed lifelessly.

Farris shook himself. It was over. He was shaking and drenched with sweat. He checked his watch. The fight had lasted less than ten minutes. "Stecher, you stay here. I'm going to see what happened at HQ."

He grabbed a jeep and raced over. By the time he got there, the fires were out and medics were treating the wounded, who were laid out on the ground. Some of the wounds were horrible and a few men were missing limbs. A trio of ambulances pulled up and men hopped out and started putting the wounded on stretchers. A couple of the wounded were moaning and one man screamed until some hastily injected morphine took over. A row of blanket-covered bodies lay a few yards away.

He found a wounded Lieutenant Sawyer trying to direct things. Sawyer's head and left arm were wrapped in bandages. Sawyer looked grateful to see Steve arrive.

"How bad are things?" Farris asked.

"Six dead and fourteen wounded. One of the dead is Captain Lytle. I think he caught a Jap shell with his chest. Jesus, what a mess. You were right. He should never have built here."

Steve agreed quietly. There was no changing what had been done. Lytle had paid with his life for his stupidity, and killed five others. More than a dozen men were wounded thanks to him. It was a helluva mess.

Sawyer sat down on a white rock. "You okay?" Farris asked, wondering if the young lieutenant counted himself as one of the fourteen wounded.

"I'll be fine. It's just starting to sink in, that's all. These wounds are bloody cuts, nothing serious. Medic says I won't even get stitches to go with my Purple

Heart. By the way, Steve, you realize you're the senior lieutenant. That means you command this fucked-up company until somebody else is assigned."

"Aw, shit," Steve said and sat down on a rock beside him. Sawyer was correct. If by only a few weeks, he was the senior lieutenant. And as to somebody else being assigned, that could take quite a while.

"So what are you going to do?"

Farris smiled grimly. "Act like I belong, I guess. First, we continue to take care of the wounded, then we arrange to bury the dead. I guess the Thirty-Second Infantry has a cemetery, but I have to admit I never gave it a thought. And right after that, I want what remains of the headquarters moved to a much better, less obvious spot. We will not repeat Lytle's mistake."

Sixth Fleet headquarters was in a state of confusion as frantic reports flowed in. So far, at least twenty attacks on American towns and military bases along the coast of California had been reported.

Once again, Japanese cruisers, destroyers, and submarines had darted in, fired a number of shells at mainly civilian targets and raced away into the night, leaving hundreds dead and wounded and multitudes of fires burning up and down the Pacific shore. The coast of California was in panic and there were reports of several large-scale exoduses from the coastal cities. It appeared that several hundred thousand people were moving inland. Where the people would go, nobody seemed to know.

It was another reminder of what skillful warriors the Japanese were. At least no battleships or carriers had been involved. These were pinprick raids, although the towns and cities hit were in an understandable state of panic. Dane could just visualize the recriminations, the newspaper headlines, and the angry citizens. Where's the navy? Where's the army? Didn't we have some planes? What the hell are our tax dollars going for?

Just as important, everyone wanted to know just how the Japanese had managed to get at them with literally hundreds of American planes in the air at all time looking for them. Someone suggested that our patrol patterns had become predictable, which meant the enemy could time them and slip through unnoticed. Another suggestion was that the Jap ships were pretending to be American escorts shepherding dummy convoys.

However, the Japanese had not gotten away unscathed. At least three destroyers and one cruiser had been sunk, along with a pair of submarines. Sub kills were harder to confirm, but the one just off where Tim's nephew was stationed was definite. The smoking hulk was still somewhat afloat and experts were trying to tow the thing ashore where it could be examined. A numbers count showed that the Japs had lost the actual battle but won the public relations war.

A quick phone call had confirmed that Steve had indeed been involved in the fighting, but was safe and that he now commanded the company following the death of his CO.

Steve had then cheekily invited his uncle and Amanda over for a cookout on the condition that Amanda bring a friend for him. Tim sighed. Didn't Steve know there was a war on? He replied that he thought it would be a little while before things calmed down enough for him to take another day off. He didn't tell his nephew that he'd been meeting Amanda each evening, going for walks and dinner, although he was quickly running out of money.

As predicted, physical contact between them had been minimal. A few kisses were about it. The more he thought about it, the more Tim thought the idea of another cookout on the beach was a splendid idea. Maybe in a week or so things would calm down a little bit.

Wilhelm Braun cheered the news of the Japanese attacks and the subsequent panic that was causing thousands of civilians to head for the hills and perceived safety. However, he was convinced that in a few weeks the panic would wear off and most of the refugees would sheepishly return to their homes. After all, it wasn't as if the Japanese had won a great victory. They hadn't, but it was a slap in the face for the arrogant Americans, and Braun loved it.

He and Krause celebrated the news by getting a little drunk on some cheap American whisky bought in a shabby bar filled with sailors. They couldn't afford better. They were painfully aware that what had seemed like so much money a while back was proving inadequate for their current and future needs. Their communications with comrades in Mexico had become even more terse and infrequent. Braun and Krause were of the opinion that his superiors in Berlin were disappointed with their results so far, and that they were on their own, at least until they actually accomplished something.

Braun had begun to think that either getting jobs in a defense plant or actually doing something with

Swenson Engineering might become necessary. Working in a plant had its merits. They might have access to areas that might otherwise be restricted, which could put them in a position to cause damage.

That lovely thought was quickly crushed when they watched how packages, even mundane items like lunchboxes, were checked by guards admitting workers to their job sites.

They had discussed assassinating prominent Americans but found the ones they'd like to kill, like Nimitz or DeWitt, too well protected, while civilian targets like Governor Olson or his probable replacement, Earl Warren, were not important enough. The deaths of politicians would not affect the American war effort. There was also the uncomfortable truth that, in order to murder someone with a rifle, the killer had to be within two hundred yards of his target and even closer if he wanted to use a pistol. Using a gun meant a high chance of discovery, capture, and subsequent death, which neither man wanted. Nor could they figure out a way to get a bomb anywhere near a human target.

Reluctantly they considered robbery as a means of funding their operations, but that carried its own inherent dangers. They might be recognized, or they might leave clues that local and federal police might follow. They were soldiers, not professional criminals, and might easily make mistakes.

A final alternative was gradually becoming the most attractive, at least to Krause. They would do as much damage as they could with the resources that remained. When these ran out, they would simply abandon their base in San Diego and head into the American heartland where, they hoped, they could disappear, picking up new identities and living quietly until Germany won the war. Braun balked at the thought. He admitted it might someday become necessary, but was convinced that they still a duty to perform and orders to obey.

They returned to the apartment above the phony engineering company, pleased that they had made a decision.

Krause sat down heavily on a tattered overstuffed chair in their living room above the shop. "So, what will our target be this time?"

Braun smiled knowingly. "With the chaos caused by the Japanese bombardments, I believe the Americans will be looking outward, not inward. Thus, I am comfortable with another attempt on their trains. Perhaps this time we'll get lucky and hit one loaded with people. That will get their attention."

Krause nodded agreement and raised his arm in salute. "Heil Hitler," he said and then added sarcastically, "Heil Japan."

Braun shook his head. "Fuck Japan."

Farris and the other company commanders snapped to attention when the grim little major entered the room. They were in a small office in what had been their battalion's headquarters. Farris thought in the past tense because he'd heard rumors of big changes afoot.

The major nodded. "At ease and be seated, gentlemen. I am Major George Baylor and I'm fresh from the Thirty-Second Infantry. I will be this battalion's commanding officer. Major Harmer is being reassigned back east."

This was said with a half smirk. Harmer had been

a good buddy of Captain Lytle's all the way back in Pennsylvania. When Lytle didn't feel like drinking alone, he drank with Harmer. In the opinion of many in the unit, Lytle completely dominated the older Harmer. There were other rumors that Harmer owed Lytle money from back in civilian life. Farris felt that many complaints against their late and unlamented company commander were backstopped by his good buddy from back home. At least this Baylor character looked like an officer. Despite a lack of height, he looked fit and trim, and carried himself with what some called a command presence. Farris smiled to himself and wished he could do that. Maybe command presence was something that grew on you.

Baylor continued. "I'm sure you've heard rumors that the battalion is moving; well, they are correct. In a few days we will commence packing up and heading north. The powers that be have decided that the campaign in Alaska is moving in dangerously slow motion and needs to be goosed along. They are also seriously concerned that the Japs in Anchorage may be getting desperate and are going to attack what few troops we have in Fairbanks. They've already made a small move part of the way up the road in that direction."

Baylor paused to let his comment sink in. "Gentlemen, that means at least six thousand Japs are headed toward an American force that is much smaller and in large part consists of civilian volunteers, along with Negro construction troops. You may not be aware, but there are no roads to Alaska, although one is being built. The engineers have been told to cut out the niceties and just plow through the trees as fast as they can so a line of vehicles, or even troops on foot, can get through before winter shuts everything down. Also, there is no rail line up there, and sending troops by ship is an obvious no-no what with the Japs controlling the ocean. And while there is an airfield up there, it is small and jammed with planes bringing in supplies for the troops who are already there, along with other support personnel who can expand the little base.

"That means we go by truck as far as we can and then we walk. Maybe that will give us a chance to improve on our recon skills which I understand are nonexistent. That doesn't matter to the army. We are listed as recon and as recon we will go and as recon we will fight. Any question?"

Farris raised his hand. "Yeah, Major, when do we leave?"

"Two to three weeks, which will give you some time to get your men in shape and learn some basic combat skills."

"What about our current tasks, like patrolling the beaches and walking the tracks?" inquired another company commander.

"If you can work it into your training schedule, do it. Otherwise I don't think we can get too worked up about Japanese invaders. Saboteurs are another problem, and I'm not pleased that we're cutting back on those patrols. Try to find some way to combine the two if you can. Smaller patrols works well for me. Any further questions? Good. Go back and give your units the good word. Farris, stay here. I want to talk to you."

Steve waited impatiently while the other two company

commanders, both first lieutenants, walked out. One glanced at him with what looked like pity. When they were gone, Baylor invited him to sit down.

"You've done better than well, Lieutenant, which is why I'm keeping you on as commander of A Company. We'll get you a bump to first lieutenant to give you some credibility with the others, but I am impressed with the way you handled that burning tanker, and the shelling of Lytle's HQ. I've read your reports and memos. Lytle forwarded them on to the division, probably hoping we'd use them to replace you because he thought you were such a pain in the ass. Fact was, we were going to replace him. We knew he was an incompetent lush, but we had other more important things on our plate. Sadly, we didn't do it soon enough and good men died because of that decision.

"By the way, you were the only officer in the battalion who tried to do anything about this miserable state of affairs. All the others were quite happy to let things slide along. I will be riding a few people's asses real hard to see who's good and who isn't, but I don't think I'll have to worry about you. Now, who do you want for a first sergeant, since that person was wounded?"

"Easy, sir, Stecher."

Baylor made a note. "No surprise. Stecher's short a stripe but we can take care of that, and it's going to strip your old platoon of leaders, but I'll juggle some bodies and make it work. Got any questions?"

Farris grinned. "No, sir."

Baylor smiled grimly and held out his hand. "Oh, but you will, Lieutenant, you will."

※　　　※　　　※

Once more unto the breach, thought Braun. Once again they were lying in wait for a train to come rolling by. Nor did it bother him that he was quoting Shakespeare. Even though he was English, the Bard was one of Braun's favorite writers. Also, he wasn't Jewish like so many so-called artists were, even the long dead ones.

According to the schedule, a passenger train from the town of Riverside would be along in half an hour. It was getting dark, which made their chances of success good in Braun's opinion. Also helping them was the obvious fact that fewer Americans were patrolling the rails since the Japanese attack on the coast. If he saw someone, he would make a short piercing whistle, which would freeze Krause in place. Two and everything was all clear. Three meant run like hell.

Braun kept a careful watch as Krause crawled along the embankment with the explosives and detonator. He smiled. It was good to have Krause around to do the shit work. He was getting too old for that nonsense.

Since he knew where to look, he was able to follow Krause in the dark as he laid the explosives. Done, and the sergeant began to crawl back to Braun. In the distance they heard the sound of a train.

Once he got back, Krause grinned, his teeth white in the dark. "Damned thing is early. Less time to be discovered, eh?"

Braun agreed. They waited expectantly as the sound of the train drew closer. A few moments later, they could see the single bright eye of the light on the locomotive. Sooner than expected, the train, obviously speeding, was on them. Braun counted twelve passenger cars and he hoped they were all crammed with people and not running empty.

The train was going so fast that the locomotive had almost made it across the detonator before it went off, separating the locomotive from the coal car. The locomotive miraculously stayed on the tracks, while all the cars behind flew down the embankment and landed in a screeching, dusty, smoking jumble. The sound of tearing metal and breaking wood was quickly punctuated by the screams of injured and dying passengers.

All of the cars had toppled on their sides and one had flown on top of another in a ghastly pileup. People were scrambling out of doors and windows. The unhurt dragged the injured and laid them on the ground. Some were attempting first aid.

A success, thought Braun. "Time to go."

He and Krause ran to the Ford wagon. As they approached, they saw motion. "Damn," snarled Krause. Both men drew their weapons.

Three men were hunched over the back of the car. One had a jack and another held a length of hose. They were going to steal the tires and siphon his gas, leaving them stranded by the scene of a train wreck that they had caused.

The three looked stunned when the two armed Germans approached them. "Police!" snapped Braun. "Get on the ground." The men complied. They were very young, in their teens, scared, and looked like they were Mexicans. Braun recalled reading in the paper that there'd been a lot of problems with thieves from Mexico. The prisoners looked at their captors. They were nervous and confused and gauging their chances to make a break.

Krause took a deep breath. "We got here in time. They did nothing." In the background, sirens could be heard. "We have to leave now."

Braun winced. Krause had been speaking in German and the three Mexicans were puzzled by what they'd heard. He looked in the back seat of the car and the trunk that the crooks had pried open. A couple of sticks of dynamite were visible. He'd brought extras and now regretted it.

"Lie on your faces," Braun said in the bad Spanish he'd learned in Mexico City. They did as they were told. Braun shot the first two men before they realized what was happening. The boy in the middle started to get up, but Braun killed him before he could get to his knees. Krause looked shocked, but quickly accepted the necessity of killing them.

"Damn, damn, damn," muttered Braun.

Krause looked toward the wreck. "Do you think the shots will attract attention?"

The noise coming from the wreck and the sound of sirens was very loud, almost deafening. "No, but like I said, we have to leave immediately."

"And them?" Krause asked, pointing at the three wide-eyed corpses.

"We have no choice but to leave them. It will be a present for the FBI." He laughed harshly. "Perhaps it will drive them crazy trying to figure out what these three had to do with the train."

CHAPTER 14

AMANDA AND TIM HEARD THE POLICE SIRENS AND the screams as they left the little restaurant. As they turned the corner they saw a crowd of sailors and a bunch of Mexicans dressed in exaggerated outfits that were referred to as zoot suits. The two sides were brawling with fists, clubs, knives, and broken bottles. The zoot suits were a type of uniform worn by young Mexicans to show they were tough. With extremely wide lapels, stuffed shoulders, and baggy pants, they were a caricature of a man's business suit and, in Tim's opinion, looked ridiculous. Amanda agreed and had laughed when she'd first seen them lounging on street corners.

Dane was in uniform and had a .32 caliber revolver tucked in a shoulder holster under his jacket. The gun made the jacket bulge and the waiter at the restaurant had looked in surprise.

Before dinner they'd gone to a movie and watched John Wayne and Claire Trevor in *Stagecoach*. He'd seen it before, but Amanda hadn't.

Tim and the others had taken to carrying a weapon after the several confirmed acts of sabotage that had culminated in the destruction of a passenger train a couple of days before. He'd made a quick trip to the site with Agent Harris and discovered nothing new in the saboteurs' modus operandi, with the glaring exception of the three young men who'd been shot to death.

As they decided and as he told Amanda, he and Harris felt that the three young men had probably stumbled onto the saboteurs and paid with their lives for their bad luck. She'd earlier teased him about carrying a weapon, but now, as the rioters seemed headed toward them, it seemed like a good idea.

Dane shifted the pistol so that it was visible and he could take it out quickly. A couple of young and nervous-looking members of the Shore Patrol trotted by. Armed only with billy clubs, the Shore Patrol had a reputation for being poorly trained, and this pair looked it. Dane hurriedly grabbed the closest one, who looked angry until he saw Dane's rank.

"What the hell's going on, sailor?"

The young man stopped and swallowed. "Sir, a rumor's going around that some Mexicans caused that train wreck the other day. A bunch of sailors were killed, and apparently some of these fucking zoot-suiters—sorry, ma'am—were bragging about how great it was that Americans got killed."

The sailor turned and trotted toward the brawl, which now included more than a hundred fighters. A number of men were already on the ground, bleeding and cut. It looked like the relatively few Mexicans were getting the worst of it. Sirens were howling louder and more sailors from the Shore Patrol were arriving along with San Diego police.

Amanda grasped his arm. "I'm a nurse. I should be doing something."

He squeezed her hand. "Wait until they stop killing each other. It looks bad, but it's happened before and unless someone goes crazy with a knife and guts someone, or uses a gun, it'll mainly be cuts and bruises. Most of them are probably drunk, which means you won't be able to work with them until they are either unconscious, strapped down, or at least partly sober."

Amanda recalled a number of frantic Saturday nights in the emergency ward of the hospital in Honolulu. She'd seen the results of bar brawls and small drunken riots, but never the fight itself. It was hypnotic to watch grown men behaving so foolishly and dangerously. And Tim was right, sometimes injured drunks had to be strapped down so they could be helped.

A rioter in a torn zoot suit emerged from the pile and staggered toward them. There was blood pouring down his face from a cut above his eye. He lurched toward them. The smell of alcohol was heavy, he was clearly drunk, and there was fury in his eyes.

Dane pulled his weapon and pointed it at the Mexican's head. "Stop right there."

The drunk blinked and said something in rapid Spanish. He stepped closer, lurching unsteadily.

Amanda gasped. "You're not going to shoot him, are you?"

Dane swore. He had made a big mistake. They could have run and easily outdistanced the staggering drunk, but now it was too late and he had a gun in his hand. Shit.

The drunk took another step closer and howled in fury. A couple of his teeth were broken. Dane reversed the weapon and smashed it down on the drunk's nose, crushing it and sending blood gushing. The zoot-suiter staggered and fell on to his hands and knees. A pair of sailors raced over, ready to finish off the drunk.

"Get back to your quarters," Dane snapped. The two sailors saw the gun and that he was an officer. They ran off as quickly as they could.

Dane looked around and quickly holstered the pistol after wiping it off on a handkerchief.

A police officer approached and took control of the drunk, handcuffing him. "Nice job, Commander, and I didn't see that gun. Obviously, this clown fell and hurt himself. You were leaving now anyway, weren't you?"

Dane thought it was a great idea and led Amanda away from the scene.

"Well done," Amanda said with an exaggerated sigh, "my hero."

"Yeah, now let's get far away from here."

As they walked down the street, a score of police and shore patrol ran by them. The rioters were now outnumbered by the cops, which, they thought, was the way it should be.

"The Mexicans didn't do it, did they?" she asked.

"Nope. Somebody must've picked up on the police finding the three dead bodies and the story got turned around to where they were Mexicans shot by the cops for sabotaging the train. We're trying to get the papers to run a retraction, but it'll be on page twenty if at all."

Sometimes he thought he told Amanda too much of what was going on, but their relationship was deepening and he felt no reason to keep secrets from her. It was almost as if they were already married. Screw the navy. He wondered what his boss, Captain Merchant, was saying to the other nurse, Grace. They were spending a lot of time together as well.

Amanda took a deep breath. "So this is what passes for normal in Southern California. Take me someplace nice and buy me a drink, Tim. After that we'll find a place near my luxurious barracks and you can kiss me goodnight eight or ten times."

He laughed. The thought of making out like a couple of teenagers had marvelous appeal.

Shore leave on the clean white beaches of Hawaii by the small city of Hilo was something that Masao Ikeda had only dreamed of in the past. To the average educated Japanese, Hawaii was a beautiful and exotic place that was held by the American imperialists and far out of reach. Before the war, Hilo had a population of just below twenty thousand, but most of them had departed when the Japanese arrived. Their absence didn't matter to the Japanese conquerors. Hawaii was indeed a paradise. That a boy from a small village north of Tokyo could be in such a place was a wonder. It was marvelous to watch the waves and even better to swim in them and try to surf through them on his belly, all the while giggling and laughing like a child while his fellow pilots did the same thing.

He could see the volcano called Mauna Loa rising majestically in the distance. It wasn't the beautiful and symmetrical sacred Mount Fuji, but it would do for today.

Even better, he was a full-fledged member of Japan's

military elite. Military intelligence had reviewed his data and the testimony of witnesses and concluded that he had shot down seven American fighters. He was truly an ace. No more teasing from his comrades. He was a warrior and his comrades accepted him as such, while the replacement pilots looked on him with awe.

Another pleasant surprise came when his squadron was assigned to the carrier *Kaga*, one of Japan's largest. On it was his old friend, Tokimasa Hirota. He and Toki came from the same village and had been friends in school. Only terrible nearsightedness kept the energetic and athletic Toki from becoming a pilot like Masao Ikeda.

Toki was not jealous. That was not in his nature, and over numerous bottles of sake, they discussed families and the village. After a number of good laughs about life in the Imperial Japanese Navy, Toki grew serious.

"Masao, just how do you think the war is coming?"

Ikeda was surprised. "We are winning, of course. The Americans are everywhere on the run and will soon sue for peace. Why?"

Toki shook his head. "Do you know what I do? I am on Admiral Kurita's staff and work as a communications expert. I see top-secret messages that no one else does. They leave me very disturbed when I read them. I code and decode them for Kurita and his staff. Sometimes I think they believe I'm either invisible or a mute and incapable of understanding what the messages say. If the Americans could decode our messages they would be gaining in confidence. Thank God they can't."

Masao did not like this sudden turn in their conversation. "Should you be telling me this?"

"I have to. I don't want to, but I must. I must tell someone and you are my friend. It preys on me. I know the truth, and the truth is we are losing badly to the Americans and soon it will become apparent to all. If something dramatic doesn't happen, Japan as we know it is doomed."

Masao gasped in astonishment. "You're joking. We've won victory after victory."

"The battle for Midway was the last one. We are trading them carrier for carrier either sunk or too badly damaged to continue. We have sunk four of theirs, and, while only one of ours has been sunk, three are so badly damaged we may not see them for years, if ever. We have only a couple under construction while the Americans may have dozens. By the end of next year they will have far more carriers and battleships then we will."

"Ours will be better."

"No, the ships will be equal. They are all made of inanimate steel and we all know that the American ships will be well built and designed. Also, ships are only as good as their crews. Have you seen the replacement pilots they've sent out for the men we've lost over San Francisco and elsewhere?"

Masao grimaced. "Children, practically babies in diapers. It will take a long while to make them good pilots like me." He laughed. "I didn't mean that to sound so conceited, but they really aren't good pilots yet."

"And maybe they never will become good pilots, and that's one of my points. The Americans are turning out pilots and planes by the hundreds, by the thousands, and we are struggling to make good the losses we took in the abortive attack on Mare Island. Or haven't you noticed that we don't have a full complement of either planes or pilots?"

"But we burned San Francisco."

Toki shook his head angrily. "A handful of small fires that were put out quickly."

The sake was making Masao even more stubborn than usual. "We destroyed ten of their planes to one of ours."

"That data has been reviewed and it is somewhat less than three to one. Those are further losses we cannot sustain since airplane construction is very low in comparison with the Americans. And did you notice that the Americans came at us with newer and better planes? You sent shells into a P47 and it laughed them off because it is a flying tank compared with the Zero. They have that fork-tailed demon and another new carrier fighter as well. Soon the kill ratio will be one to one and that will destroy us."

"Then what about our victory at the Panama Canal and the fighting for Alaska? We destroyed the canal and our army is advancing toward Fairbanks."

Toki started to laugh, but stopped when he saw how serious and angry Masao was becoming. "My friend," he said gently, "the canal is open again. We damaged it, but that's all. As to Alaska, the army advancing toward the capital is only five or six thousand starving and poorly equipped men. Theirs is a suicide mission."

Masao was aghast. "That cannot be. What about the supplies and troops we landed when our ships outdueled the Americans and won a great victory over a larger fleet?"

Toki shook his head sadly. "Perhaps not even the emperor knows the extent of that disaster. All the ships sent to help the army were sunk and no supplies reached the soldiers. We lost nine warships and six transports and all for nothing. It is like the recently finished series of raids along the California coast. We shelled a few towns, set a few fires that were quickly put out, scared a few thousand civilians into running for the mountains, and in return we lost four destroyers, a light cruiser, and three submarines, all ships that we cannot replace."

Masao flipped his empty bottle into the bushes. "Are you certain that things are so bleak? If it is true, what is Admiral Yamamoto going to do?"

"He will redouble his efforts to find the *Saratoga* task force and destroy it. Perhaps then the Americans will be humiliated and ask to negotiate. However, I doubt it. I've listened to their broadcasts and their hatred of us is strong."

"I didn't know you spoke English."

Toki chuckled. "One of my many skills, or faults if you prefer. One other point. Have you gotten laid since coming here?"

Masao grinned happily. Another type of virginity had been eliminated in a navy-run whorehouse in Hilo. "Several times, with maybe more to come. Why?"

"Tell me, when you fucked those Hawaiian women, did they squeal with delight? Did they writhe like snakes and wrap their legs around you and happily pull your manhood into them? Were they proud to be mounted by an Imperial Japanese eagle, or did they just lie there like a slab of meat while you pumped away? Were their eyes open? Or maybe they were open but looking aside and not into your face."

Instead of answering, Masao found another couple

of bottles of sake. He opened them and passed one to his friend. "Well, I did notice a definite lack of enthusiasm on their part, but, after all, they are whores."

"They're not whores, Masao, they are slaves."

Masao nearly dropped his bottle. "What?"

"When we first set up this base, we searched for local prostitutes, but there weren't enough of them and the few we did find ran off. Either we weren't paying enough or they didn't want to be identified as collaborators. So we sent out recruiting parties to kidnap young women, preferably virgins, who were then raped and made to comply. They were told that if they didn't fuck for the emperor, their families would be killed. Even that hasn't stopped a number of them from either running away or committing suicide."

"I didn't know that," Masao said softly, wishing he'd never sat down with his old friend. Ignorance is such bliss. Nor was there any reason to doubt Toki's version of things. He had access to so much inside information.

Toki belched. The beer was beginning to get to him. "I hope you noticed that the base is surrounded by barbed wire and watch towers. If you step outside, you would very likely be killed by angry Hawaiians. You would be chopped to pieces by their machetes, even though we would exact a terrible vengeance. You have a fifteen-year-old sister and someday I'm going to marry her. What would you do if the Americans kidnapped her and made her spread her legs for them?"

Masao felt fury growing. "I would kill and kill again until someone killed me."

"As would I," Toki said. "And this is what our empire has come to. We lie about battles and we rape young women. We are losing this war in more ways than one and someday the Americans will have their turn at vengeance. Yamamoto himself said we would run wild for only a while. He also said it might be necessary to take Washington in order to bring the Americans to the conference table and that is clearly impossible."

"Toki, what do you suggest?"

His friend took a long swallow of sake and belched again. "Learn English."

Bear Foley lay on the floor of the forest on a bed of pine needles. His large body was covered by a brown woolen army blanket with an overlay of moist leaves and twigs. As long as he didn't move, it made him damn near invisible. It amused him that so many doubted that a man as large as he was could move like a whisper through the woods.

Well, he could. And he could lie like he was and not even quiver for as long as it took to complete his stalk. Bear had been a hunter since he could walk and quickly learned to kill game both for his own food and to satisfy wide-eyed hunters from the States down below. A number of times he'd made the big game kill and the so-called hunters from down south took home a trophy and a bunch of lies. He'd made a good living and had a great life until the damned Japs came, tearing up the land and killing his friends. Now he stalked and killed them.

Since Germany was as much an enemy as Japan, it was slightly ironic that his weapon of choice was an 1898 model German Mauser that his father had smuggled over from his stint in World War I. His daddy had told him it was one of several thousand Mausers that had been adapted by the krauts for use as a sniper rifle. Bear had practiced with it for so long it was like an extension of his arm and eye. Dad had died of the Spanish Influenza in 1918 and left the weapon to his large son who cared for it lovingly. It was his only real connection with his dead father.

In fact, he laughed, the only thing he caressed more tenderly was Ruby Oliver's luscious body.

He told himself to get back to reality. A handful of Japanese stood in plain sight only a couple of hundred yards away from where he was lying in the woods. He was on a knoll looking down through the trees to a clearing. Peering through the rifle's scope, he could see that they were like the other Japanese soldiers he'd been observing. They were dirty, thin, and, with the exception of their officer, looked very hungry and dispirited. In the distance he heard gunfire. The first time it had happened, he'd been convinced that other scouts had been discovered, or maybe someone was shooting at him from long range. It took a while before he realized that the Japs were shooting up Alaska's forests in search of game they could kill and eat. He thought their incessant and undisciplined firing was scaring off more potential food than they were going to kill.

In Bear's opinion, the Japanese soldier was a major disappointment. From what he'd read in the news and heard from other people, they were supposed to be great at operating in the jungle, which meant they should be able to do well in Alaska's forests. Since it was generally agreed that the average Jap was less than human, they should have had no problem moving like cats through rough terrain. Not the Japs he'd seen.

They did not move through the forests with anywhere near that level of skill. Instead, they were downright clumsy and noisy, always talking and sometimes yelling to maintain contact with their comrades. Worse, their gear rattled. Not the thing to have happen while you are stalking big game that walked upright. He'd been told that their shooting wasn't very accurate, though he was not going to take a chance. In his opinion the Japs would never make anything of high quality. He'd concluded that their ferocity in battle was what made them so damned dangerous, not their technology.

Colonel Gavin would be pleasantly surprised to find out that the Japs were in such bad shape physically. Bear wondered about their morale. They could be desperate, and desperate men could be very dangerous. Hell, even a cornered rabbit would bite. The Japs weren't yet cornered, he thought, but if they were having trouble feeding themselves they could soon be as desperate as any cornered animal.

Gavin would also be surprised to find out that the enemy had managed to drive three Type 95 light tanks up the road toward Fairbanks. Where they'd gotten the fuel, he didn't know. For that matter, he'd been told the Japs had no armor, that it had all been destroyed by the navy. These tanks must have been brought ashore with the first group, or maybe they got off the transports before they were sunk, or maybe retrieved after the ships were sunk. It didn't matter. The only important thing was that three of the beasties were clanking toward Fairbanks. They were miserable-looking things, each had a small cannon, and they too rattled and sounded like they would fall apart if they hit a pothole in the road.

A Japanese officer was haranguing the men below him. He slapped them several times. The blows were hard enough to stagger the soldiers, but they just stood there and took it. Bear growled. Anybody do that to him and the guy would get his head stuffed up his ass along with that big sword the shit of an officer carried. It was no way to treat men, not even Japs. American officers wouldn't dream of beating their men like that.

Bear sighed as he looked at the tableau below. Should he or shouldn't he? What the hell, he decided. He held the Mauser to his shoulder and looked into the scope. The officer's head was clear as a bell in the crosshairs. Normally, he'd aim for the chest, but it was obscured. He gently squeezed the trigger and, as hoped, the sound was largely muffled by the ground and the earth he'd piled around the barrel.

The officer's head exploded and the dead man dropped like a rock. The soldiers around him ducked for cover. A couple of them returned fire, sort of, shooting in all directions. Enough fun, Bear thought as he got up and sprinted away. That was the third Jap he'd managed to kill on this patrol. He retrieved the small motorcycle that had carried him down the road and through the forest. Like his rifle, the bike's engine was muffled. The Japs were only about seventy miles away from the American lines. It was time to talk to Gavin.

Dane and Harris looked through the one-way window at the little man in the chair. He was slight, bald, and had a pasty complexion. Not exactly an advertisement for a German superman, Dane thought. A dirty and badly scuffed briefcase lay by the German's feet. It actually bore the emblem of the old Imperial Germany and not the swastika.

"Are we really going to make a deal with this guy?" Dane asked.

"Well now, that depends, doesn't it? Frankly, I hope this little man does have something interesting to say. I got a telegram from J. Edgar telling me to get off my ass and get this sabotage thing solved, so I guess that gives me carte blanche to do whatever I have to."

"You heard from Hoover himself?"

Harris chuckled. "And why the hell not? Seriously, he and I go back a long ways, even before there was an FBI for him to take over and shape into his image and likeness. You do recall that Hoover was head of the Bureau of Investigation before it became the FBI, don't you?"

"Sort of," Dane admitted.

"Well, I was one of his very bright young agents back when the Bureau was small. I helped him a lot and taught him a lot, and sometimes he's a little bit grateful."

"I bet you also know a lot, which is why he tolerates you."

"Damn straight. He wants agents now who are straight-arrow and wear a suit well, not some rumpled old fart like me. But he tolerates me because of our shared history. Well, at least he does so far. I'm one major screw-up away from retirement, which is beginning to look more and more attractive. Now, you want to talk to this guy or to me?"

Dane said that Harris should lead the questioning. They walked into the interrogation room and took seats across from the German. The man seemed a little surprised to see a naval officer, but quickly recovered.

Harris took out a notebook. "Let's get through the formalities. What's your name and occupation?"

The man was in his late forties, early fifties, and clearly uncomfortable. "My name is Johann Klaas and I work for the German embassy in Mexico City, or at least I did until the Mexican government shut it down and put us in house arrest pending travel arrangements to get us safely back to Germany. My position would best be described as an accountant. I was in charge of the embassy's money."

Dane thought the man's English was excellent, but then, the man was a diplomat of sorts. He did look very much like an accountant.

"What do you want from us?" Harris asked.

Klaas took a deep breath. "Asylum."

Harris pretended to make a note in his book. "I understand you faked a heart attack just before embassy personnel were to be repatriated back to Germany. Is that correct?"

"Yes. During my time in Mexico City I made some friends and one was a physician who detested the Nazis for what they were doing to the Jews. He gave me some medicine that made me very ill and then confirmed that I was having a heart attack when I was sent to the hospital. As a result, they left for Germany without me with the understanding that I would follow if and when I was well enough to travel. Hopefully, that will be never."

"Why do you wish to defect?" Dane asked, earning a quick glare from Harris, who clearly wished to control the conversation.

"I am not a Nazi. This may come as a shock to

you but many, many Germans are not Nazis and are horrified at what is happening to our country. It is especially true in the diplomatic corps. Yes, we applauded when Hitler gave us back our dignity and pride, but we did not desire war and we did not want the slaughter of our enemies and the massacres that are happening to the Jews."

Harris smiled wickedly. "I dare say there will be more of you denying you were Nazis when you lose the war."

Klaas smiled. He had bad teeth. "Of course. However, I have two other reasons for wanting to leave Germany. First, my late wife and I had two children. One is a daughter safe in Brazil. The second is a son who was an officer in the German army, what you call the Wehrmacht. He was killed just before Christmas fighting the Russians. Actually, he wasn't fighting when he was killed. One of his comrades wrote and told me he had frozen to death because the buffoons in Berlin hadn't planned on a long war; therefore, there were no winter uniforms for the men."

"So you want revenge on Hitler," Harris said.

"In a way, yes, but more than that. I want to help destroy the barbarians who've stolen my beloved Germany. Before he died, my son wrote several letters in which he described in vivid detail the atrocities being committed in the name of Germany and Hitler. He told me of mass rapes of scores of women at a time, and how even reluctant soldiers were required to participate, actually given orders to assault innocent women by their officers, in particular the SS. He told of systematic looting, and the indiscriminate slaughter of thousands of civilians simply for being Slavs or

Jews, again with reluctant soldiers being required to participate so that none could ever be blameless."

Klaas shook his head sadly. "The army of my beloved Germany is behaving like the most savage of barbarians because the Nazis believe that the Slavs are less than human. The Jews, of course, are being treated far worse. There are even rumors that all Jews will be exterminated, if you could believe that."

"You're right," said Harris. "I've heard those rumors and they are a little far-fetched."

"You are aware, aren't you, that Jews are being imprisoned, beaten, tortured, and denied a right to earn a living?" Klaas asked.

"Yes," Harris said.

"Well, Agent Harris, my mother was Jewish, which in the eyes of the Nazis, makes me Jewish as well, even though I know only a little of it and have never practiced the faith. My mother's family was what was referred to assimilated Jews. We considered ourselves Germans, not Jews. Many even volunteered to fight for the Kaiser in the past war. It doesn't matter to the Nazis. If I was to go back to Germany, I'm reasonably confident I'd be thrown into a concentration camp. You can see that I am not a strong man, so it would be a death sentence. The fact that my son was in the army might have helped me, but he is now dead. Two men on the embassy staff were Gestapo and they told me they looked forward to getting my Jewish ass back to the Reich so they could take care of me."

Klaas shuddered. "I was a Jew who handled the Reich's money; therefore, I was doubly cursed in their eyes."

Dane was surprised—no, stunned. This was all new

to him. What the hell was going on in the world, he asked himself. He had been concentrating on Japan and not enough on the Nazis.

Harris put down his notebook. "You've made a good case for letting you stay, but there's no way I can prove anything you've said and it still sounds like you're just trying to save your own skin."

Klaas was unperturbed. "I understand your position fully, and yes, I am trying to save myself. So let me offer you a quid pro quo. If I tell you something important, will you be willing to let me live in the United States at least until the war ends and I can get to my daughter in Brazil?"

Dane could see that Harris's eyes were lighting up. "It sure as hell would help."

Klaas sat back in his government-issue folding chair. "I can give you the man who is wrecking your trains."

Harris and Dane moved Klaas to a more comfortable conference room. It was furnished with a polished wooden table and very comfortable chairs. Coffee and rolls were provided. Klaas seemed quite relieved and more comfortable with his improved status.

He set down his coffee. "A short while before Mexico declared war on Germany, I was informed by one of the resident SS officers, who was an extremely fanatic Nazi, that English-speaking Germans on the staff were going to support Japan by entering the U.S. and engaging in acts of sabotage. That these acts would also support Germany was obvious."

"Who was the SS man?" Harris asked.

"His name is Wilhelm Braun. He's very murderous and I've heard that he killed Mexicans for amusement while with the embassy. That, of course, cannot be proven. Braun required money to set up a station in Mexico City and another in Monterrey. He took just about all the cash we had on hand and drained some other bank accounts. The ambassador went along with this. He had no choice. Along with Braun, a total of six men were involved and I have no idea which of them is at what city and what their addresses are. I also have no idea who crossed into the United States, although Braun most certainly did, and I rather doubt that he's alone."

Harris refilled Braun's coffee. "How is he communicating?"

"At first by mail and telephone. When that became dangerous, he began using a shortwave radio. He broadcasts pretty much in the clear since he does not have one of our encoding machines."

Encoding machines? Dane and Harris looked at each other and wondered the same thing. Who knows about them, and could they get their hands on one?

Klaas laughed. "I can read your minds. The machine at the embassy was destroyed and they are so complex that no one will be able to replicate one or break the code. If we Germans do anything correctly, it's devising codes."

We'll see, thought Dane. "So this Braun character sends messages in the clear?"

"Pretty much," Harris said. "Although he will generally say vague things like 'our objective is near,' or 'Plan A is being implemented.' He must know that any radio message might be overheard so he might be saying things that are truly innocuous on the surface. I can give you his radio frequencies and broadcast timing schedules, and you can decide that for yourself."

"Outstanding," said Harris, rubbing his hands. "Now, any idea what is objective is, other than derailing trains?"

"Yes. Some of my colleagues are quite chatty when talking among themselves; ourselves, since they considered me one of them. Tokyo has pressured Berlin, who is urging Braun to find the location of the *Saratoga* and her task force. Germany's little yellow allies seem to think her destruction would make the Americans think more favorably on a peace treaty."

"What do you think?" Dane asked.

Klaas sniffed. "I think the idiots in Tokyo are as insane as Hitler and his friends."

"Can you describe Braun for us?" Harris inquired.

Klaas reached down and put the worn briefcase on the table. "It was a gift from my daughter," he explained wistfully as he opened it. He pulled out a file folder and a number of photographs spilled out. He picked one from the pile. "Here is Wilhelm Braun."

The man in the picture was clean-shaven and looked perfectly ordinary. He had no distinguishing characteristics. Harris took the photo and said it would be copied and circulated. He added that Braun could easily disguise himself by changing his hair, growing a beard, or stuffing his cheeks with cotton when he went out. Klaas gave him other pictures which he said were the rest of Braun's crew. He followed that with Braun's radio frequencies and schedules.

"How did you get all this?" Harris asked, suspicion evident in his voice.

Klaas smiled. "When we were interned in a Mexico City hotel awaiting transportation to Germany, a number of the staffers had nothing else to do except gossip and brag. I copied down what they said, and stole the pictures from the trash. They were to be shredded and thrown out, of course."

"Can you give us any possible aliases he might use?" Dane asked.

"No. I don't think anyone on the staff gave him phony papers. I believe that would have been someone hired from the outside. Perhaps the Mexican police could help you."

Harris snorted. He had a very low opinion of Mexico's police forces. Far too many of them thought that accepting bribes was part of their job description.

Harris appeared to think about Klaas's future, but Dane thought he'd reached a decision a long time ago. "We will grant you asylum, Herr Klaas, but with conditions."

"Of course."

"You will remain in San Diego with us to help in the search for this Braun person, and you will help monitor transmissions between him and his associates in Mexico. You will also assist in translating since few of my staff speak anything other than minimal German."

"Again, of course. And when my job is done, then what?"

Harris answered. "You'll get a new name and a place to live, unless you truly want to go to Brazil."

Klaas's eyes misted over. He was clearly thinking of his daughter. "Brazil. Please."

Although Amanda loved spending as much of her spare time as she could with Tim, she and the other two nurses had bonded thanks to shared experiences and looked forward to seeing each other socially.

Even though they worked and bunked together, it was pleasant to just get away and talk.

Also, there was the intriguing matter of Mack's will. In response to a message from their local attorney, Morton Zuckerman, they met at Zuckerman's office. It turned out that Zuckerman, a heavy-set jovial man in his late forties, was related to Richard Goldman by marriage and had insisted on telling them all about it in previous meetings.

Zuckerman's secretary, a very pleasant and attractive lady named Judith, also in her forties, told them he had a client, a tenant, and the meeting was running late. No problem, they said, and chatted in the reception area. After the meeting they would go out to dinner. Amanda would see Tim later that evening. Finally, the door opened and a solid-looking middle-aged man came out. He glared angrily around the room. He looked over the three women with ill-concealed hostility and familiarity before he stomped out, limping slightly.

Zuckerman's secretary laughed. "Pay no attention to him. Mr. Zuckerman has to deal with all kinds of jerks. He's a foreigner who runs a business and isn't making much money at it. I think he thought that everyone would get rich off of government contracts, but it hasn't happened in his case. He wants his rent reduced and Mort already did that once. I think that man just simply doesn't like dealing with Jews." She shrugged eloquently. "It comes with the route."

"I thought he was undressing me," Grace said, and the others nodded. Amanda wondered if he could mentally undress three women at the same time.

"He even does that to me," Judith said and smiled. "Maybe he should get a girlfriend, or at least get laid."

"Y'know," Grace said. "Both Amanda and I have boyfriends. So why don't we fix Sandy up with Prince Charming?"

Sandy scowled with mock anger. "Just now I am not that hard up. However, see me in a week."

"Never would be better," Amanda said. She was going to arrange a meeting between Sandy and Tim's nephew. Sandy had been a little plump before crossing the Pacific and was rapidly gaining back the weight. Perhaps a boyfriend would help her keep it off.

Amanda continued. "Did you see the look in his eyes? Along with undressing us, he looked absolutely murderous."

"I doubt that very much," said Zuckerman, who'd heard most of the conversation. "He's an immigrant having a tough time because of the war, which would make anyone angry."

They entered his office and sat around his desk. Zuckerman and Grace lit up cigarettes. "As you probably guessed, I do have information regarding Mack's will. First, advertising for heirs in the appropriate places has resulted in no one who claims any relationship to Mr. Garver, AKA Mack. Therefore, that is no longer a legal issue. He did have an ex-wife but the terms of the divorce are clear. She is owed nothing. The state of California, those greedy banditos residing in Sacramento, is another matter. Mr. Goldman has negotiated with them and they are willing to be reasonable. In return for thirty percent of anything over one hundred thousand dollars in cash, stocks, or anything else of value in the box, you three will keep the first hundred thousand, and seventy percent of anything thereafter."

Amanda nodded. "That almost sounds fair."

Zuckerman agreed. "Someone in Sacramento must be having a bad day. But yes, it does look like the best we can do. Nor are the police in any way interested in something that happened in the middle of the ocean. Mack's death will be listed as accidental. More important, the next time you are in San Francisco could result in your seeing the contents of the box rather than having to wait years until a court sorts this out. Someone from the state will be watching over your shoulder, of course, but that's life."

They agreed that the decision was a good one. Like little kids, they wondered what was in the box. Realistically, they knew that it would be at least several weeks before they could manage to take the time off and arrange travel. While there hadn't been any major battles recently, there were still a large number of casualties from previous engagements who needed their attention. The safe deposit box and its unknown contents would have to wait.

Krause was pleasantly surprised when Braun showed up with a Mexican woman who looked like she was in her late twenties. A little plump, but not all that bad looking, he decided. In fact, she looked better the more he stared at her. It had been a reluctantly celibate existence for both of them since moving to San Diego.

Braun grinned. "Her name is Juanita Morales and she's going to entertain us tonight."

Juanita looked around their apartment and decided she'd seen worse. After all, these were two men living together, so what did she expect? She'd come from

Escondido in northern Mexico as a small child and recalled dirt floors and sharing them with a goat, so what did she care if the place was littered? The men did not appear queer and only wanted sex. As long as they paid, that was fine by her. They talked like they were foreign, but she'd been told by "Bill" that they were Swedes, whatever that meant.

"Okay," she said. "Here's what I'll do. Normally I charge by the trick, but since there's two of you and I'll bet you want me to stay all night and play with you until you get tired, it'll be thirty dollars and I'll do anything you want, but I don't get hurt. Oh yeah, you got to use rubbers unless I'm sucking your cock. It's going to be more if you want all of us doing it at the same time."

They negotiated down to twenty dollars and they each gave her ten. They also assured her that there would be no threesomes.

"Let's get started," she said and stepped out of her dress and underclothing. She was voluptuous and Krause stared, getting aroused. She had large, full breasts with dark nipples and he couldn't take his eyes off them. Juanita laughed at him.

Braun had rank, so he went first while Krause went to the garage downstairs. Krause was second and was pleased that Juanita was somewhat exuberant when his turn came. He had the feeling that paying her ten dollars each for the night was an overcharge. Braun had found her at a bar frequented by sailors, and the idea of going with someone who wasn't in the military and had his own place appealed to her. He also said there was no pimp in the picture to complicate matters.

Juanita didn't get tired of their alternating until it was almost dawn. This was just as well since the two Germans were exhausted. She finally serviced them orally and asked to be driven home, and Braun said he would do it. She asked if she could come back some time and they both agreed.

Krause went to bed and slept in until midafternoon. Braun had gone directly to bed after returning. It had been a good night and they agreed that they needed a day off. Krause realized he'd left his cigarettes in the Ford and went down to the garage. He'd just put the pack in his shirt pocket when something on the back seat caught his eye. It was a woman's purse. Damn it to hell, he thought as he realized the implications. He raced upstairs.

"Was it necessary to kill her?"

Braun shrugged. "I thought it best. She was a lot of fun, but she'd seen us, our place, and God only knows what else she might have noticed."

"How did you do it?"

"Easy. I told her I'd give her five more dollars if she'd let me take pictures of her naked on the beach. When she thought she was posing, I shot her in the back of the head and left her there. Don't worry, there was nobody around."

Krause grudgingly accepted the need to maintain secrecy, but some aspects worried him. For instance, would anyone miss her? Or would someone recall her going off with a middle-aged white man in a Ford, which might be something unusual for a hooker who specialized in sailors?

Braun caught the worried look on Krause's face and misunderstood. "Don't worry, Gunther, we'll get us another playmate sometime soon in the future. Maybe the next one I won't bring back here. By the way, here's your ten dollars back."

Harris was pleased. For once his request for information and help from local police had gotten results. Generally there was no love lost between the FBI and the San Diego cops and he'd been afraid that his asking for cooperation had wound up in a waste basket. Most of the local cops were extremely territorial and he was the outsider. They even thought he talked funny, originally being from out east and all that.

He'd pressed the point with his local contact, a detective named Flaherty. He'd said he was looking for possible saboteurs and maybe that had gotten their attention and enabled them to look past their prickly pride. Or were they prideful pricks, he wondered? Flaherty said he'd keep an eye out. It helped that the cop was a good guy and that Harris was the one who'd told him about the possibility of sabotage and murder by Germans. Harris had worked with Flaherty before and there was a level of mutual respect.

The woman on the slab looked up at the ceiling through lifeless eyes. She was naked. Her body was pale and there were a number of bruises and cuts. Harris wondered if they were from crawly things gnawing on her after she died and decided he didn't want to know.

"Where's her clothing?" he asked and was informed that she'd been found naked on the beach yesterday morning by a couple of very surprised hikers.

Flaherty volunteered that she was probably a local whore and their immediate assumption was that she'd gotten killed by a jealous boyfriend. What had made Flaherty curious was the fact that she'd been shot by a nine-millimeter bullet to the back of the head, just what Harris had asked the locals to be on the lookout for.

Flaherty held a handkerchief to his nose. The body was getting a little ripe. "I took the liberty of circulating her photo around some areas on the assumption that, looking Mexican, she was probably a prostitute. I was right. A couple of her coworkers gave me a name, Juanita Morales, said she worked alone, and said she left with a middle-aged white guy the night before she was found."

"Anything more about him?"

Flaherty sniffed. "Nah. They were all busy earning a living and didn't notice anything special about her new friend. They said he was kind of nondescript, frankly."

"Great work, detective."

"You think the killer's the guy who's wrecking your trains?"

"I would put serious money on it," Harris said. "I owe you."

"What do you want me to do with the body?" Flaherty asked. An autopsy would be performed, but that would confirm the obvious—death by bullet to the head. The police would keep her prints and a photo on file as a matter of course.

"Just give Miss Morales a decent burial. She may have died actually helping her country."

"She's Mexican," Flaherty said with a slight grin.

"Okay, helping our country."

Harris drove away with the bullet in a paper bag. An hour later and back on base, he and another agent were peering through microscopes, comparing the bullet recovered from the woman to the bullets extracted from the border guards and the Mexican kids.

"Son of a bitch," Harris snarled, although he was not surprised. The grooves on the bullets had all matched. Whoever the saboteur and killer was, he was still on the loose and still killing.

CHAPTER 15

TIM ROLLED ON HIS SIDE AND LOOKED AT AMANDA, who was lying on her own beach blanket and looking contentedly at the full, billowing clouds. He thought they were cumulus but wasn't sure. She knew he was staring at her and smiled slightly. She hoped he liked how she looked in her new two-piece bathing suit. Both Sandy and Grace insisted that it accentuated her very slender figure, while the light blue color went well with her lightly colored hair.

"Honey," Grace had said, "if I had a flat belly and perky little breasts like that, I'd wear one of those suits too."

However, Grace added, she didn't. Her figure was more on the voluptuous side and she really needed something to help tuck in her tummy. Like most women, she wore a girdle when out in public. Amanda generally did, too, although she didn't think she needed one. Not wearing a girdle was liberating but it scandalized older women, which she sometimes found amusing. Where was it written in law that women, especially slender ones, had to wear a heavy and constricting girdle that made a woman sweat and itch? Grace said it made it so much harder for a man to undress her if she wasn't willing, so maybe that was a selling point.

Sandy sat a few yards away from them with Steve Farris. They seemed to be hitting it off. After some initial shyness, there was now a lot of laughter coming from their blanket. Grace and Merchant were somewhere off on their own. The difference in rank was too much for them all to be comfortable, especially Steve, who was still only a first lieutenant, and Merchant, the Army's equivalent of a full colonel. Amanda thought that the military's fixation with rank was silly, but it was something they had to live with.

Amanda rolled onto her side so she could face Tim. "Like what you see?"

"Immensely. You're beautiful."

"I'll bet you say that to all the women who lie half naked on a beach with you."

"I'd even say it if you were totally naked."

She giggled. Sandy and Steve turned to see if they were missing something, decided they weren't, and went back to their own conversation. Amanda liked what she saw of Tim in a bathing suit, even though it was baggy and too large for him and admittedly borrowed from a friend. He was muscular and had told her that he worked out at one of the base gyms to relieve stress. She thought that lying on a California beach was a much better way of alleviating stress. The only mildly disturbing factor was the presence of several destroyers and patrol craft at the opening to San Diego Bay. She rationalized their presence by thinking that they would have been there in peace-time as well.

"Tim, every now and then you have a good idea and this is a wonderful one. Your nephew seems like a nice man and it looks like he and Sandy are hitting it off."

The four of them were on a beach a mile south of San Diego and it was a Sunday afternoon. A number of other couples had similar ideas, which meant there was little real privacy. Steve's unit was through packing, and his battalion had been given the weekend off, which was why they were near San Diego and not Steve's small base. On Monday they'd be heading north and on to the vast wilderness of Alaska to confront the Japanese army that was slowly approaching Fairbanks. Steve was less than thrilled and Tim shared his worry. After all, the woods up north were filled with angry, hungry, and fanatic Japs.

"Will you ever go back to Hawaii?" Tim asked.

"No," she said softly. "That part of my life is over. I wanted to spend a year or so there on a kind of lark that turned into a tragedy. From what I've heard about the horrors of living on the Islands, especially Oahu, I wonder if anyone will ever want to go there on vacation again. I'll continue nursing here until I get the chance to go back east and then on to med school. Do you think I can make it and become a doctor?"

"Easily," he responded.

Nor would she have much trouble getting into any med school. Not only was she very bright and well educated, but her nursing experience would help her immensely. And it would not hurt at all that her father was a senior surgeon on the staff at Johns Hopkins in Baltimore. But would she like it as a woman doctor in what was a man's world?

She sat up and brushed sand off her pale skin. "Let's go in the water. I can't stand too much sun."

She'd earlier explained that her badly sunburned body was pretty well healed, but that her new skin was still very tender. The doctors explained that she might be susceptible to sunburn for quite some time, perhaps forever. Therefore, her time on the sun-drenched beach would be limited and infrequent, unless she wanted to wear clothing, which struck her as silly. Why go to the shore if you had to stay dressed? Today was just too nice to spend indoors and, besides, even southern California weather couldn't be wonderful all the time, especially with winter on the horizon. She would take a few chances and enjoy life.

They waded in and then swam out beyond a large seaweed encrusted raft that shielded them from being seen by anyone on the beach. No other swimmers were in the area so they were deliciously alone. The water came just up to their chests and they stood comfortably, letting this day's fairly gentle waves splash around them. If the sea had been any rougher, they wouldn't have been able to stand out there. They would have had to climb onto the raft.

Pleased by the privacy, they slipped into each others' arms and kissed tenderly, then passionately. Tim was aroused and didn't care if Amanda knew it.

She nuzzled under his chin. "I guess you really do like me."

Tim kissed the top of her head. He slid his hands down and lifted her up, squeezing her bottom. So far she'd permitted him very few liberties and he wondered what would happen today, out of view and already half undressed.

She read his mind. "You're a very good man, Tim. Someday you and I will make love, just not right now."

"I understand."

"No, you don't. I was hurt once, betrayed by someone I loved very much, and I thought he loved me."

The light dawned. "Is that why you came to Hawaii? Not just for the sailing and not just on a lark?"

"Partly," she said and wiggled against him, arousing him even more. "The young man in question, and I will never tell you his name because you might want to challenge him to a duel, said he wanted to marry me and when I wouldn't go to bed with him, told everyone I had. Then he spread it around that I had done some strange things with him. Look, there are a lot of people who do and that's their business, but they keep it quiet. When he broadcast such lies, I felt like my reputation and trust had been destroyed."

"People don't want to believe the truth, do they?"

"Not when salacious tales are so much more fun. And there's no way I could deny it. I tried, but people preferred to believe the more interesting lies. Tim, I'm no saint. A long ways from it in fact, but I do consider myself a private and discreet person."

"Is that why we're hiding behind a raft in the middle of the Pacific Ocean?"

"Absolutely," she said and kissed him hungrily, teasing him with her tongue.

She pulled back and smiled. She slipped out of her top and guided his hands across her small and firm breasts. He hoisted her farther up, thankful for the ocean's buoyancy, so he could kiss and nibble them. Her breasts were beautiful and delicious, tasting like salt water. She groaned with pleasure and let him shift the bottom of her suit so he could caress her even more intimately. After a few moments she groaned and shuddered, almost clawing at his shoulders.

She smiled tenderly and pulled his swim trunks town to midthigh. It was her turn to caress him, and she did until he climaxed.

"Who taught you to do that?" he asked.

She laughed softly and licked the inside of his ear. "You did. Just now."

"I love you," he said softly.

"I know, Tim, and I love you too. Now let's get dressed and go back in."

"Can we come back?"

She grinned wickedly. "Perhaps later if I get hot."

This trip with his men was much different from the earlier trip to California, thought Farris. Way back then, he'd been a total rookie with a cast of misfits under his command, along with an NCO who held him in contempt and a pair of drunks as company and battalion commanders.

Since then, he'd been promoted, given an under-strength company to command, seen combat and felt that he'd grown immensely. That did not, however, make him pleased as the long column of trucks rattled north. Taking on the Japanese army in the woods of Alaska was quite frankly frightening. Since receiving word that they'd be heading north, both he and the new battalion commander had been driving the men hard. They'd worked on their marksmanship, their conditioning, and their ability to operate in dense woods as a unit.

They'd also watched with a mixture of sadness and relief as a fresh and innocent-looking unit took over what Stecher referred to as their beachfront property. Leaving was a little bittersweet for Farris. After all the time watching for enemy ships and complaining about being lonely, he'd finally met someone. He and Sandy Watson had hit it off. They'd promised to write and he wondered if he could finagle some telephone calls from up near the Arctic Circle. She'd let him kiss her a few times, but stopped him when he tried to go a little farther. "When you come back," she'd told him.

Steve was delighted that Uncle Tim had found someone as nice as Amanda, although both he and Sandy had been amused by the fact that they'd gone behind that raft thinking no one would notice. Sandy insisted they really weren't going to go all the way because Amanda had said they wouldn't. They'd made jokes about all the splashing and waves coming from behind the raft. Amanda and Tim had gone out there three times during the afternoon. What the hell, let them all be happy, Steve thought. Let everyone be happy. There's a war on and tomorrow everybody could be dead.

There had been other casualties before they set off. One company commander and three lieutenants had been shipped off either for being utterly incompetent, for toadying too much to the previous regime, or both. No loss was the consensus. They were going into combat and nobody wanted jerks commanding men.

They'd been issued cold-weather gear including flannel shirts, field jackets, and fur caps that, in Farris's opinion, made them look like Cossacks. Stecher said that barbarians in training was more like it.

Even though it was still fall according to the calendar, the weather was noticeably colder the farther north they went and there was wet snow on the ground. Steve wondered how the Japs liked freezing. He felt they'd gotten their reputation as jungle fighters, not winter fighters. The major reminded them that the Japs had been fighting in China for years and north China was far from tropical. No matter. He hoped they all froze their little yellow asses off before the column got to Fairbanks.

This, Farris was told, was the road that was supposed to ultimately link the U.S. with Fairbanks. Instead of building a proper highway, the engineers were now concerned only with hurriedly blasting and bulldozing a way to get troops and equipment to where the fighting would soon be.

The muddy dirt road was so narrow that pine boughs slapped against the canvas-sided trucks and they could see down valleys and ravines that could kill them if the drivers lost control and sent them tumbling over the edge. Some of the bridges over rivers and bogs were well constructed, while others looked like they'd been slapped together. Worse, they creaked and swayed when the trucks crossed over them. It didn't help their morale to be told that construction on the road would soon shut down. The miserable weather would require it.

When they paused for periodic breaks to stretch and relieve themselves, Farris saw that the scenery was both magnificent and frightening. It looked as if they were surrounded by mountains. He no longer had any thoughts of camping and fishing.

Farris was not happy to be told that the Japanese were reported to be within fifty miles of Fairbanks. He had no idea how many of the enemy there were, but one would be too many.

After what seemed like an eternity, the trucks stopped and they all piled out, looking around in confusion. They'd run out of road and would have to hoof it.

"How much farther to Fairbanks?" Farris asked a civilian engineer who was lounging against a bulldozer. A handful of Negro soldiers clustered around him. They all looked amused at the new arrivals.

The man stopped and thought for a moment. "I reckon maybe seven hundred miles."

Farris gasped. "What?"

The engineer roared with laughter. "Gotcha, Lieutenant. It's ten miles or so. Unless you guys are really out of shape, you'll make it before nightfall."

They did, even marching into camp in decent order. The commander, Colonel Gavin, greeted them, clearly delighted to see reinforcements. He shook Major Baylor's hand and went around encouraging the men and shaking still more hands, including Steve's. Farris was impressed by Gavin. Maybe they did stand a chance against the Jap army.

Masao Ikeda stood on the flight deck of the *Kaga*. He did not walk to the edge like others did. He was not afraid of heights when flying twenty thousand feet or more in his Zero, but there was something about hanging over the ocean that unsettled him. Being afraid of anything was unmanly, and admitting to something as simple as fear of heights would subject him to merciless teasing from his fellow pilots if they ever discovered it. Anytime he had to be near the edge, he always made sure that an antiaircraft battery was beneath him, providing an illusion of stabililty.

The wind was cold and refreshing as the *Kaga*, her smaller sister, the *Shinyu*, and the rest of their task force headed north. Masao was tired. In the last few days, he'd spent long hours cooped up in the cockpit of his fighter practicing the skills that would enable them to kill Americans and return safely. He sensed rather than saw that his friend Toki was standing behind him.

"How was your day?" Toki asked. "How well did your new pilots perform?"

Masao laughed harshly. "Like clowns in a circus. I cry for them when I think of them going up against the Americans. Of course, I know my commanders felt the same way when I first started out and look at me now."

"Are you saying there's hope for them?"

Masao lit a cigarette and drew deeply. He felt that smoking made him look more mature. He grinned genially. "Yes, just not much." One new pilot had crashed after aborting a landing and was in sick bay with a broken leg and a ruined career. "Now tell me, Toki, is it confirmed that we are heading to Alaska to rescue our men?"

"Yes, but it is not a rescue mission. The men on the ground are doomed. Our goal is to prolong their lives a little longer. Of course we're not telling them that. We're saying this attack is to enable them to take Fairbanks and spend the winter there until there's either peace or they are rescued by the navy next summer. They will die before either happens."

"That doesn't make sense."

"But it's bushido. We are going to help them take more Americans with them when they die. Tell me, do you wish to die? Do you have a death wish?"

"Of course not. I have to get home to prevent you from marrying my sister. If you live a hundred years you will never be worthy of her even if she is a snotty, argumentative little brat. However," he said, turning serious, "I will gladly forfeit my life for Japan if I have to. Well, maybe not gladly, but I will anyhow."

"Would you be willing to die if the situation was hopeless and surrender was an option?"

"Surrender is shameful."

Toki smiled. His friend had not answered the question. "Do you think the soldiers in Alaska should surrender rather than face death for no reason? They cannot be rescued and their deaths will not bring victory to Japan."

"I don't know," Masao reluctantly admitted. "Tell me, do you have any good news to cheer me up?"

"Not really. The *Akagi* was sunk."

Masao gasped. "Your information is wrong. The mighty *Akagi* was damaged, but was sent to Japan for repairs. She will soon return to the fleet."

Toki shook his head. His expression was grim. "American submarines found her and finished her off. There were few survivors."

Masao felt like he'd been punched in the gut. At thirty-seven thousand tons, the *Akagi* had been one of the largest carriers in the Japanese fleet, which meant that almost all the remaining Japanese carriers were of the smaller classes. Only his current ship, the *Kaga*, was anywhere near the *Akagi*'s size. Yes, the Japanese

Navy had a number of carriers, but they were smaller than the American fleet carriers, and did not carry the number of planes the larger Japanese ships could.

Far more important, so many of the lost carrier's crew had been his friends. He'd never experienced anything like this painful and personal sense of loss before.

"She was sunk in Tokyo Bay," Toki added. "Our navy thinks they got the sub, but they aren't certain and it really doesn't matter at all. The Americans will trade a sub for a carrier every day. Who wouldn't? A few more disastrous trades and the war will be over."

Masao sagged. The implications were obvious. If American subs could enter the hitherto safe waters off Tokyo and sink Japan's ships, then his beloved nation truly was in dire straits. But were they actually losing the war or was this just a temporary setback? He wished he could talk to Yamamoto, but that was clearly impossible. The admiral was almost a god.

Toki lit his cigarette and offered one to Masao, who had finished his. Masao took it if only to give himself a chance to think.

Toki took a deep drag and exhaled. "There is extreme pressure on Yamamoto to end the war by winning a great victory, which is one of the reasons for this foray to Alaska. When we attack, it is hoped that the Americans will come out and chase us. When they do we will ambush them again."

"Do you think that's possible?" Masao said hopefully. He realized that he was fully acknowledging the accuracy of what Toki was telling him, however depressing it was.

"I think it is no more likely than that we will win a great victory in China."

Masao stifled a groan, drew deeply on his cigarette

and choked. The Japanese army had been fighting the corrupt, disreputable, but enormous Chinese army for what seemed an eternity. It had been a source of jokes for the pilots and others in the navy. The army had started the war and now weren't competent enough to finish off poorly armed and even more poorly trained and led Chinese hordes.

"Masao, I will now speak treason. If given half a chance, I will surrender rather than die for no good reason, and I hope our leaders will as well. Admiral Kurita has talked with Yamamoto and others and is hopeful that negotiations will bring an end to this war, even if it means that we will have to give back much of what we have conquered. In short, we might have to admit defeat in order to preserve Japan."

Masao said quietly, "I have a better idea. The situation means that we must create a victory so that talks can begin."

When the Nazis came to power, one of the first things they did was strongly encourage those of the minor nobility in Germany to stop using "von" in front of their last names. It was an attempt at egalitarianism that annoyed the erstwhile Johann von Klaas and it was one of the first things he reinstated when he defected to the Americans. Of course, important people in the Nazi hierarchy, such as von Runstedt and von Ribbentrop and von Papen, were powerful enough to simply ignore Hitler's pressure. Klaas's usage of the title seemed to amuse the Americans. More important, they had accepted him as well as his minor title.

FBI Special Agent Harris looked up from his desk. "Found them, Herr von Klaas?"

Von Klaas almost bowed before forgetting that Americans didn't do that. At least he hadn't started to give the Hitler salute. It was something he'd avoided as much as possible in Mexico and would have been more embarrassing than bowing.

"Sorry, but no. The messages were in English, not German, which makes sense. Anything in German would have attracted undue attention."

Harris smiled. "It also means I don't need you to translate, Herr von Klaas."

"Then send me to Brazil, Agent Harris."

"Soon," Harris replied. "Now, what was in the messages?"

"First, let me say that Braun and his comrades are very clever. Like I said, they transmitted in English, which would not have attracted any attention unless we were looking, and the messages were not coded. They are hiding in plain sight. The messages are extremely short and we've been unable to track them to any specific location."

"No surprise."

"The messages contained symbols and vague terms like objectives and resources, which would mean nothing to somebody not looking. If we weren't looking at that frequency and those times, the verbiage would be totally innocuous and appear to be conversations between the representatives of a couple of businesses. However, we are looking and I believe Braun and whoever might be with him north of the border are beginning to run out of money."

Harris laughed. "Bloody marvelous. Couldn't happen to a nicer bunch of Nazi swine."

"Although Braun is clever, I think that the men

Braun left behind in Monterrey and Mexico City may have pretty well spent all they were given, which was about fifty thousand dollars. Perhaps it was too much money and too much temptation for them to resist. Braun was lamenting that things were getting tight where he was, and that they should send him more of what he referred to as resources. Their response was that things were tight for them as well and reminded him that he had not fulfilled his end of the contract, whatever that was, and that he shouldn't expect more until he does."

Harris nodded thoughtfully. "Either more sabotage or, more likely, he's to provide information on the location of the *Saratoga*'s task force. Do you really think they've run out of money?"

Von Klaas shrugged. "Braun is a very smart man and I believe he took at least one other man, likely Krause, with him. Krause is not stupid and he would not be profligate. As to the ones he likely left behind in Mexico, as I said, they are idiots and could easily have gone through the money I gave them."

"Then what will they do to get more?" Harris enquired.

"Agent Harris, I haven't the foggiest idea."

The five sailors were engrossed in their game, high-stakes poker. The pot was at several hundred dollars and might go higher, which fixated them. A couple of them had never seen that much money all at one time.

What they were doing was illegal and might get them court-martialed if caught, but the chance at heavy action was worth more than what they considered the remote risk of punishment. If the police or shore patrol burst in on their basement room, they could expect time in jail or the brig, and be busted in rank, but that was a chance they were willing to take. It was also why they'd posted a guard outside the door.

Thus, they were stunned when two masked and armed men burst in, guns pointed at them.

"Put your hands on your heads and stand up."

It was awkward, but they complied, almost too shocked to speak. One, a sailor whose cousin had been standing guard, was worried and asked about him.

"Your friend at the door is taking a nap. Whether he wakes up or not is largely up to you. Now, turn and face the wall and disrobe completely."

"What?" one of the gamblers exclaimed.

"Shut up and do as you're told. We could kill you all here and leave you and no one would notice for days, but we won't unless you force us to."

Sullenly, the men stripped down. They were told to stand naked and facing the wall with their hands stretched up as high as they could. While one robber held a gun on them, the other scooped up the money and stuffed it into a cloth laundry bag. The second man then rifled through their clothing and found a little more money along with a small cache of weapons.

"I guess you don't trust anybody," the first man cackled. "Can't say as I blame you."

"We'll get you, you prick," snarled one of the gamblers.

"Actually, you won't. First, you have no idea who we are and where we're going and, second, you were performing an illegal act. What are you going to do, run to the police and admit that you got robbed while committing a crime? What do you think they might say when you asked them to get you your money back? That would not be smart. No, you will write this off as a cost of doing business. You might want to get a better man as a guard. It was very easy to take him down, although I don't think he's badly hurt."

The second man gave the money bag to the first and then scooped up the gamblers' clothing. "This will ensure that you don't leave for a while," the first gunman continued. "We'll leave your clothing just a ways down the alley."

With that, Braun and Krause departed. They were laughing and almost exhilarated. They took off the bandannas that served as masks and turned the reversible jackets they'd been wearing inside out. They got on a San Diego bus and sat separately, even going past where they'd pulled off the holdup. No one was in sight. Braun thought the gamblers might still be looking for their clothes. It would be a while before they found them in a trash container, and they would not wander around naked for the same reason that they would not go to the cops.

Two hours later, they were in the apartment above Swenson Engineering. Braun laughed and held up a wad of cash. "A little over two thousand dollars. Well, along with the other heists we've pulled, this ought to keep us in money for at least a little while."

The two men had spent time scouting out a number of such high-stakes games and in a two-night period following a payday, they'd hit four of them. They now had more than ten thousand dollars to keep them going.

"Yes," said Krause, "but we can't do it again. The next time they'll have real guards on lookout and others watching the guards. They'll catch us and we'll have our asses kicked and then we'll be thrown into the ocean as shark bait. The next time we're short of cash, we'll have to come up with something new."

"Suggestions?"

Krause grinned. "I suppose we could always rob a small bank in a small town."

"Those are Japs," yelled Stecher. Farris took half a second to confirm that the planes screaming only a few feet overhead were indeed Zeros before throwing himself prone and beginning to crawl to a culvert.

Machine guns chattered and bullets ripped into the American camp at Fairbanks. Men ran in all directions, stunned by the suddenness of the attack. Some were chewed by bullets and left sprawling. Farris could hear screaming.

"What happened to our radar?" yelled Stecher. "And where the hell are our planes?"

Farris saw that the handful of American fighters and transports lined up along the still inadequate airstrip were being shot to pieces. So too were fuel dumps and other storage facilities. He didn't bother telling Stecher that radar was inadequate and maybe pointed in the wrong direction, but he did wonder just why no American planes or spotters had caught sight of the oncoming Japanese horde.

Plane after plane swept over the base, strafing and bombing without much in the way of resistance. A few antiaircraft guns opened up, but they didn't stop the Japanese. A couple of enemy planes were hit and one crashed into a warehouse, resulting in an explosion and fire that quickly consumed the entire building. Farris wondered if the Japanese pilot, his plane damaged, had directed his plane there.

A pair of American P47s did make it into the air and a couple more Zeros were shot down before the American planes went down in flames too.

It was over as quickly as it had begun. Farris checked his watch. He thought the raid had lasted no more than fifteen minutes. A grim-faced Colonel Gavin began shouting orders and yelling at a major who looked like wanted to be anyplace else on the planet. Perhaps it was the major's fault that the Japs had gotten so close, although overall responsibility for the base was Gavin's.

Ambulances had begun to pick up the wounded and the dead, while shocked but unhurt GIs crawled out from where they'd been hiding. Stecher grabbed Farris's arm and pulled him.

"Come this way."

Farris did as directed. In a little while they stood with a bunch of others around the wreckage of an airplane, a Japanese Zero. The tail was burning brightly. The gas tank had exploded and fires were consuming it.

"Look in the cockpit," Stecher said, laughing. "That's a fucking Jap."

Indeed it was, Farris thought. The man had been burned to a crisp and was little more than a charred and blackened skeleton. His white teeth seemed to be laughing at them. Should I feel sympathy for him, Farris wondered. After all, didn't the pilot have a family? Or friends? Where there people who would mourn for him when they received word that he'd gone on a final mission?

So, should I feel sorry for him? Farris asked himself.

Fuck no.

CHAPTER 16

A TALL, RANGY MARINE LANCE CORPORAL WALKED into Harris's office and almost saluted, stopping quickly when he remembered that he was seeing a civilian, and not an officer. His face was pale and there was a large white bandage on his head. He looked around curiously at the decrepit furniture that was clearly a bunch of castoffs.

The FBI, recognizing its lack of numbers and communications limitations in the San Diego area, had convinced the navy to give them a group of offices on base and, by design, these were down a drab hallway from where Dane worked. As usual, the last to show up got the crummiest in the way of chairs, tables, and desks. Harris did not complain. It was how the game was played and, besides, he didn't anticipate spending a whole lot of time in the office. Once the problem of the saboteurs was solved, he would move on to other cases.

"What's your name, son?" Harris asked softly to try and gain the Marine's confidence. The young man had telephoned earlier and said he wanted to meet. Harris guessed him as in his early twenties.

"Eppler, sir, Lance Corporal Lee Eppler."

"Great. Now close the door and sit down." Eppler did as directed and Harris continued. "Now tell me what you have on your mind."

Eppler took a deep breath as if what he was going to say was difficult to admit. "Sir, there are rumors all over the place, and me being here talking to you confirms one of them, and that's that the FBI is actually here on base. The second rumor is that you're chasing saboteurs like the ones who derailed those trains."

"We haven't announced that any saboteurs derailed anything."

"You don't have to, sir. A whole bunch of people were working on clearing wrecks, treating injured, and stuff like that. They could see things and they listened to you guys talk. The trains were sabotaged."

Harris was intrigued. He was also a little pissed that there were no secrets on a naval base. Despite the war, San Diego was still a small town full of gossips.

"Okay, son, what do you know about sabotaging trains?"

"Seriously, sir, I don't know anything specific. But something strange did happen to me. Last weekend, some guys I know slightly offered me twenty bucks if I'd be a doorman at some kind of big-money card game. I was to keep unwanted people out and give a warning if the cops were in the area."

Harris smiled. "Does the military really give a shit about card games?"

"Generally no, sir, but there was going to be a ton of money in this one, maybe thousands of dollars, so nobody wanted to take chances. Since I send almost all my money home, I knew I could use the twenty bucks. At any rate, I didn't do a very good job. While I thought I was keeping watch, somebody sneaked up on me and knocked me cold." He fingered the bandage on his skull. "The medics said I was lucky to get away with a few stitches and a mild concussion. When I came to, I was tied up and gagged. There was yelling in the room where the action was. I couldn't hardly believe it, but the bad guys were telling the gamblers to strip. Finally, two guys came out with a bag that I later learned contained the money. Like I said, maybe as much as several thousand dollars."

Harris whistled. "That is a good-sized haul and one hell of a poker game for a bunch of swabbies and jarheads to be playing."

Eppler laughed. "Yeah. My so-called friends must have been pros in real life. The bad guys also had the players' clothes with them. They talked among themselves for a second, and that's why I thought of calling you."

Harris leaned forward. "Really?"

"Yes, sir, they were speaking German."

A few moments later, both Dane and Merchant arrived. Harris had summoned them since Eppler was part of the military and, therefore, under their jurisdiction. Also, he was likely to be impressed with their rank. He was right. Eppler seemed momentarily nonplussed but quickly got over it.

"How did you know they were speaking German?" Merchant asked.

"Both my grandparents came from Germany and my mother speaks it fluently. After a number of years talking to the old people, a little of it rubbed off on me, so, yes, sir, I did recognize it as German."

"What were they saying?" Dane inquired.

"I really couldn't tell completely, sir. I picked up a lot of words, but I don't know all that much. It did sound like one, the older of the two, was telling the other guy, who was a little younger but bigger, to hurry up."

Dane smiled. "Did you see them?"

"I pretended I was unconscious. They had guns and had already hurt me. If they thought I was listening and watching I was afraid they'd kill me, so I played dead."

"Good move," said Harris.

"But I did sneak a look as they were leaving. They'd taken off their masks so they wouldn't look weird on the outside, and I got a decent look at the bigger guy."

Merchant smiled happily. "Could you pick him out?"

"Don't know, sir, but I'd sure as hell be happy to try."

Dane opened a folder filled with photographs which he then spread on the table. "Is he in this group?"

Lance Corporal Eppler looked over the array, staring intently. He fingered several photos, paused, and smiled. "This is the big guy."

Harris, Merchant, and Dane grinned at each other. The young Marine had picked out Wilhelm Braun's associate, Gunther Krause.

Now what? they thought. First, Harris asked if Eppler had gotten his twenty and was told, no. "Hell no, sir, and I have no problem with that. After all, I really didn't do my job very well, did I? Actually, the guys in the game first thought I was in cahoots with the bad guys until they realized that I was actually hurt. Then they drove me on base and dumped me at the hospital, right by the emergency room. I managed to stagger in under my own power."

"What did you tell the medics?" Harris asked.

"That I fell and hit my head on a curb."

"They believe that?" he continued.

Eppler grinned. "Not for a moment, sir, but a lot of guys get drunk, fall down, and hurt themselves. Also, they had more important things on their minds. There had been a couple of stabbings, so they patched me up, gave me some aspirin, and put me on light duty for a couple of weeks. I kind of like light duty."

Harris continued. "Okay, Lance Corporal Eppler, here's what's going to happen. You are not going to tell anyone about this conversation or what you saw at the card game, or you will spend the rest of your life in a desert counting scorpions. I don't think your gambler friends are going to be talking to you about it, so don't worry about that. If they do, we'll take care of them. Same thing with anyone else in your outfit, particularly your officers and NCOs. If they get too nosy or don't believe that you got hurt falling down, Captain Merchant is going to give you a note on Admiral Spruance's stationery saying that they are to butt out, only a little more polite. Big thing, young man, is that you saw nothing, remember nothing, and this conversation never took place, got that?"

Eppler swallowed. "Got it, sir."

"Good," said Harris and slipped him a couple of twenties. "Maybe the night wasn't a total loss."

When the Marine left, they looked at each other. Dane started. "For supermen, those two Germans aren't too fucking smart, are they? Jesus, if Eppler had been better at security, the krauts could have gotten hurt, if not killed. Maybe the gamblers would have fought back as well."

Harris disagreed. "If security at the game had been better, they wouldn't have tried. It does show, however, that the two Nazis are getting desperate. Jesus, from crashing trains to robbing gamblers? What a comedown."

"I think we are genuinely closing in on them," Merchant said, "and they are running out of time and options. Maybe we can get them and roll up the whole bunch, including the people in Mexico."

Dane and Harris looked at each other. They had a preposterous idea they'd been discussing between the two of them. Since Harris was the civilian and couldn't be chewed out by Merchant, he responded. "Y'know, Captain, just maybe we don't want to do that, at least not right now."

Farris's small company was one of several ordered out on patrol. They were out doing recon work even though they still didn't know all that much about it. Fortunately, they were assisted by a dozen Alaskan Volunteers led by the large man named Bear, and the Alaskans' tracking skills were immensely better than theirs.

The Alaskans wore white cloths over their regular clothing, which annoyed Farris since his men hadn't been issued any winter gear like that. When he asked Bear about it, the Alaskan had simply laughed. "We took the sheets off our beds and cut them up. Beats the hell out of waiting for the army to come through with the right kind of gear."

A chagrined Farris decided he'd have his men do the same thing when they got back to base.

The Americans were helped by the fact that a couple of inches of wet snow had fallen, which meant that anyone travelling through the area would leave tracks. A light snow continued to fall, rendering visibility poor, but that worked both ways.

Colonel Gavin did not think there were large numbers of Japanese too close to Fairbanks just yet, but he was not going to take a chance. Along with Farris's troops, several other company-strength patrols had been sent out to probe and upset any Japanese scouts who were trying to assess American numbers. Gavin had openly wondered why the Japanese hadn't coordinated an attack on Fairbanks with the carrier raid that had caused so much damage to their meager resources. Had Japanese infantry attacked during the chaos, the American force could have been forced to give up the city and the base, or at best, suffered serious casualties. Farris could visualize hordes of screaming Japanese emerging from the forests and chopping American soldiers with their swords and overrunning them while they cowered in their foxholes.

Now, supplies to replace what was lost were arriving in a thin but steady flow, and these included a new squadron of P47 fighters. Because of the need to ship material to supply existing forces, additional manpower was given a lower priority. A trickle of reinforcements, including more men from the 36th Infantry Division and a handful of Marines, continued to arrive, taking the last miles on foot as the engineers attempted to lengthen the highway from the south.

The advance paused and a soldier near them lit

up a Chesterfield. "Put it out," snapped Bear. The soldier with the cigarette glared at him.

"What the fuck for?" the GI snarled. "You ain't my mommy. Hell, you ain't even in the real army. And besides, it ain't nighttime so nobody can see the glow in the dark."

Bear matched the soldier's glare and the GI wilted. "Because you can smell cigarette smoke a mile away in the woods, that's why, jerkoff, and that would alert the Japs that you're coming so they can blow your worthless ass away."

Farris was about to support Bear when the soldier simply nodded and put out the cigarette he'd been puffing on. "Pass it around," Farris said, "no smoking."

"But we'll die," lamented another soldier in a falsetto whine, bringing nervous laughter. Even Bear chuckled, while the GI who'd been scolded just turned away.

"The same thing with matches at night," Farris added, "but you already know that. And keep the talking down, too."

At Bear's suggestion, they were formed up with two platoons in front and a third bringing up the rear. The understrength company still didn't have enough men for a headquarters platoon. Stecher controlled a slightly overstrength squad that passed for one.

Even though there was no intelligence confirming that the main Japanese force was near, the patrol was a strong one because of a real concern that a decent number of Japanese might possibly be close by and could easily overwhelm a smaller patrol. At least that was the theory. Farris seemed to recall that Custer had more men than he at the Little Big Horn and a fat lot of good it had done him and the Seventh

Cavalry. Of course, the Seventh didn't have radios or
air support, which might have proven useful.

One of the scouts emerged and gave the signal to
halt. They froze. The scout had found footprints in
the snow. "The Japs tried to cover their tracks," the
scout explained, "but they did a lousy job."

Now moving with utmost caution and letting the
scout and Bear lead, they followed the tracks. Both
civilians estimated the Japanese force at maybe a
dozen men, an augmented squad.

Again they called a halt. Bear pointed at a thicket
about a hundred yards away. The dense forest and
falling snow prevented them from seeing it sooner.
"They're in there and they can see us," Bear said.

Just as Farris was about to ask what the Japanese
were waiting for, rifle and machine-gun fire rippled
from the thicket, crashing into trees and bushes, tearing off branches and bark. The Americans dropped to
the ground. Farris grabbed his helmet and tried to
melt into the earth. He got a mouthful of snow for his
efforts. With macabre humor, he hoped it wasn't yellow
snow from where some Jap had pissed. He and his
men started to recover from the shock of being fired
on and began searching out targets. Close to seventy
men soon responded with rifles, carbines, and light
machine guns and BARs. Farris, almost overcome with
excitement and fear, managed to remember to order
the rear guard to keep facing the rear. He wanted no
surprises creeping up on them.

"Are they going to retreat from there?" Stecher asked.

Bear grinned. "Retreat to where? We're between
them and safety. If anything we're pushing them back
to Gavin."

Someone screamed and the call went out for a medic. One of Farris's men had been hit. The Japanese fire began to slacken under the intense American shooting, and then it stopped. American soldiers crawled closer, maintaining a high rate of fire, shredding the thicket.

Farris's radio man said that Major Baylor wanted to know if they needed artillery support. Farris said it would be nice if they knew precisely where they were, but no thank you.

More soldiers crawled to the thicket and hurled in grenades, which exploded with loud *crumps*. Again, there was no response. The damn Japs were either dead or waiting for them to get closer.

"Now's the hard part," Bear said with a feral grin. "Somebody gets to go in there. Kind of like hunters in India I read about going into the jungle after a wounded tiger."

Farris swallowed. "You coming with me?" he asked.

Bear grinned. He was openly pleased that Farris was going in himself instead of letting others take the risk. "Wouldn't miss it for the world, Lieutenant."

Cautiously, Farris led a line of soldiers the rest of the way across the small clearing and toward the thicket which now consisted of mangled trees. There was silence. Farris's heart was pounding as he pushed his way through. He halted as he saw his first dead Jap a few yards in and a second one just a few feet farther away. They had been hit by multiple bullets and were now just bloody human wreckage.

More troops filed in and Farris was pleased to see that they kept themselves spread out and were looking for survivors instead of gawking at the first dead Japanese soldier most of them had ever seen.

They passed through the rest of the thicket. Quick shots finished off a few Japanese soldiers who might yet be alive. One of them exploded as the bullets detonated the grenade he'd been hiding, sending gore over the nearest soldiers. Tim angrily ordered his men to shoot all the corpses, no matter how badly mangled they were.

In all, they found eleven bodies, including one sergeant who'd killed himself by stuffing the barrel of his Arisaka rifle into his mouth and pulling the trigger with his toe. Farris made the cold-blooded decision to not bury them. It would take too much time and, besides, the ground was probably too frozen to dig even a mass grave for so many dead bodies. They searched the bodies for identification and info, such as anything resembling orders and some letters home. It was all chicken-scratching to Farris, but maybe someone like his uncle could decipher it.

Bear pointed at the bodies. "What do you see, Lieutenant?"

"Along with a bunch of dead Japs, I see Japs who are scrawny and in rags. Hell, they must be desperate." Then he thought that a desperate enemy could be the worst kind.

Bob Hope and his troupe's arrival at San Diego coincided with the astonishing news that the U.S. Army had landed in North Africa. The war to liberate Europe was on. The news was met with mixed reactions by the troops. Some were jealous that they weren't in on the action, while others were thankful that the fighting was taking place far, far away.

All of a sudden, place names like Oran, Bizerte,

and Tripoli were being used as if the speakers knew where the hell they were. And who the hell was Dwight Eisenhower, the American general in command? With a name like Eisenhower, he sounded more like a German.

Amanda and Dane sat on the ground about a third of the way back from the improvised stage, and quietly wondered how many GIs actually knew where North Africa was in the first place. Still, it was a damn good feeling to be finally striking back instead of taking it in the groin for so very long.

Tim thought Amanda looked striking in a white blouse and blue slacks. She'd worn slacks instead of a skirt so that she didn't accidentally give some sailors a show. That apparently either didn't occur to Grace or, more likely, she didn't care as she sat with Merchant and happily exposed an expanse of thigh. Tim hoped he and Amanda could find a quiet place later on and become at least as intimate as they had in the surf. Since then, he was back in the monastery and she in her nunnery. And now they were part of a huge crowd of people. Damn.

Twenty thousand jubilant soldiers, sailors, and Marines were packed densely on the field in front of the large wooden stage. Hope was there along with Frances Langford who, Amanda decided, really didn't have all that good a voice, and slapstick comedian Jerry Colonna, who Dane admitted wasn't all that funny. A man named Les Brown led what he called "Les Brown's Band of Renown" with okay talent.

But what the hell, the fact that, with the exception of Hope, the talent wasn't all that talented didn't matter. They'd made the effort to entertain the troops and the troops appreciated it with noisy enthusiasm for every poorly sung song and every bad joke. Better, it was a break from routine and everyone was having a great time listening to Hope tease all the brass who were in the front few rows and taking it with apparent good humor. Like they had a choice, Amanda whispered.

Hope pointed to the generals and admirals. "How many of you have ever seen an enlisted man before?" he said, drawing gales of hoots and laughter. "Well, you've struck the mother lode this time." Hope would never go beyond gentle teasing, which was part of what made him so compelling and likeable.

Hope ragged on about the bad food, the miserable accommodations (unless you wore a star on your shoulder, of course), how lousy the weather was in southern California what with the almost constant sunshine, and what it was like to get Montezuma's Revenge along with other maladies from a trip south of the border to Tijuana. Hope had been touring for the USO since May 1941, well before the formal start of hostilities. He informed the troops that there was no way he was going to slow down. Hell, he reminded them, he wasn't even forty years old yet.

"I'm going to go to England, and Churchill and this Eisenhower guy will be in the audience. Then I'll go to North Africa and do a command performance for Rommel, except we'll be commanding him, of course, and he'll be watching from a prison cage."

That comment brought cheers and he continued. "When I started these shows, I said I'd take them as close to the front lines as possible. Little did I know that part of the front lines would include San

Diego. Y'know, that's got to change, and real soon."
More cheers. "Here's a thought. Next year at this
time why don't we have this show a little bit farther
west? Like Tokyo."

Still more cheers. "And we'll have Hirohito in the
audience as well." He grinned widely and wickedly.
"Don't you think he'd look absolutely wonderful in
prison stripes?" He struck a thoughtful pose. "Yes, a
prison-striped kimono."

The show ended to wild applause and the happy
crowd filed out. Amanda and Tim waited for the field
to empty. She was far from the only woman present,
as many nurses and female military were present along
with a handful of wives and local girlfriends. Still,
girl-hungry young men stared at her. Some glared,
apparently resentful that she'd found an officer to
care for her. Amanda decided she didn't care.

As Dane stood up, an envelope fell out of his jacket
pocket. "Oops," he said. "I totally forgot I had this
on me. Can't have other people seeing this." He was
annoyed at himself. He'd left in such a hurry after
meeting with Harris that he'd forgotten the pictures
were in his pocket.

"Am I other people?" she teased.

Tim smiled. He'd gotten in the habit of talking with
her about almost everything, and security be damned.
Who the hell was Amanda going to talk to? Tojo?

He handed her the envelope. "Here. These are
a couple of photos of some interesting characters."

"Your saboteurs?"

"Possibly. No, it's likely them. We may have gotten a break."

Amanda happily opened the envelope. She liked

it when Tim trusted her enough to show her things like that. She stared at the first picture and paled. "Tim, oh, my God."

"What?"

"I've seen this man."

"Wh-where?" Dane stammered. This was incredible. She looked at him sadly. "I don't remember."

CHAPTER 17

AT FIRST, NEITHER SANDY NOR GRACE COULD
identify the man in the photo either, although they
too were certain they'd seen him somewhere. All three
agreed that they'd never seen the second man. But
where had they seen the first man, was the maddening question.

Dane had quickly contacted Harris and they all met
in the FBI office close to Tim's. The photos were on
the table, staring back at them. Both Tim and Harris
were stunned that the women might have been close to
the German, and the women were frustrated that they
couldn't recall when, where, or why. Harris was pacing
and it was clear that his frustration was growing as well.

Finally, it was Grace who broke the spell, clapping
her hands and laughing. "Oh shit. Now it's coming to
me. He was the creep in Zuckerman's office who looked
so angry and like he wanted to undress us right then
and there."

"Yes!" exclaimed Amanda, and Sandy chimed in as
well.

This required a quick explanation of why they were in Zuckerman's office in the first place, and Harris took notes. He was mildly curious about this Mack character and what might be in the safe deposit box, but that was a job for the state of California, which seemed to have it covered.

First thing the next morning Harris, Dane, and a couple of other agents went to Zuckerman's office. The additional firepower was present on the off chance that they might run into Braun just as Amanda and the others had. If so, Dane had specific orders to stand back and he pledged to obey.

Dane was mildly amused when the lawyer and his secretary, Judith, arrived together, and were conversing with a degree of intimacy that went beyond a working relationship. He wondered if there was a Mrs. Zuckerman or if the secretary had a husband, and decided it was none of his business.

Inside his office, Zuckerman looked at the picture and nodded. He handed it to Judith who agreed. "His name is Olaf Swenson and he rents some property from me," Zuckerman said.

"What do you know about him?" Harris asked.

"Not all that much. I know that he's a Swedish engineer who started up a small business and is working doing something for the navy. He works with another foreigner who might be Swedish as well. Swenson is the one who pays the rent, and his money's always been good. He pays on time and in cash."

"He's a jerk." Judith glared. "He's rude and obnoxious. It's obvious he dislikes Jews. He probably can't stand the thought of having to pay money to one."

Harris nodded grimly. "That's because he's German and a Nazi and SS to boot."

Zuckerman recoiled as if he'd been struck. "A Nazi? Here? That can't be. I would never do business with a Nazi. What is your proof?"

Harris was about to respond that the FBI didn't need proof in wartime to arrest someone, but thought better of it. "It's true, Mr. Zuckerman. These photos are those of a part of a group of Nazis left behind in Mexico when the war started. These two have come north to commit as much sabotage as they can. I normally wouldn't give you all that information, but I want you to understand what we're all up against."

The lawyer shook his head as if to clear his mind of the shock. "I believe. How do I evict the sons of bitches?"

"Hopefully, we can do it for you," Harris said. "Now, please give me the address of the property."

After the agents left with the address and all other information they possessed, Judith hugged a disconsolate and sobbing Zuckerman. "I can't believe I rented to Nazis. I can't believe I had anything to do with the filthy swine. After what's happening to my family in Europe, it's almost impossible to comprehend."

Zuckerman's last letter from his Aunt Hilda in Austria had been smuggled out and informed him that several of his family had been ordered to report to a new work camp in Poland. His aunt added that she hadn't yet been swept up, and said she'd received a postcard saying their relatives had arrived at a place near the town of Auschwitz and were doing well.

Aunt Hilda used subtle phrasing in her letter to fool anyone reading it. It was clear that she didn't believe it at all, and that their relatives were likely doomed. As was she, Zuckerman thought.

Judith sat beside him on the office couch. She cradled his head to her bosom and rocked him and kissed his forehead. She too had relatives back in Europe, although in France where she hoped they were safe. That is, if there was any place in the world where a Jew could be safe.

"Look on the bright side, dear," Judith said as tears ran down her cheek. "Now you have the chance to destroy him." She stood up and straightened her dress. "And we are going to do exactly what that nice FBI man said we should do, aren't we?"

Zuckerman managed a smile. "You're right. A little vacation is more than in order."

Caution, patience, and a strong sense of paranoia were vital assets for any agent working behind enemy lines, and both Braun and Krause possessed all three in abundance. They had spent much time observing the goings on in the neighborhood near Swenson Engineering. They observed the actions and routines of the area regulars and quietly memorized them. They knew who their neighbors were and who their friends and customers were. This, of course, meant that they too were known quantities to those same neighbors, and they went out of their way to maintain friendly, even cordial, relations, even cheering American victories when they were announced. We're all in this war together, aren't we?

Like any neighborhood or cluster of businesses,

there was a pattern to life and any deviation from that pattern attracted attention.

Thus, the presence of the two unmarked cars with two men in each was immediately noted by the two Germans. One car was in front and down the street and the other in the rear of the building and down a ways. The occupants of both vehicles appeared to be interested in Swenson Engineering, and were quickly identified by the two Germans as a menace.

Instead of driving onto their property, Braun and Krause drove past and around, parked a little distance away, and observed. They were quietly thankful that the Ford didn't have the Swenson Engineering sign attached at the moment. After a while, the two men in one of the cars were spelled by two more men in another car. It confirmed to the two Germans that they'd been discovered.

Braun sighed. "They are not very good at their jobs. They are either FBI or local police and it doesn't matter. We've been betrayed and now we have to run."

"Where to?" asked Krause.

"Wherever you want," Braun said. "As we previously discussed, we are going to split up and go our own ways. Our part in this war is over. We have no way of notifying the people in Mexico who will doubtless soon be arrested if it hasn't happened already. We have phony identification that should enable each of us to fashion a life. When Germany is victorious, we can each, separately, find our way back to the Reich for whatever is due us. Since we failed, I doubt it will be much of a reward," he added bitterly, thinking that their reward could be years in a prison camp as the Reich didn't tolerate failures.

Krause was silent. He'd been listening to the radio and reading the newspapers and if they were only half correct, the Third Reich was in grave danger. The offensives in Russia had stalled and a second Russian winter was upon the German army. Also, the Americans were in North Africa helping the British and there was a massive buildup of American forces that the German navy was unable to stop. No, German victory in his opinion was far from a foregone conclusion, and Braun's dreams of returning to Germany might never come true. Defeat seemed far more likely. He also felt that Japan would sooner or later feel the wrath of the Americans.

Nor did Krause think it would be all that easy to disappear, even in the vastness of the United States. If the American government had their names, they likely had their pictures, and he'd seen photos of wanted men on the walls of post offices and in the newspapers. He could envision some small child telling his mommy that the man in line to buy stamps looked just like the man glowering from the wanted poster, the man accused of espionage. Oh, that would be wonderful, he thought.

"We will need money," Krause said.

"Fortunately, we have some. There's almost seven thousand dollars in the safe deposit box at the bank. Since it's in another name, I doubt that the police are watching it yet. I suggest we get the money, split it up, and disappear. You will leave first, as I have a job to do."

Krause nodded slowly. He knew he was being cheated. He'd counted the money when Braun wasn't looking and knew there was more than twelve thousand dollars, not seven. He didn't like the thought of Braun screwing him and leaving him on the run for the rest of his life. Krause thought he understood what job Braun was going to do. But what could he do about it and how could it work to his benefit?

"All is quiet on the Pacific Front," joked Captain Merchant. "And I like it that way."

Dane couldn't complain either. Work, if you could call it that, was falling into a routine. He now had a staff of two and they did much of the initial work, leaving him to analyze what they had written down. One of his staff was Nancy Sullivan, the half-Japanese daughter of the store owner in Bridger. She'd been raised by a Japanese mother, and both spoke and read the language far better than he. She could also write it, which he couldn't at all. Going to work for the navy had transformed what Dane thought was a shy young girl into a bright and cheerful young woman who exuded considerable confidence. This further confounded those who thought all Japanese women were shy and submissive.

Getting Nancy onto the base had taken a little help from Merchant and Spruance, but she had proven invaluable, even if she did draw some strange glances from others. She puzzled them. Was she Japanese or not? As long as they left her alone, she was content and safe, while her mother prudently remained in hiding somewhere near Bridger.

The second staffer was a different story. He was a recently commissioned ensign who had majored in Japanese and Asian studies at Harvard and, in Dane's opinion, might be able to write poetry in Japanese but couldn't order food in a Japanese restaurant. The ensign was clearly frustrated that a young college student was so much more knowledgeable than he. It also meant he was relegated to routine clerical tasks, which thoroughly annoyed him.

Nor was Amanda all that busy either. There had been no major fighting in some months, and that meant empty beds in the hospital, while those that were occupied contained patients who were either mending or were stabilized. As a result, they had plenty of time to be together, but no opportunity to be intimate. Their time at the beach had not occurred again. Amanda had hinted that she might be willing to go away with him for a few days, but where? Only Merchant had his own place off base and Grace now spent a lot of time there. He and Amanda joked that they did not want to share the place, even if Merchant would agree to it. They supposed they could go farther away, perhaps to Arizona, but both were essentially on call and neither wanted to take the chance of being absent if something important occurred.

Dane was staring at a wall when the phone rang. He answered and a deep voice responded. "Commander Dane?"

"Speaking."

"I wish to make a bargain with you."

"Do I know you?"

"In a way. My name is Gunther Krause and my companion is Wilhelm Braun."

The information took Tim's breath away. "How did you get this number?"

Krause chuckled. "It was easy. I asked the base information for the name of the navy person who was working with the FBI. I didn't know you by name, but I assumed there had to be someone working as liaison with them. They gave me your name and number right away. You really ought to be more careful with your secrets. After all, there is a war on."

"What do you want, Mr. Krause?"

"I wish to go free. In return for information of tremendous value to you, you will have me pardoned of all crimes I might have committed, and you will permit me to live the rest of my life in the United States."

"I don't think I can do that."

"Of course you can't. However, you can send the request to your government and they can do it. In return for that and as a good-faith down payment, I will now tell you what Herr Braun is planning to do."

Wilhelm Braun parked his car in front of the building that housed Zuckerman's offices. He got out, looked around, and saw nothing out of the ordinary, nothing to arouse his primal instincts. He was focused on the idea of killing Zuckerman the Jew. He knew his hatred was making him careless, but it didn't bother him. He wanted to kill and Zuckerman the Jew would be an easy target. He looked forward to seeing the look of horror on Zuckerman's face. Perhaps he would rape his secretary while the Jew watched before putting both of them out of their misery.

The Jew was the only one who knew he was here, and therefore, it must have been Zuckerman who turned him in to the police. He did wonder if it had been the supposedly highly vaunted FBI who'd been watching his building; since whoever it had been was so obvious. Perhaps the FBI had had to farm out the task to local police who were far less skilled than Hoover's Bureau. It seemed likely but right now it was terribly irrelevant. He would be on his way out of San Diego in a very few minutes.

He shifted so the pistol in his belt was within easy reach. Once he'd sworn his life to his Fuehrer and, later in Mexico, had wondered if he had the courage to die for the Reich. Now he knew. He did have that strength. But he would not die alone and hopefully not today. Zuckerman and his whore of a secretary would die today and burn in the hell that all Jews deserved.

Braun despaired that he and Krause had done so little to help Hitler. A couple of trains wrecked meant nothing. They and their contents had doubtless been replaced in a matter of minutes by America's incredible production capabilities. Nor had he had any success in finding out the location of the surviving American carrier. Should he make it back to Germany, he thought, he did not want to return knowing that he would be punished, not rewarded. Therefore, he would not ever return to Germany. He would disappear in the United States. Still, it behooved him to do as much damage as he could, for his own satisfaction if nothing else, before disappearing.

He entered Zuckerman's outer office. Good, he thought, it was empty. No clients were waiting. A sign on the whore's desk said she was out. If she stayed out she might be lucky and remain alive. No matter. He would not stick around and wait for her after killing the Jew. He heard sounds coming from the inner office indicating that Zuckerman was inside. Perhaps he was screwing the bitch? The thought made him smile as he pulled the Luger from his belt. Perhaps he would be able to kill them as they were fucking their little Jewish brains out.

He pushed the door open and stood in surprise. No one was behind the desk.

"Hands up," came a shockingly stern voice from behind him. "FBI. You're under arrest."

Braun started to turn. "Don't even think of it," the voice said. "Now drop the gun."

A side door leading to a bathroom opened and Braun was aware of another agent to his left and still others now to his rear. Braun didn't move. He was frozen with indecision.

"Braun, my name is Harris and I'm willing to make a deal with you. Work with us and you won't hang or be shot."

Braun laughed harshly but didn't lower his weapon. "No, all I'll do is spend the rest of my life in a small cell while Jews like Zuckerman run the world. No thank you."

Braun wheeled and fired. The shot went high, smashing into the wall. Harris was the first agent to shoot and his bullet took Braun in the chest, flinging him over the desk and onto the floor. The other agents shot quickly, riddling the German's body. The gun fell from his hands and Harris kicked it away.

Harris walked over and stood over Braun. He was breathing shallowly. The others hurried in and began checking him over, but it looked like a useless gesture. Harris was shaking. It was one of only a few times he'd pulled his weapon and the first time in his career that he'd ever shot anyone. He felt nauseous but kept it down. His other agents were responding similarly.

Thank God they'd been available instead of the local sheriff's retired buffoons he'd had to use to stake out Swenson Engineering. Of course, he felt hugely disappointed that Braun was dying, which meant that he could not be turned or pumped for information.

"Braun, do you have anything to say before you die?"

The Nazi smiled grimly as the light faded from his eyes. His voice, however, was surprisingly strong. "Yes, Heil Hitler and fuck you."

"Banzai!"

The shouted cry came from their front and chilled them even more than the cold, wet snow did. The Japanese were within shouting distance. Only thing was, Farris thought, they couldn't see them in the woods. The Japs were hidden by the soggy wet snowflakes that would have been beautiful under other circumstances. Today, the lovely flakes were a deadly camouflage, hiding their fanatic and implacable enemy.

"Banzai!"

Farris was sweating in the cold and began to shiver. He wiped his forehead with his hand. The damn Japs were working themselves into a frenzy. They had come down all the way from Anchorage and now they were finally here, on the outskirts of Fairbanks and with the town behind them. Gavin had his small army arrayed so that multiple strongpoints would provide overlapping and concentrated fire. No one had any real idea how many Sons of Nippon were out there, but the consensus was at least as many as there were Americans.

Damn it to hell, Farris thought. Why wasn't the road from the south open yet? The engineers only had a few miles to go and then troops and armor could come flooding down it, instead of arriving in little trickles like his company had. Soon, he thought, please God soon.

At least Stecher should be happy. He'd been looking for Japs to kill and now they were just a little ways away.

And why didn't the defenders of Fairbanks have enough artillery to pound the enemy in the woods, and why didn't they have enough planes to bomb and strafe the enemy? Because nobody thought this would happen and now good men were going to pay with their lives for somebody's miscalculation.

"Banzai!" and this time a chorus of voices echoed the cry. How damn many of them were there? Farris had an almost overpowering urge to urinate. Or crap. Or hell, maybe both. This would be the first time he and the company had been even close to real combat. He couldn't count shooting at that sub as combat, although the shells the sub fired at them had come disconcertingly close, and taking on that Japanese patrol had been laughingly one-sided. No, this would be personal.

Major Baylor walked by, calm and upright, just as if he was inspecting them on a Saturday morning before going on weekend pass. Farris knew that it was the major's first time in combat, along with Gavin's, but Baylor couldn't show nerves to his men and be their leader. And I can't either, Farris thought.

"Keep lots of ammo ready, make sure your grenades are easy to reach, and keep your bayonets fixed," Baylor said. "Oh yeah, aim for the guys with the swords. Those are their officers."

The thought of sticking someone with a bayonet or being hacked to pieces with a sword swung by a crazy Jap made Farris want to throw up. He patted the pocket of his field jacket. He'd just gotten a letter from Sandy down in San Diego. Yeah, he thought absurdly, Sandy San Diego. She'd been warm and polite, but noncommittal, which, he supposed, was the way it should be. They'd only gone out a couple of times and he hadn't even made it to second base. Still, he was glad someone from the female side of the tracks was writing to him.

"Banzai!"

"Either attack or shut the fuck up," someone yelled and Farris agreed. Do something!

They got their wish. "Oh Jesus, here they come!"

Shapes became dimly visible in the whipping snow. The enemy had gotten to within a hundred yards of them thanks to the crummy weather. Now they were so close he could see expressions on their faces. All hell broke loose as every American soldier opened fire with everything he had. There were a dozen men in Farris's bunker, and along with their rifles, they had a pair of BARs and a .30-caliber Browning machine gun. They all opened up and chopped into the onrushing Japanese.

Farris worked his rifle as rapidly as he could. Aim, fire, work the bolt, aim, fire, work the bolt, and every five bullets, change the clip. He saw Japanese soldiers tumble and fall. Some got up and tried to continue and were shot again and again until they finally fell and stopped moving. Some ran past his little fortress, while others, many others, were headed straight toward him.

"Jesus, they got tanks!" someone yelled, and Farris thought it was Stecher in an adjacent bunker. Two awkward and ugly metal shapes noisily clambered into view. Their machine guns belched fire and their cannon boomed. Shells from the tanks hit near his bunker and raised clods of mud and debris. Somehow, Farris recalled that Japanese tanks were supposed to be miserable, but these looked like monsters to him.

One of his men started hurling grenades and the first wave of Japanese faltered. Still more grenades filled the air. The man who'd thrown the first grenade grabbed his face and fell backward, screaming. An American artillery shell landed in front of one of the tanks, showering it with dirt and making Farris fall back from the shock. Machine-gun bullets raked the tank, but did no harm. An American jumped out and ran through shocked Japanese and up to the tank. Jesus, Farris realized, it was Stecher. The sergeant pried open the driver's hatch and dropped in a grenade. A moment later, the tank exploded, blowing Stecher aside like a leaf.

The second tank hit a rock and threw a tread. Instead of staying safe in their iron hull, the crew jumped out and began running insanely toward Farris.

An officer with a glistening curved sword waved it and urged his men on. Farris aimed and shot him in the chest.

"Good one, Lieutenant," one of his men said.

But here were just too many Japanese. They swarmed on to Farris's position. Some continued past, while others howled and attempted to jab and stab at the men in the trench. A couple of Farris's men panicked and clambered out of the bunker and began running to the second line of defenses. Farris too thought it was time to leave but he couldn't. A dying Japanese soldier had fallen on him and he was stuck under the body. Other Japanese jumped or fell among Farris and the remaining Americans and it became a killing fest, as men on both sides used fists, knives, and teeth. Farris grabbed one Japanese soldier by the throat and strangled him until something hit him on the top of his head and he fell to the muddy bottom of the trench. More bodies piled on him and he tried to claw his way up. There was an explosion and something slammed into his shoulder. He blacked out as excruciating pain overwhelmed him.

Gavin's second defense line consisted of any soldier who could fire a weapon, along with the Alaskan Volunteers and a number of other local people who'd signed up for the duration. He watched in horror as the human wave of enemy soldiers ignored brutal casualties that would have stopped a normal army and overwhelmed much of the first line. Of course they would ignore their own casualties, he thought angrily. They came here to die.

Many of the forward bunkers held out, but others could not. Fleeing American soldiers ran toward him, comingled with charging Japanese.

Gavin's people began firing as quickly as they could, even though they were aware that some of their shots might hit their own men. It was that or die themselves, he thought bitterly.

His artillery, mainly 105mm pack howitzers that had been carried to Fairbanks by mule the last few miles, fired as rapidly as they could, shooting over sights that were set as low as the gunners could make them. "Open sights" was the next order he heard and never thought he would hear in his lifetime. It meant the enemy was almost too close to shoot at.

Gavin was in an open bunker with Bear and Ruby, among others, and they kept shooting, mowing down the Japanese who wouldn't, couldn't, stop charging. Bodies piled up in front of them in a writhing mass. Ruby was beside him, blazing away. Gavin recalled telling her that women shouldn't be on the firing line, and her telling him to go screw himself.

A screaming Japanese soldier stood directly in front of him, a grenade in his hand. Ruby shot him and he fell backward. The grenade exploded, shredding the Japanese soldier.

Both Americans and Japanese hurled grenades as if they were snowballs in a schoolyard fight. Yet another Japanese soldier appeared a few feet away and someone cut him down with a burst from a BAR.

"This can't go on forever," Bear said, gasping in pain. There was blood on his leg and he was having a hard time standing.

A Japanese soldier jumped the sandbags and stumbled forward. Gavin fired, but he clicked on an empty chamber. He was out of ammo. "Down," Ruby ordered, and shot the Japanese in the head as Gavin ducked.

Gavin reloaded, wheeled, and looked for a new target. There weren't any. The ground in front of the bunker was piled sometimes three deep with Japanese dead and dying. He looked at the other positions in the second line and saw much the same thing. The firing was dying out and all around an unnatural silence was beginning to fall. Two tanks were burning in front of his first line, and another had been destroyed to his right. The Japanese armored threat was over, but what about their infantry?

Gavin clambered to the top of the sandbags and looked farther. The few Japanese soldiers left were still screaming their fury, but running aimlessly and were cut down as he watched.

Bear climbed up and stood beside him despite the wound in his leg. "Fuck me, colonel, if we haven't just run out of Japs."

Gavin grunted and gave the order for his men to move out. It was time to retake what they had lost.

A thin wave of men and a handful of women moved slowly across the battlefield. A grenade exploded and a man screamed. A Japanese soldier had just killed himself and taken an American with him.

"Make sure they're dead," someone yelled. "Kill them. Kill the fuckers!"

Gavin wanted to stop it, but couldn't bring himself to do it. His men had a right to protect themselves from Japanese lunacy.

As they moved to the original defense line, their walk was punctuated with sporadic gunfire as guaranteed death was delivered to the Japanese. Their wounded were put out of their misery before they could kill more Americans. Japanese prisoners, Gavin thought ruefully, would be few and far between. It might not be what the Geneva Convention said was correct, but blame belonged with the Japanese.

As they reached the outer line of bunkers, American bodies began to be found among the Japanese. Some had tried to retreat and been shot and hacked for their efforts, while others were clearly facing toward the enemy. Gavin seethed. He wondered what else he could have done to save his men. He had little artillery, no armor, and the weather had stripped him of any air cover, or even the ability to shoot the Japs at long range. The sight of so many American dead would haunt him for the rest of his days.

A number of bunkers had been bypassed by the Japanese human wave, and the Americans inside them were too shocked to do anything but wave feebly in relief.

A few yards in front of the first defense line, a dead American sergeant lay sprawled and mangled in front of a charred Japanese tank. He looked vaguely familiar. What had happened? Had the American killed the tank? He hoped they would somehow find out. The dead American might just deserve a medal.

They came to a trench filled with Japanese bodies. The arm of an American soldier, recognizable thanks to his skin color and his uniform, pointed to the sky.

"Poor bastard," Gavin muttered and looked away.

"Hey, the guy's hand just moved!"

Gavin and other soldiers moved quickly and feverishly to pull Japanese bodies from the trench. Several American bodies were removed, but they were clearly dead. Finally, they came to the man who owned the arm. He was breathing but covered with blood. A medic jumped into the hole and started to treat him. Like the sergeant by the tank, the GI looked familiar. Gavin finally put a name to this face—Farris. He'd been one of the first to make it through from the south.

The medic looked up in dismay. "Jesus, Colonel, I sure as hell hope not all of this blood belongs to this poor guy."

CHAPTER 18

DANE'S CURRENT JOB WAS TO SIT BY THE PHONE and wait for the late Wilhelm Braun's assistant, Krause, to call back so he could give him the answer from Washington. The FBI was ready to trace the call, but it was assumed that the call would be brief and from a pay phone, and, therefore, effectively untraceable.

Dane didn't think Krause would be unhappy with the response. Harris had bumped upward the German's suggestion that he be given a full pardon and freedom in return for information that would lead to the destruction of the Japanese fleet, and gotten the only possible response possible—go for it. Dane recalled that Churchill said something to the effect that he would praise the devil in Parliament if it would ensure victory against the Nazis, and this was indeed a devilish pact.

In Dane's opinion, Krause was a saboteur and a cold-blooded murderer of Americans, and he was going to go free in return for his help. So be it. If it saved American lives, it would be worth it. If Krause was going to be punished, it would be in another life. If he cooperated, the United States would have no interest in his future. Nor did his efforts have to result in the enemy's destruction, which was a vague and subjective term. All Krause had to do was make a good-faith effort.

Amanda had also agreed as they discussed it over dinner at a local restaurant. "I've seen too many wounded young men. Do whatever can be done to end it, Tim, even if it means paying such a price." She had paused thoughtfully. "In fact, I don't think it's much of a price at all."

The war had also gotten even more personal. Dane had heard from a friend that his nephew Steve had been badly wounded in the battle against the Japanese in Alaska, which the radio and newspapers were trumpeting as a great victory. It had been reported that the Japanese army assaulting Fairbanks had been annihilated. This was no surprise to Tim as he'd predicted there would be few if any prisoners taken and this had been borne out.

It had indeed been a victory but at a great price. Several hundred Americans had been killed or wounded in the final battle. He had no idea how bad Steve's wounds were or if he would recover. If using a Nazi like Krause helped end the slaughter, so be it. Amanda's friend Sandy had been informed that her erstwhile boyfriend had been wounded, but seemed strangely unconcerned, leaving Tim and Amanda to think that any ardor they'd felt was cooling rapidly.

It was difficult for Dane to think of either Braun or Krause as spies and saboteurs. After the shooting, Harris had taken him on a tour of the two men's quarters above their phony engineering company, and what Dane had seen was sad and banal. The two Nazi supermen had been living in a small two-bedroom flat above a nondescript shop filled with what could only be described as junk. An old truck was in the first-level garage, while the upper living level was filled with cheap furniture, dirty laundry, unmade beds, and littered floors. Nor did it look like they did any cooking. Carry-out food containers, much of it from local Chinese restaurants, filled stinking wastebaskets to overflowing.

Both Amanda and he had laughed over the so-called glamorous and dramatic life of a spy as seen in movies and written about in novels. Comparing it with the reality of dirty underwear on the floor of a small apartment was a letdown. The two Germans were slobs, not supermen.

A bedroom closet in the Germans' apartment was stuffed with enough detonators and dynamite to blow up a city block if improperly handled. The two Germans did know what to do with the stuff, but Dane and Harris shuddered at the thought of someone breaking in, poking around, and causing a tragic accident.

When the phone finally did ring, it surprised Dane and he jumped. "Commander Dane," he answered a trifle pompously.

"Krause, Commander. My sources have informed me that your president has concurred with my wishes."

"Yes, and how did you find out?"

"Because my associate in the Swiss embassy was kind enough to phone me. He has in his possession a letter agreeing with my wishes, signed by Roosevelt and General Marshall, which he will retain on my behalf. You will receive another original if you haven't already, and you will give me a photographic copy. All I have to do is make a good-faith attempt to divert the Japanese fleet to a location of your choosing and I can live my life at peace in the United States. Perhaps I'll even become a citizen. Since battles are unpredictable, it is accepted that there is no guarantee that you will destroy or even defeat the Japanese, but that is your concern, not mine."

The German's confidence annoyed Dane. "Krause, you do realize that you will be incarcerated for the duration of the war so you cannot change your mind and possibly try to contact your old Nazi buddies, don't you?"

Krause chuckled. "Of course. I never thought you would be so stupid as to let me go free just now. Goodness, wouldn't it be awful if I changed my mind and tried to warn the slanty-eyed Japs? The letter from Roosevelt said I would be kept at a residence on the naval base at San Diego where I could monitor what is happening and where you could watch my every move. Remember, it might just take more than one contact with the fools Braun and I left behind in Mexico for things to happen."

"Are you ready to turn yourself in?"

"Do I have a choice? Of course I am."

"I'll arrange to get you. Where are you?"

Krause laughed hugely, further annoying Dane. "I'm downstairs in your lobby. Your security is still pathetic."

Two days later, Harry Hopkins flew in from Washington D.C., where he observed Krause from behind a one-way window. "Calm-looking bastard, isn't he?"

"Why wouldn't he be? He's lived up to the first part of his agreement," said Spruance. "He sent a message to Mexico by shortwave. Commander Dane here watched him."

"What did he say and how did he say it?" Hopkins asked Dane.

"Sir, the message was sent shortwave and in Morse code. He told me he usually sent the messages since the now dead Braun was poor with telegraphing the code and made a lot of mistakes. He told his men in Monterrey that, quote—The customer you wish to contact is ill and will be recuperating at a spa in the Gulf of California in about three weeks and will be there for about a month. It is anticipated that several other family members will also be present. If you wish to make contact, please make plans immediately—unquote."

"And this went out in plain English?" Hopkins asked, bemused.

"Yes, sir," Tim responded. "A very simple, innocuous message that no one would give a second thought to."

"Clever. Admiral, will the Germans in Mexico be picked up?"

Spruance turned to Dane who answered. "Not just yet, sir. We may have to send and receive other messages, and, also, picking them up might alert the enemy. However, the FBI has men down there watching them."

Dane hoped that the agents in Monterrey would be a little smarter than the local cops who'd let themselves be discovered by Braun and Krause while watching Swenson Engineering.

"Very well," said Hopkins. "Now we can begin planning at this end."

* * *

Admiral Yamamoto read the message from the navy's headquarters in Tokyo with a combination of delight and concern. The *Saratoga* had been found and she was in bad shape. She needed significant repairs that would take several weeks. What her precise problems were and what caused them were not mentioned, nor were they particularly important. What was important was that she would be in North American waters and the message warned that an attack on her would be dangerous.

He laughed at those concerns. Dangerous? War was dangerous. So too was crossing the street in downtown Tokyo. Doing nothing was even more dangerous and could even prove fatal. Danger was a chance to be taken.

As before, he was on board the *Yamato* and his guests were Admirals Kurita and Nagumo. Both men had read the reports and both had serious doubts about their validity. Still, they had toasted the good news that the American carrier had been located with some of Yamamoto's limited supply of good scotch.

"Can we believe this?" the dour and somber Nagumo asked. "How can we risk our carriers on such flimsy information?"

Kurita nodded. "And it may well be a trap to get our carriers close to American planes and guns."

Yamamoto took a deep breath. Neither of the other admirals had ever been a gambler, yet gambles were sometimes necessary. The Japanese Navy had to do something to break what had become a stalemate in the Pacific. Granted, the Imperial Japanese Navy had been victorious in so many battles, but, as he'd said earlier, the United States was getting stronger and smarter each day. It was not the time for caution. It was the time for aggression, and yes, for taking chances. However, taking chances and being reckless were not the same thing.

Yamamoto smiled. "We will seek out and destroy that carrier and, by doing so, we will send American hopes reeling. And I believe we can do it without risking our fleet."

"How?" asked Kurita. He commanded the battle-ships and these were most vulnerable to American land-based planes. They had to get close to shore for their guns to be effective. Nagumo commanded the two carrier divisions.

"It is quite simple," Yamamoto answered. "We will attack the Americans quickly and suddenly, and with overwhelming strength. We will conserve the fleet by risking it. Nor will we take half measures. It will be an all or nothing toss of the dice, just as we did at Pearl Harbor."

Nagumo persisted. "And if it turns out that the Americans are too formidable?"

Yamamoto smiled and took a healthy swallow of his scotch. He openly hoped that the war would end soon so he could get some more. Perhaps he could arrange for a few cases to be sent to him as war reparations from the British.

"The Americans are in disarray," he said. "They are trying to defend far too much. While I mourn for the men lost in Alaska, their defeat was ordained and has nothing to do with what we shall accomplish in the Gulf of California. The army made a terrible mistake in landing at Anchorage. We, the navy, will make no such mistakes."

Nagumo shook his head. "I urge caution. Your plan is good, but I disagree as to the possible price. It may well be unacceptably high. One carrier for one of theirs is a fair price; even two of ours for their last one would be acceptable. But what if the price was higher? What if we lost three? And don't forget that they don't have to be sunk to be out of the war."

Yamamoto squirmed inwardly. Outwardly he was his normal, composed self. "We will continue to plan for the attack. We will also, however, confirm what we have been told and attempt to evaluate the risks involved. But mark my words, I want that carrier destroyed."

Lieutenant General John DeWitt was again trying to control his anger. Once again, he thought, this son of a bitch Hopkins was trying to tell him how to run his army, his command, and all the way from Washington, no less. Worse, he had to take it. Admirals Spruance and Nimitz were obviously trying not to laugh at his discomfiture, but he wondered how loudly they'd guffaw once they were alone. He was being mocked and there wasn't anything he could do about it.

The navy was trying to take over the army, and that was intolerable. There was a war on and DeWitt had been tasked to protect the people of the West Coast from invasion, while the navy's assignment had been to keep the Jap fleet from our shores. In DeWitt's opinion, the navy had failed miserably while the army had succeeded in defeating the Japs in Alaska, so why was there this rush to give the sailors even more authority?

Nimitz tried to be conciliatory. "General, I know how much you must dislike this arrangement, but I assure you it is only temporary."

"You have no idea what I am thinking, Admiral," DeWitt snapped with more anger than he'd intended.

"Enough," said Hopkins. "The situation requires one commander, at least for the time being, and that one commander is going to be Admiral Nimitz. Quite seriously, General, if the command structure is that distasteful, then a replacement for you can be found."

Bluff called, DeWitt thought, and pulled back. "Of course I will comply and obey, Mr. Hopkins, but I do wonder at the necessity of it all."

Hopkins sighed. "It's because the president has signed off on a risky and daring venture that requires all people to be not only on the same page, but reading the same word and understanding the same meaning. We may have an opportunity to cause great harm to the Japanese and it is essential that army and navy efforts be coordinated to the utmost. There can be no mistakes, no confusion as to who is in charge, and no missed or misunderstood communications."

DeWitt was somewhat mollified. More than anything, he wanted the Japanese to pay for Pearl Harbor and the Philippines. At least the destruction of the Japanese force that had landed at Anchorage had been not only an army victory, but a nationwide morale booster. Of course, he had to admit that the navy's smashing of the Japanese reinforcement force had played an important role as well.

Nimitz continued. "Simply put, General, we hope to trap at least a large part of the Japanese fleet near our shores and either defeat or destroy it. We hope we have led the Japanese to believe that the *Saratoga* will be in the Gulf of California in a while, and we absolutely need the army's planes to help support the ambush we hope to spring."

DeWitt still had his doubts. "But what you are

asking, moving hundreds of planes from bases in California and elsewhere to spots where they can cover the Baja, will leave much of the West Coast naked and defenseless. Should the Japanese decide to attack other than where you think, it could be catastrophic. Not only that, but we will have to move large numbers of engineers and mechanics to bases that don't yet exist. And will the Mexicans even cooperate, since we'll be operating on their land?"

Hopkins sipped his coffee and made a face. It had gotten cold. There were no stewards available to get him a refill. They were all alone in the room. Secrecy had its drawbacks.

"The decision to strip other cities of their defenses was made by the president, who understands the risks involved. It is a chance that we have to take. As for the Mexicans, they will cooperate or they will regret it for a thousand years."

"I understand," DeWitt said.

Hopkins continued. "And if this should succeed, I guarantee you that you will get a prominent place in the historical record as well as a fourth star."

DeWitt glared. "Do you really think I'm such a prick that all I want is another star? Of course I'd like to be promoted. I'm just as human and ambitious as the next man, but my first love is for my country and my second is for my command and the men in it. I've sworn to protect the West Coast and I'm damn well doing it to the best of my ability, no matter what some sob sisters think of my methods, and your inference that I can be bribed by another star is disgusting."

Hopkins sat back, astonished by the outburst. "I apologize."

"Don't bother," DeWitt said, his anger spent. "You can have anything you want. I will cooperate more than fully. Just one thing about my future. If this fails and results in another navy disaster, just keep my name out of it."

The crews from the movie studios in Hollywood had no idea where they were going or why. They only knew that the U.S. Navy wanted them for a special project and that was good enough for them. As a result, several hundred men had volunteered, been put on a navy transport and shipped to the east coast of Mexico, across from the Baja Peninsula. There they found a tent city waiting for them, along with a number of barges that had been lashed together just offshore. They were confused by the sight and were further disconcerted by the presence of a number of antiaircraft batteries being built along with rude airstrips in various stages of construction.

Captain Bill Merchant called the assembly to order. They'd first thought of meeting in a large tent, but the air inside was stifling. Instead, they met outside by the waters of the Gulf of California. Merchant also thought that a little morale building was in order, so he'd brought in enough bottles of beer to lubricate the citizens of a good-sized city.

After thanking them for volunteering and getting everyone a cold one, Merchant got down to business. "You people are all supposed to be the best set designers and builders on the face of the earth. You've made magic out of movies by convincing people that they were watching Robin Hood in a real castle, a little girl traipsing through Oz, and, maybe most dramatically, setting fire to the city of Atlanta in *Gone With the Wind*. Gentlemen, you have dazzled and impressed countless millions of people with your ability to make things look real."

He paused and took a deep swallow of his beer. It was a Schlitz and he didn't particularly like Schlitz, but it was cold and the Baja was torrid.

"We, the United States Army and Navy, want you to build a fleet out of those barges. You will have all the plywood and paint you need, and when you are done, we want anybody flying over real quickly to see a pair of aircraft carriers, a handful of cruisers, and a bunch of destroyers sitting out there in the bay. I wouldn't mind if there were dummy models of planes on the decks of the carriers."

A hand was raised. "You don't want them full-sized, do you?"

"Nope. Maybe half or three quarters will do. They can't be too small or somebody doing a flyover will notice."

The first man rose. He had a big grin on his face. "The suckers we build are going to be lures or maybe bait, aren't they?"

"Yep, and we're going after real big yellow fish from the Land of the Rising Sun."

Another hand. "When the hell do you want these m chers made?"

Merchant grinned. "I was thinking a week ago. But, since the sun is beginning to set, I think tomorrow morning is a better idea. When we start, though, we're going to work like hell and pretty much around the clock. In the meantime, we have a bunch of dead cows that have been carved into steaks, and a whole lot more beer, and unless anybody has any objections, let's get started."

❋   ❋   ❋

Bear clutched his rifle and ducked as the grenade went off not more than fifty yards away. He looked up and laughed. "Another damned Jap just went to meet his ancestors." The other men in his group smiled appreciatively, but nervously. When would the last Jap be dead?

Almost all the Japanese Alaskan force had been killed in the suicidal attack on Fairbanks, but a few hundred had been left behind for various reasons, usually involving their inability to move because of earlier injuries or illness. Clearing them out of their nests and hidey-holes was both time-consuming and dangerous. Maybe the Japanese remnants weren't very mobile, but they were, as he liked to say, very hostile.

Rifle fire to his left made him duck again until he recognized the sound as that coming from an American Springfield.

"Got him," someone yelled.

Good work, Bear thought. Once they cleared out all the Japs, Ruby could head back to her home at Anchorage. She said she had some things to clean out and then added that she thought she was through with the restaurant business. She'd told him she'd had enough of waiting on a bunch of drunken lechers who tried to paw her and then left lousy tips. She would stay with Bear. She told him it would be fun hibernating with him during the cold, snowy winter. He thought he would burn up a lot of firewood keeping it warm enough so they could romp naked, but decided it would be well worth it and, besides, Alaska had a lot of trees. Come summer they would worry about making a living and other long-term stuff.

More shots and this time he dropped to the ground.

He recognized the sound of a Japanese rifle, followed by a rain of shots from Springfields. A moment later came the *crump* sound of a grenade going off, followed by yells from American soldiers. Another Japanese fanatic had decided to swallow a grenade. Jesus, he thought, what crazy people. Who would ever prefer death to surrender and living? Then he thought about the atrocities committed by the Japanese on American POWs and captured civilians and wondered just what he would do if confronted by the choice of dying or surrendering to Japanese mercies. Damn, he thought. What a hell of a way to run a war.

Farris had spent much of the time since he'd been wounded floating in and out of consciousness. He'd dreamed sometimes, and the dreams were often terrible. He kept seeing Stecher being blown up and then a montage of Japanese faces, their mouths open and all of them screaming that he should die. What was worse was that he couldn't force himself to wake up, as he could as a kid with a nightmare. He'd heard people's voices saying that they were keeping him sedated until his injuries had healed enough.

Injuries? What the hell were they talking about? He felt like he was underwater and trying to reach the surface. His mind strained and reached for the light. He opened his eyes and blinked. The room was dimly lit and he had trouble focusing. He looked around and saw another bed, but it was empty. The room was stark and sterile and obviously a hospital.

Then he realized he was looking through only his right eye. Oh Christ, he wondered, have I lost an eye?

He mumbled something and a man appeared and

stuffed a drinking straw in his mouth. "Drink this. You've got to get yourself lubricated before you can talk properly."

Farris did as he was told and the cold water was an elixir. "Drink all you want, buddy, just take it slowly. I don't want to have to clean up your puke."

With each successive swallow, he felt his strength returning. A distant memory recalled his aunt watering her potted plants and how some of them would perk up almost immediately. He decided that's what he was, a house plant, a house plant with one eye.

Shit and double shit.

He tried to move and realized that his left arm wasn't responding. He reached over with his right and found his left side was swathed in bandages. He gingerly checked his head and the left side of his face was also bandaged. Damn it, was anything working? He groped between his legs and was relieved to find that everything seemed at least present and accounted for in that department.

Another face appeared and this was clearly a doctor. His nametag said so. "I'm Doctor Greeley and you're in a military hospital in Vancouver, British Columbia. You were wounded a couple of weeks ago and were flown down here for treatment once your wounds had stabilized. You are very lucky."

"Am I blind?" Farris managed to say. His voice came out raspy and he wondered if he could be understood.

The doctor took a deep breath. "Not really and maybe not at all. Obviously you can see out of your right eye, but we are a little concerned about your left. We are also concerned about your left arm. We're not totally certain what happened, but you may have lost some use of your left side as a result of being buried under a pile of bodies. Maybe you were pinned for too long and there was some nerve damage or other problems resulting from oxygen deprivation or something else we don't quite understand. Tell me, do you recall what happened to you?"

Farris closed his eyes and tried to remember. At first it was snapshots, then he saw Japanese, like in a movie, screaming and yelling, and coming straight at him. Only this time it wasn't a nightmare. Then he was inundated and buried under a pile of flesh.

"I remember," he said. "I just wish I didn't have to."

"Good reasoning. But it does tell me that your mind is working and that is a very good sign."

"If my mind worked all that well in the first place, I wouldn't have gotten myself into this stupid situation. By the way, Doc, what am I doing in Canada?"

"Kindly recall, Lieutenant Farris, that Canada and the United States are allies, and that we Canadians have pretty good doctors and hospitals. We use anesthetics and some of us have been known to clean our hands and our surgical tools before operating, even though we're not sure why," he said with obvious sarcasm.

"Either that or we could have left you up north in the care of some well-meaning medics who would have called on an Eskimo shaman if they needed a second opinion. Which would you prefer?"

"I think I like it here. What happens next?"

"That's somewhat up to you. Now that you are fully conscious and likely to stay that way, we are going to wean you off of morphine and then arrange for you to be flown south, either to San Francisco or San Diego. Not that it matters to the military, but do you have a preference?"

"San Diego, if you can arrange it. I have an uncle down there and maybe a girlfriend, a nurse, and she can maybe take care of me."

Jesus, he thought. Would Sandy even want to see him if his arm was crippled and he had only one eye?

"Excellent choice. I'll put you in for Kansas City and see what the army comes up with."

"Doc, when I get out of this bed, you know I am going to have to kill you."

Greeley smiled. "Ah, but you'll have to catch me first, which would mean you are quite well indeed. By the way, you have some mail." He handed Steve a thin bundle of letters and left.

After Greeley left, a male nurse took pity on his fumbling one-handed attempts to pry open the envelopes and did it for him. The first letter was from Colonel Gavin praising him for his bravery and hoping he would recover quickly. He was also being put in for a medal. Stecher was getting the Silver Star, posthumously, of course.

The second was from Dane, also hoping he'd get well and come down to San Diego. He added that there was a surplus of beer and steaks. Well, Farris thought, that was a plan.

The third was from Sandy and he looked at it hesitantly. She hoped he was well. Hell, if he was well he wouldn't be in a hospital. She wanted him to come down to see her. She was friendly but curiously noncommittal. She said they'd started something very nice, kind of like Amanda and Tim, and she wanted to know where it would end. Well, so did he, but he wondered just what lay under the bandages. Did he have an eye? If not, would he get a glass eye? He's seen people with glass eyes and they looked so terrible and out of sync with the rest of a person's face. Maybe he'd just wear a patch. Or was he so scarred under the bandages that he'd scare her away? Tim had mentioned a buddy of his who'd been burned when the *Enterprise* sank and whose scars were very slowly disappearing. Was he going to be like that or would his situation be even worse?

Damn it to hell. First, though, he had to get out of the hospital and out of Vancouver, no matter how friendly the natives were, and go south. In order to do that, though, he had to quit feeling sorry for himself and start working what was left of his body into shape.

Krause was bored to tears. But, he consoled himself, at least he was alive. He had been billeted in a rather pleasant two-bedroom bungalow on an American naval base and he was being treated with at least a small level of respect. The Yanks had made a promise and he was relatively confident they'd live up to it. He had decent food, comfortable furniture, and even a small garden that he found surprisingly pleasant to work in. The house had once belonged to an officer who'd been killed in the Midway debacle. A shame, he thought, but at least he could put the house to good use.

Of course, the Americans didn't trust him any farther than they could throw him. He'd done his part and now wanted to be released from this genteel captivity as soon as possible. He was guarded by military police under instructions to keep conversation to a minimum, although he was permitted a radio and local newspapers that kept him abreast of the course of the war.

The news reinforced his decision to throw in with

the Americans. Germany was not succeeding against the Soviets and had not expelled the Americans and the British from North Africa. He was convinced that Hitler had not succeeded on either front because the German army simply didn't have the numbers or resources to fight both the Soviets and the Americans. It would take a while, but Germany would be defeated. So too would Japan. Yes, he thought, he had definitely made the right choice.

Every day either Harris or Dane would come and visit. The occasions were not social. Today was Dane's turn.

"Commander, I'm bored."

"Forgive me for not caring," said Dane. "At least you're still alive. There are those who feel you should be hanged."

"For what?" Krause said incredulously, even though they'd had this conversation several times. "Are your people angry because I helped derail a couple of trains? Please, those were all acts of war. What do you think British and now your bombers are doing to trains and other targets in Germany? Trust me, they are not making distinctions between freight trains and passenger trains. Nor are they avoiding civilian areas when you and the British bomb German cities. Luebeck, Rostock, and Cologne have been severely damaged and many civilians have been killed or maimed. Even Berlin itself has been bombed.

"And don't bring up the issue of those poor Mexican boys. They were criminals and they would have betrayed Braun and me. They were unfortunate casualties of a cruel war. Wasn't it an American who said that war was hell?"

"You weren't in uniform, which is a violation of the Geneva Convention."

"And you are not a signatory to that ridiculous document, even though you did agree to abide by it, a distinction that confuses me. I also have it on good authority that you and your so-called Allies are sending saboteurs in to France and elsewhere and I am quite certain that they would not be so stupid as to wear American or British uniforms."

Dane glared at him. "Is this all we're going to do, rehash old arguments? If so, I'm going to leave you to feel sorry for yourself."

"Of course not, Commander, and I assure you I am not feeling sorry for myself. I have a suggestion that will help expedite the process of drawing the Japanese into your trap. Are you interested?"

"Of course."

"You are building a mock carrier task force down in the Gulf of California, are you not?"

Somebody has a big mouth, Dane thought, and then realized that maintaining such secrecy on a huge base was virtually impossible. Besides, who could Krause tell, and, more important, what would encourage him to? Information was his lifeline to a life of freedom.

"Of course we would be interested in any ideas you might have."

Krause smiled, looking almost pleasant. "I knew you would. So, here is my idea. You had me tell the Japanese that one of your carriers, the *Saratoga*, would be in the Gulf. Well, they say that Yamamoto is a gambler. Therefore, why not make it double or nothing?"

CHAPTER 19

AMANDA LOOKED STERNLY AT HER FRIEND. "WELL, make up your mind. Are you in love with him or not?"

Sandy grimaced and wiped away a tear. Her eyes were red from crying. "I don't know. We only went out a couple of times and now he's badly wounded."

Grace inhaled deeply on her cigarette and smiled as she exhaled a perfect smoke ring. "Let's face it, Sandy dearest, you are afraid that you're going to wind up with a war hero who's a cripple and so badly mangled that you won't want to be seen with him, much less wind up screwing him, even with the lights off."

Amanda smiled. "You do have a marvelously tactful way with words, Gracie."

"The hell with tact," Grace said. "I think it's time to be blunt. When young Mister Farris went north, Sandy moped and then did what she does best at a time of crisis, she ate. Sandy, did anyone ever tell you you're getting fat again?"

"I am not getting fat," Sandy said loud enough for

the handful of the others in the restaurant to hear. They stifled grins and turned away.

"All right," Sandy said and wiped away another tear. "You're right, I am gaining. I'll stop eating, so don't call me a baby."

"Good," said Amanda. "Now what are you going to do about Steve Farris? If he's coming down here, you are going to have to meet with him and deal with whatever problems he has. That is, if you want to have a future with him. Even though you two aren't married and maybe never will be, that for better or worse thing still counts. Maybe it's even more important before you get married, or even begin to take each other seriously. And, by the way, if he's on his way down here, he can't be all that badly wounded, can he?"

Sandy had gotten a brief note from Steve, written with obvious difficulty and just delivered. In it he said he was having trouble with his left arm and eye, but was otherwise okay and looked forward to seeing Sandy. All of this said that he wasn't an amputee and strongly implied that he wasn't confined to a wheelchair. But was she really looking forward to seeing him? He would be coming down by train in a few days and said he was delighted that a wounded army officer was being sent to recuperate in what was essentially a navy town.

Amanda pressed her. "Sandy, you are a nurse, remember? You've seen some sights that nobody should ever have to see. You've worked on patients so badly mangled it's a miracle that they're still alive. You've seen men missing limbs and eyes and faces, and you've seen relatives who've sucked it up and decided that they would take care of their son, their brother, their husband as best they could. You've heard grown men cry for their mothers and dying boys say they didn't want to die a virgin. Steve got a medal for what he did, but those people are heroes too."

Grace laughed. "And don't think it was such a big thrill making love to Mack's old and withered body."

"It wasn't?" Sandy said angrily. "I would have thought otherwise from all the noise you two made."

"Well, actually it was. Not as good as Captain Billy Merchant, mind you, but quite nice."

Sandy took a deep breath. "You're right, of course. I'll be a big girl and deal with it as it happens. And I'll skip dessert, thank you."

Amanda smiled and turned away. Sandy's situation had brought out her own unspoken fears. What would she do if Tim was badly wounded, crippled, blinded? He'd seen so much action it was a wonder he was still alive. Sometimes she thought it would be easier dealing with someone's death. Then, when she thought that way, she realized her thoughts were stupid.

The two Australian cruisers were a mass of flames. So too were the pair of transports the fools had been escorting. Masao Ikeda turned his plane for another strafing run on the almost helpless targets. An anti-aircraft crew on one of the cruisers was still firing at them. He dropped his Zero's nose and his guns obliterated the response.

Aichi E13A seaplanes had spotted the ships earlier in the day. The cruisers were tentatively identified as the heavy cruiser *Canberra*, ten thousand tons and four turrets each with two eight-inch guns, and the light cruiser *Hobart*, seventy-one hundred tons and eight six-inch guns, and they were now burning and sinking. Australia's navy had been small and now, he thought happily, it was even smaller. Rumor had it that Australia's food situation was becoming as desperate as Hawaii's, so maybe this setback would cause Australia to think twice about continuing to fight the Japanese Empire.

A number of lifeboats and rafts were in the water and some of the other Zero pilots, mainly the newer ones, thought it was great sport to strafe the helpless little boats. He watched in disgust as bullets ripped through the flimsy craft, sending men into water that was rapidly turning blood red around their floating bodies. He heard the pilots exulting on their radios and contemplated telling them to shut up. He didn't, though. Let them have their way for a little while. Besides, even though he now had a dozen kills to his credit, they might not obey him. Their blood lust was up.

In earlier times, Masao had thought that way as well, but not now. He had seen far too many men die to think kindly on the idea of slaughter as a sport. Killing the helpless was not the way of the warrior. Nor was it right for the gunners on the cruiser to have kept firing, forcing Masao to kill again. There was no shame in retreating to fight again another day. The Australian gunners had been fools and it would be justice if they were dead.

The newer Japanese pilots were not the same quality as the men they were replacing, the men who had fought and died for Nippon, the men he mourned as lost companions. The men replacing them were children in comparison, a point he'd frequently made to his good friend Toki.

The *Canberra* rolled on its side and then on its back. Australian sailors tried to cling to the slippery hull but it bounced obscenely in the water and they were thrown off. God help anyone trapped inside, Masao thought and permitted himself a shudder since no one could see him show weakness in the cockpit of his plane. When I die, he thought, let it be fast.

An hour later, his plane and all the rest of the pilots were safe on the *Kaga*. Two Zeros had been shot down by enemy fire and both pilots lost. They had been new pilots and now they would be replaced by two more who were even less well prepared.

Masao took a long drink of water and walked as close to the edge of the flight deck as his fear of heights would let him. The mighty ocean swells were hypnotically beautiful and deceptively peaceful. One could look and never see war.

"Don't jump," a familiar voice whispered from behind him.

"Go to hell, Toki," he cheerfully said to his friend. Masao was glad to see him. There hadn't been much opportunity to visit in the last several days.

"We may already be there, or haven't you noticed? The men and the ship are wearing down. We need a long and slow refit in a harbor that actually has facilities and where the people don't want to kill you like they do on Hawaii. And admit it, wouldn't you like to walk on the ground just one more time before you die?"

"Yes, but I don't plan on dying just yet."

"Who does, but we are in a war," Toki said.

"Which is why we cannot surrender to our desire for luxuries," Masao answered. "We must harden ourselves and be stronger than the Americans. Our time will come. Then we will have geishas or even American or Australian maidens to service us," Masao added facetiously.

"And they'll be as enthusiastic as the whores, or slaves, in Hawaii. By the way, that little piece of happiness and sunshine near Hilo has been abandoned. Apparently, Hawaiian guerillas overran the place and freed all the slaves. Now you can't even go there and just sit on the beach. We bombed and strafed the island, doubtless killing a number of the enemy, but that was an exercise in futility."

"Enough," Masao said sharply. "Please tell me you have some good news for a change."

"Well, it is news, but I won't be the judge as to whether it's good or not. Apparently, we have somehow located the American carrier, the *Saratoga*."

Masao beamed. "Excellent. Now we can strike at her and kill her. And then perhaps we can go home and get laid by a proper Japanese woman."

"What happened to your American or Australian women? Regardless, it might not happen. Just because we found the damned carrier doesn't mean she's in a position where she can be attacked. Apparently she is off the Mexican coast, in a body of water called the Bay of California. It is near enough to San Diego for surface planes to protect her. Neither Admiral Kurita nor Admiral Nagumo thinks she would be worth the price. Yamamoto of course disagrees. He reminds his admirals that Japan was willing to lose two carriers at Pearl Harbor in order to destroy the American fleet, and should be willing to lose a carrier or two in order to wipe out the final vestiges of American power in the Pacific."

Masao grinned. "Just so long as one of the carriers sunk isn't the *Kaga*. I'm very tired of having to change ships because the previous one was sunk. Seriously, what do you think will be the decision?"

"Apparently our revered Admiral Yamamoto is torn. Attacking the *Saratoga* while she is being repaired is one option. Another is to wait until her repairs are complete and hit her with a host of submarines. The exit from her sanctuary is relatively narrow and could easily be covered by our submarines. A number of them are already on their way to blockade the gulf."

Masao pondered for a moment. "A good plan, but not good enough. The Americans will surely be looking for our submarines, whether they suspect that we know where the carrier is or not. No, the only way to be certain is to use our planes. I suppose we could use our subs to trail the *Saratoga* once she does emerge and take her on the high seas when she's away from any help from land-based planes, or even their subs. But the American carrier is much faster than our subs, and that means we would run the always present risk of her escaping. If that were to happen, the chase would begin all over again."

Toki laughed. "You should have been an admiral. Those are exactly the arguments that are raging. Yamamoto does not want to run the risk of having to chase her again."

"Well, I am smarter than most people think, and better looking, too. But what do you think will happen?"

Toki took a deep breath. "I believe Yamamoto is

looking for the slightest excuse to attack her while she is in Mexican waters."

Dane came up with the basic phraseology for the second message and Krause modified it only slightly. The message said that not only was the client recovering in Mexico, but that the client would shortly be visited by his twin brother and suitable gifts should be provided for the siblings.

Krause was happy. He could see himself one step closer to being free to disappear in the vastness of the United States. He was more and more convinced that Germany would lose the war. He felt that the offensive against the Soviet city of Stalingrad which had begun in June would prove to be a catastrophe.

"According to your newspapers and radio," Krause said, "Hitler will lose in Russia and he will lose in North Africa, even though your advances have been slow and poorly managed at best. The German Army in North Africa cannot be reinforced or kept well supplied. You will simply overwhelm Rommel or whoever is in command. In a way, it is like your situation in Alaska, although that seems to have taken a turn for the better."

"I'll relay your thoughts to Roosevelt and Marshall," Dane said drily. "I'm sure they'll be gratified to know of your approval."

Krause ignored the gibe. "When will you arrest the men I've been communicating with in Mexico?"

"Not my call. I suppose, though, that it will happen when they and you are of no further use. Who knows, maybe we'll get lucky and they'll all be killed resisting arrest. Why, are some of them your friends?"

Krause paused for a moment. He was visualizing their faces and remembering the times they'd had together.

"Friends? No. I will concede that they are, or were, comrades in arms. But after all is said and done, if they must become casualties, then so be it." He laughed. "It's not as if I have a choice in the matter. If anybody has to be a casualty, I would much prefer it be them and not me."

Farris sat in an uncomfortable chair in the darkened hospital room and looked at the doctor shining a light into his bad eye. He put a hand over his right eye and used only his left. What he saw was blurry and bright, but at least it was sight. He reached over with his left hand and picked up a pencil on the third try.

"Damn it."

"Keep working at it," the doctor said and left. Farris thought the doctor had been useless, telling him nothing he didn't already know. He could see out of his left eye, just not very well. Sometimes he thought he would be better off wearing a patch but the doctors said he should try to strengthen his eye and his vision by using it. Sometimes he got headaches, but they would be a small price to pay if he could regain much of his vision. An eye doctor suggested that he might wind up wearing glasses when his vision stabilized. Damn, that meant he would look like Clark Kent, without the ability to turn into Superman. Would Lois Lane, Sandy, want such a creature? Did he want Lois Lane? The doctors informed him that there would also be scarring and that half of his left eyebrow no longer existed. This was hardly a big deal when he considered some of the others recovering in this and other hospitals. At least he was alive. Stecher wasn't.

Use of his left arm had returned somewhat. He would perform tasks that didn't require skill, like picking up something large, but other tasks, like picking up a pencil or turning the pages of a book or newspaper were still difficult at best.

His trip to San Diego had been interrupted by more vital traffic, and he found himself convalescing in San Francisco. He'd been told that he would be treated for a while, maybe a few weeks, and then likely discharged if he wanted it. He'd served his country well, an overweight major had told him, and he'd gotten his wounds and medals. The major said that Farris was a hero. Steve almost told the major to go screw himself. He knew he wasn't a hero. He also wasn't certain he wanted to be discharged. He'd been scared to death during the final Japanese attack. Stecher had been the real hero and Steve was glad that Gavin had put the sergeant in for a medal. The poor bastard had wanted so much to kill Japanese in revenge for their killing his brother, it was a shame that he'd gotten himself killed just when it seemed like he was coming to grips with his personal tragedy.

A PFC with a clipboard came in. "You Lieutenant Farris?"

"I am."

"Well, sir, I got orders from some Canadian doctor in Vancouver to put you on a bus to Kansas City."

"Are you kidding?"

The PFC grinned. "Yes, sir. One of the docs who was looking you over put me up to it. His cousin is the guy in Vancouver who treated you. Actually, you're scheduled to go by train to San Diego and it leaves in two hours. Can you be ready?"

Farris laughed and almost jumped out of his chair. "Damn right I can."

Even the normally dour Admiral Nagumo was stunned by their good fortune. Not one, but two American carriers would soon be in the Gulf of California.

"I cannot believe that fortune is finally on our side," Nagumo said.

Even Yamamoto grinned. "What happened to your normal state of pessimism?"

"Perhaps it is overwhelmed by the possibility that we may actually be able to bring this war to a conclusion favorable to Japan before the full might of the United States is brought to bear against us. That possibility would make even a corpse giddy. But tell me, what convinces you that this is not a trick designed to draw us into an ambush?"

Yamamoto stood and looked out at the large map of the Pacific that dominated his conference room on the battleship *Yamato*. He too had been wondering the same thing. Was it too good to be true? There was a saying he'd heard in America—if it seems too good to be true, it probably is too good to be true.

After a long moment, Yamamoto answered. "For one thing, the source is Germany, our ally. For another, I believe we can verify the existence of the carriers."

Nagumo nodded sagely. "But what if our attempts at verification are discovered? That will induce the Americans to depart the area, won't it?"

"Indeed, and that is why we must be extremely circumspect. Germany has volunteered to provide the eyes that will confirm the existence of the two carriers and I have accepted their offer."

Nagumo was clearly unhappy. "I would prefer that Japanese eyes do the confirming. I do not trust our Nazi allies. They detest us almost as much as they hate Jews."

"Agreed, but we might not have a choice. If we use a floatplane from a sub, we run the risk of it being discovered and the Americans will know we are on to them and will flee. Nor can we get any surface ships close to the Gulf of California without being discovered by American planes and radar."

Nagumo nodded. "You are right. We do not have a choice. But I do not like the idea of putting our destiny in the hands of the Germans."

"Nor do I," Yamamoto said, "but we are not in a position to choose our friends."

Yamamoto walked over to the map of California that was taped to the wall. It amused him that it clearly said it came from a *National Geographic*. Still, it was an excellent map. He fervently hoped that the Americans had trouble getting decent maps of Japan.

"Once the presence of the carriers is verified, we will attack them with overwhelming force and sink both them. We will lose planes and possibly even ships, but it will be more than worth it. We will distract them from protecting the carriers by using our battleships and heavy cruisers to bombard Los Angeles and San Diego. The bombardment will come first, which will cause the Americans to divert planes to protect their cities and the civilian population."

"Will you notify Tokyo of your intentions?" Nagumo asked.

Yamamoto bristled. "No. I command the fleet and I do not need permission from anyone to do battle with the Americans."

Nagumo nodded solemnly. "Keeping the attack a secret with only the fleet aware of what we hope to achieve will keep our plans even more secure. While the Americans cannot read our codes, there might be a blabbing mouth in Tokyo and news might somehow reach our enemies. As much as I would prefer that we receive blessings from Tokyo, I agree that this is something that we alone must do."

Yamamoto smiled. He didn't need anyone's permission or blessing, but it still would have been good to receive. Now if only the existence of the American carriers could be verified. Their destruction would result in Japanese control of the Pacific for at least several more years. The longer the growing might of the United States Navy was kept at bay, the more likely the Japanese Empire would emerge from this war with an honorable peace that would provide Japan with both economic and military security.

There was another problem that could arise should they be victorious. There would inevitably be calls from the hierarchy in Tokyo to make additional punishing attacks on the United States. Perhaps there would be pressure on him to invade Australia and Oahu, stretching his slender resources. These would have to be dampened and tempered with reality. What some called "victory disease" could prove fatal.

Still, Yamamoto thought, he would use the fleet to make selective attacks on the United States after the victory in the Gulf of California.

❋　　❋　　❋

Juan Escobar was a proud man who was both mystified and angry at what had happened to his once proud and orderly world. An aristocrat who considered himself more Spanish then Mexican, he deplored the fact that crude, illiterate peasants of Indian descent had done so much to change his world. Not only did he no longer receive the respect that was his due as a descendant of the conquistadores, but he saw thinly veiled contempt in the eyes of many from the lower classes. Even worse, these communist-inspired cretins had almost destroyed his beloved Holy Mother Church's influence in Mexico with their liberal and egalitarian ideas.

Yes, there currently was a shaky accord in place between the Mexican government and the Church that promised to end the fighting, but his beloved Church remained in a seriously reduced role, and Escobar did not like that. The Church represented God and, therefore, should be in charge. His late uncle had been a bishop and had been adamant about the Church's proper role in the world. He believed that all governments should be subordinate to the Papacy. He knew that some laughed at him and called his beliefs archaic, but he knew that his way was the truth.

It had come as no surprise to the fifty-year-old Mexican Army colonel that he found himself drawn to the ideas of Adolf Hitler and the Nazi Party. Hitler knew what to do with the communists. Mexico needed its own Hitler. He held onto the now fading hope that it would someday be a man named Juan Escobar. Even though Hitler did little to support Catholicism, Escobar was confident that the Nazis would change when victory over utterly godless communism was theirs.

Escobar had even rejoiced when Germany declared war on the United States. Perhaps Mexico would join with Hitler and attempt to get back the lands stolen by the U.S. a century before.

Thus, he had been aghast when Mexico had declared war on Germany instead of on the United States. Still, he could do his part to ensure that Germany won. Too bad it meant having to help those repulsive little yellow men from Japan. Whenever he had doubts about what he was doing, he reminded himself that the friend of my friend is my friend as well.

Which was why he found himself bobbing up and down in a stinking little fishing boat off the city of Mazatlan and trying not to speak with the boat's filthy, foul-mouthed, and sweaty captain any more than necessary. Fishing was a major industry in the area and the Gulf of California teemed with fish, including manta rays and numerous species of whales. Escobar cared nothing about the fish. All he wanted to do was get back to his home in Mexico City, have a drink, and have his mistress visit. He had flown to Mazatlan by private plane and had hoped to take the plane over the area where the American ships were said to be hiding, but his German source informed him that he might be shot down if he was spotted. The area was patrolled by both American and Mexican planes. The new American occupiers still permitted fishing. People had to eat. Thus, an innocuous fishing boat was the best alternative.

The waters in the Gulf of California—he still preferred to call it the Gulf of Cortes—were calm. The night was clear and the little boat chugged its way north and west to where the enemy waited, allegedly grouped against the western side of the gulf. Escobar's instructions were succinct. He was to count and categorize American ships, especially and logically the larger ones, and under no circumstances was he to risk being discovered.

Ergo, he could not get too close, which was fine by Colonel Escobar. He considered himself to be as brave as the next man, but it had been decades since he'd seen combat, fighting against the American intruders in 1916.

The predawn light poured across the waters. On another day, he would have reveled in its beauty. A rare fin whale surfaced and splashed mightily. Despite his anxieties, it brought a smile.

In the distance, shapes began to emerge as the light grew better. He took out his binoculars—German of course—and focused on the distant objects. When he realized what he was seeing, he understood why the Japanese were so anxious. Clearly silhouetted were a host of American warships. His jaw dropped. Jesu'—two of them were aircraft carriers.

American patrol vessels were only a couple of miles away. He could not get closer, nor did he feel that he had to. He directed the slovenly Mexican monkey who owned the boat to return to Mazatlan and promised him a bonus if he hurried. The money belonged to Germany, so he was inclined to be generous.

The next night he was in his apartment enjoying an excellent French white wine. He had just completed and sent the message to his German associate, a man he'd help hide after the German embassy had been closed down. The German had been extremely grateful and promised that the Third Reich would take care of Juan

Escobar when the war was over and the Axis nations triumphant. Escobar didn't want money. He was already rich. He just wanted his world put back in order.

In an apartment a few blocks away, a thoroughly tired Roy Harris and two other FBI agents stopped listening. An observer on the street noted that all the lights in Escobar's apartment were out. The colonel had doubtless called it a day. The Mexican's phones had been tapped ever since the Germans, whose phones were also tapped, had contacted him. Harris had even managed to fly to Mazatlan in another small plane and had seen Escobar take the fishing boat out. He'd contacted the fleet and told them that the little boat's trip was not to be interrupted. If necessary he could be chased away, but nothing more.

"Should we kill him now or later?" Agent Walt Courtney asked cheerfully.

Harris smiled. It seemed like such a great idea, but it wasn't going to happen. For one thing, the Mexicans, always touchy, would be thoroughly angry if the U.S. preempted their right to take care of their own traitors. Only a handful of people in the Mexican government were even aware that the FBI was actively working in their country.

"Later," Harris said, "and we'll let the Mexicans do it. By communicating with the Germans and running errands for them, he's just proclaimed himself a traitor to Mexico. Maybe they won't put him in front of a firing squad. Maybe our Mexican allies will make him work at hard labor in a Mexican prison for the rest of his life and be guarded by those peasants he hates so much."

Agent Courtney appreciated the thought. "And just

maybe he'll get himself cornholed each night by his jailors or fellow inmates. I kind of like that idea."

Harris decided he did too. Nobody likes a traitor, even though the actions of this jerk might just change the course of the war.

"Crowley, get your pink young ass in here and close the door!"

Lieutenant Ron Crowley, executive officer of the *Shark*, rolled his eyes and smiled. His lord and master was pissed. Again. It had not been the best of patrols. They'd sunk a pair of smallish five-thousand-ton merchant ships, but nothing else. They'd fired a pair of torpedoes at a Japanese light cruiser, but they'd either missed or been duds. Almost insultingly, the cruiser hadn't seemed to notice.

It was night and the sub was running on the surface. Her hatches were open as she swapped fetid air for fresh, recharged her batteries, and let the crew take turns standing out in the open and enjoying the simple act of inhaling and exhaling. Of course, everyone on deck had to be watching carefully for any sign of Japanese planes or ships. Lieutenant Commander Torelli, the *Shark*'s skipper, was adamant about that. As he told everyone, especially new crewmen, there would be no repeat of the time when, en route to San Diego, she'd been spotted and depth charged. Now he wouldn't even let the men throw their cigarettes into the water lest some keen eyes pick them up and realize that an American ship might be nearby. Dumping garbage was done very discreetly, using weighted bags.

Crowley picked his way through the passageway. The lights were off so not even the hint of a glow would make its way out, but there was no problem, the XO knew every step, nook, and cranny by heart as did all of the crew.

"Present and accounted for, Skipper," he said as he entered Torelli's cramped quarters.

"Tell me, young Lieutenant, which did you like the most up in Alaska—waiting and waiting or sinking that destroyer?"

"Is this a trick question? I loved sinking that Jap and so did you. It's what we're out here for, isn't it?"

"Maybe not, Ron. We just got orders and they are more of the same. We are to hurry up and wait. We are to take up station and patrol an area off of San Diego and look for the Japanese fleet, which may be coming just over the horizon. But when we do spot the slanty-eyed yellow pricks, we are not to attack. In fact, we are not to do anything except stay out of the way and make sure we are not spotted. When we deem it safe, we are to report in and that's it. It was strongly implied that if we were spotted we would be in more trouble than we could ever imagine even if we should manage to survive the encounter."

Crowley sat on a small stool. With both men seated in the tiny cabin, their knees were almost touching. "I suppose they have their reasons, Skipper. It sounds like they want to do something sneaky to the Japs and I can't see anything wrong with that."

Torelli grinned. "I can't either, but I don't like letting them off scot-free if we do find them."

Crowley looked at Torelli in surprise. "Are you implying that we might not obey orders? I don't know about you, but I don't want to be court-martialed or spend the rest of my life supervising KP."

"Don't fret, Ron. I'm crazy, not stupid. We will obey both the letter and the spirit of the orders. But I want to be totally prepared if we do get the opportunity to hit Hirohito's fleet. I want every torpedo inspected and inspected again. I want to eliminate the possibility of duds as much as we can."

Crowley declined to remind his captain that they'd been working with the torpedoes since leaving the base at Mare Island. The problem with malfunctioning torpedoes had not gone away. The navy hierarchy out east in Washington's BuOrd was adamant that there was nothing wrong with the torpedoes and that the sub skippers were the ones screwing up. The men on the subs felt just the opposite.

The navy's highest brass had come down with a firm directive that the sub crews may not tamper with or try to improve the torpedoes. Torelli, like a number of others, had quietly and privately thought that the brass in Washington should go screw themselves. Admiral Lockwood, now firmly in charge of American subs operating in the Pacific was on the side of the crews and generally looked the other way when they tweaked the torpedoes. After all, they were the ones who had to deal with the after effects of dud torpedoes, which included highly enraged Japanese warships coming down the throats of their American tormenters.

"What's happening now, Lieutenant?" asked one of the crew as Crowley emerged.

"Just the usual, we hurry up and wait. After all, this is the navy."

CHAPTER 20

AMANDA DIDN'T KNOW WHETHER TO BE ANGRY or amused. Perhaps a little of both was in order. She had made an offhand comment to Tim about doing more to help the war effort and here she was, in a skimpy two-piece bathing suit, sitting on a beach blanket with the ocean in the background as Captain Merchant took a picture of her and Gunther Krause, who was also in swim trunks and enjoying himself hugely.

Thankfully, Tim had the good grace to look uncomfortable. Both he and Merchant were also in trunks and if any of the handful of people in the area were watching they all looked innocent and innocuous. Just a group of friends enjoying a pleasant day, they would conclude. They were where she and Tim had frolicked not so long ago, only now the beach was almost deserted.

Merchant took another moment to focus the camera. He'd taken several pictures already. "Amanda, smile

a little more warmly and try to give the impression
that you actually like Krause."

Krause laughed. "I actually am very likeable once
you get to know me."

"Shut up and snuggle," Merchant said and Tim
glared.

Amanda put her head on Krause's shoulder and
he put his arm around her waist. Tim seethed. If
his hand got too close to her breast he was going to
break it. He had noticed that the Nazi was peering
down the front of Amanda's too-loose top. Damn it.

One of Krause's contacts in Mexico had informed
them that the Japs wanted to know just who the
source inside the U.S. Navy was. Specifically, who had
provided the information on the carriers' location?
When Tim had mentioned the problem to Amanda
over lunch, she had suggested it be a fictitious person
in Nimitz's staff, a civilian and a woman, and someone
who'd been having an affair with Krause. The idea
made sense and it had been a short leap to getting
Amanda to volunteer. Yes, she wanted to help her
country defeat the Japs, but did she have to do it
with a Nazi's hand around her body and with Tim
breathing fire out of each nostril?

She took a deep breath and smiled at the camera.
She realized that her objections were idiotic. What she
was doing was nothing in comparison with what soldiers,
sailors, and Marines were doing in actual combat. How
could being pawed and leered at by a Nazi prisoner
compare with being shot? She had made Merchant agree
to the caveat that her real name would not be used
and he had agreed. A letter would go down to Mexico
from Krause telling his friend that he was engaged to

the lovely Patricia Barkley, photos attached, and that he was a lucky man. The note would casually mention that Patricia Barkley worked for some admiral. It was hoped that this would more than satisfy any doubters and be of no interest to anyone reading it.

"Enough," said Merchant. The camera and film went into a container. The film would be developed immediately and the letter and photos would go out this afternoon.

Krause helped Amanda to her feet. Tim noticed that his hand brushed her bottom and her eyes widened slightly. Krause never saw the punch coming. It hit him in the pit of the stomach and he doubled over, gasping and vomiting lunch. The second punch struck him on the side of the head and dropped him to the sand where he spit out blood and something white that might have been part of a tooth. He rolled onto his side and got up groggily.

"Once again, my hero," said Amanda, smiling sweetly.

Merchant shook his head. "That's going to screw up German-American relations, you know, and maybe leave a mark on this asshole."

Krause managed to straighten up and shook his head. "No, it won't. I deserved it, but I have no regrets."

Amanda glared at him. "And I need a swim. Nothing personal, Herr Krause, but I feel just a little dirty and want to clean up. Tim, come with me."

The water was a little on the cool side, but comfortable enough. "Tim, you have been very good and I want to be just a little bit bad. I did what I thought was right in having those pictures taken, and have no regrets. I just can't stand remembering him touching me. Only you get to do that."

Tim grinned. "Does that mean we're going behind the raft again?"

"Indeed it does, sailor boy."

Toki and Masao were beside themselves with joy, as was the entire crew of the *Kaga*. The carrier's skipper, Rear Admiral Jisaku Okada, had just used the loudspeaker and made the formal announcement on behalf of Admiral Nagumo who was en route from meeting with Yamamoto. The Imperial Japanese Navy would strike hard at the two American carriers now in the Gulf of California. All the rumors were now confirmed as facts.

The *Kaga*'s crew had responded to the good news with jubilation. Cheers resounded throughout the ship and men slapped each other on the back in un-Japanese shows of exuberance. Even the most hardened of NCOs were seen to be smiling, however briefly. Bottles of sake were brought out and they all talked about the implications of the coming assault. Shouts of "banzai" were heard throughout the ship. This would be a day of celebration. Tomorrow they would sail off to war.

"This is a magnificent opportunity to end this war," Masao said.

Toki laughed. "I thought you were a warrior who wanted it to go on forever. Don't tell me you've had your fill?"

"At least for a while," Masao admitted. "I would like to go home, see my family, walk the earth, smell the flowers, and convince my sister that you are a complete and utter fool."

"But it won't happen for a while," Toki said. "Too

many people have plans for us once we've destroyed the Americans."

"You are very confident that they will be destroyed. How many of our carriers will be sent against the two Americans? My guess would be four or five."

Toki grinned and then turned somber. "All of them. We have eight carriers ready to use and we will overwhelm the Americans. Sadly, it will mean that we will lose men and planes. The Americans will doubtless defend their ships with desperation."

"Carriers at anchor and under repair cannot launch planes," Masao said.

Toki took a long swallow from the bottle in his hand. "Which means that the Americans will have taken the planes off their ships and will launch them from ground strips. It may also mean that other planes will be at ground bases and will protect their carriers. Of course, Yamamoto will distract them and hopefully stop that from occurring."

"How will he do that?"

Toki smiled smugly. "Kurita's battleships and a couple of smaller carriers will first attack San Diego and Los Angeles. It will cause the Americans to hold back their planes and attack Kurita's ships. We may lose some old battleships, but their day is over anyhow. It is now the time of the carrier. When the battle is over, we can get on with consolidating our hold in the Pacific."

Somehow a pair of fresh bottles had appeared in their hands and they swallowed happily. "And how will we do that?" Masao asked.

"The plans for after our victory are simple but elegant. We will finally occupy the island of Oahu, which will probably surrender without a fight when they finally

see how hopeless their situation has become. Then we
will land more army troops to take back Alaska, and a
large force will be sent against the Panama Canal. The
Americans will squeal like pigs being castrated."

"Excellent," Masao said. He thought his voice
sounded funny and concluded that he was getting a
little drunk.

"And finally, we will land an army on Australia and
end that nuisance. With total control of the seas, we
might just decide to bypass MacArthur's forces now
fighting ours on New Guinea and force Australia to
surrender without an invasion. Don't you think it
would be wonderful if MacArthur lost yet another
army like he did in the Philippines? Of course, he
would become our prisoner, which would further
shame the Americans."

Masao thought it all sounded wonderful. He also
thought he was going to have a terrible headache in
the morning. He sincerely hoped he would not be
required to fly for at least a little while.

Merchant smiled. "Admiral Spruance would like to
borrow your brain for a little while. He promises to
return it reasonably intact."

Tim wondered what this was all about as he walked
down the hall to Spruance's office. To his surprise,
Admiral Nimitz was also present. He started to report
formally, but Nimitz told him to relax and take a seat.

Spruance began. "Once upon a time, we didn't have
enough intelligence about Japan. Now we may just
have too much. Everybody and his brother now has
ideas as to what the Japs are going to do. The ONI
is inundating us with contradictory data, which means

we have no clear indication or consensus regarding Japanese intentions. So, since you are our resident expert on Japan and since you are just down the hall, what the devil do you think Yamamoto would do, and don't tell me you haven't been thinking of it."

Dane managed a smile. "It's on everyone's mind, Admiral, and yes, I have been giving it a lot of thought. I think Yamamoto will hit us with everything he has, and that includes carriers and battleships and anything that floats. The Japanese have been hoping for what they refer to as a decisive battle to knock us out of the war, or at least win a victory for them that will make us think about negotiating. They know they cannot fight a war of attrition with us. They may have sunk more ships and knocked down more planes of ours than we have of theirs, but they cannot replace their losses while we can easily replace ours. Therefore, Yamamoto will see this as a golden opportunity to inflict a major and decisive defeat on us. Frankly, sir, I don't think he has a choice."

"A banzai attack?" asked Nimitz.

"Yes, sir, a full-bore hell-for-leather banzai attack, but with ships and not infantry."

Spruance nodded while Nimitz remained impassive.

Tim continued. "Latest intelligence says they have eight or nine carriers available, although some of them are of the small, escort variety. We want to lure as many of them as possible to the Baja and we might just get all of them. They could hit our decoy fleet with as many as five or six hundred planes. Since they don't fear a carrier attack from us, I don't think they'll leave very many planes behind to cover the carriers."

"What will they do with their battleships?" Nimitz asked.

Tim took a deep breath. This line of questioning was far more than he'd expected, but he had an answer. "Apparently, and based on what they did at Midway, the Japs like fairly complex battle plans to keep us off balance and confused as to their true intentions. When we were fighting off Midway, a Jap force split off from the main force and bombed Dutch Harbor in Alaska as a distraction. I think they will do the same thing with their battleships this time. I believe they will bombard San Diego and maybe a few other places in an attempt to draw our planes off from protecting what they believe are our carriers. They may even support the bombardment force with planes from their smaller carriers."

Nimitz stood and Dane started to as well, but was waved back to his seat while the senior admiral paced. "I agree that they will attack with a major portion of their forces, but I disagree as to using their battleships and cruisers as bombardment forces. We believe they will hold those back to protect their carriers from our inevitable counterattack, as well as keeping some aircraft to protect them as well. Or am I thinking too much like an American and not like a Japanese, Commander Dane?" Nimitz laughed. "You don't have to answer that, Commander."

Tim was thanked for his thoughts and left. Nimitz looked at his friend and fellow admiral. "He pretty well nailed it, didn't he?"

Both men were among those who had access to the Ultra intercepts detailing what the Japanese were up to. The fact that the Japanese military codes were largely broken was one of America's most closely held secrets. As long as the Japanese suspected nothing, the U.S. held a major trump card.

Spruance grimaced. "Of course, knowing what the Japs are going to do and doing something about it are two different things. At Midway we knew what they were up to and still lost."

"We cannot let them know or even suspect a thing," said Nimitz. "But I am concerned about such a large concentration of carriers and planes, as well as their plans to bombard cities. Dane was only half right. Yes, they will shell San Diego, but Los Angeles will be hit as well. Morally, we must warn the people, but if we do that and the cities are evacuated, the information will get back to the Japs. We cannot be certain that all enemy spies have been gathered up, or that some consular staffer from a neutral country might spill the beans about his being sent away to safety, with the result being that the info is somehow relayed to Japan. We must do nothing until the last minute, even though many innocent people will die as a result."

Both men thought for a moment about the rumors they'd heard regarding the German bombing of Coventry, England. Rumors that said that Churchill knew about it through their codebreaking efforts, but had to let it go forward without interruption lest the Nazis figure out that their mail was being read. As a result, more than a thousand British civilians had died. Both men wondered if their silence would be worth it. Would it help end the war? Only time would tell.

Spruance sighed. "Radar will give us several hours warning of the approach of their surface fleet."

Radar towers, like those that lined the English Channel, had been constructed on high ground overlooking the Baja, San Diego, Los Angeles, and other cities.

They could spot ships and planes up to two hundred miles out. That would mean a number of hours for battleships, but less than an hour for airplanes.

"There will be chaos when the sirens sound," Spruance said. "There still aren't anywhere near enough bomb shelters, and I don't know what can protect anyone against a fourteen-inch shell. People will literally try to run for the hills and there will be a stampede. People will die. God, I hope this is worth it. We will do everything we can, but we simply cannot let the Japs stop the attack on the decoys. We will not have enough ships and planes to halt them."

"The Japs will probably focus on attacking military installations, but who knows where the shells will land. I know it's futile, but I wish we hadn't sent the Midway survivors, the cruisers and destroyers, to Pearl Harbor instead of here."

Nimitz looked out a window where he could see the bay. Two heavy cruisers and four light ones, along with a handful of destroyers, were all that the navy possessed at San Diego. There were other ships in San Francisco and Puget Sound, but they would have been inadequate in the first place, and likely would have been sunk if they'd attempted to move them south to San Diego.

"We play the cards we were dealt," Nimitz said grimly. "But if they actually do hit us here with all the planes that their carriers have, we are in trouble."

"Then we'd better start shuffling planes down here from up north as soon as possible," Spruance added.

"Are we ready for that?" Nimitz asked.

"Do we have a choice?"

Down the hall, Merchant asked Tim how it went.

"I gave them my frank opinion and said that the Japs were going to hit us with everything, and including the kitchen sink. Only thing, I don't think they quite believed it. Nimitz asked if I thought he was thinking too much like an American and not like a Jap. He told me not to answer that, so my career's intact, although, if he'd pushed, that's exactly what I would have said. Unless we start thinking like Yamamoto, he's going to keep beating us."

Lieutenant Harry Hogg, USAAF, had been called Piggy since the day he was born. Mom said he'd been a chubby baby and the name had stuck, even though Hogg was a slight and slender young man of twenty-three. When he was younger, he thought he'd like to kill dear old mom, but then realized that the nickname was inevitable given his last name.

Hogg stood by his twin-tailed P38 fighter and looked around at the Mexican terrain. The land was barren and rugged, but, somehow, engineers had managed to lay out a number of airfields scratched into the hard surfce of the earth. His landing had been scary as his plane used a lot of runway and this dirt field had all of about six inches leeway. Taking off was going to be a joy as well. He and the other P38 pilots were safe for the moment and damned glad to be down on mother Earth.

Some people he knew went on vacation to Mexico. This, however, was not going to be a vacation. An NCO had directed him to a series of tents where there were cots set up for the pilots and mechanics. There was food, and it was neither plentiful nor good. When asked how long they'd be at this abomination, Piggy and his fellow pilots were told they'd be there as long

as the Army Air Force or the United States Navy said
they should. That was another thing. Army and navy
pilots were intermingled and more and more planes of
all types were coming in, including P39, P40, and P47
army fighters and navy Wildcats. Hogg had seen many
others fly overhead and on to other fields that were out
of sight. Quietly, they were told they shouldn't be in
Mexico for more than a few days. Sure, they all thought.
The word "soon" to the military could mean an eternity.

Everyone felt that something big was up, but nobody
was quite certain what. There were what appeared to
be a couple of carriers out in the bay, but they looked
way too small, even misshapen.

Fuel had been brought in, but not all that much of it.
To Piggy, this meant that the facility truly was temporary
and that suited him just fine. It looked as if there was
only enough fuel for two or three full flights of thirteen
hundred miles each, which was the P38's range. He'd
only recently completed training and, while anxious to
take on either the Germans or the Japanese, knew he
was good but had doubts as to whether he was good
enough to duel with an experienced enemy pilot. From
what he and the others had heard about the Japanese,
they flew their Zeros with consummate skill. Piggy loved
his twin-tailed fighter and looked forward to using it
against the enemy, just not any time real soon. Some
of the twin-tailed planes had been stationed in Alaska,
but they'd been withdrawn after the Midway debacle.

Senior officers quickly informed all the pilots that
there would be no training or orientation flights. They
wanted to minimize the chance that the planes would
be seen by unfriendly eyes although, obviously, they
might have been spotted flying in. Hogg and the other

pilots all looked at each other. The need for secrecy meant that the Japs *were* coming and they were going to try and spring a trap on the dirty yellow bastards.

When asked if they would have some time to go into town, the pilots were informed that there was no town. They were also told not to drink any water that hadn't been boiled or any food that had been cooked in local water. The same held true for the local booze. Montezuma's Revenge was spelled out in great detail and Hogg decided he would take no chance on having a case of the raging shits while trapped in the cockpit of his plane. Even if he and the plane made it back, he was told that both would have to be hosed down.

A ragged cheer told him that the tent designated as the mess hall had opened for business. Piggy was a healthy young man and he hadn't eaten since morning.

He entered the tent and grabbed a metal tray. "What's today's main course?" he asked one of his fellow pilots.

"Shit on a shingle. What else?"

"If I asked you to leave San Diego, would you?" Tim asked.

Amanda smiled tenderly and patted him on the cheek. "No."

"I didn't think you would." They were seated on a park bench and had a view of the bay. It was almost empty of warships.

"And don't even think of asking. I'm a nurse and I'll stay here and do my duty just like you will."

Tim thought there was a big difference between a naval officer and a civilian nurse, but prudently kept his opinion to himself.

She squeezed his hand. "The big battle's going to come and very soon, isn't it? And it's going to take place around here, right?"

"That's the rumor."

"Tim, you know more than that."

"Not really. A lot of people think that there will be fighting around here, and, yes, I'm one of them, which is why I had hoped you would consider leaving."

"Well, I'm not going. Do you really think the Japs are going to target civilian areas and places like hospitals? I don't think they did that when they attacked Pearl and Honolulu."

"Civilians were killed, weren't they? I seem to recall hiding in a shelter with a beautiful but frightened nurse while everything exploded around us."

"I wasn't frightened, I was terrified. But you'll be here, too, won't you?"

"No."

"What?" she said. She was shocked. "Where are they sending you now?"

Tim took a deep breath. He'd hated the thought of telling her and had been putting it off. "Spruance is going to take over from Halsey. It seems that Bull has gotten another attack of his skin infection and, while it's still mild, Nimitz can't take the chance of his being incapacitated during the middle of a battle."

"So let me guess, he's taking you along with him."

Tim nodded solemnly. "Yes, and some other personnel, including Merchant. Seems he wants at least some of his regular staff with him, and that makes sense. Who knows, maybe he'll want me to translate surrender terms to Yamamoto."

"That's not funny and it doesn't make sense," she

said, wiping away a tear. "Jesus, Tim, how many battles have you been in? Haven't you done enough?"

"I can think of a lot of guys who've done a lot more, so no, I haven't done enough. I'm not being noble and I'm scared to death for the both of us, but the curse of the military is that you can't let down your comrades, your buddies."

Which was why Amanda knew she couldn't leave San Diego when others remained behind. "When will you be leaving?"

"Two or three days. Why?"

She stood and pulled him to his feet. "Then we'll have to act quickly, won't we?"

"This, Skipper, is a torpedo."

"Thank you, Lieutenant. I would never have known."

Crowley ignored Torelli. "And this is a torpedo without its clothes."

He lifted off the metal sheath covering the warhead. "And this is the part of the torpedo that we are to never ever touch or change under penalty of death or something worse."

Torelli looked at the torpedo's innards. There it was, the mechanism that was supposed to guide the weapon under the hull of an enemy ship and, in response to the enemy ship's magnetic field, detonate the torpedo, thus breaking the back of a supposedly doomed vessel. Problem was, it frequently didn't work even though the bastards at BuOrd said it did and that any problems were caused by submariners who were too stupid to follow instructions.

The same problems continued even if the electronic widget was disconnected and the torpedo used as an old-fashioned impact weapon. All too frequently that didn't work either, as they'd found out in highly unauthorized tests against Japanese merchant shipping. The damned torpedoes just weren't dependable and couldn't be counted on. Using the torpedo as originally configured often resulted in the fish disappearing. The consensus was that the torpedo was running low, but why? When used as an impact weapon, they'd literally heard the torpedo clanging against the hull of an enemy ship, but without a resulting explosion.

Crowley pointed to the impact trigger. "Based on my highly unscientific knowledge of engineering I think I see the problem."

Torelli grunted. Crowley had a degree in engineering. "I know all about problems, young Lieutenant. What's the solution?"

"I think the trigger mechanism is too weak and needs to be strengthened. I can't prove it without seeing a torpedo that's failed after hitting, and there's a snowball's chance in hell of that happening out here, but I think the trigger mechanism is too fragile and probably collapses instead of causing a detonation. If we strengthen it, we might correct the problem."

"We could also get court-martialed," Torelli said.

Crowley glared at him. "We'd have to survive in order for that to happen, and what do you think our chances of that would be when we're told to stop staring at Jap ships and begin trying to kill them?"

Torelli eyeballed the offending mechanism, looked up and smiled grimly. "At any rate and assuming our survival, I'll bet we could arrive back at San Diego without any altered torpedoes left, couldn't we?"

CHAPTER 21

AMANDA LAY NAKED ON THE BED AND LOOKED up at the ceiling and the bare light bulb that was, mercifully, off. The only light in the room was from a night light in the bathroom. She was covered with sweat and, for the first time in her young life, she was sexually satisfied, at least for the moment.

She was also married.

After their conversation in the park, they'd found a pliant justice of the peace who owed FBI Agent Harris a favor for something or other, and then got a county clerk friend of the JP to ram through a marriage license. They had the feeling that such goings-on weren't all that rare with so many tens of thousands of servicemen and women in the San Diego area, and many in various stages of shipping out, coming back, or just plain wanting to live in the moment. She wondered if the justice thought she was pregnant and decided she didn't give a damn what the silly little man thought.

The justice had married them the evening before. Maybe some navy regulations had been bent or broken, but Nimitz said he'd take care of them, and that Tim had little more than a day to get the hell back. Grace and Merchant had been maid of honor and best man. It had been pleasant and swift. As a girl growing up, Amanda, like all her friends, had dreamed of a big church wedding with her starring as a beautiful bride wearing a flowing white dress. A dozen bridesmaids in matching dresses would accompany her, and hundreds of her and her parents' friends and relatives would dine at an elegantly catered reception that most people couldn't afford while an expensive band played on. She'd even decided that Lester Lanin's high society band would be just perfect. She would be appropriately thankful that her father was a well-to-do doctor and then go on a honeymoon to Europe with her Prince Charming.

Funny how war changes perspectives and values, she thought. She recalled a sermon in which the minister said something about "when I was a child I thought as a child, but now I am an adult so I think like an adult." Fairy-tale weddings might have a time and a place, but now the world was at war and fairy-tale weddings were no longer that important. And who wanted to honeymoon in Europe with Hitler in charge?

Instead, it was far more important for both of them to pledge themselves to each other, and who cared whether it was in a small office in California or in a magnificent European cathedral? And who cared whether the honeymoon was on the French Riviera or one night in a small apartment in San Diego? She and Tim were married.

The apartment was Merchant's. He was roughing it in Tim's bachelor officer's quarters for the duration. Amanda was certain that Grace would find some way to provide him with a level of solace, although probably in a parked car.

She giggled softly and Tim stirred. He'd been a very gentle lover. The first time they'd been tentative and a little awkward, but there had been no pain. The second time was much, much better as they learned so much about each other. The third was an explosion of exuberant passion that left them gasping, shocked and delighted. Neither was concerned about the possibility that she might get pregnant. Without quite saying it, both of them hoped it would happen. If something happened to Tim, at least there would be another Great Dane to carry on.

He was staring at her. "You are so beautiful, my dear Amanda."

"And so are you, my dear Tim." She followed up the statement by caressing his chest while his hands moved across her breasts and down to her still-moist thighs. She let her own hands travel downward and found that her new best friend was also awakening.

One more time, she thought a few moments later as he entered her. One more time and he'll have to go back to the damn war. She wrapped her arms and legs around him and drew him deeper, deeper, deeper. Damn, damn, damn, she thought in tandem to his stroking inside her.

Steve Farris and Sandy had their meeting. From the beginning it was awkward. Sandy was pleased that Steve had not been maimed, and he said that she looked great, but it became clear that whatever spark there had been before he had gone to Alaska had been extinguished. There was nothing either one had done or said; rather, they simply realized that they had little in common. After a polite conversation, they parted. Sandy went back to work, while a slightly disconsolate Steve wondered what was going on.

Getting onto the naval base early the next morning was fairly easy. A man in uniform, even an army uniform, using a cane and with a Purple Heart and a Bronze Star on his chest, opened a lot of doors. He was just about to enter Tim's office building when a woman's voice hailed him.

"Lieutenant Farris, how are you?"

He turned in surprise. At first he didn't recognize the slight young woman with the dark-rimmed glasses. Then he noticed the oriental shape of her eyes and smiled.

"Nancy Sullivan," he said, quickly recalling the daughter of the store owner in Bridger. After Stecher had discovered Nancy and her mother at her father's store, he had been reluctant to go the store on future occasions, which left Farris with the honors. On several occasions he'd struck up brief conversations with the slight young woman with the glasses. "I am fine, and what are you doing here?"

"Thanks to your uncle, I work here now. Apparently there cannot be enough people fluent in Japanese."

"Speaking of my uncle, I'd like to see him."

Her face clouded. "Ah, he's not here. He and a number of others are, well, away."

"I'll bet that's because there's a war on, isn't it?"

Nancy smiled. "Tell you what. Buy me a cup of

coffee, and I'll tell you what's happened since you went to Alaska. Tim's very proud of you, by the way."

They had two cups each. Steve heard that Tim and Amanda were married, which delighted him, while Nancy was saddened by the death of Stecher. "There was so much hate in that man, but it seemed to be coming out."

"Does it bother you that he died killing Japanese soldiers?"

She looked at him quizzically. "No more than it bothers me that you killed some of the enemy. You keep misunderstanding me and, for that matter, many American people of Japanese descent. I am an American, not Japanese. Japan is a strange and predatory land across a very large ocean, and, like all Americans, I cannot understand this perverse code of behavior called bushido. It is insane. Maybe someday I'll go visit and look up my ancestors, just like my father would like to see his ancestors in Ireland, but not until my country, the United States, has defeated Japan."

"Sorry," he said sheepishly.

"Don't worry." She smiled widely, then reached across and patted his arm. He noticed that she had a number of light freckles across her cheeks. Not too many Japanese had freckles, he thought. It made her look very attractive.

Nancy stood. "Even though almost everybody's gone from the office, I really should get to work."

"Would you like to go to lunch with me?"

"I'd like that a lot," she said, and Steve began to think that the day might not be a total loss after all.

At that moment, the sirens began to howl.

✳   ✳   ✳

Harris yawned. Sitting in a car and looking at an apartment building in Mexico City was worse than dull. He had enough seniority to dump these jobs on more junior FBI agents, but no, his informant in the Mexican Army had been specific. He and he alone should be at the expensive-looking apartment building at eight o'clock in the morning on this date. He was told he might appreciate Mexican justice being served, and the thought indeed intrigued him.

A few minutes after eight, Juan Escobar, colonel in the Mexican Army and informant for the Nazis and Japanese, stepped through the door. He was in casual civilian clothes and seemed well satisfied with himself. Harris recalled that Escobar had a mistress, and it seemed logical that he'd spent the night with her. He clearly looked smug after getting laid and Harris envied him.

So what did that have to do with him and the FBI? Maybe he was going to watch Mexican police arrest Escobar for providing aid to the Germans and the Japanese? That was a pleasant enough thought, but why did they think it was necessary for him to be there to watch?

Escobar stood near the curb and looked around as if he didn't have a care in the world. He was obviously waiting to be picked up by some junior officer. Harris stiffened as the colonel was approached by two men in equally casual clothing. His mind registered the sight of the pistols being drawn. They were jammed into Escobar's gut while he began to protest, a look of terror on his face. The men fired rapidly and Escobar's eyes widened and then glazed over.

As Escobar toppled to the ground, blood pouring from

his chest, the men took his wallet and watch. One more shot to the chest to make certain he was dead, and the men ran down the street and around the corner. A few stunned people came out and slowly began to approach Escobar's body. Harris quickly shook off the shock of the murder. He had been told that justice would be served and he couldn't argue with the brutal fact. Also, he had to admit that faking the robbery might actually mask the fact that it had been an assassination by other members of the Mexican military.

He waited only a few seconds to gather his nerves and drove back to his office in the American Embassy. He didn't want the Mexico City police wondering what an American FBI agent was doing so close to the killing of a respected Mexican Army colonel.

The somewhat grumpy woman assigned as his secretary had taken a message from someone who refused to give a name, only saying that Mexicans don't like traitors either. Harris crumpled the paper and threw it in the wastebasket.

He thought he should talk to the ambassador before leaving to go back to the U.S., but just then someone loudly announced that the Japs were attacking California. The hell with the ambassador, Harris thought as he ran out of the embassy, he had to get a flight back to California as soon as possible.

Amanda had just arrived for her shift at the hospital when the sirens began to scream. Oh God, she thought. What should she do now? Patients were staring at her as if she knew what to do. Some could be moved, but many could not. But where to go? Was anyplace safe? Worse, there was an appalling lack of shelters.

The supervising nurse solved at least part of her problem. "Get as many as you can down to the basement and stay with them. I'll take care of the ones who can't move."

Amanda and another nurse managed to get a good twenty men down from the second floor and to a room in the damp and claustrophobic basement. Another dozen wounded made it themselves, some even joking how Japanese bombs and shells motivated them to get their butts out of bed and made them forget their little aches and pains.

When everyone was pretty well settled on the floor of the basement, Amanda went back upstairs. The sirens were still wailing, but did that mean enemy shells or bombs? Or maybe—please—maybe it was a false alarm. She'd endured bombs, shells, and false alarms in Honolulu, what seemed an eternity ago. Just a couple of days earlier, she'd relished discovering so much about herself and Tim, and how much they enjoyed making love and thinking about the future. What the hell was happening to her little world? Tim was off to somewhere dangerous and she was under enemy fire in San Diego. Where was God in all this mess?

"Our ships are leaving," someone yelled. She dashed to a window. Sure enough, the handful of American warships that had remained in San Diego Bay were steaming as rapidly as they could toward the open sea.

She asked a navy captain whether or not the departing ships were going to take on the Japanese, and got an answer that surprised her.

"Sure hope not. Two cruisers and half a dozen destroyers aren't going to stop the Jap navy," he said. "They'd get killed. The navy's just trying to get those little ships out to safety. That is, if there is any place safe."

Thunder boomed in the distance. "Our shore batteries," the captain said. Amanda recalled that Tim had told her there were eight- and ten-inch guns in batteries on Point Lomas overlooking the entrance to the bay. More distant thunder told her that the Japs were within range. This was confirmed by giant splashes in the harbor, some frighteningly close to the fleeing warships.

"They must have spotter planes up," the captain said.

"So why don't we shoot them down?"

"Good question. I don't know where the hell our planes are. It's as if we don't have any."

A massive shell hit a destroyer. The explosion lifted it out of the water. It landed and capsized. Amanda watched in horror as men tumbled into the water. A new sound intruded. Planes, Jap planes. Antiaircraft guns began firing and adding to the din.

Amanda was no fool. Her place was with her patients, not where bombs and shells might be falling. She ran downstairs where most of them waited stolidly. She gave them all the information she had, which seemed to please them. Nobody liked to be kept in the dark.

"Thank you, Nurse Dane," a sailor with his arm in a cast said, grinning. The announcement that she was married had caused great amusement. A couple said they were heartbroken and wondered why she'd dumped them, and she'd replied that she still loved them all.

Something exploded nearby, and the building shook. The lights went out, but they'd brought some flashlights. Another sailor laughed nervously. "This place wasn't built on a low-bid contract, was it, ma'am?"

Another explosion and pieces of the false ceiling began to tumble down. "Get under something," she hollered.

Half the men had done that already, but it did motivate the rest to take cover under anything they could find. Desks and tables were the favorites. She looked around for something to hide under.

She was already flying across the room when she realized that another explosion had occurred, and this one terribly close. She hit the wall with enough force to knock the wind from her. She gasped for breath and felt pain surging through her body. Debris was falling on her and she couldn't move. As she felt consciousness ebb, she heard screams and realized at least one voice was hers. Then it became dusty and dark.

Farris and Nancy cowered in a long slit trench. It was filled with men and women, civilians and military, and even a few children. The Japanese were pounding the base. A shell landed nearby and showered them with dirt and debris. A child began to scream in stark terror.

Antiaircraft batteries nearby began to fire. Farris risked looking up and saw a pair of Japanese planes, the damned Zeroes, fly low overhead. It was obvious that Jap carriers as well as their warships were very close.

A Zero streaked across the bay, only a few feet above the water. The antiaircraft battery opened up with its twin 20mm guns. The plane flew through the shells and fired its machine guns, riddling the battery. Men staggered out and fell, some quivering.

"Where the hell are our planes?" a Marine sergeant asked. Then he saw Nancy. "Hey, she's a fucking Jap."

The enraged Marine threw a punch that Nancy ducked. Farris grabbed the man and pushed him against the wall of the trench. "Do that again and I'll kill you."

Nancy grabbed his arm and pointed to the destroyed antiaircraft guns. "Some of those men are still alive."

Farris climbed out of the trench and ran to the ruined battery, with Nancy right behind him. While most of the gunners were shredded meat, two men were still alive. He grabbed one and she grabbed the other. The two men moaned at being roughly man-handled, but there wasn't time to be gentle.

Farris pulled at his wounded man. He was too big to carry, so he dragged him. The pain to his damaged shoulder was excruciating, and he felt it pop. Incredulously, he saw Nancy managing to drag the other man the few dozen yards to safety. Halfway there, the Marine sergeant and another enlisted man arrived to help them with their burdens.

They managed to get the two wounded men into the trench. People moved away to give them room. "How's your first aid?" Nancy asked. Farris and the Marine sergeant admitted theirs was okay but that was about it. Even in combat, Farris hadn't had to treat wounds.

"Then my skills are better," she said. "Living in a place like Bridger made us all very independent. Let's get organized; start helping me."

Steve's left arm was again limp and useless. All he could do was watch while Nancy and another woman did what they could for the wounded men.

"Sorry about being such a jerk, sir," the Marine sergeant said. "I didn't realize she was an American."

"Don't worry about it."

"I think your shoulder's been dislocated."

Farris agreed with the diagnosis. The Marine pushed him against the wall of the trench, grabbed his wrist, and jerked. The pain was excruciating and he nearly fainted, but the shoulder popped back in.

The Marine offered Steve a cigarette. "That woman is something else."

"Yeah. She sure is."

The explosions in and around the base represented both fear and an opportunity for Gunther Krause. For a while he had been having second thoughts as to whether the Americans would honor their agreement or, once he was no longer useful, discard it and him as well. Now, as the shells fell on the base and in the city, he knew the answer. The government would need a scapegoat for the burning mess that was the San Diego Naval Base and that person's name would be Gunther Krause. The Americans would manage to blame him for the devastation and the slaughter.

When he agreed to help the Yanks lure the Japanese, he had no idea it would result in so much destruction to an American city. No, he thought ruefully, there would be no freedom for him. If he managed to escape the firing squad or noose, they would put him in a place where he'd never even see the light of day.

When the shelling started, his two guards had left the house and run to a slit trench, assuming that he would follow. If he was smart, that is where he would be. But if he was really smart, he thought, he would take advantage of the chaos and confusion. Maybe he didn't like the idea of spending the rest of his life on the run, but it beat a firing squad by a lot. He quickly packed the suitcase they'd allowed him to bring with him and ran outside. He was dressed in civilian clothes. The American military didn't want him defiling their uniforms and that suited him well this morning.

His two guards had left their jeep in the street. He got in and drove off. As he approached the gate to the base, he saw people in uniform running in and trying to get to their posts, while others, mainly civilians, streamed out. The guards weren't in the least bit interested in who was leaving and only looked quickly at those entering. As long as you were white, in uniform, and not Japanese, you were okay. He parked the jeep and simply trotted out and into San Diego. Crowds were headed out of the city and he joined them.

Krause had only gone a few blocks when he saw that, incredibly, his bank was open. He entered and asked to open his safe deposit box. A Hispanic female clerk named Maria helped him. She explained, angrily, that their idiot of a manager wouldn't let them close the place, not even for a Japanese bombardment. If she didn't need the job so much, she'd walk out. She added that the pay was lousy and she was thinking about quitting and going to work in a nearby factory like her husband did. She said they'd lived in the town of Grover, a ways north of San Diego, and had been shelled out of their homes by the Japanese. It looked like it was going to happen again. Krause wanted to strangle her.

Finally alone in the booth, he emptied the contents of the box. He now had more than ten thousand dollars and three sets of identification. He also had a

.32 Colt revolver. Krause happily departed the bank, found a car, hot-wired it, and drove off inland along with much of the population of San Diego. He was confident that the police would have too much on their hands to worry about a stolen car, especially when they would recover it shortly. He was uncertain as to exactly where he would go, but east would be the general direction and then he would take a Greyhound bus to somewhere. Kansas City sounded like a nice destination. He would be a German refugee who'd fled Hitler before the war. Yes, that would get him sympathy. Maybe, he thought, he would make it after all.

He laughed. The Third Reich was doomed to a slow death in the frozen steppes of Russia and would ultimately be trampled by the vengeful Soviets, but there was no reason for a similar fate to befall him.

Admiral Chester Nimitz clutched his chest and tried to hold back the tears that threatened to spill down his cheeks. In the background, his aides, his staff, were imploring him to go to a shelter. A couple had even tried to pull on his arm, but he had shaken them off. However horrible this was, it was something he had to see, especially since he had caused it.

Nimitz recalled an old phrase: "What hath God wrought?" No, this time it was: "What Hath Chester Nimitz wrought?" It was his decision to try to lure the Japanese fleet to California and now he had them. He laughed bitterly and recalled another saying: "Be careful what you wish for, it might come true." He now had to accept the possibility that the name Chester Nimitz would go down amid the host of history's fools.

Custer and whoever had led the Charge of the Light Brigade and demanded the assault on the Somme would welcome him as a failed comrade-in-arms.

Through the window of his office, he could see small boats moving fearlessly through the attack, picking up survivors from the sunken destroyer. There were precious few sailors being pulled into the boats, and Nimitz assumed that many of them were dead already.

Another enemy salvo crashed onto the base, destroying a warehouse. Something in it exploded with a roar. The hospital had collapsed and he hoped the patients and medical personnel had gotten out. The shore batteries had already been silenced. Japanese ships and planes were shelling and bombing with impunity, and he had invited them in. Intelligence said that at least six and possibly eight enemy carriers were approaching the Baja, so where had the planes bombing and strafing the base come from? Either the Japs had more carriers than anyone thought, or they were using anything that would float and hold planes.

Regardless, the full fury of Imperial Japan was descending on San Diego and Los Angeles, which was also being bombed and shelled. The Rose Bowl stadium had been shelled and the "HOLLYWOOD" sign had been blown off the hill. The handful of fighters he'd held back to provide a token defense had been shot down.

Another explosion rocked the area. A bomb or shell had hit a fuel depot and resulted in billowing flames surging skyward.

"Admiral, let's go."

It was one of his aides. This one was brave enough to be insistent. Nimitz allowed himself to be led down the stairs to a place that was, theoretically at least, safe. If the enemy force approaching the Baja was not destroyed, or at least defeated, his name would be reviled.

Nimitz paused. He had a horrible thought. What if Yamamoto had seen through the trick and no Japanese fleet was actually going to the Baja? Perhaps they would turn around, or even head north, attacking and devastating other coastal cities as they went. Perhaps they'd seen through his clumsy ruse and knew that there were no carriers in the Baja. If the Japs made such a fool of him, the word "reviled" wouldn't begin to describe the contempt he would endure.

Belowground, in his reinforced concrete bunker, his staff looked at him, relief evident on their faces that he'd finally joined them. He made a mental note never to scare them again. A second mental note was that whatever happened, he would endure it.

"What's the latest?"

"The Jap surface fleets are turning back, sir. Either they're out of ammo or out of targets."

"Neither," Nimitz said. "They're trying to lure us out. They want us to send all our planes after them and we're not going to do that. How many planes attacked here and Los Angeles?"

"Maybe thirty apiece," another aide said. "We think they have a small carrier off each city. Allowing for typical pilot exaggeration, we shot down an estimated twenty of the enemy."

"A heavy price for a decoy," the admiral thought out loud.

Another aide looked at him eagerly. "Sir, radar on the hills overlooking the Baja report that the enemy

carriers are within their range. They also report that
the Japs are close enough to start launching large
numbers of planes."

Nimitz sat down in leather admiral's chair. Despite
his many doubts, the Japs were going to attack. Perhaps
this wouldn't be such a bad day after all.

Toki ran up to his friend and embraced him in a
most unJapanese display of affection, a wide smile
on his face. "Today is the day, my friend, go bravely
and sink their ships."

Masao slapped him on the back and laughed. It
was a good day to be a Japanese warrior, a samurai.
"Make up your mind. A while back you were certain
we were doomed because the Americans were so
powerful. Now you seem confident that we'll defeat
them. Which is it?"

"Of course I have doubts. Nothing is certain in
life, except, of course, death."

They were standing on the flight deck alongside
Masao's Zero. The deck was humming with pilots waiting to be given the word to take off, while mechanics
performed whatever last-minute wizardry they did to
make sure that the magnificent Japanese planes flew.

Finally, the order was given and pilots eagerly
climbed into the cockpits of their planes. Along with
Zeros, the *Kaga* was going to launch all of her Aichi
D3A dive bombers with their five-hundred-fifty-pound
bombs, and her Nakajima B5N torpedo bombers with
their Type 91 torpedoes that had warheads containing
more than five hundred pounds of explosives. Just
about every plane from every carrier would be involved
in the attack. Only a handful of Zeros would remain

behind. Some had wondered about the wisdom of that decision, but the revered and infallible Yamamoto had said that fortune favors the bold. The Americans could not attack the Japanese fleet because they had no carriers at sea, although they would surely have some land-based planes guarding their ships. Ergo, there was no need to retain planes to fight off any American planes.

With a roar, Masao was airborne. The sight of the vast aerial armada took his breath away. A mighty host of planes was headed toward the American coast. He exulted. In a short while the two American carriers would be at the bottom of the Gulf of California.

As he and the others drew closer, they could see dots in the air. Yes, the Americans were rising to meet them. Good, Masao thought, victory would be even more complete when they were all shot down.

Soon he was both high enough and far enough along to see the distant shapes of the American ships. They appeared to be dead in the water. Something nagged at him. They didn't look quite right. He dismissed the thought. After all, weren't they in the Gulf for repairs? That must be why they looked strange.

He wiped any distractions from his mind. There was no time for daydreaming. First, he had to fight his way through a surprising number of American planes that were racing to meet him. The more of them to shoot down, he thought happily.

Lieutenant Harry Hogg had similar thoughts as he and his fellow pilots waited for the order to take off. It seemed like they were going to wait for the Japs to get real close before taking them on, which seemed like a dumb idea. He'd much rather get them as far out as possible.

When the order finally came, he and hundreds of others took off from dozens of hastily scratched-out fields and flew over the waters of the gulf. He laughed as he thought that his P38 probably cleared the end of the runway by a hair. Now where the hell were the Japs?

Radar directed them toward the Japanese air fleet. After a few minutes, they didn't need radar. The sky was filled with enemy airplanes.

"Jesus, look at them all," Harry announced. For many this was their first combat flight and radio discipline was lousy.

"Every fucking plane in the world," someone said with awe in his voice.

"Shut up and remember your orders," snarled the major. Yeah, Hogg thought, our orders.

There was no longer time to think, only react. Planes swirled and turned. Tracers streaked through the air as the two immense forces mingled in a giant lethal dance. A Japanese plane appeared for an instant in front of him and Hogg fired a short burst, missing. Damn it to hell, he raged. Another Zero appeared and it exploded, shot down by somebody else. A P47 spiraled downward, missing one of his wings by mere feet. He urged the pilot to bail out but saw nothing. He couldn't watch. He had to take care of himself and follow his damned orders.

More planes exploded or tumbled to the sea. He shot at a Zero and it burst into flames. He yelled with happiness until the major again told him to shut up and remember his orders. Fuck the major, he thought. He had just shot down a Zero.

Suddenly, he was through the swarm. He looked about and saw that a number of other twin-tailed planes had also cleared the brawl. They formed up and headed west. They had their orders. Hogg wondered if other squadrons had similar orders.

Torelli and the *Shark* had lain low while the Japanese battleships and cruisers headed toward San Diego. Other than sending a quick burst of information describing what they'd seen—four battleships and eight cruisers, along with a dozen destroyers—they'd honored their orders and stayed submerged.

It annoyed Torelli that he hadn't been able to tell fleet headquarters that the biggest, baddest battleship in the world had just roared over his sub as they hid below the waves. Like everyone, he'd heard rumors that the Japs had a monster ship with bigger guns than anyone else had, but hadn't lent any credence to them. Now he knew that everyone's nightmares were true.

He figured the enemy battleship at seventy to eighty thousand tons, far more than anything the U.S. Navy could throw against it. He dreaded the thought of what the shells from her mighty guns might do to San Diego and the naval base, much less what they could do to an American warship.

When the sound of ships' engines faded and he thought it was safe, he ordered the sub to periscope depth and looked around. Nothing. He raised the radio antenna and immediately got a signal from Pacific Fleet. The gloves were off. Now any Jap ship was fair game. Los Angeles and San Diego were being bombarded.

"I wonder why we couldn't attack before?" Crowley asked.

"Ours not to reason why and all that high command type bullshit," Torelli answered with a smile.

"Any chance we'll get a shot at that big one?"

"If we do, will our torpedoes work?"

Crowley grimaced. "We've done our damndest."

Torelli patted his young executive officer on the shoulder. "Then get them loaded and ready to shoot."

CHAPTER 22

DANE'S FLIGHT TO TASK FORCE 18 HAD BEEN uncomfortable, cramped, and exhausting, but surprisingly short. The American fleet wasn't hiding anymore. It was on its way.

As to comfort, there simply wasn't enough room in the PBY for all the additional people and their gear. They couldn't move for fear of interrupting something important being done by the crew, and sleeping was done in fits while seated. They tried to find room for Spruance to rest, but he insisted on sharing their mutual discomfort.

Dane considered it a real miracle that their pilot found the small fleet in the vastness of the Pacific. When Dane looked down on it, he was both impressed and disappointed. The *Saratoga* and the *Essex* looked tiny and puny and only began to take on substance when they flew much closer. The two new battleships, the *North Carolina* and *Washington*, however, were sleek and deadly-looking creatures. Too bad they were already obsolescent, he thought. They looked like wolves straining to get among the sheep. Too bad the Japanese weren't sheep. He also counted a good dozen destroyers in a loose circle around the carriers and battleships. Once it would have been an impressive array, but that was all changed.

The PBY put down alongside the *Saratoga* and the men were taken by launch to the carrier. Dane was mildly surprised to see the PBY crew with them. Merchant told him they couldn't take the chance that the plane might be spotted on the way back and enemy fighters vectored back to the carriers. It made sense but it was a shame to see the perfectly good flying boat quietly sink beneath the waves.

Task Force 18 was so named because its predecessors, TF 16 and 17, and been destroyed either in the battle of Midway or its aftermath. Using the names of the predecessor units would have been bad luck and sailors were very superstitious.

Spruance's group crossed the crowded flight deck, where planes and pilots awaited the word to go, and went to the flag bridge. They were greeted by Halsey, who looked like hell. He appeared exhausted and what was visible of his skin was covered by scabs. His skin disorder, psoriasis, had indeed flared up and the man appeared to be in agony. In Dane's opinion, the belligerent little admiral looked far worse than when he'd last seen him in San Diego. He wondered if the psoriasis was caused by the intense pressure and responsibilities of command. He wondered if his thoughts were unkind. Halsey was a brave and capable man. The two admirals spoke quietly for a few minutes and Halsey left, his head down.

When Spruance returned to the group, his expression was grim. "Halsey's going to sick bay. He's turned command over to me. Nothing, however, is changing. We are steaming toward the Japanese. We will be in range in a very short while, much sooner than I expected. As soon as radar shows them launching their planes to strike at our dummy carriers, the *Saratoga* and *Essex* will turn loose our planes and hit them with everything we have."

Merchant asked the first question on everyone's mind. "When will Admiral Halsey resume command?"

Spruance sighed. "Not for a while. I think this battle's going to be mine."

Merchant continued. "Then what about Japanese radar? Do we still assume they don't have it on their ships?"

Spruance paused. If the Japanese did have radar on their ships, the American force could be steaming into another ambush. His men needed to know what they were up against, but they weren't cleared to know too much.

"Just like us, Captain, very few of their ships have radar, and, just like ours, it isn't very reliable. All indications are that their ships do not carry long-range radar if any at all. I know it's dangerous to presume, but we have no other choice."

A young ensign burst in on them, saw Spruance, and saluted. "Sir, we just got word that the Japs' carriers have launched their planes. They all appear headed for the Baja."

Spruance paused for a moment and appeared to look upward. Dane wondered if he was seeing a chance at redemption or the likelihood of losing more carriers.

Or maybe he was praying. Finally, he smiled. "We will attack immediately."

As soon as the shelling appeared to stop, rescue parties began swarming over the smoking ruins that had once been a major naval base. In most cases, the buildings had been emptied, and their occupants fled to shelters or trenches like the one that had protected Farris and Nancy Sullivan.

Not so the hospital. Originally a three-story office building located on a rise outside the base proper, it had been struck and devastated by several Japanese shells. The temporary wooden buildings and Quonset huts surrounding it had been smashed and were burning. The stench of scorched flesh filled the air, gagging rescuers.

As an officer who'd volunteered to help, Farris was given a dozen sailors and Marines who didn't seem to notice that their commander was from the army and that he was having trouble with his left arm. There were lives to save and no time for bullshit.

Farris's shoulder now ached and he could hardly lift his arm. So much for getting better, he thought. Worse, though, was the information from Nancy that the hospital was where Amanda worked. Since she had not shown up to help with the injured, they could only presume that she'd been in the building when the shells hit. Even though he'd only met her a couple of times, she was now family and Steve was deeply upset that she might have been buried in the hospital.

A few people, most of them badly injured, had been found alive and carted off on stretchers, and Nancy had helped carry them. When he mentioned it, she shrugged it off, explaining that she'd studied Japanese fighting methods and that leverage more than compensated for brute strength.

More frequently, though, what they found were dead bodies or, worse, parts of bodies. One of the sailors near Farris pulled on a human leg and screamed when it came out of the rubble without the rest of the body. Farris tried to calm the young man down and sent him off when he couldn't stop shaking. Unfortunately, the finding of bodies and partial bodies was all too common. He wondered if the hospital had been targeted intentionally and then dismissed the thought. Even though there were large red crosses on the buildings, he doubted that the Japanese could even see them. No, these were more likely random shots with tragic consequences.

"Lieutenant, over here!"

Farris scrambled over to where a small cavelike opening appeared in the debris, possibly leading to the basement. He stuck his head in. His spirits sagged as he smelled dust, smoke, blood, excreta, and death. If Amanda was in there, God help her. Regardless, the tiny opening would have to be enlarged.

Nancy was beside them. "Just make it big enough for me and get me a flashlight. I'm a lot smaller than you guys and can make it where you can't. I only wish I hadn't worn a skirt."

The men nodded enthusiastically and began digging. Farris noted that nobody seemed to care anymore that she was part Japanese. Hell, everyone was too busy carrying dirt from the rubble.

A few moments later and Nancy slithered in through the slightly enlarged hole. She carried a flashlight and wore a helmet that looked incongruously large. Someone had slipped her a set of fatigues that, hopefully, would provide some protection from contact with the rubble; she wasn't concerned about modesty, saying if somebody wanted to see her skinny legs, let them look. A rope was tied around her waist. If something happened, maybe they could pull her out. At least they'd know where to find her.

Inside the cave, she turned on the flashlight and recoiled. A man's face was staring at her. His eyes were wide open but unseeing. She checked under his chin for a pulse and found none. A few other limbs protruded from the rubble. She checked and found no signs of life. She began to think that this was a dangerous waste of time. But she continued to look and scrambled farther in. She saw an arm sticking out and she felt for life.

"Oh, Jesus," she said and began to crawl back.

Another few moments, and her head popped up in the sunlight. She saw Farris. "Get me some canteens and begin opening that hole real fast."

Masao howled with glee as one of the evil looking twin-tailed American fighters broke in half under the impact of his guns and plummeted into the sea. It was his third kill of the day, and, even better, it appeared he was through the American planes defending the carriers.

His was not the only plane to break through to the enemy ships that were now nothing more than fat targets anchored in the bay. Others were ahead of him and beginning their bombing runs. Large splashes rose near the American ships and a couple of bombs struck

the carriers, sending debris skyward. Masao thought the
carriers looked strange and the flying rubble different
than what he expected. However strange, he thought,
the American carriers were going to die. He noticed
there was no antiaircraft fire coming from them and
he wondered why as he began his run. Perhaps their
guns had been removed as part of the repair process.

"Abort, abort," came the order over his radio. "Those
aren't real ships. Pull up! Pull up!"

Masao hesitated only for an instant before obeying.
Even so, his momentum carried him over the "carriers"
and he had the sickening realization that they were
indeed dummies. Where then were the real American
carriers? Had the Japanese planes been lured to this
site so they could duel with the American planes, or
was there a more sinister reason? If it was to be a
duel of planes, he was confident that the American
fighters were no match for his fellow Japanese, even
though so many of the pilots were inexperienced
replacements.

The radio crackled again, and this time his commander's voice was almost frantic. "All planes, return
to your carriers. The Americans are going to attack
our carriers."

Stunned, Masao turned and joined hundreds of others as they began to chase the American fighters who,
he now realized, had let them slip through on purpose.
He could see the American planes gaining altitude
and disappearing in the direction of the carriers. He
was astonished at the speed of the American planes
and the altitude at which they were flying. Perhaps
Toki had been correct—the Zero was indeed obsolete.

"The carriers are under attack," the shrill voice

came over the radio, but how, he wondered? The
American planes were in sight and still a ways from
them. The truth dawned. If they had just attacked
the dummy carriers, then where were the real ones?
They were now attacking the Japanese carriers, that's
where. He howled his rage and vowed vengeance on
the Americans.

Toki stood behind Admiral Nagumo on the bridge
of the *Kaga* and tried to make himself small and
unnoticed, and to a large part, he succeeded. The
admiral was obviously conflicted as he received the
information that the American carriers weren't in the
waters off the Baja as expected. Both the American
and Japanese airplanes were now en route to the
Japanese carriers, with at least some of the Americans
due to arrive ahead of the Zeros.

Toki listened as other staff officers outlined the
dilemma. The Japanese planes had already made a
long flight to California and now were headed back.
They would have some fuel, but not enough to sustain
a long fight. Thus, they would have to be refueled,
and if the Americans were in the area, that would
be both dangerous and chancy. Staffers argued about
their options. Some said the Zeros should destroy
the Americans using what fuel they had and take a
chance on ditching.

Nagumo finally made the decision. All carriers
would be ready to receive planes and refuel them as
quickly as possible. It had to be done that way. If
Japanese planes were forced to ditch, they and their
pilots were as good as lost. So too might the carriers
be lost without planes to protect them. Nagumo said

the ambush was a serious setback but he was confident that Japan's superior planes, pilots, and sailors would prevail, turning the situation into an opportunity for a decisive victory. After his uncharacteristic optimism earlier, Toki was not so certain. Nothing had gone right this day.

In the meantime, the fleet would prepare to defend itself against the Americans flying in from the east. They would meet a storm of antiaircraft fire that would hold them at bay until the Zeros closing in on them took over. It meant, though, that the carriers would be on their own for at least a little while. Toki found that idea very disturbing.

Toki joined the lookouts peering through binoculars, searching for first sight of the Americans approaching from California. This would be the first time he would truly see combat. Watching as pilots departed and returned wasn't the same thing. He felt nervous, afraid. Did everyone feel that way, he wondered? At any moment he could be blown to pieces and he decided he didn't like that at all.

A scream tore him away from his thoughts. A sailor was looking upward and pointing, and not toward the east. No, Toki thought, it can't be. He heard others saying the same thing out loud, uselessly protesting against the obvious. High above, little dots were becoming larger ones. Enemy aircraft had found the carriers and were falling on them like hawks attacking a rabbit.

Antiaircraft guns were turned upward and began firing maniacally. Many of them couldn't shoot, however. They'd been poorly positioned and couldn't aim at a plane diving from above. The lead American dive bomber was hit and fell apart, but the second made it through, dropping its bomb in the ocean a few dozen yards off the *Kaga*'s bow, raising a spray of water that washed over the deck, sending several crewmen overboard to their deaths. Toki wrenched his eyes away and looked up again. Another bomb was falling and he threw himself onto the deck and curled up. A second later, the bomb struck the flight deck and exploded, causing fuel and ammunition to flame and detonate in a cloud of fire, but fortunately not coming too near him. He got up and could see dozens of men lying prone as flames consumed them.

A second bomb struck the stern, penetrated, and started another conflagration. Japanese planes were prepped belowdecks, which meant that large quantities of fuel and ammunition were stored below. Toki stood up, but an explosion from the guts of the ship threw him against a bulkhead. Finally, he got to his feet and looked to see if the other carriers had been hit. Perhaps Japan and Nagumo would be lucky and only the *Kaga* had been damaged. No, he sobbed, it would not be. The *Shokaku* and *Junyo* were also burning furiously.

An American dive bomber, its bomb gone, flew low and strafed the flight deck, starting more fires. Another explosion, this against the hull, and an enemy torpedo bomber flew insolently over the stricken carrier. The great ship convulsed and began to list.

Lieutenant Harry Hogg's orders were to fly in the general direction where someone thought the Jap carriers might be. What a great idea, he thought sarcastically. He and his buddies were headed out in the middle of the world's largest ocean in the general direction of China with the whole Jap air force chasing their asses, and they were supposed to somehow find enemy ships. Worse, he wasn't carrying a bomb or torpedo. He and the others were supposed to kill the Jap planes protecting their carriers.

I'm going to die, he thought. Either I'll be shot down or I'll run out of gas, ditch, and float away. He figured he had more than enough fuel to make it back, but his orders were to find the Jap fleet. There was, he thought, one chance in a million of that happening.

Son of a bitch, he thought, and there they were. At least he could see smoke arising in the west from something that had to be ships. He laughed. Maybe he couldn't bomb a carrier, but he could sure make life miserable for them.

As he drew closer, he could see several carriers on fire. No sense going after them, he exulted. They were already hurting. Harry spotted a smaller carrier that seemed to be untouched, signaled the others with a wave of his arm, and began a strafing run.

For the first time in his brief career, he fired his guns on an enemy ship. Almost oblivious to antiaircraft fire, he took his Lightning low and quick over the length of the flight deck. Something thudded against his plane and he realized he'd been hit. He checked the controls and everything was working. Well then, he exulted, it was time to do it again. He'd just finished a second run and was relishing the sight of many fires burning on the deck, when he felt a sudden and brutal jolt. None of his controls were working. For that matter, his chest was covered with something wet and sticky. His fading mind was still trying to process this when his shattered plane cartwheeled into the ocean.

Masao grimaced as the twin-tailed American plane died under his guns. The tiny *Soryu*, the smallest carrier in the attack force at only twenty thousand tons, was in flames, along with her larger sisters. He watched in dismay as other American planes found her and attacked. He gained altitude and looked for a carrier that hadn't been damaged, but didn't see one. In a short while he would have to put down and refuel, but where?

His radio crackled. He was ordered to fly in a new direction where the cowardly American carriers were supposed to be hiding. He looked at his fuel gauge. He fervently hoped that the Americans weren't too far away, and, with equal fervor, hoped that he'd have a place to land his plane. All he saw now were burning Japanese carriers and the wide ocean.

Dane wondered if everyone else on the *Saratoga* felt as naked and exposed as he did. Almost all the carrier's planes had gone to attack the enemy carriers, with only a couple in the air to warn of oncoming Japanese.

Radio traffic told of several enemy carriers burning and dead in the water. He recalled one pilot from the Battle of the Coral Sea exulting, "scratch one flattop," a phrase that had become immortalized. How many flattops had been scratched this time and how many remained unscratched? How was the battle over the Baja going? The two battleships and the destroyer screen sailed in front of the two carriers as a buffer, but how many Jap planes might find them? All the Japs had to do was figure out which direction the American planes had come from and fly back up that way. Jesus, talk about your fog of battle.

Once again Dane was agonizing over Amanda's safety. The bombardment of San Diego and Los Angeles, obviously designed to draw off American planes, was over. Was she okay? At least she was in a hospital, but did the damned Japs care about that? Hell, maybe they couldn't even see a red cross at long range.

A terse announcement said that enemy aircraft were approaching. So much for being invisible, he thought.

Masao saw the two American carriers at the same time the other Japanese pilots did. There was no time to organize a proper attack. The pilots were on their own. Once again, he checked his fuel. He sucked in his breath. If the gauge was even remotely accurate, there was little possibility of him making it back to the fleet, if any of it even still existed. The battle had become a horror. Instead of another magnificent Japanese victory, it was clear from what he'd seen and heard that the empire's carriers were being destroyed and with them any real chance of Japanese victory in this war. Toki was right. It was all turning into ashes. He had said he was willing to die for the empire, but not uselessly and most certainly not without taking Americans with him. Now Masao knew what he had to do.

Masao flew over the first carrier, quickly identified her as the *Saratoga*, and dropped his bomb. It missed the ship by a hundred yards, confirming that it was very difficult to hit a moving target, however large.

He cursed and moaned. He would never see his family again. He hoped there was an afterlife so they could all be reunited. He didn't even care if silly Toki married his equally silly little sister. It would serve them both right. Maybe they would have a boy child and name him Masao. He prayed that would happen.

Masao only had a few moments left. American planes chasing him and his companions were gaining rapidly. He climbed for altitude, turned, and began his dive. His ashes would never be sent to the Yasukoni shrine, but his parents had hair and nail clippings. They would have to do.

"Banzai!" he howled as the *Saratoga*'s bulk grew larger in his eyes.

Dane and Merchant watched in helpless horror as the Japanese plane plummeted down and toward them. Tracers from a score of antiaircraft guns sought it out, but most missed. Those that did hit tore pieces from its wings and fuselage, damaging it, shaking it and maybe even killing it and its pilot, but not stopping its deadly plunge.

"He's killing himself," Merchant yelled. "You're right about them, Dane. They're all crazy!"

The dying Zero smashed into the flight deck near the bow of the carrier. Even though the suicide plane was almost out of fuel, there was enough to cause a large explosion.

Dane had thrown himself prone and felt heat and debris fly over him. Something heavy landed on his back, knocking the wind out of him. All around him, men were yelling and screaming. Was this going to be the sinking of the *Enterprise* all over again? If so, where was Spruance? Wasn't he supposed to rescue the admiral? He couldn't think straight. Something was terribly wrong.

Tim pushed himself to his hands and knees and

vomited. His body wasn't responding and he collapsed. What was happening? He looked for Merchant and saw him lying near. A large piece of metal protruded from his chest and the expression on his face was blank and lifeless.

Tim felt a hand on his shoulder. It was Spruance. "I'll help you again, sir," Tim managed to say. His voice was mushy and it sounded as if it came from another room rather than from his own body.

Spruance smiled kindly. "This time it's my turn to take care of you, Dane."

Tim was dimly aware that he was being put on a stretcher. He knew he was hurt, but why didn't he feel any pain? "Are we sinking?"

The admiral had gone to check on others, so the medic responded. "Sinking? Not a chance, Commander. Damage control is doing its job. There wasn't any problem with our hull and the fires are coming under control. Like you, we'll need some good repairs, but we'll be all right."

Tim wanted to ask some more questions, but the medic had jabbed him with morphine. He fought it for a moment, but decided it was far better and nicer to let it do its job.

"Abandon ship." The command was repeated until it stopped abruptly. The electricity on the *Kaga* had just gone out. Toki fully understood that the flames had won. The mighty carrier was in its death throes. Explosions rocked her and flames billowed skyward. The rumblings of more explosions from below deck made the *Kaga* seem like she was alive, not dying.

Abandon ship or be burned alive were Toki's choices.

He had already donned his life vest, so, looking down at the ocean and hoping that he wouldn't be sucked into the carrier's still-spinning propellers, and praying that he'd be picked up, he jumped.

Hitting the sea felt like hitting a wall. He blacked out and came to with a number of others from the carrier, some swimming and others flailing desperately. An empty life raft floated by. He grabbed onto it and climbed in. He offered his hand to several others still in the water, but only a couple joined him. The rest shook their heads solemnly and a couple managed to say they'd rather die than live with the shame of defeat.

One of the men with him said he too would join the others in dying if it appeared they would be rescued by Americans. Toki didn't know what he would do. Overhead, the once-invincible Zeros circled and then, one by one, crashed in the ocean. The planes soon disappeared under the water and no pilots emerged. Toki visualized this happening all over the battle area. He knew he would never see his friend Masao again and he mourned for him, but only for an instant. Now he just wanted to live and go home to his family and Masao's little sister.

After a few hours, he and the two others were alone. But then they weren't. A destroyer maneuvered slowly through the waters, its crew searching and looking. They were spotted and the ship came close enough for them to see that it was an American. Toki's companions moaned and slid off the raft and into the sea. They gasped and bobbed a few times and then disappeared.

Toki made up his mind. Only fools chose death when life was at hand. They had killed themselves for no good reason. He stood and waved a handkerchief that he hoped was white enough. With the skill of a dancer, the destroyer was maneuvered beside him. A row of armed Americans stared down at him.

"I speak English," he yelled. "I surrender."

There was silence from the angry-looking Americans. "Why the fuck should we save you?" one of them finally asked.

"I am Admiral Nagumo's chief aide," he said, lying only slightly. Like most Japanese sailors, he had received no instructions regarding how to behave if he actually was taken prisoner since it was assumed he would choose death instead. Thus, there was no reason to discuss or plan for the unthinkable.

There was a quick conference and an officer leaned over. "First, you will remove all your clothes, and I mean everything. After you've stripped down, you will then climb up the ladder which we will lower to you. When you make it to the deck, you will lie on your belly with your legs spread apart. We will examine you and tie you up. Understand?"

Toki understood fully. He too had heard tales of Japanese soldiers trying to take Americans with them as they killed themselves. "I understand. But may I take my wallet? It has my identification and pictures of my family."

He thought the American might have smiled for a flickering instant. "Bring your damned wallet," was the response.

Once again Torelli felt the freight train pass over him, shaking his sub like it was a toy. Jesus, that Jap battleship was big. And fast. Worse, it was going to be moving away, which meant a stern shot and a quick one.

He ordered periscope depth and all bow tubes open. They would simply fire off all four torpedoes the first clear chance he got. He looked through the lens. The battleship was a mountain and moving rapidly. He didn't bother to look for escorts; he just assumed they were there.

The shot was as good as it was going to get. "Fire one," he ordered, then two and three and four. As soon as he heard the sound of the torpedoes leaving, he ordered an emergency dive.

"What now?" Crowley asked. His eyes were wide with tension and fear. They heard splashes and then depth charges exploded. They were close, but not close enough to do damage. It looked like the Japs were more interested in clearing out than in attacking him.

"We wait," Torelli said.

They listened through the rumble of the depth charges. Finally, they heard a different sound. An explosion, but what? They all looked at each other. Had they actually managed to hit the monster? If so, what damage, if any. Maybe it was like shooting a rhinoceros with a peashooter? Probably the damn thing wouldn't even notice.

Yamamoto felt the battleship quiver. He barely heard the explosion and saw nothing. The battleship's massive superstructure blocked his view and insulated him from any sound.

"Torpedo," announced a grim-faced aide a moment later. "No apparent damage, sir."

Yamamoto nodded. It was what he expected. What

else could go wrong this terrible day? He had been totally outwitted and outfought by an American Navy he had thought was, if not dead, then moribund and too frightened to take risks. Now all he could do was try and salvage something out of the burning wreckage that had once been the pride of the Imperial Japanese Navy. Four of his prized carriers were in sinking condition and were being abandoned. If they didn't sink on their own, they would be torpedoed by their own ships, a totally inglorious and shameful end to their careers. Two other carriers were seriously damaged, burning furiously, and might also be lost. Worse, if there could possibly be a worse, the carriers lost were the largest and most powerful the Imperial Japanese Navy possessed. The only carriers remaining were the smaller ones now being categorized as escort carriers.

Nor did it matter that the American carrier they'd sought for so long, the *Saratoga*, had at least been very badly damaged. The few Japanese pilots who had survived the attack on her reported her burning and, in their opinion, likely to sink. Yamamoto was not so confident. The Americans were magicians at saving and repairing ships and, besides, what did it matter if the *Saratoga* was sunk? The Americans had many others under construction. They would join up with what was thought to be the *Essex*-class carrier that had accompanied the *Saratoga* and do so well before Japan could recover from today's disaster.

His thoughts returned to the doomed pilots. At least four hundred of them had been lost and that toll was likely to go higher. Four hundred highly trained carrier pilots could not be replaced. At the current rate of pilot graduation, any damaged carriers were likely to be repaired and ready long before the pilots were trained according to traditional standards. Thus, those standards would have to be relaxed, which meant that new Japanese carrier pilots would be lambs to the slaughter. Nor could the even larger number of planes lost be replaced in the foreseeable future.

Yamamoto accepted that the defeat was his responsibility. All decisions had been his. He would go to Tokyo and personally apologize to the emperor for his failure to bring victory to Japan. It wouldn't matter that this was just as he had forecast that summer before the attack on Pearl Harbor. He had accepted command of the fleet and the blame was his. He would offer his resignation to the emperor and the prime minister. He didn't think they would take it, although he now wished they would. He would let them change his mind about resigning, of course, and do his utmost to save the empire, but he would also try to convince Tojo and Hirohito of the need to negotiate a peace with the Americans. The British could be ignored, but not the Americans. The war in the Pacific would largely be a naval war and the Imperial Japanese Navy would be overwhelmed by the U.S. Navy if it went on much longer.

In order to do this, he thought, the Americans would first send forces to reestablish a forward base at Pearl Harbor, which would also rescue the Hawaiians from their near starvation. The blockade of Australia would be lifted and Japanese garrisons in the Solomons would have to be abandoned. Japan would have to pull back or be destroyed. It was his duty to convince the government of this inevitable fate.

Captain Miyazato Shotoku commanded the *Yamato*.

He now approached the admiral with eyes down. He was clearly shaken and seemed almost afraid to speak.

"What is the news?" Yamamoto asked softly. From the man's expression, it could not be good.

Shotoku took a deep breath and swallowed. What he had to say was painful in the extreme. "We were struck by one American torpedo. It has jammed our rudder. We are stopping so we can send down a diver to determine whether it can be repaired. Otherwise, we can only steam in very large circles. We are not optimistic about the outcome. It is very likely that we will not have the tools and equipment to effect the repairs. I believe it can only be done in drydock."

Yamamoto sucked in his breath. It was almost the same thing that had happened to the German super-battleship, the *Bismarck*, in May of 1941. Unable to retreat and doomed to steam in circles, she had been surrounded by British ships and blown to pieces. Would the same happen to the *Yamato*, the pride of Japan? It was unthinkable. At least he'd had the dubious pleasure of watching as the Yamato's mighty 18.1-inch guns fired over the horizon at San Diego. But would that be the ignominious end of her military career? Not if he could help it.

"The *Kongo* will take the *Yamato* in tow if quick repairs cannot be made," Yamamoto said to Captain Shotoku. "We cannot sit here and wait. The Americans will be here shortly."

Shotoku nodded and left. Orders would be made for the battleship *Kongo* to tow the larger *Yamato* out of danger. The two ships' rate of speed would be slow and they would be vulnerable until they were out of range of American land-based planes. In the meantime, Yamamoto gave instructions that he and his staff would transfer to another ship, the destroyer *Umikaze*, which was close by. At less than one tenth the size of the *Yamato*, he and his staff would be cramped, but they would get away to fight another day.

But the crew of the *Yamato* would not be so fortunate. He had no illusions. It was extremely likely that the American planes and ships would find and attack the two battleships with overwhelming force. The gambler in him estimated the two battleships' chances of survival as one in fifty.

Many of the *Yamato*'s crew would not look at him and those who did showed faces full of dismay, disappointment, shock, and anger. Japan had been defeated. How could that be? Yamamoto had no answer. All he knew was that the men of the *Yamato* would likely all die within the next few hours unless a miracle occurred, and he did not believe in miracles. He accepted their anger at him as his due. He had failed.

The floatplanes reported that the navy fighters and bombers had ceased their attacks on the two Japanese battleships. One, the *Kongo*, was reported to be down at the bow and barely making headway, while the other, the monster *Yamato*, still steamed slowly. The *Kongo* had been towing the *Yamato*, but they had separated.

American pilots confirmed that the *Yamato* was moving in a wide circle to starboard. Skillful ship handling had enabled the *Yamato* to lengthen the distance between herself and both the coast of California and the approaching American carrier. At the rate she was moving, however, it would take an eternity for her to make it to safety.

The United States Navy in the Pacific was again down to one aircraft carrier, the *Essex*, and she was just about out of ordnance. Her bombs had been used up and so too had her pilots. A couple of planes had crashed while trying to land on the *Essex*, which caused Admiral Spruance, now on the battleship *Washington*, to call a halt to the attacks. The *Essex* would be resupplied and her pilots rested before she resumed the fight.

Thus, the older battleships and Admiral Jesse Oldendorff entered the field of battle. The *Colorado* and *Mississippi* had been augmented by the *Pennsylvania*, a survivor of the attack on Pearl Harbor. The admiral now flew his flag on the *Pennsylvania*, which he considered appropriate when he thought of her history and her resurrection from Pearl Harbor. Admiral Nimitz's foresight in moving his squadron from Puget Sound to join with the *Pennsylvania* at San Francisco caused Oldendorff to smile. He wanted nothing more than to strike back with his battleships before they were sent to a museum. The defeat of the Japanese squadron off Anchorage, while satisfying, had not been enough. He and the ships' crews all wanted a shot at the enemy, battleship to battleship. It didn't matter if the *Kongo* and *Yamato* were damaged; he wanted his ships' guns in at the kill.

"Greene, how far can an eighteen-inch gun fire?"

Commander Mickey Greene rubbed his still-raw jaw. It was a hell of a question and nobody really knew the answer. Nobody had ever seen an eighteen-inch gun and had no idea of its range or velocity. A really good gun of that size had been considered an impossibility. Once again, the Japanese had been underestimated.

"I've got to guess at least twenty-five miles, sir, maybe closer to thirty."

The admiral turned to the rest of his staff. "All of which means we'll be within range of her guns before we can hit her. Assuming, of course, that the monster has any guns left that can fire after all the punishment she's been taking."

Greene swallowed. Of course the *Yamato* would have weapons left. No matter how many times the ship had been hit by bombs and torpedoes, she was still afloat and moving and had to be presumed dangerous.

Oldendorff gave the orders. "We will concentrate on finishing off the *Kongo*. The *Mississippi* and *Colorado* will go to port and we will go to starboard. She'll be between us and we'll bracket her quickly."

It almost wasn't necessary. The American ships opened fire on the badly damaged *Kongo* at just under twenty miles. Colored dye showed which splashes came from which ship and within only a few minutes, the battleships' fourteen- and sixteen-inch shells began smashing what was left of the *Kongo*. Several explosions ripped through the Japanese battleship and she began to list to port. There was no return fire and no sign of lifeboats being lowered. Nor were any Japanese sailors jumping from the doomed vessel into the ocean. If there were any living souls on the *Kongo*, they had determined to go down with her.

Or maybe their officers wouldn't let them run, Greene thought. The Japanese were all nuts, so their sailors would likely obey such an order and die at their stations. He saluted their bravery, but not their common sense. Why the hell would anybody want to die when they could live? At first he had wanted to

die when he saw the mess the fires had made of his
face, but that went away. Yeah, he would be scarred
and they would remind him of his ordeal every day,
but most of the worst had faded and he would live
a reasonably normal life.

The *Yamato* was nearly forty miles away from the
destruction of the *Kongo*. Even though over the horizon, smoke from the numerous fires slowly destroying
her was plainly visible. Vectored in by the pall and
the guidance of the floatplanes, the three battleships
again began their dance. At twenty miles, they opened
fire. Again the brightly colored splashes guided the
shells until they too smashed into what had been the
massive symbol of Japanese might.

There was no response and the American ships continued to move in closer until they were firing at only
a few miles, point-blank range. The three American
ships formed a line so their shells wouldn't hit each
other, and prepared to launch torpedoes.

"The damn thing won't sink, won't stop," muttered
Green.

Oldendorff heard and nodded. "We may be pumping
shells into a corpse. If the torpedoes don't kill her,
we'll just pull back and let her steam in circles for
all eternity. For all we know, her engines are so well
protected we haven't done a thing to them."

They moved closer, now only a couple of miles
away. Through binoculars, Green and others could
see the utter destruction on her deck.

Wait! Was that motion? Green stared at the stern-
most turret on the ship, the "D" turret. Yes, it was
slowly turning and her guns were rising. The sons of
bitches had been lying low. The three guns pointed

directly at the *Pennsylvania* like three massive eyes and then fired.

All three giant shells slammed into the *Pennsylvania*. The American battleship was well-armored but not against this. Two shells penetrated her hull and a third struck her superstructure. The ship reeled from the titanic shock. One, the shell that struck her superstructure, obliterated all traces of life there, while one of the shells that pierced her hull found one of her magazines. A few seconds later, the *Pennsylvania* exploded. She broke in half with the two pieces floating briefly before slipping beneath the waves and taking her entire crew with her.

In a vengeful fury, the crews of the two remaining American battleships ships first pounded the surviving turret into rubble and then fired every shell and torpedo they had, reducing the Yamato to a burning hulk. After an eternity, she rolled on her side and sank.

They had redeemed the *Pennsylvania* and sunk the mightiest battleship in the world. But at what cost?

CHAPTER 23

FARRIS FOUND IT DIFFICULT TO PUSH THE WHEEL-
chair with his left arm in a sling, so he let Nancy
Sullivan help out, enjoying the slightly erotic feel of
her body against his as they pushed along the long
corridor.

Once again the hospitals were full. What the newspapers were calling the Battle of the Baja or the
Miracle of the Baja had been a complete American
victory, but there still had been many casualties. Farris pushed past wards full of heavily bandaged men,
some of whom were terribly maimed. Farris could
not help but think of his good fortune in surviving so
much fighting with nothing more than a bum shoulder
that was going to keep him out of combat. Instead,
he would be assigned to a training command in the
Fourth Army, an assignment that he'd requested instead
of a discharge and was fine by him. He'd had enough
combat for several lifetimes. Besides, he'd just found
Nancy and didn't want to leave her.

All of America was enjoying the incredible, almost miraculous victory. Five Japanese carriers were confirmed sunk and two more were badly damaged and probably out of the war for good. The battleships *Yamato* and *Kongo* had been found and sunk, at the cost of the *Pennsylvania*. A huge relief convoy was en route to Hawaii stuffed with supplies and medicine. Was the end of the war in sight? Based on his firsthand experiences with Japanese fanaticism, he thought it unlikely.

"Would you mind hurrying?" Dane asked.

Farris declined to answer. This had been a daily ritual for a couple of weeks now, complaints and all. Dane was still in a brace while his broken back and fractured ribs healed, but at least he was no longer in that massive and ugly-looking cast that had confined him to bed. He'd been informed that his war was over too, and that he would be given a medical discharge. Numerous doctors said he was damned lucky he wasn't paralyzed. The debris that had hit him on the *Saratoga* had broken his back. Just as the army couldn't take a chance on someone with a bad shoulder going into combat, the navy couldn't do the same for a man whose back would take a very long time to return to normal.

"Are we there yet?" Dane mockingly whined in a kid's voice.

Farris laughed. "Be still."

"In a couple of weeks I'll be able to walk and then I'm going to kick your ass."

"I look forward to it," Farris said, meaning it.

"I still outrank you."

"Screw your rank," Farris said genially while Nancy giggled.

They pushed open the double doors to the cafeteria. It was between meals and only a handful of people were present. Dane took control and pushed his wheelchair toward another one. He parked alongside, and he and Amanda embraced as best they could under the circumstances. Both her legs were in casts from foot to mid-thigh. They kissed and others in the cafeteria either watched approvingly or turned away to give them a semblance of privacy.

After a moment, Amanda completed the ritual by awkwardly hugging Nancy and again thanking her for finding her under the rubble and staying with her until she could be dug out. Both of Amanda's legs had been badly broken but were healing, and she would be out of the casts in a couple of days. It would be a while before she and Tim could resume life together, but it was on the horizon. They'd already discussed just how they'd manage sex when they were released, and decided that, like porcupines, very carefully would be it for a long while. That was fine by them. They just wanted to be together.

"Guess what?" Amanda said, changing the subject. "Grace came back from San Francisco with everything we wanted to know about Mack's safe deposit box." She and Sandy had give Grace power of attorney and she'd gone north to meet with Zuckerman, Goldman, and a rep from the State of California.

Dane didn't really care. That was part of her life, not his. Still, he was more than a little curious. "Are we rich?"

"I really don't know. They found only thirty thousand dollars, which is below what the State of California said they'd tax, so it belongs to us. They also found some stock certificates, and Zuckerman suggested that I keep the stocks while Grace and Sandy split the cash. Apparently they really need the money while I don't. He thought the company was a good one doing a lot of work for the government. He says International Business Machines should be worth quite a bit some day. He said that we should hold on to it and wait. Regardless, we now have a thousand shares of IBM."

Tim thought he approved. "We'll have plenty of time to think about it. First, we have to get out of these things, and then we have to learn how to walk again."

Amanda nodded solemnly. "And we'd better figure out how to make love without breaking anything. At least we'll have a place to live when that time comes."

After Merchant had been killed, Farris had continued making rent payments on Merchant's apartment, on Dane's behalf. The landlord didn't care who rented as long as someone paid, and Tim had the feeling that Steve and Nancy had spent some intimate time there as well, and why the hell not? Grace hadn't wanted to live there. Too many memories, she'd said and, after a few drinks, wondered why the men she liked kept getting killed.

Nancy nudged Steve and they walked away to give the newlyweds some more privacy. "I think we have a couple of hours before the two lovebirds have to be back in their wards. Any idea how to spend that time?"

Steve almost leered, causing Nancy to blush and laugh. "I can think of a few," she said.

The ride from Fairbanks to Anchorage was depressing. First, Ruby and Bear had to wait for a convoy to form up. Even though the army was reasonably confident that any remaining Japanese were either dead from wounds, starvation, or exposure, there was always the nagging possibility that one or two were lying in wait for an opportunity to kill themselves and anybody else in the name of the emperor.

When they finally got to the ruined little town, it was even more depressing. Even though the army was setting up shop and building an airbase, Anchorage itself was a burned and broken shell. Ruby had a difficult time convincing a couple of young MPs that she was the owner of the pile of charred rubble that had once been her restaurant, her one and only source of income. In the ruins, she found very little of worth to her.

While she was looking through the debris, she was approached by a man who said he was a real-estate speculator, and would she sell to him? They haggled right then and there and he ended up paying cash for the property, giving her what she felt was about a third of what it was worth. She didn't care. It was time to move on with her life.

She did talk to the army and pointed out where she'd seen the Japanese shoot and kill the men they'd pushed into the water. She was somewhat gratified when her information resulted in divers finding several bodies. They would continue to search for others. The murdered young men would be going home, she thought with a good deal of satisfaction. And so would she, only it wouldn't be Anchorage.

"We should live in Fairbanks," Ruby announced.

"And do what?" Bear asked. His world was changing, too, and he wondered what the future would bring.

"Well, they're building a new airbase up there as

well, and the road to the south is now open. If we play it right, we might have enough money to open a bar and restaurant, and you can make some cash guiding officers out into the wilderness to do some big-game hunting, Alaska style."

"That'll do for the summertime," Bear said, "but what will we do in the winter?"

Ruby smiled. "Why, we'll do what everyone else does up here in the winter. We'll drink ourselves silly and screw our brains out."

He smacked her on the bottom. "Damnation, why didn't I think of that? What the hell are we waiting for?"

Admirals Chester Nimitz and Ray Spruance were the toast of the nation, a fact which perplexed them because of their innately shy natures, and annoyed Admiral King, who rather relished publicity. Their pictures had graced the covers of *Time, Life, Collier's*, and the *Saturday Evening Post*. Even Nimitz had to acknowledge that Yamamoto and what remained of his fleet were clearly on the ropes. The Japanese were pulling back and, from the intercepts they'd gotten, were going totally on the defensive.

The one-sidedness of the wide-ranging fighting still stunned Admiral Nimitz. The *Saratoga* was already back in action after some miracle-working by repair crews in San Diego and, in the next few months, would be joined by no fewer than three fleet carriers and nine escort carriers. Additional new battleships were on the way including one *Iowa*-class monster that might even be a match for the *Yamato*'s remaining sister ship, the *Musashi*. Most felt that the day of the battleship was over, but maybe the *Musashi* would fall prey to the guns of the *Iowa* and her sisters. The admirals thought that would be suitable justice for Pearl Harbor and the destruction of so much of San Diego and Los Angeles.

More than three hundred American planes had been shot down in the battle, but more than half of their pilots had been recovered and most of those rescued would return to service. Not so with the Japanese. Intercepts said they acknowledged four hundred and fifty planes and pilots lost. Even the Japanese admitted that they could not replace the quality of the men who'd died in the battle. In future plane-to-plane encounters, the edge would now belong to the United States. The American pilots had not died in vain.

Enough melancholy, Nimitz thought. There was a duty to perform. After a lot of investigating and haggling, it was finally determined that one torpedo from the *Shark* had damaged the *Yamato* sufficiently that she could not flee to safety, thus causing her destruction. Yes, planes and gunfire had ultimately sunk her, but it was Torelli's torpedo that had slowed her down to the point where the planes and ships could catch and kill her.

All he had to do was remind Torelli that neither he nor his crew were to say anything about modifying their torpedoes. He still could not fathom why the brains at BuOrd in Washington couldn't get it through their heads that something was wrong with their expensive toys.

Juan Camarena was one of a number of army officers who despised the incompetence, corruption, stupidity, and greed of so many of his fellow officers in the Mexican military. Ever since Mexico first won her independence from Spain in 1821, the nation had been wracked with revolutions, coups, and theft on a monumental scale that sometimes made his beloved country a joke. Now, just when it seemed like events were coming under control, his nation was forced to choose between the United States and Hitler's Germany.

When pushed, Camarena would admit that he didn't give a damn for either nation. The United States had stolen Mexico's northern provinces a century before and turned them into the states of Texas, California, Arizona, and New Mexico, among others. Germany, under Hitler, had become a monster. So too had Japan, and the Land of the Rising Sun posed a greater threat to Mexico than did Germany.

Camarena and his associates hated the United States. However, his government had decided to side with the Americans against Germany. He thought he saw expediency in this decision as the U.S. was so close and Hitler so far, but he saw absolute evil in Hitler. Camarena almost couldn't comprehend the reports of Nazi atrocities he was getting from diplomats and others in Europe. Nor could he abide the idea of a militant and expansionist Japan being victorious. If they defeated the United States, Japanese ships would then be able to cruise up and down the western Mexican coast without any interference from the joke that was the Mexican Navy. Mexico would be dominated by the yellow-skin savages even more than she was by the gringos north of the border. Therefore, backing the U.S. was the lesser of two evils and Camarena dedicated himself to that purpose.

Camarena and his allies had engineered the killing

of the traitor, Juan Escobar. It pleased him that the American FBI agent, Harris, had been able to observe justice being served. Unlike so many Americans, Harris seemed to play fair. The police had closed the case. They'd quickly concluded that Escobar the traitor had been killed in a street robbery gone very badly awry.

That left the Germans who'd been left behind in Mexico and who had been directing Escobar's moves on behalf of the Japanese. At first the Americans wanted them left alone, but now they gave the go-ahead to dispose of them. Camarena was glad. He would take care of the human garbage, not for the United States, but for Mexico.

First, Camarena had a series of notes sent to the remaining Germans from someone who identified himself as a friend of the late Escobar. The notes said that the Mexican police had found out about the Germans' activities and would arrest them shortly if they didn't flee. Since they weren't in uniform, they would be shot or hanged as spies. The "friend" suggested that they move to a place in the country and suggested just such a place.

Thankful, the remaining Germans moved out to a small one-story house in the middle of a field about fifty miles from Mexico City. Camarena was a captain in the Mexican Army and his companions were all officers who felt like he did about the Nazi filth.

There were a total of eight well-armed Mexicans in on the raid, not a great numerical advantage, but they hoped that a middle-of-the-night assault would catch the Germans either asleep or exhausted from their daily bouts of drinking. At least this night there were no whores in the house.

There was only one guard stationed fifty yards down the dirt road leading to the shabby house, and Camarena took care of him personally. He snuck up on the half-drunken idiot and sliced his throat. He gave a signal and the others rushed the windows, smashed the glass, and threw in hand grenades that exploded with a roar.

Incredibly, not all the German swine were killed by the blasts. Two men staggered out the door. Their clothes were torn and they were disoriented and bleeding badly. Camarena's men quickly gunned them down. Camarena led his men into the house. Inside, it was a pile of broken furniture and mangled bodies. They counted the pieces and decided they had gotten all of the Germans. The house was a long ways away from other houses and the bodies might not be discovered for some time.

As they drove back to Mexico City, Camarena decided that he would telephone Harris and let him know that the garbage had been taken out. Harris and others like him needed to know that Mexico didn't need help doing everything.

EPILOGUE

HARRIS TURNED HIS RENTAL CAR ONTO THE LONG, winding driveway that led to the compound's elegant main building. Once the place outside Atlanta had been a farm, but it had been rebuilt a few decades earlier in a style reminiscent of the antebellum South. The people who'd done the renovations hadn't been able to enjoy them. They'd lost the property in the Depression, and it now had new owners. It reeked of money.

The old man on the rocking chair on the wide porch looked vaguely familiar to Harris. His body was thicker and the hair, what was left of it, had gone gray. Of course, twenty-five years will change a man. It sure as hell changed me, Harris thought. He parked the car and got out awkwardly. He was overweight and having problems with his knees. The doctors said it was arthritis and old age. Screw the doctors.

"What took you so long?" the old man asked.

"I had better things to do." Harris answered.

"Are you taking me back?"

Harris plunked himself down on a chair beside Krause. "Why the hell would I do that? You didn't break any laws by running away. We were going to turn you loose anyhow, just not quite so soon."

"I'm Gunnar Kuess now. I used the ID I had and made myself a new life. I'm from Norway and I became a U.S. citizen a number of years ago. I'm a good American. I even voted for Nixon and Goldwater, and I was devastated when that little piece of vermin killed Kennedy. You may be able to invalidate my citizenship and send me back, but my wife was born here, as were my two children, so they are safe."

"Guess what? We don't much care. The government would find it very embarrassing. Besides, a whole lot of people think you're a hero for turning against Japan and Hitler."

Krause was puzzled. "Then why are you here?"

"First, I'm hot and would really like a beer, and second, I'm long retired from the FBI. Hoover can go screw himself as far as I am concerned. This is a private job. Did you see the movie *The Longest Day*?"

"Of course," Krause said with a laugh. "I'm a big John Wayne fan, and it told me a lot about the invasion of Normandy and what a fool Hitler was. I also read the book. I've read quite a number of books about World War II. What a tragedy. How could people get duped by Hitler? And, yes, I am including myself."

"Good, 'cause we're coming up on the twenty-fifth anniversary of the Battle of the Baja and there's going to be a movie about it, along with a companion book. The producers and writers want input from all the major participants, including those who took part in the planning of what was referred to as the 'Immaculate Deception.' I found Dane and Farris very easily since we exchange Christmas cards. You, however, took a little longer."

But not much longer, Harris thought. It was almost as if Krause wanted to be found. He'd run from California to Georgia, posed as a refugee, and gotten a job in a gas station. No problem there, since he was too old to be dodging the draft and had papers saying he was from Norway. He was a decent mechanic and proved himself to the owner. After a few years he married the owner's daughter. Krause was an even better businessman than a mechanic and now owned a chain of quick oil-change shops and was, if his current house was any indication, quite well off.

"What if I don't want to talk to anyone?"

"You might not have a choice. Look, if an over-the-hill retired FBI agent can find you all by his lonesome, anyone can. And believe me, people will wonder about the man who turned his back on Hitler and helped the United States."

This was not quite true. Although finding Krause hadn't been all that difficult, Harris had contacted a lot of friends and called in a lot of markers to do it.

"Besides," he continued, "most people consider you a hero. You're the ex-Nazi who found redemption by helping us win the Battle of the Baja, even though it was more likely you were just protecting your own ass. Regardless, your real name is going to be plastered all over the place. I think you'd be a lot better off making the announcement yourself instead of being hunted down and trapped by a horde of reporters. Sooner or later, Krause, it's going to happen."

"True enough," Krause said. "Are the people producing the book and the movie paying you for your efforts?"

"Quite a bit, thank you. Does your family know about your little secret?"

Krause sighed. "My wife knows and my late father-in-law did as well. I think my children suspect that there is more to their old father than meets the eye. They are both adults and not stupid. Not like their old man was." He smiled.

"Are they here today?"

"Yes, and doubtless wondering who you are and what you want."

"Want to call them and you can make your announcement? Then we can all talk."

Krause stood. "I'll do that right now. No point in waiting."

"While you're up, get me that damned beer."

The following is an excerpt from:

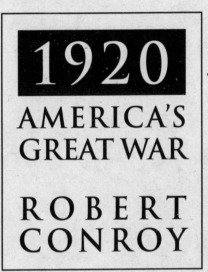

1920
AMERICA'S GREAT WAR

ROBERT CONROY

Available from Baen Books
December 2013
hardcover

PROLOGUE

How could this have come to pass? Reggie Carville wondered. He was a captain in the British Army and was about to become a prisoner of the German Army and its demented leader, Kaiser Wilhelm II. Instead of victory, he and many tens of thousands of British soldiers would be guests of the Hun until they were repatriated back to England.

What a humiliation. What a terrible, horrible way to end this dismal year of 1914. He and thousands of others were squatting in the damp and clammy mud of southern France, waiting their turn to give up. It seemed so strange to be able to look across a field and see the German soldiers they'd been trying to kill just the day before standing in plain sight. He could almost hear their laughter, and his humiliation ate at him. The British Expeditionary Force, the BEF, would soon cease to exist.

Of course, Carville thought, *it was far worse for the French.* At least the British force had remained intact. Not like the French Army; it had utterly disintegrated after its defeat on the Marne and the subsequent capture of Paris by the Germans.

And who could blame the poor French soldiers who'd finally thrown away their weapons and run like rabbits? Poorly led and poorly trained, they'd been directed to charge into the rain of bullets coming from the German machine guns. They'd been told that *Elan*, the spirit of the warrior, would carry the day. Machine guns would be as nothing in the face of Gallic courage. Instead, they died in bloody heaps, their bodies broken and the *elan* of the survivors evaporated. Hell, Carville thought, they were still wearing their traditional red and blue uniforms, which made such splendid targets. The British wore khaki and the Germans a field gray, both of which served as far better camouflage.

Ironically, the Germans hadn't been much smarter in the early days of the war. They too had marched across bloody fields in mass formations. But they quickly learned the error of their ways.

In a curious twist of linguistic irony, Field Marshal Sir John French commanded the British forces operating in France. He was widely considered to be overtimid and did not get along well with either his own officers or his allies. Carville wondered if a more aggressive leader might have avoided this debacle. Perhaps not, he concluded. There'd been too many Germans and too few British, although three hundred thousand Brits hardly counted as a trifle. They and their French so-called allies had confronted more than two million Germans.

Carville was attached to Field Marshal French's headquarters as a junior aide and could have avoided any contact with the fighting, but his upbringing and training demanded otherwise. On several occasions he'd gone to the front and watched as highly-trained British soldiers fired their Enfield rifles with a speed and accuracy that made the Germans think they had many more machine guns than existed. In front of the British, it had been the Germans who'd died in heaps. Too bad there were only a few hundred thousand British soldiers in the entire army and too bad they were all going to have to surrender. What, he wondered, would happen to poor England without an army? At least the Royal Navy was largely intact and could probably defend the nation from a German invasion.

Being part of the headquarters' staff, Carville knew things that others didn't. He knew that, months earlier, their French allies had been informed that the German Army on the Marne had split and that a counterattack on the German westernmost flank would stop them in their tracks.

But no, the old-fashioned French generals rejected the notion because they didn't quite trust the sources. Much of the information had come from pilots who'd seen the German mistake, but they simply hadn't been believed. People who fly planes are all mad, don't y'know. The commander at Paris, General Joseph Gallieni, had begged for permission to attack the exposed German flank, but had been denied. Sit tight and wait, he'd been told. When the Germans were defeated at the Marne he could attack their retreating forces. Carville's own leader, Marshal French, had also been reluctant to authorize a risky breakout.

Of course, the British and the French had been

defeated at the Marne and Paris taken after a short but bloody siege that saw many landmarks, like the Eiffel Tower and Notre Dame, in ruins. The British and French armies had retreated south, hoping to reach the Mediterranean and rescue. Instead, they had gotten no further than the city of Clermont. The French army had disintegrated while the British stayed intact and continuously bloodied the noses of the Germans.

Carville felt pity for the French soldier, the *poilu*, and contempt for his leaders. Of course, he wasn't all that fond of the English leaders who'd led him to this surrender field. In his opinion, Field Marshal Sir John French was a horse's ass.

Carville also knew that the Germans were exhausted and at the end of their tether. Their armies were in disarray and their supply lines had been unable to keep up with their army's needs. The German Army was in rags and almost out of food and ammunition. One good push and they'd either be stopped or defeated.

One problem—the French army no longer existed and the British Army was in even worse shape than the Germans. Victory, Carville concluded, would go to the side that was least exhausted. Wellington had prevailed in battle and called it a near-run thing. Well, this campaign had been a close one, but the result had been defeat, not victory.

Carville saw Sergeant Smith—the sergeant pronounced it "Smeeth"—staring at him. "Well, sergeant, are you ready?"

"Oy, but I'll fookin' hate it."

Carville grinned. Smith sometimes affected an outrageous accent when he felt like it. He and the dimunitive, wiry and outspoken Smith went back several years. Smith was a consummate professional soldier of the King. "I can't think that anyone's looking forward to a German prison camp," Carville said. "Can't imagine it'll be for too bloody long, though."

Smith nodded glumly. "Oy don't give a shit how long it be. Oy've lost too minny mates to take kindly to Germans. Hate the bastards, I do. Next time I hope their lordships in London gives us at least a fookin' fighting chance to kill the Kraut fuckers."

Carville clapped him on the shoulder. The little man had killed more than a dozen Germans with his Enfield. As a sniper, he was almost a legend. In fact, the only better shot Reggie Carville knew of was Reggie Carville.

Whistles blew and men formed up. Carville nodded at Smith and returned to headquarters. They would march out, turn in their weapons, and be returned to their encampment. Officers would be paroled to live in local hotels, and the enlisted men would be kept at the camp until arrangements were made. Carville didn't think they would take long. The Germans didn't want to have to house and feed three hundred thousand Brits any longer than they had to.

What really concerned Carville was the thought of the world with Germany as its only preeminent power. England had been defeated. France and Russia had been crushed. There was no one left to be a real rival to Imperial Germany and the ambitions of the half-mad and half-crippled Kaiser. The United States was a possibility, but they seemed more than content to hide behind their ocean moats and listen to their president, Woodrow Wilson, proclaim how terrible war was and how important it was that the United States stay out of it.

Carville sighed at such naiveté. What was one to do when the town bully attacks you? Someday, America and Woodrow Wilson were in for a rude awakening.

Later, as he marched through the German lines, he saw how fatigued and dispirited they were. They looked at their late enemies with dull, dispirited eyes. Their faces were gaunt, their uniforms filthy and torn. *Damn it,* Carville thought. *We could have had them.*

CHAPTER 1

His horse was near collapse and the six armed men chasing him were gaining steadily. The old and scrawny mare's chest was heaving and her whole body was covered with sweat and foam. It hadn't been such a great horse in the first place, and was thoroughly outclassed by the well-bred cavalry mounts pounding behind him and gaining with every stride.

Luke Martel would soon be helpless on the ground, confronted by a half dozen German lancers—Uhlans—who would like nothing better than to spit him like a rodent on one of their spear points. The Uhlans's uniforms and weapons were archaic, but archaic or not, their lances could impale human flesh with ease.

Since he was pretending to be a civilian, Martel was armed with a Colt revolver and not his more powerful .45 automatic service weapon. Even though he thought lancers were an anachronism in twentieth-century warfare, the revolver he carried was an inaccurate weapon and carried such a light round that it might not stop a horse, much less a human being.

That assumed he could hit either if forced to fire at a gallop from his staggering nag.

The river and safety were to his right, maybe a quarter of a mile away. But first he had to reach the river and, second, he had to cross it without getting captured or killed.

He looked behind him. His pursuers were momentarily hidden from view. A curve in the dirt track that passed for a road gave him an opportunity. Another curve was just in front of him. He slipped from his horse and slapped it hard on its flank. Freed of its unwelcome burden and motivated by the slap, the mare lurched forward and behind the curve where it disappeared from view.

Just make it a little farther, Martel begged his horse. He clambered up and behind some rocks to his left and away from the river. When the Germans realized he was on foot, he hoped they would logically assume that he'd headed directly for the river and salvation. He counted on their logic. If nothing else, Germans were so bloody damned logical.

He began to backtrack in the direction of his approaching enemy. Again, he hoped their orderly minds wouldn't expect him to do anything other than run like hell from them and their damned lances, which any reasonably sane human being would do. Of course, a reasonably sane person wouldn't have gotten himself in this mess in the first place.

Martel could hear the pursuing horses clearly now and, seconds later, they thundered past as he hid behind a rock. The lancers' faces and their gaudy uniforms were covered with dust and grime, but the Germans were grinning, laughing, and riding easily, their lances canted slightly forward. The well-conditioned German horses seemed to be enjoying themselves as well. They were hunters after the ultimate prey.

And then they were gone. But they would be back. A moment later, he heard a gunshot. He presumed they'd found his exhausted horse and put it out of its misery. Too bad, he thought. The beast had served him well.

Now the Germans were confused. They returned to a point where he could see them again, and broke up into three pairs. They began to comb the ground between the road and the river. From his perch on the rocks and behind some thin bushes, Martel could see them searching along the riverbank that was a lot closer than he'd thought. It was maybe only a couple of hundred yards away. Of course, it might as well be a hundred miles with the Germans patrolling between him and it.

After maybe an hour, the Germans formed up and returned back down the road. Had they truly given up, or were they going back for more men to conduct a more comprehensive search? If the latter was the case, someone with a brain might figure out that maybe he hadn't run directly for the river, but was waiting for an opportunity to make a move.

Martel decided it was time to get the hell out of there.

He clambered down from the rocks and, after looking as far down the road as he could, ran across. The ground was sandy and open and he felt like he was totally exposed and could be seen for miles.

He ran hard. The river was in front of him. It didn't look deep, and he knew that it oftentimes wasn't. Maybe he could dash across without having to swim.

He heard a shout from behind him. The bastard Germans had spotted him. They weren't as dumb as he'd hoped. They'd circled back along the riverbank and not the road. And now one of them was less than a hundred yards away and coming hard.

Martel ran as fast as he'd ever run in his life. Almost immediately, he was in the river, splashing in water that was knee deep and getting deeper. He could hear the sound of the German's horse breathing behind him and he could almost feel the lance going into his back and coming out his chest.

He threw himself into the water as a Uhlan roared past him, jabbing down. Martel rolled away, lunged upward, grabbed the cavalryman's boot and jerked hard, causing the German's horse to stumble and the rider to fall into the water. The Uhlan dropped his lance and tried to stand up, but fell back to his hands and knees.

Martel kicked the German in the head and pushed himself onward. He thought about grabbing the German's horse, but the animal was already trotting back to the riverbank.

At some point, he'd be in the middle of the river and safe. At least that's the way it worked in theory. The international boundary was the middle of the river. Maybe, though, the Krauts wouldn't be too concerned about such niceties as international boundaries with countries for which they had utter contempt. They might also be enraged that one of their own had been humiliated, another reason to disregard vague boundaries.

Two more mounted Germans had entered the water and were plowing towards him. The German he'd kicked was standing unsteadily, dazed but apparently not seriously hurt.

Martel could hardly breathe as he pushed himself onward. The water that had been up to his waist was growing shallower and he looked up. The rocky north bank of the river was just before him. He turned around and saw that the mounted Germans had picked up their comrade and were withdrawing to the south bank. One turned and glared furiously at him and made an obscene gesture. What the hell had just happened? Maybe he would live long enough to see his thirtieth birthday.

Now on his hands and knees, gasping and vomiting dirty water, Martel reached the north bank and crawled through the sand and mud. He didn't consider himself safe, not yet. Along with their ridiculous but deadly pig stickers, the Uhlans carried carbines. Would they fire across the border? Well, there wasn't much he could do about that except gather himself and continue to run like hell.

"Where you goin', boy?"

Martel looked up. Several rough-looking white men with rifles, mounted on scraggly but tough-looking horses, had emerged from the brush that had hidden them and were staring hard at him.

"I'm an American," he managed to gasp.

"That's what they all say," said a lean and wiry man in his thirties who appeared to be their leader. "Now tell me just why the fucking Germans chased you all the away across the Rio Grande and into Texas."

Martel stood up and tried to regain his dignity. "Because I'm an officer in the United States Army, and the fucking Germans didn't like me snooping around them and their camps in Mexico this spring of 1920. Now who the hell are you?"

That seemed to amuse the man in charge who grinned amiably before spitting on the ground. "First off, my name is Marcus Tovey and I'm a Texas Ranger just like all these fine young gentlemen who are accompanying me, and anybody who's being shot at by the fucking Germans can't be all bad."

Luke Martel noted that the cowboy was carrying a Winchester 30-06 carbine and that he was wearing a badge. "That's an old weapon," Luke said.

"It'll still kill," Tovey said. "So we are now going to take you to our post and let you prove your tale. Then you can try to answer a question for me?"

Martel relaxed. "I'll try."

"Then tell me, young soldier, just what the hell are the Germans doing along the Rio Grande and the boundary of the state of Texas this spring of 1920?"

—end excerpt—

from *1920: America's Great War*
available in hardcover,
December 2013, from Baen Books